Lone Operative

D1551718

Allan Strange

Cross Peanut and there are consequences.

He doesn't do prisoners.

There are no half measures.

Lone Operative

Poke in the Eye Publishing LLC

chair leg was sliced in two. Chuckie fell backward onto the floor as the chair gave way. Peanut heard the sickening sound as Chuckie smacked his head on the concrete floor.

Chuckie shook his head to clear it as Peanut placed the tip of one sword under his chin and the tip of the other just pressing against his groin. Chuckie gaped at him with dazed, frightened eyes. He knew it was bad, really bad. There was no mercy in Peanut's voice.

'It's tell-the-truth time, fat guy. Tell me about Janice-Rose.'

'You promised!' Chuckie pleaded.

Peanut's voice was flat, hard. 'So sue me. What you sow, you reap. It's in the bible somewhere, Chuckie. It's called *consequences*, fat boy. Now tell me about Janice-Rose.' He stabbed the sword lightly into Chuckie's neck, drawing a trickle of blood as Chuckie felt the other sword stab slightly into his groin. He jerked back in pain and winced, his face now a mask of terror.

A sudden hammering on the door gave Peanut a start and he spun around.

'Police! Open up!'

Peanut spun towards the glassless window, then stopped. A figure in black had jumped onto the fire escape. Dressed in bulletproof armor, his automatic rifle was pointing directly at Peanut. The door behind Peanut burst open, the dead body shoved aside. Two police in bulletproof armor carrying automatic rifles stormed in.

'On the floor! Now! Now!' Peanut dropped his swords and dropped to the floor with his hands stretched along the floor. This was not good. Arrested in a room with two dead guys, both killed by the swords he had just dropped. And a fat guy missing both his ears. This had the death penalty written all over it. His. Would Libby take a rain check, he wondered? Then again, why would she bother? He was as good as dead.

Chapter 2

A knee was jammed into his shoulder blade and his face was pushed into the floor. The smell of old polish, spilled booze, and something sweet and sickly like old vomit crawled up his nose. He fought the reflex to gag. He felt his hands getting cuffed behind his back and the knee and the hand on his head were lifted. He knew why they did it. It was just to stress the point about who was in charge and that he had to do what *they* wanted. It was much easier to interview shit-scared, belittled suspects.

He was left lying face down on the floor when he heard a noise and twisted his head toward the sound. A pair of ugly brown shoes came into view with thick black socks sticking out the bottom of a set of brown pant legs. Then the elegant shapely legs of a woman came into view. Nice shoes, not too high in the heel, made more for use and practicality than fashion. He twisted his head further and craned his neck. A dapper man and a lady glanced at him. The man was stocky, mid-fifties, with a lined tough-looking face. He was dressed in a dark brown suit, white shirt, and black tie. His grey hair was short, almost a crew cut. A fed. Couldn't be anything else, dressed like that. Peanut thought he looked like a walking turd.

The woman was in a dark blue skirt and jacket and a plain white blouse. The skirt was made of a light material and it fitted her ass snuggly. Every muscle and twitch was on display with no sign of any pantie line. Her jacket was open, exposing her gun in a belt holster. He twisted so he could see her face. She was pretty. Her white, almost alabaster skin was framed by elegantly cut brunette shoulder-length hair. Her pale, cold blue eyes were hard and she examined him like he was part of the scum embedded in the floor. She didn't seem all that old, maybe late twenties or even thirty, but she was clearly the one he should worry about. She was in charge, that much was evident when she raised her hand and signaled goodbye to the armed men.

'Thanks, guys, we'll take it from here. Little muggings won't give us any trouble. And thank Jim for us too, please.' Her voice was calm and professional. It was the voice of someone in control, well used to having her orders obeyed. The armed men left, nodding to her politely as they filed through the door. She turned to the guy in the brown suit.

'Christ, it stinks in here,' she said.

The guy chuckled.

'Welcome to the other side,' he said.

Peanut could hear the departing squad's footsteps clattering down the stairs. The woman prodded him with her toe, none too gently, but not worth complaining about either.

'On your feet,' she said.

Brown Suit stepped forward to give him a hand up, but Peanut rolled, drew his knees under him and flicked himself upright.

The man stared in surprise. The woman merely shrugged at her partner. From his ugly brown suit coat the man pulled out a gun in a plastic bag. He slipped on a pair of deposable plastic gloves and removed the gun. Peanut felt his heart drop. They were going to kill him.

The man then bent down, put the gun against Chuckie's temple and pulled the trigger. Peanut registered the look of surprise on Chuckie's face in the split second before he died. The explosion was loud in the small room and he watched as Chuckie's body jumped, twitched once and then lay still. More blood joined the congealing blood from Chuckie's severed ears and leaking thigh wound. Peanut felt no emotion at the death. The Turd-in-a-Suit had just done what he was going to do anyway, just not with a gun.

Peanut was helpless as his hand was forced open and the gun put in his palm and his fingers closed around the butt. The gun fired again and the warm barrel was placed in his other hand. He knew he was being framed when he saw the gun being put in the plastic bag and labelled. His hand and wrist were then swabbed, and the swab put in another labelled bag. He knew they'd taken a sample of the residue from the firing of the gun. They were thorough, he gave them that. This was one murder charge that he wouldn't be able to escape. He glared at them. The woman gave a fleeting smile, her cold blue eyes and blank face revealing nothing as she addressed Peanut.

'Neville Walker Patterson, I am arresting you for the murder of one Gerald O'Conner, also known as Chuckie. You have the right to remain silent, but anything you say may be used against you in a court of law. You have the right to have an attorney present before and during questioning. You have the right to have a court-appointed lawyer to represent you before and after questioning.' Then she turned to Turd-in-a-Suit.

'We'll get the SOC team in to deal with this mess,' she said. 'Make sure those swords don't go missing. We need them matched to the wounds.'

Peanut figured that SOC meant Scene of Crime. The Mona Lisa wasn't as well framed as he was. He was fucked. It wasn't a matter of *if* he got the death sentence, it was now a matter of *when*. What the fuck had he done to deserve this sort of treatment from the feds? The woman glanced at him as she turned towards the door.

'You! Come with me. Now!' she commanded.

Peanut followed her out of the door. She grabbed his arm as they walked down the stairs and he wondered why. He was just as stable on his feet with his hands behind his back. Maybe she thought he would run? They emerged into the fading sunshine and the cool breeze wasn't as noticeable at street level as it was upstairs. The woman guided him to a black SUV, opened the back door and watched as he climbed in. She walked around the other side and got in beside him. The SUV moved out into the traffic, with Turd-in-a-Suit following in another car, driving away from the city. The driver glanced in his rearview mirror at the woman.

'Is Peter coming to the camp? I see he's following us,' he asked.

'Yeah, I think so,' she replied.

That told Peanut the name of the Turd-in-a-Suit. Peter. Asshole.

The woman glanced across at him. 'They call you Peanut, don't they?'

'Yeah.'

'We'll call you that as well,' she said.

Peanut shrugged.

'Suit yourself.'

'We will. As of now, your ass is ours. You've just been recruited. From now on you work for us. Any attempt not to fulfil your obligations will result in you being charged with Chuckie's murder, or maybe accidentally expiring. No one will ever give a toss about a shitty little killer like you. Do I make myself clear?' Her words were blunt.

He refused to look at her and stared out the window as he replied.

'I assume you mean expiring as in dying and not the breathing in and out kind?'

She didn't so much as glance at him, her cold blue eyes surveying the passing traffic.

'Guess.' She turned to him and gave him a baleful stare. He now had the distinct feeling that the bitch didn't like him. He wasn't feeling all that loving towards her either. 'Do what you're asked and you won't have any problems. It's that simple.'

Peanut grunted.

'So, am I working for the good guys or for another piece of shit like Chuckie?'

'We serve our country, but that doesn't necessarily make us the good guys and since you're already a murderous little asshole, you'll fit right in. As I said, you've been recruited. You will obey orders, no matter what they are. Clear?'

'Crystal. And thanks for the loving endorsement. Incidentally, I wasn't Chuckie's murderer until your Turd-in-a-Suit friend Peter shot him. Do I get any choice in this?'

'No.'

The black SUV wound its way out into the verdant Virginia countryside, where the vivid green pastures and trees had new leaves forming. He paid attention to the road signs, making a mental note of where they were going.

'It won't do you any good,' she said when she noticed.

'What?'

She snorted, exasperated.

'Christ! Fuck the bullshit! You're checking where we're going.' She sighed. 'And I thought you were smarter than that. Did it not cross your little criminal mind that if we were worried about your seeing where we were going, you would have had a hood on?'

'So, either you have something to stop me running away or this is just a one-way trip?'

She reached over, shoved him forward, undid one of his handcuffs, leant across in front of him and cuffed him to the grab rail. He could smell her hair as she leant over him and he had to admit, the expensive shampoo and perfume did smell nice, especially after the stink of the building.

'Whether it's a one-way trip or not is up to you. If you don't do as you're told, this could be the last time you'll see this countryside. I suggest you take a good look, just in case. It'll be your choice.'

He breathed a quiet sigh of relief. They weren't going to kill him. At least not yet.

'So where are we going?' he asked.

'Home for the next two months,' she said. 'Tell me, why did you cut off Chuckie's ears?'

'They were wasted. He wouldn't listen.'

'Were you going to kill him?'

'Yeah.'

'Torture him?'

'Only until I got what I wanted. I'm not a total sadist. But he deserved to die.'

'He did. He was holding Libby, wasn't he? And knowing Chuckie, someone would have been twisting her tits. That fat prick got off on that shit.'

Peanut was stunned but he hid it. They knew it all. Who the fuck were these people and who the fuck was this bitch? His mind was racing.

'Yeah,' he mumbled.

'It would have been a quick stab in the heart, then?' she asked.

'Eventually, yeah.' He paused. 'What's your name?'

'Amanda Carolyn Hiller. Hills is what I answer to. But you will call me either Mam or Ms. Hiller.'

'Yeah? And if I don't?'

'You won't use your nuts for a month.'

'Thanks for the warning, Ms. Hiller, but I didn't have any usage planned.'

'No problem.'

They lapsed into silence and Peanut watched as the SUV turned off Highway 66 and onto Highway 81, heading south. The light was disappearing and in another hour it would be dark. As they sat in silence, the hum of the SUV's tires on the road was almost soothing.

But Peanut wasn't being soothed; he was thinking and thinking hard. They needed him for something, otherwise he'd be sitting in a police cell, awaiting trial and then death row. That could still happen.

'Why me?' he asked in a quiet voice.

As she turned towards him her mouth puckered into an evil-looking grimace.

'Because you fit.'

Chapter 3

'What'd you mean, I fit?'

Hiller ignored the question.

'You robbed Harrisons. We haven't figured out how yet, but we will.

'Nah.'

She sighed again. 'We have your DNA.'

'Yeah? Then why don't you charge me?' he asked.

'We're not the police. They don't know who robbed Harrisons, but we do. We intend to keep it like that. Besides, we have your ass for cold-blooded murder and torture. You really should have left his ears on.'

'Hey! I didn't know you were coming or me and Chuckie would have worn fucking bow ties! Besides, I've been thinking about that. You won't take me to court in case I start talking and if any journo or lawyer starts investigating, they'll soon find a flaw.'

'You're right. We won't. But leave and you'll be wanted and hunted for cold-blooded murder. We'd say that you're extremely dangerous, a killer, and should be shot on sight.'

She turned and stared at him, her cold eyes letting him know exactly what she thought.

'This whole performance today is just so we can have you hunted down and killed if you do decide to run away. Not that you will. Did your mom get her ring back?'

'Don't know what you're talking about.'

'The ring you stole from Harrisons,' she said.

Peanut shook his head and looked out at the darkening countryside. How the fuck did they know he'd got the ring back?

'Don't worry,' she said, 'we're not going to charge you with the robbery. Gerald Harrison deserved it.'

'He's a thieving prick.'

'I agree with you. So did your mom get her ring back?'

Peanut shrugged. It was pointless fudging; they knew everything.

'Yeah,' he said.

'That's nice. Maybe you're not such a complete piece of shit after all.'

'Lady, the last thing I want is a ringing endorsement from you.' He paused. 'So how does me getting mom's ring back make me fit?'

'We have a vacancy for a skilled thief. You're it.'

'Excuse me?'

'We need a thief, and a good one. You stole the ring back and we don't know how. That took the sort of skill we need. You fit the profile. You're a perfect fit for an upcoming job.'

'And if I decide that I don't fit the profile?'

'That decision is above my pay grade.' She glanced sharply at him, her eyes cold and calculating. 'But I wouldn't recommend you do that. One of our many skills is that we're experts in making unwanted, troublesome pieces of shit disappear.' They sat in silence for a minute and Peanut thought about what he had heard. It raised a question.

'How do you know about the ring?'

'We have contacts with the police, especially the detective branch. We found out that Harrison had complained about a robbery, but the detectives investigating found no sign of forced entry. No fingerprints, no DNA, nothing. And because the ring was locked in a safe, a secure digital one, it couldn't be done. They thought Harrison was lying to get the insurance money, despite him showing them photographs of the ring. So, they told him that they couldn't find anything and that he had to claim insurance. With no evidence, the insurance company turned him down. He is one pissed-off guy.'

'Good. It couldn't happen to a smellier piece of shit.'

'Was the ring worth that?' she asked.

'How much did he say?'

'He said he paid twenty for it, but it was worth at least forty to fifty.'

'He's lying. The ring was appraised last year at a second-hand value of sixty. The total retail value is over one hundred thousand. Harrison didn't want to look like a complete turd. He'd seen that valuation.'

'Your mom was desperate for cash?'

'Not now. I sold the ring for her in New York. I got sixty-five. Problem over.'

'That guy she was with was a loser, wasn't he? Used to beat her up, we hear.'

'Yeah.'

'Still around?'

'Not now,' said Peanut.

'He disappeared?'

'Yeah.'

'You sure he won't come back?'

Peanut grinned.

'Not unless he's Jesus.'

She scowled at him. 'You really are a murdering little piece of shit, aren't you?' He turned and looked at her. For the first time she really noticed his eyes. Black, no mercy, a killer's eyes and she heard the cold anger in his voice. It suddenly unsettled her.

'Yeah, I'm a murdering little shit. Just like you and your dressed-like-a-turd pal, Peter. Think you're better? You're not. It'd pay for you murdering thugs to remember that.'

The blow was fast. His cuffs meant that he couldn't dodge quickly enough and get his free hand into place. It was a swift decisive punch to his testicles. His groin exploded into pain, doubling him over against the cuffs, leaving him buckled in agony, just hanging in pain. He used his training to control his breathing as he straightened up slowly. He heard her faintly talking in the background.

'Get one thing straight, you little piece of jailbait shit, I am several levels above you and always will be. Insult me again and the next time you won't walk away.' Her voice was harsh, uncompromising.

Peanut didn't respond. What was the point? They were going to do what they wanted with him anyway. But fuck talking nice to the bitch! The pain slowly subsided, but the dull ache remained. He was still recovering when he noticed the driver staring at him with a concerned look in the rearview mirror.

Peanut stared out of the window and concentrated on making it as difficult as possible for her to hit him again.

'So, how did you do it?' she said as she tried to re-start the conversation.

Peanut sat making sure he was twisted in his seat, ready to defend himself against any further blows, yet knowing it was probably useless. She was trained. She would know how to inflict pain, anywhere. But he didn't have to talk to her. He was completely fucked, and he knew it.

'Cat got your tongue, eh? We know how you got in. Peter was intrigued. He cased the area. The building next door was pretty close and around the back there was a right angle of walls. He surmised that you climbed up the angle and went in through the toilet window. Those old brick walls are pretty rough and there was plenty of foot grip. He checked, and the window had been forced and it had a rough edge. A bit of sharp metal was sticking up and he found a stain. It looked like blood. We got a DNA match to your jailbait brother. The gap between the buildings was only five feet and he found an old door that had recently been removed and was obviously used to cross from one building to the other.' She paused for a second. 'So, how did you crack the safe?'

Peanut was looking out of the window, still controlling his breathing. The ache in his nuts was still there, but it was slowly easing. Even so, he didn't want to talk to the bitch. He now had a bad feeling about all of this. He might be better off dead.

She didn't ask again, just gave him a long look, then turned away and looked out of the darkening window. She pointed at some disappearing town lights.

'Woodstock. Not to be confused with the real deal where the festival took place. The celebration of a generation of losers. They all wanted to change the world and they changed nothing. But hey, they all got stoned, drunk, screwed each other and had a good time.'

Peanut noticed the lights. He knew exactly where he was. He knew this town. His mom had gone to the real Woodstock and he knew that this town wasn't it. His mom had always sounded sad when she talked about it. As if something precious had been lost since then, stolen, like hope had gone. He supposed the realities of life crept in and then the stress of day-to-day living killed whatever hopes they once had. They branched off onto Highway 33 at Harrisonburg, leaving the lights of the city behind. The occasional lights of farmhouses began to disappear. He checked the dash clock—it wasn't late, just eight o'clock. They slowed down and the SUV turned onto a gravel road. Ten minutes later, they stopped outside a set of high steel gates. The driver pushed a button, the gates opened, and they drove through.

They pulled up outside a long wooden building that resembled a large bunkhouse. Peanut sat still as she leant over and released his handcuffs. The sweet smell of her hair didn't do it for him anymore. If he ever had the chance, he would kick the ball-bashing bitch in the cunt. He had a quiet hate building for Ms. Amada fucking Carolyn Hiller. But deep down he also had a feeling that this could get worse, a whole lot worse. He took comfort in knowing that somehow, they needed him, but after he'd finished whatever the job was that they wanted him for, his life would most probably be over. The driver got out, swung the door open and bundled him out, turning him around and shoving his face against the car before fastening the handcuffs again.

Peanut could smell the forest, the scent of rotting leaves, lush grass, and the woodland. It reminded him of holidays long ago in the country, good times with his mom. He sensed a movement. Hiller was standing beside him. She pointed at the building.

'Move.'

He walked towards the steps leading to the porch and climbed them. She prodded him across the porch to the door. The driver opened it and they went in. A substantial desk filled the space in front of him. The musty smell hit him as soon as he walked in—it was if the building had been closed up for a very long time.

The guy sitting behind the desk wore a dark green uniform. Peanut didn't know what it was. He had never seen one like it before. No markings, no name, no identification, just the insignia of a corporal on the shoulders. Ms. Hiller signed a form and the guy handed over a key. She took Peanut's arm and marched him to a door at the far end of the desk. The driver opened it and Peanut was led along a passageway to a door that had the number nine on it. His cuffs were released and he was shoved inside. The door closed behind him and he heard the lock click. He tried the handle, but it was locked. In the gloom, he groped around the door frame and found the light switch and turned it on. It was a plain ten-by-ten-foot room with one single bed, a desk and chair, a toilet, a washstand, and a shower in the corner. He sat at the desk and stared up at the bars on the outside of the high window. It was a prison from which there was no escape, but at least he was still alive—for now, anyway. He consoled himself with the thought that after all the trouble they had gone to, he must be worth something, but how much? What value did they place on a good burglar? He felt a slight hope building. Maybe it wasn't so hopeless after all.

***

Amanda Hiller sat in the lounge down the hall.

'What do you think?' she asked the driver.

'You shouldn't have hit him in the nuts.'

'Sorry. I just don't take cheek from smart-ass creeps like that.'

Chas sighed. They needed Peanut and Hill's attitude towards him was not making things easier.

'Lose the judgment. We know nothing about this guy other than he is excellent at breaking and entering and is famous for putting the fear of God into some seriously bad guys. Chuckie wasn't the first to come off second best.'

'With all due respect, I don't think he's Miss Mary, Queen of Goodness and Light. He was in there with Chuckie and two of Chuckie's henchmen, both dead from stab wounds and he was starting in on Chuckie,' she said.

'Don't judge him by that. Chuckie and his mates deserved all they got,' said Chas.

'Yeah? It's the sort of company he keeps. He's a fucking piece of shit.'

'No, he's not and he's not a creep either. I repeat, we know nothing about this guy, other than he could be very useful. He has the perfect skill set for what we want. He's absolutely perfect to get the job done. What we do know is that his mom's a hard worker and an honest woman. She just has a bad habit of picking the wrong men. His older brother Danny is in jail for minor offences including fighting, and Peanut has sorted out three tough guys, probably more.' Chas thought for a minute, noting Hills's skeptical face.

'Chuckie was the last. Remember, he never picked those fights—they picked him. But I think that smack in the nuts just might make our job a little bit harder. Do me a favour, try to be polite to him until we get the full measure of this guy, okay? We need to see just how deep he goes. If he's nothing more than a murdering little shit, we'll cut him loose.'

Hills nodded in agreement, but as far as she was concerned, Peanut had already been dealt his first lesson and he was still a piece of shit. She had already decided that it would take a lot of convincing to make her change her mind, no matter what Chas thought.

Chapter 4

The door clanged open and Hiller stood there.

'Breakfast. Move, if you want fed.'

Peanut stood up, walked to the door and turned around with his hands behind his back, waiting to be cuffed.

'You're on trust. Break it and you'll be put in leg irons. You first, I'll follow,' she said.

Peanut stifled a grin. She didn't trust him enough to let him walk behind her. She was correct in thinking that. Hiller followed him along the hallway, before pointing at the door leading into a dining room. He noticed that she stayed at least three paces behind, far enough back to give her time to act if necessary, but also close enough to close the distance quickly. He gave a wry grin. She was wrong on both counts.

He peered into the room. There were solid, square wooden tables and chairs and enough room for twenty people or so. With the walls panelled in light cedar, it was a warm, welcoming room. There were four other guys sitting at tables, all in the same dark green uniform worn by the guy at the desk the previous evening. The driver and the turd looked different in uniforms instead of suits.

Hiller walked Peanut over to a buffet where a cook stood waiting behind the counter. He was fat and middle-aged, his obvious baldness covered by a chef's hat. He stared at Peanut and raised a bushy grey eyebrow. Peanut stared back. He heard Hiller sigh.

'Tell Herman what you want,' she said.

'Scrambled eggs and toast,' Peanut said.

The cook looked at him as if he was weird.

'That's it? No bacon, beans, sausages, chops or fillet steak?'

Peanut thought for a second.

'Nah. Just plenty of scrambled eggs and three slices of toast, please.'

Hiller leant forward.

'Two poached eggs and three rashers of bacon for me. One slice of toast. Thanks, Herman.'

The cook turned and disappeared out of sight.

Peanut walked over to an empty table, sat down and glanced around the dining room. The driver finished his meal, took his plate to the buffet and then came over. Peanut noticed that despite being around the fifty-year age mark, he was sturdy, only five-ten but solid, not fat and strong-looking with wide shoulders. His dark hair was short, almost a crew cut, but he had friendly brown eyes. He grinned at Peanut.

'Welcome to Camp Pain, Peanut. I'm Chas Ficher, the boss here. We'll have a meeting after you finish your breakfast.' He turned and walked out of the dining room and it was almost as if a signal had been given. Over the next minute, everybody went out. Peanut was left sitting by himself while Hiller sat at a table on the far side of the room, pouring over her tablet. Peanut sat quietly, waiting and watching. He was looking out of the window, when Herman came to the buffet.

'Foods up, folks,' he called.

Peanut's eggs were delicious. Herman could cook, no doubt about that. Something had been added to the eggs but he didn't know what it was. He took his plate back and he noticed Herman out in the back of the kitchen.

'Thanks, Herman,' he called out, 'that was great.'

A muffled 'okay,' drifted back to him as he turned and walked over to the coffee machine. He noticed Ms. Hiller was looking at him strangely.

***

Hills was confused. She was trying to figure him out. No criminal she had dealt with had ever said thanks unless there was a reward. It wasn't in their nature as they only used people for their own ends. That's the way criminals' minds worked, but that little piece of shit had thanked Herman. It showed consideration and an ingrained politeness and a sense of courtesy that was nearly always absent in criminal behaviour. She had studied criminology when she joined the force and what she had seen since had confirmed those studies. She wondered if Chas could be right about him, that perhaps her initial judgment was wrong. Then again, the little murdering shit might just be a good actor. Psychopaths could be polite.

Peanut noticed the trees surrounding the camp. It was a well-secluded area but if this was escape proof, he couldn't see it. The high fence with no wire outrigger would be easy to scale. He had noticed it wasn't electrified, but maybe it had low current in sections so they would know when someone climbed in or out. There was no road or walking track around the fence, which meant it wasn't patrolled. For all of Hiller's talk, this was not a secure place. So, why was his room so secure? Bars on the windows, a cell for a room—what was this place? He was still wondering about it when Hiller walked towards him.

'Meeting. Let's go,' she said. Peanut put his cup back on the buffet counter and followed after Hills.

Chas Ficher and another guy from the dining room were sitting at a large oval table that dominated the small conference room. Peanut noticed his swords and the sheath were lying on the table. Chas had two gold stars on his uniform lapels and the other guy had three stripes on his arm. *A fucking sergeant*, Peanut thought. *All I fucking need.* Solid, with a shaved bullet head, he looked like a drill sergeant. He knew then that this had to be a military or police outfit. But Hiller wasn't in any uniform. So, what was she? Hiller gestured him towards a seat. She sat down several seats away, as if she didn't want to be part of it.

The driver leant forward.

'As I said, I'm Chas, and this is Boris Weber. You've already met Amanda Hiller. Sorry about the sore nuts, but Hills was just expressing her displeasure at your comments.' He grinned. 'It pays to keep some things to yourself around here, and around Hills in particular. Many lads have found themselves flat on their backs after making inappropriate comments, generally about her ass.'

He grinned at Hiller and Peanut noticed that she scowled back and was clearly not amused.

'So, it's not one big happy family then?' asked Peanut.

'No, we're not a family. We work for Uncle Sam, semi-military in structure, but we achieve what Uncle Sam wants by working for and with each other. We expect robust debate but always structured towards achieving the goal. Personal abuse is out.'

'Yeah? My nuts tend to differ.' Peanut's expression was sour.

Chas laughed, but the sergeant didn't. Peanut knew the sergeant was eyeing him up, assessing him. The stony, staring eyes of the sergeant were meant to unnerve him, but Peanut hid his discomfort and his face remained inscrutable.

Chas continued.

'No doubt you're wondering why you are here. Well, it would help us all if we exchanged information. Whatever you tell us will go no further, especially not to the police—unless, that is, you decide to leave without our permission.'

Peanut said nothing. This sounded like the butter up before the hard sell.

'Okay, you first. Why am I here and why the stitch up?' asked Peanut.

'You were going to kill Chuckie. No loss. The police knew he had killed at least five other people anyway, at least two of them women. The true tally would probably be much higher.'

16

'I had heard that Chuckie was an equal opportunity killer. He was nothing more than a piece of shit. Incidentally, the tally for dead women is at least three, not two,' said Peanut.

Chas was surprised. 'How do you know?' he asked.

'I knew one of the women he killed.'

'They were all low-life pieces of shit that he killed, apart from the women, so the police weren't going to try too hard. They suspected Chuckie had a line into the department as he always got his fat ass out of the way of official raids pretty quickly. With him dead, that line is now out of action. So why waste a body? We needed a hold over you, and turning Chuckie into a carcass was a heaven-sent opportunity. So, we used it,' Chas said.

Peanut was still puzzled.

'You didn't answer the question. Why me? You have endless tough guys serving in specialist groups like the Seals and the Green Berets. Why the fuck pick on me?'

'Because you fit. We need your burglary skills. Under that unassuming look, you're a skilled burglar. But it's more than that. You can fit in anywhere without being noticed. You're the sum total of a nondescript person. Nobody would ever give you a second glance. You're still young enough to act like a teenager, and with the right clothes, you could probably walk into the White House and not be accosted. If they spotted you, asking you to leave would be the only response.' Chas paused for a second and smirked. 'You also seem to be very good at making unwanted pieces of shit disappear. So, there are three reasons why we want you on the team.'

'You mean you kidnapped me up just to steal something?' Peanut asked.

'Correct. That's the number one priority. Don't you get it? Everybody assumes that because of your small stature, you're inconsequential. Nobody notices you or thinks you're a threat in any way. Nobody would think you were going to steal something or do anything until it's too late. Like Chuckie.'

'So, what now?' asked Peanut.

'We'll train you and use you. Hence the hold over you.'

'I could still fuck off?' Peanut said.

Chas shook his head.

'And leave your dependent mother? Don't talk shit, Peanut. You're all she's got.'

'Yeah, I suppose,' replied Peanut thinking they really did know it all.

'We've been truthful, now it's your turn. What exactly did Chuckie want you to do?'

'The conversation never got that far. Libby screamed and I reacted. Me and Chuckie were getting along fine until you lot of assholes poked your noses in.' Chas and Ms. Hiller looked angry for a second at being called assholes, but Chas eventually gave a wry grin.

'So, what do you think he wanted?' asked Chas.

Peanut grimaced. 'A cop killed.'

Chas, Boris, and Ms. Hiller sat bolt upright.

'Who?' Hills blurted out.

'As I said, the conversation never got that far. I assume it was the bent prick that he'd been dealing with.'

'Would you have killed him? The cop I mean?' asked Hills. Peanut turned and gave her a hard stare.

'Ms. Hiller, did it look like I was agreeing with Chuckie when you spoilt our little good times party?'

Hills stared at Peanut's hard, bleak face for a second or two and then slowly shook her head. She remembered Chuckie lying on the floor, smeared in his own blood, both his ears cut off and bleeding from a wound in the groin. The only one being killed in that stinking apartment was Chuckie. It wasn't a negotiation that she had seen; it was the prelude to a murder. She had once been attached to a rapid response team and was well used to seeing the carnage that anger and guns and alcohol could cause, but up there, in that stinking apartment, there was no anger, no hate. There was nothing but cold-blooded torture and a murder that was about to take place.

Chas took control again. 'Okay, Peanut. How did you steal the ring out of a locked safe? And a late-model digital one at that.'

'Why is it so important to know? It's not like you are into stealing jewellery, is it?'

'No, but as we're going to use those burglary skills of yours, maybe we could make use of the technique. It wouldn't hurt to tell.'

'It was simple. I knew I could climb the wall of the building next door; if I could do that, then I could get across. But that would put me above the Harrisons jewelry store, not in it. So, I went into Harrisons while it was open, looking at watches and rings and paced out where to put a camera if I wanted to see the numbers entered to crack the safe. The rest was easy. Those upstairs rooms above the jeweler are cheap flats and the building next door was used for storage. I went up the corner of the wall, as you figured, in through the bathroom window, ripping my finger, again as you know; then took a door off its hinges to span the gap between the buildings.'

Chas shook his head. 'Sorry, Peanut, the window opposite was six feet higher. That wouldn't work. You're talking bullshit.'

Peanut just grinned.

'When I went up the corner, I first climbed onto the roof, attached a rope to the vent and let if fall past the window. When I was back inside, I fastened a couple of screws into each side at the front of the door, attached the rope and shoved it over, jamming the back of it with more screws into the window frame. The rope held the front of the door up. I walked out on the door, put an old chair on it, stood on it and opened the window. It wasn't latched so I went in. The woman who lived there worked the night shift at the hospital. I measured out where I wanted to cut through, lifted the carpet, cut the floorboard, and bingo, I had space down to the ceiling. I drilled a tiny hole and inserted the camera, wired it into the power circuit for the lights, attached a sender, checked the image, screwed the patch of floorboard down and replaced the carpet. By the next morning I had the code.'

'Shit! So how did you get into the store?' Chas was stunned.

'The same process. Just lifted up two more boards and then the ceiling panel and shimmied down a rope. Easy.' He chuckled as he elaborated. 'If that tight prick Harrison had spent a couple of hundred bucks and put in an internal intruder sensor alarm, he would have saved himself a fortune.'

Chas grinned at Peanut's comment and glanced at Boris.

'Any questions, Boris?' Boris sat thinking for a moment, then scowled at Peanut and pointed to the swords.

'How much do you practice?' asked Boris.

Peanut gave a noncommittal shrug.

'Varies. Some days, not at all; others, maybe four hours. I probably average about ten to fifteen hours a week. I did a lot more training while I was learning.'

'Do you practice against other people?' asked Boris.

'Twice a month.'

'You win?'

'Yes.'

'All the time?'

'Yes.'

Boris saw that as arrogance and stared angrily at Peanut.

'Tomorrow we'll have a practice. It's not good if you to let the skills go. Incidentally, if you think the pain you got from Hills on the way here was significant, I have better skills and I'm tougher. You will suffer.'

'I take it Camp Pain's specialty is pain?' asked Peanut.

Chas laughed. 'It's the name of the camp, Peanut, Camp Payne, P-A-Y-N-E.'

'We'll see you tomorrow,' said Boris as he stood up.

Chas too eased himself to his feet.

'Well, Peanut. No point in putting it off. We need to see what we have to work on.' He turned to Hills. 'Do we have spare judogi?'

Hiller nodded, smiling as she looked at Peanut. It wasn't a nice smile; it was an *I'll kick your ass* type smile. Peanut wondered for a minute what they were talking about and then remembered that a judo uniform was called a judogi. He had never done judo in his life. A bit of jiu-jitsu was about as close as he had ever got. He hoped that his multidiscipline, self-defence skills would be enough, because if they weren't, this could hurt. No doubt about it, these hijacking assholes were out to do damage.

Chapter 5

The small gym reeked worse than the rest of the place. It had the musty smell of disuse but also the smell of layers of old sweat, lots of it. Peanut knew the moment he walked in the door that whatever they did to keep fit; it wasn't done in this room. The smell of locked-up mustiness was too pervasive. This room hadn't been used for a very long time.

Chas walked around the room opening the windows, letting the cool clean smell of the forest and budding trees waft in on the spring breeze, making the room at least usable, if a bit chill. A punching bag hung on a stand stood in a corner, dusty and unused and another one, swinging on a rope in another corner, was also unused. The room was only thirty by thirty feet square and there were no weights, no benches, no parallel bars and no matts on the floor.

Peanut dragged one rubber-soled boot on the polished wooden floor and realized he had plenty of grip. He was still in his jeans and tee shirt as his small stature meant that none of the judogi fitted him, not even close. He was glad. The tight-fitting jeans and shirt would make it difficult for Hiller to get any sort of grip. She was standing beside Chas and smiling. It was the way she was smiling that worried him. Was it for real or just bullshit? He was already a murderer, so it was no skin off their noses if he died. He would simply disappear. Nobody knew where the fuck he was, and apart from the SWAT team, those who had seen Hiller at Chuckie's place were dead. A grave dug among the trees would be his fate. Peanut waited. It was too late to change things and that annoyed him. He hated being jerked around by people he didn't know. Maybe he'd better play it cautiously until he found out a bit more. He decided that was the wisest option.

Chas clapped his hands.

'Let's go, folks.'

Hiller moved in front of Peanut. He had already decided that defence was the best option. Until he knew more about things, not just how good this bitch was, but who these pricks really were, it was the only option. After all, he might wind up in the hospital, or dead.

The kick was swift. Hiller lashed out and aimed for his stomach. It was part of a one-two movement. The main kick followed even quicker, low to his kneecap. Dirty. He turned and jumped. The stomach kick missed and the kneecap kick sailed into the air. She landed and lashed out with a neck chop. He had anticipated that and deflected it. Then he surprised her by moving in close, sweeping and shoving. She staggered back, recovered, and lashed out again, but he had moved out of range, guarding, blocking, and stopping her attacks. He sized up her standard rapidly. She was good, but not good enough. Good enough to immobilize a third-year martial art's student, and maybe an average fourth-year student, but she was nowhere near his level of skill. She paused for a second after her attacks had been blocked, then came at him with a vengeance. Three rapid-fire kicking and punching attacks followed. Then she exhibited cunning, making a ploy of false feints, with a killer punch thrown in as she tried to grab his clothes. Peanut saw the openings and ignored them, easily batting her hands aside. After ten minutes, she stood back, frustrated, sweaty and now angry, very angry.

'Is that all you are going to fucking do? Just fucking block?' she yelled.

'Hey, it works for me. I'm not hurt, and neither are you. We both win.'

Chas clapped his hands to stop the contest for a second.

'Ah, that's not why we're here. We need to find out how good you are on attack, not just defence,' said Chas.

'Even if she gets hurt?' asked Peanut.

'I don't think she'll get hurt.'

Peanut raised his eyebrows. Chas obviously didn't know much about martial arts. Anyone who can defend any attack will by definition, know all the attack moves. In this style of fighting, his compact stature was a blessing. He was a small, rapidly moving target, harder to hit, harder to defend against. His brain was in overdrive. He had a tough decision to make. He knew he could easily smash Hiller. He could do a quick rotate, upend her, and drive her head into the floor. Done at the right angle, using her momentum, her neck would snap. Or he could dump her, really hard from shoulder height so the stroppy bitch who had punched his nuts would spend at least the next week or three thinking about that from a hospital bed. Trouble was, he didn't know enough about these guys. He had the gut feeling that they were a weird version of the good guys. Even though he had been framed for murder and been smacked in the nuts, they might take exception to their pet bitch getting seriously hurt.

He moved forward. Hiller noticed the change and knew it was purposeful. When he moved, it seemed as if his body was going both ways at once. He wrong-footed her immediately, his kick low and to the shin. She wore the blow, it was light, then turned to strike. She missed the hit, her arm was deflected; a quick shove from the opposite side and she lost her balance, staggering. Suddenly her legs were gone, a rapid punch numbing her. She could feel her body, but she couldn't control it. She had the unexpected feeling of weightlessness as her legs went out from under her and her body dropped towards the floor. She felt his quick hold that broke most of her fall, but she still landed hard on her back, her head smacking the floor. She blacked out momentarily. She was hazy, winded, and numb. When she came to, she saw his boot heel just above her throat. His foot was steady and unmoving. She was helpless. She distantly heard him speak to Chas, his voice conversational, polite.

'Do I kill her now or later?' asked Peanut.

Chas shook his head.

'Neither. Stand down. You've proved your point.'

She watched his foot move away and lay there, not really knowing what had happened as she waited for the feeling to return to her body. He had hit her on a nerve point paralyzing her muscles for a second or two. She had learnt some spots on the body that could do that, but not that one. She had been dumped and dumped with ease. Then the realization hit her. He could have killed her. The offhand manner in which he had asked if he should kill her now or later unnerved her. He could have killed her with ease. She got to her feet and stood on shaky legs, unable to hide the fact that she was still groggy.

'Go and get changed, Hills, and thanks. Well done, now we know just how good Peanut is,' said Chas as he pointed to the door.

She turned and walked out, not bothering to look at Peanut. He watched her go, his face blank as he smiled to himself. Her pride had been badly dented. Good, that was part payback for his sore nuts. But only part. She still needed a lesson, a hard lesson, that bitch.

As the door closed behind her, Chas turned to Peanut.

'Depending on tomorrow and your meeting with Boris, we might not have to train you in self-defence. It might be just the technical stuff. But be warned, Boris is tough. And you'll be fighting with kendo sticks.'

'What, no swords?' asked Peanut.

Chas stared hard at Peanut and immediately thought he was joking and a half smile formed on his lips. Then he noticed the hard bleak eyes staring back at him and realized that Peanut was impossible to read. Was he joking? Or was he for real? The half smile died on his lips. Enough feedback from Hills and Peter had convinced him of Peanuts skills with the swords. Deep down, he hoped Peanut was joking or they just might have bitten of more than they could chew.

'No,' said Chas. He paused and then added, 'Tell me, why did you kill Mick Ortega?'

'That's only a rumor. My brother is in jail because of him. Ortega was working with the police. He and Danny had a disagreement and got into a fight. When Danny won, Ortega framed him. Said he had attacked him, and the police backed him up. Danny should have

21

known better than to associate with shit like that. I spoke to Ortega and he laughed at me, punched me from behind when I went to leave, then kicked me while I was on the ground. Ten seconds later, it was over.'

'Where's the body?'

'Where it should be. In the cemetery. It's three feet down on top of a recently buried homeless guy. I figured he wouldn't mind the company.'

Chas laughed. 'Okay, what about Fellows?'

Peanut gave a nonchalant shrug.

'I didn't kill him. He was the gang's drug runner. He sold to street vendors. I swiped his drugs and most of the gang's as well and pilfered a lot from the main supplier. I left Fellows mark all over it. He disappeared and I got blamed. The gang moved on after most of them were busted.'

'I remember. It was inside information to the police, as I understand it. The gang is still trying to figure out who the hell it was. Let me guess. You had a hand in it?' asked Chas.

'I got blamed because I was the last to see Fellows alive. That's all.'

'He came to kill you, correct?'

'Yeah.'

Chas knew there wasn't much point in any further questioning. He had formed his own opinion of Peanut.

'And he didn't, obviously. Which is why you're here,' Chas said. 'Let's go grab a coffee in the dining room. Herman always keeps a pot on.'

***

The dining room was empty as Peanut enjoyed his second cup of coffee. Chas had downed a quick one and then left, leaving Peanut nursing his mug, sitting by the window, watching a squirrel in the trees, and thinking that this was a pleasant place to stay. It was peaceful, soothing. Then it struck him. The locked cell doors, yet everything else was open. The unused feel of the place. The mustiness of the building, the gym, the rooms. This had once been a drug rehabilitation center. He had just solved another mystery.

The door opened and Hiller walked in. She paused when she saw him, then went and got herself a coffee before sitting down at the table. She had showered; her hair was damp, and the smell of her perfume filled his nostrils. He returned his attention to the squirrel as it jumped to another branch.

'You're good,' she said.

Without looking at her, he replied quietly, 'By the time I was eight or nine, I knew that if I was to survive, I had to have an edge. Something that levelled the playing field. I only had my body, so martial arts it was. I've learnt four different styles. I've been doing this for a very long time.'

There was quiet for a moment as she thought things over.

'Okay, so why?' she asked. 'Why attack Chuckie and Ortega and the ones we don't know about?' He glanced at her, then carried on looking out the window as he talked. She could hear the sadness in his voice.

'We had a nice neighborhood. Old time sort of neighborhood where people tended to look out for each other. Then the drug dealers started to arrive. I made some move on, but guys like Fellows, Ortega, and Chuckie kind'a dug their heels in. They thought that as they had the numbers they were invincible. They were wrong. I was hoping that Chuckie would've had the brains to move on. He didn't, so I planned to move him on, permanently.' He turned his head and looked at her sadly. 'Then you lot of stupid pricks poked your pointy noses in.' He wasn't going to tell her the real reason he went to see Chuckie: Janice-Rose.

He noticed she was annoyed. She obviously didn't like being called a stupid prick. Peanut sat quietly, once again focusing his eyes out of the window, not bothering to look at her.

'Ever get beaten?' she asked.

'In the gym? Sometimes, but not for a while, maybe a couple of years. Out in the real world, getting beaten means you're dead.'

She gave a grunt, agreeing with him.

'Yes, it does. It keeps you on your toes,' she said.

'Yeah.'

'I spoke with Chas. I apologize. I had you wrong.'

'No, you had it right,' he said.

'That you're a murdering little shit?' She gave a nervous laugh, but it dried up when she saw his face. It was if it had been carved out of stone. His blue-grey eyes were bleak, cruel.

'Yes,' he said in a flat voice.

'So, if Chas had said go ahead, you would have killed me?'

'Yes.'

They stared at each other until his cold eyes got to her.

'Why? I was on the floor immobilized. I was helpless, for Christs sake!' she said

His eyes never left her face as he replied.

'If that had been me on the floor and Chas had said to kill me, you would've.'

She was stunned. Her mind went into overdrive. Would she have killed him? She knew Chas would never do that, but what if he did? The thought badly unsettled her.

He studied her, seeing her discomfort.

'Ms. Hiller, do you believe in good and evil?'

'I'm a police officer, of course I do.'

'In my experience, being a police officer can mean something or sometimes it can mean nothing. The world is simple. If someone tries to point a gun at you, do you shoot first or go ask a judge and jury to decide?'

'I shoot first, of course. Self-defence.'

'I do the same. But as I'm not a law enforcement officer, that makes me a killer,' said Peanut. 'And I'm happy with that opinion. I didn't ask to fight you. It was something you and Chas dreamt up. If that meant your death, that decision wasn't mine. I would have killed you. Play with fire, Ms Hiller and sometimes you get burnt.'

She abruptly stood up and walked to the buffet. She didn't think Peanut was someone she wanted to get to know. Whatever had happened in his past life had turned him into an exacting and cold-blooded killer. She placed her used cup on the tray and left. Unlike the other guys in the camp, Peanut now scared her. She now knew that Chuckie never stood a chance. She wondered what Boris would make of it all tomorrow. Should she warn him?

Chapter 6

With two kendo sticks in his hands, Boris waited. No fancy white judogi, just shorts and a grey military-style tee. Peanut was still in the jeans and tee he'd been wearing when he first arrived. There were two kendo sticks lying on the floor. It had been a long time since he had used sticks. He found his swords so much better. They were lighter, quicker, and lethal, if not as sturdy because of their thin blades. But he had used sticks often enough to know that he would adapt almost instantly.

They had an audience. Chas, Hiller, the guy with the corporal stripes, and the older guy, Peter. He was again out of uniform and again dressed as a turd. Everyone had come to see him get smashed; there was no doubt about it. They had heard what had happened to Ms. Hiller and decided that this was going to be a fight to see. If he was going to be smashed, Peanut decided he would go out with a bang. When it was over, they would shoot him. There was nothing he could do about that, and he knew it.

He controlled his breathing and set himself up for combat. He was ready. He eyed up Boris. At an even six feet tall, he was not fat and had wide, strong shoulders. Peanut guessed that he used his strength instead of skill and cunning. He would soon see. Chas laid out the rules.

'When I clap my hands, the fight is over. I'll shoot anybody who carries on. Clear?'

Peanut gave Chas a bleak look—that stupid speech was for him. Would it apply to Boris? He didn't think so. As he bent to pick up the sticks, Boris attacked. Peanut saw him move. He was used to dishonest moves and he threw himself forward and down and Boris's strike missed him. Peanut scooped up the sticks and using one as a fend, he jabbed with the other and hit Boris hard in the groin. Boris staggered and his face twisted in pain. Peanut had a fraction of a second to roll clear and spring to his feet. That had been a dirty move on Boris's part. He wasn't going to let him forget it. It had also been stupid. It told him that Boris wasn't sure of himself. Boris wanted the sort of edge that a hard early hit gave. What Boris didn't know was that kendo was the first martial art that Peanut had learnt and that was why he carried the swords. It was his best discipline.

He took note of Boris's stance. It had to be a quick decisive takedown. Boris moved into attack and swung one stick while the other was in a standard defensive position ready to knock aside any attacks. That was when Peanut preformed the unexpected. It was the simplest of moves. But it was fast, just a blur of movement. He flipped both sticks together, ducked and drove forward towards Boris's face. Boris reacted instinctively and brought his sticks in to knock Peanut's out of the way. Peanut immediately swung his sticks outwards, taking Boris's sticks away as he stepped in close, really close, driving his knee into Boris's already sore groin. Swinging his sticks in, he grabbed Boris's head between his wrists and head butted him. Boris reeled backwards, staggering, dazed as Peanut executed a simple hip throw. Boris hit the floor with a thump, his head smacking the floor and the floor reverberating with the shock. Peanut could feel it through the soles of his boots. Boris lay there unconscious and Peanut swung his sticks together, placed the ends on Boris's throat, and looked at Chas.

'Shall I kill him now or later?'

'Neither.' Chas shook his head at the speed with which it had happened. 'Stand down.' Chas knew Boris had the upper hand at the start of the fight. He had seen him attack first, but the speed and ease of his defeat was total. Chas stared at Peanut and saw the bleak look. He knew if he had said yes, Boris would be dead. Hills had told him the same thing. It appeared they hadn't just hired a skilled burglar, they had hired a killer.

Chas was now delighted. He grimaced at Peanut, happy. As a team, they now had an edge, a lethal edge. He nodded at Hills. 'Check Boris, will you?'

She crouched down beside Boris as he began to stir. She knew he would be alright. It would be his pride that had taken the biggest hammering.

***

When Chas walked into the dining room, Peanut was enjoying a coffee. Chas sat down next to him.

'I need to keep fit.' Peanut said instead of greeting Chas. 'When do I get a run?'

'You and Hills can go later today.'

'Wrong. I run alone. Ms Hiller and I have history. She might shoot me in the back if I go with her.' Peanut's voice was flat and matter-of-fact.

'It's that or nothing. You need to keep fit, but it's bullshit that you need protecting from Hills.'

'There is no defense against a bullet. Only mugs believe the stupid shit that they put in the movies.'

'She won't shoot you, believe me. Hills is a total professional. We have plans for you, starting next week and Hills will be part of the team you're on. Besides, I doubt that she would go running with a gun.' Chas paused a second as if gathering his thoughts. 'I have a lot of doubt that you'll ever become a team player. Much of what we do requires teamwork, but as a lone operative, I think you would be superb. Hills will come and get you when she's ready.'

He turned away and walked out of the door, leaving Peanut wondering what he would be doing next week. It had to be the reason why he had been kidnapped, surely?

***

Peter was leaning up against the porch post, jacket draped over the rail, sipping his coffee and enjoying what was turning into a nice day. He never heard Blue come up behind him.

'Nice out. A bit of sun to lounge around in would be nice.' Peter didn't even turn. He was annoyed that his peace and quiet was disturbed and he sighed.

'Yeah.' He didn't say any more, hoping that Blue would fuck off. No chance. Peter loved the peace and quiet of the forest and Blue was intruding.

'Out latest recruit is turning out to be something special,' Blue said. 'He really dumped Hills.'

'He's a crim.'

'Yeah, maybe, but he trashed Boris as well.'

'He's still a fucking crim.' Peter flicked his coffee dregs into the long grass by the steps. It was obvious that Blue wasn't going to leave and he had no intention of wasting time talking shit with him. He turned and strode off, Blue grinning at his retreating back. For some reason, Peter seemed to have taken a dislike to the new recruit. But it was hard to tell. Peter was rude to everyone. But as an ex-Cop of many years' experience, his attitude towards the criminal element was set in stone. Blue thought about it. Peanut had never been charged with anything and apart from them arresting him as he was in the process of killing Chuckie, so did that make him a crim? Chuckie deserved everything he got and his death was justice, rough justice but still justice. So was Peanut a crim? Blue grimaced. Grumpy Peter could have that wrong.

***

Peanut sprinted up the hill, leaving Hiller in his wake. At the top he paused before jogging down the other side. He waited at the bottom for her to catch up. She was still getting her breathing back to normal when she arrived.

25

'Do you always run that fast?' she asked.

'I use the hills to put maximum strain on my body and then recover on the downhill side. It's my version of fartlek training.'

She gave him an ironic smile. 'It seems to work,' she replied.

He shrugged.

'Can we walk for a bit and chat? I need to recover,' she said.

'Okay. What do you want to talk about?'

'Nothing much, just chat. There's not much social chatting back at the camp. Boris is not much of a conversationalist at the best of times and Chas is okay, but he's a lot older than me. Blue, the corporal, is nearly forty, randy, and married, so chatting just doesn't happen,' she said.

'Chat away,' Peanut replied even though he wasn't particularly interested. Her not having enough talkative company was not his problem.

'Your mom works?' she asked.

'Yeah. Stacks shelves at night and does the morning shift on the till at the same supermarket. She's a good person and she means well but she just gets lonely for male company. Sometimes she gets sucked into the bullshit some men spin just to get her into the sack. Danny and I look out for her. But with me here and Danny inside, she's on her own and I worry about her.'

'I'll raise that with Chas. We'll need you to focus, not worry about your mother. So, no sisters?'

'Two. Maggie and Janice-Rose. Maggie was murdered. The boyfriend who killed her and her baby is in jail. Twenty-five years he got. She was pregnant at the time.'

'Ouch! That is sad. It'll be some time until he's out.'

'Yes. He'll wish he'd stayed inside.'

Hills noted the threat even though it was said indirectly. She was in no doubt it would be carried out.

'Janice-Rose?' she asked.

He didn't comment. It was his business, but then he remembered that they already knew so much, probably too much about him. If they wanted, they would find out about that too. He decided to tell her.

'I'm trying to track her down. She had a row with Mom and ran off. She had fallen in love with a moron. Now she's disappeared. I want to find her.'

'Any ideas?' she asked.

'Yeah. Chuckie. He ran women and if Janie-Rose had been forced to go on the game, he would have known. He would also have known if her boyfriend was dealing as well. That was my hunch.'

'Yeah, that line of inquiry is a real dead end.'

Peanut didn't smile. Witty puns as far as his sister went were out.

'Apart from finding Janice-Rose, have you ever given any thought to what you want to do with your life? I mean, I get a lot of satisfaction out of what we do here. I know that we make a difference.'

Peanut pulled a face. He was surprised by her question.

'I'll take your word for it.'

'So? What do you want to do with your life?'

Peanut scowled. 'Until you arrested me, I was looking out for Mom and I had a job in an electronics shop, selling stuff and assisting customers with their electronic kit sets. When they got stuck, I'd put the kit together for them or show them how. Sometimes they'd bring them in, and I'd help them solve what had gone wrong.'

'So, you know electronics?'

'Some.'

'You have a computer, obviously.'

'I have a laptop that I share with Mom. It's mainly hers, and a desk job that I built.'

'Gaming?'

'No. Not interested. Sorting shitheads out in real life is much more fun. And then I have my training and fitness.'

'Girlfriend?' she asked.

He snorted and pointed at himself. 'A runt like me? Get real. I have girls as friends. That's it.'

'That's sad.'

'That's the hand that life deals you. You live with it and you move along. I'd rather be who I am than a beefed-up jock with ten girlfriends and poodle shit for brains.'

Hiller burst into laughter and it surprised him. It was a pleasant tinkling sound. It made Peanut realize that under her hard cloak was a person, a woman, probably even a nice woman, not just a semi-military bitch. Not that it meant anything.

'Can I ask if you'd like a girlfriend?'

He stopped and stared at her. It was the strangest question. Then she seemed embarrassed.

'I am,' said Peanut, 'sorry *was*, perfectly happy the way things were before you lot came onto the scene and fucked it. Ready to run again? We have a nice hill up ahead.'

She glanced up. The hill was steep, really steep and her heart dropped. This was going to kill her. The next time he could run by himself, or take Boris or Chas. They needed a fucking workout more than she did!

***

They walked through the gate and ambled up to the camp. She was still struggling for breath and panted as she talked.

'Don't take it personally,' she said.

'What?'

'Me asking you about girlfriends. It's just something women do. We care about relationships more than men do.'

'I wasn't taking it personally. It was just a strange question, given that you lot probably still haven't made up your minds whether to shoot me or not.'

'There are no plans to shoot you.'

'If that's the case, then your recruiting technique needs sorting. It is shit.' He turned at the top of the stairs and went to his room.

He had just settled on the bed when the door swung open. Hiller stood there. She didn't have to say anything. He stood up and she followed him to the small conference room. It was the usual mob with two new guys in plain suits. They sort'a looked like the FBI. As he walked in and sat down, the new guys gave him the once-over.

'Petrov and Smythe. Department of State. They're here to help us lay out a plan for next week,' Chas said by way of introduction.

It was then that Peanut noticed a large screen on the wall that showed images of a square, three-story building. The street front was semi-Romanesque, but the sides and back were plain redbrick with square-plastered quoins. There were no easy inside corners to climb, only old cast-iron drainpipes and only one was near a window.

Petrov stood up. Tall and lean, with short hair and a thin face, he looked like an ex-basketball player. From what Peanut could see of Smythe, he was laid back and fat. An office junkie. His face said he was forty-five, but his belly said sixty.

'We've decided to move forward,' said Petrov as he pointed at the screen. 'This is the target building. The office is on the top floor, situated here.' He clicked on his laptop and the side of the building showed up. 'You can see it's typical of the times. It's well over a hundred years old. The top-floor configuration is a central hallway, three offices, one on one side and two on the other. The target office is the back one of the two.' He pointed to the back half of the three-story building. 'The office is behind these three windows.'

Peanut knew he could climb the corner with ease. The short roof over-hang would help. Petrov clicked again and the full frontage of the building came up. The roof had a high gable in the style of government buildings at that time. Peanut stared closely at the front. Behind the top balustrade was a small balcony, just wide enough for someone to stand on to change the flag. The doorway behind would open into the roof space. The stairway inside would lead to the floor below.

Easy, thought Peanut.

'Doable?' asked Chas.

Peanut was noncommittal, even though he could see it would be easy. 'Yeah, I think so. But there could be a problem opening the internal doors. Most offices are alarmed. Is the ceiling in the office modern panels or a high stud with plaster?'

'Ceiling panels, modern,' Petrov said.

'Are you sure?' asked Peanut.

Petrov was annoyed at the request but started the video. It showed the entrance into an office and modern acoustic infill panels. He played another video; this one showed the way through to the offices out the back; all had the same ceiling. Peanut was pleased. Given the building's age, he suspected the roof space would probably have an internal walkway, just to service the lighting and the roof. That was normal when buildings like this were built.

Smythe stood up.

'You have all the info, so we'll leave that with you,' he said nonchalantly. 'Any problems, you're on your own.' He pasted on a cheesy smile as Petrov packed up his computer, and they left.

Chas turned to Peanut as the door closed. 'You can get in and out, can't you? Unseen and unheard.'

'Probably. I'd like to see this building up close. Just to make sure.'

'Not in daylight. There are video monitors everywhere. You might get noticed and we know they'll scrutinize that video footage when they realize they've lost the items.'

'What is that building?'

'It's an ex-US Government Treasury building.'

Peanut didn't react but felt his heart drop. Buildings like that were built for security. What was he missing? It couldn't be that easy, could it?

Chapter 7

'What are we after?' Peanut asked the obvious.

Chas smiled. 'The Department of State did an investigation. Too many little things were turning up in the hands of people who shouldn't have had access. By that I mean restricted information. The firm that has the corner office is an investigative firm of dubious parentage, but it seems to be owned by Russians or people with Russian connections. The department's investigation showed that the firm had, most probably, in fact almost certainly, obtained some damning evidence relating to work that the department had done on behalf of Uncle Sam. For the Department of State to get evidence of the theft they'd have to apply to the courts for a subpoena to search the offices. That means they would have to reveal what the documents were they were looking for and that is what they want to avoid. As they want no public scrutiny and as they don't have sufficient evidence to apply for that subpoena, we steal it back. Simple, huh?'

Although Peanut had it figured, he saw the downside immediately. 'And if all this goes tits up, I would go to jail for theft. For a very long time.'

'Yes, it's certainly a reason not to fail,' Chas said.

'And there is no evidence that the firm is in possession of anything, is that right?' Peanut asked.

'Correct. But there is circumstantial evidence that they have it. But that probably won't get us a subpoena.' Chas paused, thinking, wondering how far to go, then continued.

'There have been conversations in which references were made to things that could have only come from the documents. Either way, the Department of State wants to know.'

'When can I see the building?' Peanut asked.

'Tomorrow night. That gives us a couple of days to get everything we need and then we'll go in over the weekend. Saturday or Sunday night will be your debut.'

Peanut didn't like what they were suggesting, but he wasn't about to say anything. He wanted to see the building first, at night.

'Hills, you and Peanut take the Chevy. Peter, Boris Blue and I will take the SUV. We leave in one hour. Pack your bags,' said Chas as he stood up.

'I don't have a bag. I'm still in the clothes you arrested me in,' Peanut said. 'I washed them in the sink and dried them overnight, but if I don't get some clean clothes, I'm going to protest by not washing. Then you will have to shoot me to get rid of the smell.'

Chas sighed. 'Hills, when we get to the hotel, take Peanut and buy him some new clothes.' Hills nodded.

'Yeah, Ms. Hiller. A nice black suit. They always look good in a coffin or on a corpse.' Peanut's voice was quiet as he glanced at the sour faces of Chas and Hiller. His quip didn't go down well. He still wanted to know the surname of the guy in the brown suit, the walking turd, Peter. He was the asshole who had framed him.

***

The Chevy Suburban cruised along the highway. Peanut was enjoying the peace and quiet until Ms. Hiller spoiled it by starting a conversation.

'You think you can do this? That building looks pretty impregnable,' she said.

'Yeah. My worry isn't getting in or out, it's getting caught. None of you pricks would put me on your prisoner visiting list.'

His bitter tone said it all and she changed the subject.

'Has Chas told you what you're after?'

'Not yet. Looks like a fishing expedition to me, more than any recovery. He's probably not sure himself,' Peanut replied.

'Only Chas knows the details. Wait until he tells you what it is.' She glanced over at him; his slight wiry frame was almost dwarfed by the large front seat of the Chevy. 'What clothes do you need?'

'Jeans, shirts, tee shirts and underpants. Socks and runners as well, if we have the time. I always buy in the boys' department,' he said. 'You'd think that they would be cheaper, but they aren't. It's a costly business raising kids.'

'You want a family?' she asked, 'like kids of your own?'

'Never thought about it. Christ! I'm only twenty-four!'

'It's your birthday next month. You're almost three years younger than me. But in three or more years, would you want to be a dad?' She was persistent. It began to annoy Peanut.

'Ms. Hiller, I haven't given it any thought. And with a charge of murder hanging over my head and a dodgy unpaid occupation stealing things for Uncle Sam, it's not even worth considering. Let's just get this job over with, huh?'

'You can call me Hills.'

'And risk another smack in the balls? I don't think so, Ms. Hiller. Let's just stick with what we know and love, eh?' He relaxed in his oversized seat and took in the scenery. The drive back to Washington had a side benefit; he now knew exactly where the camp was situated. Hiller made no further comment and he could see that she was miffed. Tough! He had no intention of becoming friendly. Polite, maybe, but why would he want to become friends? This was the only job he'd been hired for. Despite what they said, he had a feeling that the plan would be to make him disappear once it was over. Then he couldn't say anything about what he had done.

***

It was close to ten p.m. when they drove past the building. They had stopped at the hotel and dropped Hiller's bags off before they went shopping. With Uncle Sam paying, he got two pairs of jeans, two shirts, a packet with five pairs of underpants, and four tee shirts. Hills didn't say a word; she was bored. Sourcing good quality runners and socks was a bit more difficult, but two pairs of New Balance and four pairs of socks later, he was satisfied. He had clothing for not only the next week but the months ahead. He picked up a backpack and went for the dearest, a better quality one, again because Uncle Sam was paying. Once he was outside, he bundled his new clothes into it. He smiled inwardly. Good old Uncle Sam. Great fucking guy!

Peanut studied the building as Hiller drove by. The roof overhang was shorter than he expected, less than ten inches. Perfect. The gable slope was also less. All in all, he was feeling pretty good about this job. Even so, that worried him. It was clear they wanted him in and out in one night. That could be pushing things. He decided he would suggest a Saturday night intervention, just in case he had to go back.

They drove around the block and parked on the opposite side of the street. Secure behind the dark windows of the Chevy, Peanut scanned the building with binoculars. When he told Hiller they could go, she drove off slowly, heading for the hotel just as her phone rang. She pulled over and answered it. It was Chas.

'There's a meeting in the hotel bar and you're invited,' she said after she hung up.

He nodded as he watched the scurrying Friday night traffic. He loved cities. The bustle, the noise, the frenetic movement of people making money. It excited him. There was something alive in all the movement and he couldn't understand why people wanted to live in the country. Nice for a holiday, but it really was deadbeat-ville the rest of the time. Who the fuck wants to sit around and listen to the ducks quack and the cows moo?

Hiller parked in the underground parking lot and they rode the escalator up to their rooms. Peanut dropped his backpack and went back to the lobby and the adjacent bar. It was nearly empty. Across the room, at a table well away from the few people that were there, Chas and Peter were sitting and Chas stood up and waved him over.

'Excited?' Chas asked.

'Nope. Why?'

'The start of a new career. Maybe?'

'I never planned on breaking-and-entering as a career.'

Chas seemed energized as he pointed to Peanut's glass. 'Drink?'

'Thanks, but I don't. I'll have a lemon, lime and bitters and don't slip in any Vodka. I can taste the alcohol.'

Chas signaled a waiter. Peanut noticed Peter looking sourly at him.

'Peter, what's your last name? Just so I don't confuse you with someone else,' he asked.

Peter ignored him.

'It's Withers, Peanut. And yes, he is a dour prick, but he's one of the best operatives in the business. Don't mind him,' said Chas. 'Have you seen the building yet?'

'Yeah.'

'And?'

'It's okay. I'd prefer Saturday night, just in case I need a spare night to fix anything up.'

'That shouldn't be necessary,' said Peter.

Peanut grimaced. 'What say we let Mr. Expert here lead the way in and show us how it's done, shall we?'

'Not my fucking job, asshole,' snarled Peter.

'Not mine either. I was framed to do this job by you, remember?'

Peter snorted. 'So fucking sue me. I'm not going to be the one waiting for the needle on death row.'

Chas raised his hands in a peace gesture. 'Gentlemen, gentlemen. We'll get there faster if we don't bicker. When Hills arrives, we'll sort out the details.' He opened a file and pushed a sheet of A4 towards Peanut.

'That's the layout of the office. We think this back office houses the safe room. It has bars on the window.'

Peanut studied the drawing. It had been lifted off the plans. The room with the bars in the window was backed up against the wall adjacent to the central passage and the rear of the office. How secure was it? He knew he would have to check it out.

'Whatever your resident expert thinks, we go tomorrow night. I don't know enough about what's in there. I might have to get specialist tools and come back on Sunday.'

'Okay, Peanut. Tomorrow night it is.'

Peanut was surprised at Chas' swift agreement. He was pleased; it gave him breathing room.

Just then Chas looked up and gave a low whistle. Hiller had walked in, dressed up and looking gorgeous. Her hair was loose, she wore a dash of makeup and her blue dress was slinky and sexy, with a tasteful hint of cleavage. Peanut thought she looked a treat. Every muscle in her ass was visible with each step she took. It was a show and a half and Peanut noticed the men at the bar turning to look at her. Hills's smirk told him she was enjoying the attention. She sashayed over and sat down next to Chas.

'What's been sorted out, Chas?' she asked.

'We go tomorrow night.'

'Why?'

'Peanut wants time. He's studied the layout and isn't sure what's in there. He might have to get specialist tools and go back on Sunday. So, we go tomorrow night.

'Understood. What are the teams?' asked Hills.

'Peanut and you with Peanut on the inside, you on watch duty outside. Peter and I will be on watch duty a block away. We'll be wired together so we'll have constant contact.'

'Okay.'

Peanut leant forward. 'Do you mind telling me what I am supposed to be stealing, sorry, liberating?'

'You had it right the first time, buddy. You're just a thief,' Peter said sarcastically.

'There's a wanker in every room. Let's all guess who it is in here,' replied Peanut.

Peter flushed in anger and began to rise while Chas, hiding a grin, signaled for peace. He opened the file in front of him and handed a copy to Peanut.

Peanut read the cover sheet. *Interdepartmental Working Group Long Term Governmental Data Integration Plan.* Underneath that heading were smaller sub-headings regarding actions.

Data Security during Integration

Departmental Amalgamation and Redundancy.

Planned Response to Departmental Resistance to Changes

Then the biggie: *Removal/Relocation of Personnel Opposing Change/Plan.*

Peanut knew the importance of these documents. How to blow up the existing government structure in four easy steps.

'The Department of State obviously want this back?' chuckled Peanut.

'Desperately.'

'So how the fuck did they lose it?' he asked.

'They didn't. It was copied and then sent by email—and before you ask, the FBI think they've caught the guy. But he refuses to admit anything, so the investigation is ongoing. The FBI said it was sent to an individual that the department can't trace, despite their considerable resources.'

'It won't make the *New York Times Book of the Year*, that's for sure, but I bet a lot of people would like to have a look,' said Peanut.

'I don't think the author gave a shit about the *New York Times Book of the Year*,' said Chas.

'So how many copies of this have been made since—or is that an unknown?' asked Peanut.

'That's what you're going to find out. Check desks, drawers, thumb drives, anything and everything. It's advantageous that this document is so secret only a few know of its existence. Given its secrecy, we don't think multiple copies will have been run off. Its value is in it staying secret. There's no leverage if its contents become widely known. That's it, Peanut. That's what we want. What time do you want to start?'

'Ten p.m.'

'Reason?' Chas asked.

'Anybody on the street will be looking ahead to a good night, hoping to get a few drinks in and get laid. People in cars will be eyeing up the talent and those on foot will be doing the same. In the background, up high, we'll be unimportant.'

'That sounds fair enough,' said Chas.

Peter grunted sarcastically. 'Let's see if it works.'

Chas had enough of the bickering and grumped harshly at Peter. 'If it doesn't work, we'll all be out of a job. We're all volunteers, remember? There's no golden handshake with another job offer waiting. How are your job prospects looking in the cold light of day, given that you're not in the prime of your life anymore?'

Peter's face turned red.

Chapter 8

Peanut noticed Ms. Hiller was looking at him with an unflinching stare. It was unfathomable. The sort of look he had seen some women have when they were after something and trying to figure whether it was worth it or how to get it. As soon as she noticed him looking at her, she glanced away. Peanut reminded himself of his priorities. She might be pretty and tonight she was stunning, but she was still the enemy. He finished his drink.

'Get you another?' Chas asked.

'No thanks. Do meals go on our room numbers?' Peanut asked.

'You hungry?'

'Yeah. Food then bed, I think.'

'Okay.' Chas paused for a second. 'You know you're on trust here, don't you?'

'Yeah. I know.'

Chas broke the short silence.

'Hills told us about your brother. I've approached the appropriate people in the department and he's a candidate for early release. The end of next week, all going well.'

Peanut was stunned. Danny out! He knew that once he was out, Danny would be able to look after their mom, no matter what happened to him. He felt the tension ease, as if a rock had been lifted off his chest. He had been worried sick about her. He knew she would have been wondering where he had gone.

'Thanks, that really means a lot. To Mom as well as Danny and me.'

'Thank Hills. She's the one who did all the work. Even told me what to say to the officials. But she's right. We can't have you distracted. We need you focused. So, go say thank you.'

Peanut stood up, walked around the table and sat next to Hiller. She glanced at him and was clearly uncomfortable. Her look was anything but inviting.

'Ms. Hiller, I want to say thanks. Chas told me what you have done to get Danny an early release. Mom will be delighted and thank you again. It does take a lot of the worry away.'

She was taken aback and looked confused, then recovered and suddenly smiled.

'You're welcome. I said I would, so I did. Danny is by all accounts a model prisoner. He wants out just as much as they want to get the numbers down.'

'Thanks again, Ms. Hiller.' Peanut stood, ready to leave.

'Where are you going?' she asked.

'Next door for a meal. Going to find out if they can cook scrambled eggs as good as Herman can.' She gave an unladylike snort.

'Probably not. Can I come with you? I'm hungry too.'

As he followed her out of the bar and into the dining room, eyes and surreptitious glances followed her. If those turkeys watching had any idea just how fast she could dump their fat backsides on the floor, they just might look the other way. He knew he looked out of place. Hiller was elegant in her dress and high heels and she towered over him. His jeans and flat-heeled boots just didn't cut it. They sat down and the wine waiter came over.

'You drink wine?' asked Peanut.

She shook her head. 'No. You?'

'Lemon, lime and bitters please,' Peanut said to the waiter. Hiller nodded.

'The same, please.'

'Did you ever drink?' she asked.

'Not really. I saw what my dad did to my mom when he was drunk.'

'I get a feeling there are things that have happened in your life that have made you hard, am I right?'

'Don't pry, Ms. Hiller. Some things are best left alone. What are we going to eat?'

'For fuck's sake! Call me either Hills or Mandy. Please!'

'Yeah, okay. As everyone calls you Hills, we'll stick to that. So, what's to eat—Hills?' asked Peanut.

She studied the menu. 'Old favorite. Caesar Salad. You?'

'Steak burger. I need the iron.' She examined his slight frame and remembered his speed and endurance when he was running.

'I think you have stamina to burn, just quietly. And you strike me as a guy who doesn't give up. You just keep on going.'

'Isn't that what we're all doing? Trying to get ahead? Trying to make things better?'

She gave him a cynical look. 'And how does making things better fit in with you killing Chuckie?'

He stared hard at her for a second, then cleared the air.

'Chuckie raped the sixteen-year-old daughter of Mom's friend. Cheryl Alonso was her name. Nothing could be done until she lodged a complaint and when she did, a week later she disappeared. They found her body in a drum in a warehouse. There was no evidence to link her to Chuckie. I grew up with that girl, played with her out in our yard. She had hopes and dreams. She was a lovely girl and a good friend. She didn't deserve to be raped and murdered. Chuckie did. Rough justice? Yes. But justice it was. I was going to kill him and whisper her name in his ear as he died. Just to let him know what he was dying for. Then you lot fucked it. But it doesn't matter now. It's all sorted.'

Hills sat quiet, imagining the pain Cheryl's parents must have gone through. Would they feel better now Chuckie was dead? She suspected they would stand and cheer. She would, but it would never bring their daughter back.

'Yes, it's all sorted,' she said.

The meals arrived and they ate in silence. Peanut had to admit the burger was great, really great.

Hills had finished and was watching him.

'Better than Herman's food?' she said and laughed.

'Oh, yeah, but can they outdo Herman on scrambled eggs? I have my doubts!'

***

Peanut spent the next morning going over the details and the layout of the safe room. He was looking for inspiration, anything that would give him an edge. He learnt nothing more than what he already knew. He sat back and his thoughts returned to the evening with Hills. She had been fun. Work was never mentioned and they laughed about the funny things that happened at school and work and drank lemon, lime and bitters until their bladders had said enough. He had walked her to her room.

'Thanks for a fun evening and thanks again on behalf of Danny. Mom will be so happy,' he'd said to her.

'You're welcome, it was fun. Let me know if you have any luck finding your sister. If you have a rough location, we could help.' She then smiled at him. 'Shall we do this again after the job is over?'

'We'll see. That all depends on what happens tomorrow,' Peanut said. 'Goodnight.'

She gave a brief nod and turned and walked to her room. He watched her for a second before turning and walking back to his. He barely remembered getting into bed.

He got Hills to take him shopping and bought the things he thought he would need, working off a list. He knew he would need a battery drill with screwdriver and drill bits. He bought one at the local hardware store along with a one-inch hard-cutter knife and a fine board saw; both were ideal for cutting hard surfaces. Needle-nose pliers and a length of jumper wire went into the pile along with a tablet computer, just in case he needed to check any thumb drives. Last came the rope, shackles, and a length of light line. It all fitted neatly into his new backpack. He was well prepared and as the afternoon rolled around, he went back to bed for a sleep. At two in the morning, he would appreciate it.

***

It was just on ten p.m. when Hills stopped the Chevy on the street behind the building. It was quiet. There were no pedestrians, only a couple of empty parked cars. The place was deserted. Peanut sat scanning the area for a minute, then noticed Hills glance at him.

'Fingers crossed, Peanut,' she said.

'Is that for me or the team?'

'Both, silly. We are the team.'

He chuckled.

'You realize that in Vietnam crossed fingers is the sign for female genitalia?'

She frowned at him. How did he know that?

'So, what's unlucky about that?'

'It could mean we're fucked.' He grinned at her, hearing her snort as he opened the door and slid out and walked straight to the six-foot-high brick fence that ran around the sides and back of the building. He jumped up, grabbed the top, and disappeared over it.

She saw him climbing the corner of the building, using the outstanding quoins as hand and foot grips, noticing the ease with which he reached the top. He took hold of the gutter, turned facing outward and curled his body up and rolled onto the roof. She sat watching, amazed at the effortless way that he moved. She started the Chevy and drove around the block and parked on the opposite side of the street from the front. By then there was no sign of Peanut.

As Peanut reached the front edge of the roof, he had to take care. There were people on the street but nobody was looking up. This part of the town was not an entertainment precinct and after working hours it had minimal foot traffic. He swung over the front edge, his feet finding the balustrade and he climbed down onto the small flag-raising balcony. The door leading onto it opened easily, telling him that flag raising was still taking place. He closed it, turned on his flashlight and walked down a short flight of stairs to a landing with a narrow door. The stairs led on down to another door that would lead out onto the top floor. He opened the narrow door that gave access to the roof space and the central walkway that ran down the middle. Built to last out of solid rough-sawn Oregon pine, it would make his access to the ceiling above the offices easy. He closed the door and walked to where he knew the last offices would be. Reaching the end of the building he counted his steps backwards, hoping the plans he had studied were accurate.

He drilled a flat-head screw into one of the timber laths that supported the old plaster ceiling and attached the light line to the screw, then cut out a square section of the old ceiling, using the light line to pull it up out of the way. If he accidentally dropped the cut-away section, it would have smashed through the suspended ceiling panels to the floor below. Through the hole he could see the lightweight steel frames that held the suspended ceiling panels. He knew this would be awkward work. The modern ceiling panels were three feet below the old ceiling and he couldn't reach them from where he was lying. He would have to go into the hole. He stepped back, pulled the rope out of his backpack and tied a foothold eight feet from the bottom. He dangled the rope down so that it coiled on the ceiling panels with the foothold just clear of the panels. Next, he drilled a hole into the rafter and screwed in a holding bracket, before tying the climbing rope onto it. With his backpack on he shimmied down the rope, using the foothold to take his weight as he bent and removed a ceiling panel. He smiled in delight. It was the safe room. He flicked the eight feet of curled rope off the ceiling panels and down the opening to the floor below and began to descend.

35

Seconds later, he was standing on the floor of the safe room. He began his search. It wasn't hard. The room was bare apart from two steel cabinets. His lock pick had the simple locks open in seconds. In a box marked *Confidential,* he found the file and a thumb drive. He plugged the thumb drive into his tablet and began to read. It was a digital version of the file and a lot more besides. It was explosive. This the department would not want the public to know. He copied the files to the tablet, then pulled out his own thumb drive and copied the files to it, deleting them from the tablet and putting his drive back into his pocket. He put the file and the found thumb drive into his backpack and again checked the cabinets. There were two ring binders containing files in the back of the cabinet. They contained information about a secret organization that had been set up by the Department of State to circumvent the laws regarding spying and espionage against their own citizens. The name stuck out. They were called the ICT. Second page in, he realized that ICT stood for *Illegal Clearance Team.* He hunted for a thumb drive that would have those files on it, but he couldn't find it. He swore under his breath and put the folders in his backpack. He took one last look around, shuffling things aside and checking underneath stacked files. Then he found it. A micro SD card taped to the underside of a metal cash box. It was obviously the petty cash box and he picked the lock and opened it. The amount of cash in it was anything but petty. There was over ten thousand dollars. He removed the cash, closed the cash box, locked it and prized off the micro SD card, slipping it into a card adapter and then into his tablet. He began to chuckle as he read the files. He had hit gold. This tiny card was the jackpot! He copied the files to his own thumb drive and again deleted the files from the tablet, taping the SD card back under the cash box, before putting it back on the shelf. That card was the find of a lifetime. He would start to plan things when he dumped the shits that had kidnapped him.

He checked the door to the safe room. It was alarmed. The only way out was the way he'd come in. He climbed back up the rope, moving along the walkway until he was over the next room and started the same procedure. A hole cut, the rope dropped and the panel lifted, then climbing all the way down and he was in. He searched the other offices but found nothing. The desks were unlocked, the cabinets open, even the boss's desk was unlocked. He found nothing important. Using the photocopier he copied all the files from the ICT folders to his thumb drive. His earpiece crackled and he paused the copier.

'Yeah?'

'How's it going?' Hills.

'Good. Thirty minutes or so to go. Lots to look through.'

'Okay.' He restarted the photocopier and kept feeding the files in. The last page went through and he checked the drive. It had the lot. He climbed back up, replacing the ceiling panels, and climbed back down into the safe room, replacing the folders where he'd found them. Panels replaced, he packed his gear and felt relieved as he stood on the walkway and walked back to the door that led to the stairway. He paused and took his thumb drive and the cash out of his pocket. He did a quick search and then hid them in a niche under the walkway. He would retrieve them later. Now he had to get away. That was always the most difficult part of any operation. Going out the walkway door he went down the stairs. On the ground floor, he stood next to one of the windows facing the street and checked the Chevy sitting across the road. He knew immediately that something was wrong. Hills had her hand against the window. He could see her crossed fingers. Why was she doing that? He remembered the crossed fingers conversation. Was Hills telling him they were fucked? He stepped back from the window and pressed *talk* on his radio.

'Hills, do you copy? Over.' Silence. As he watched, her fingers uncrossed and re-crossed.

'Hills here. How long until you are finished? Over.'

'Ten, fifteen minutes. Will come out of the front door. Will call to make sure the way is clear before leaving. Copy that? Over.'

'Copy,' she said after another lengthy pause.

He had it figured. Someone was in the car with her and was monitoring everything. The darkened side windows were stopping him from seeing in. He sprinted up the stairs, opened the door and went onto the balcony, glad that only the side and back of the Chevy were facing him. He quickly climbed onto the roof, ran to the end, swung down and once again used the quoins to climb down before swinging over the wall. His only weapon was the battery drill. He fitted a four-inch long quarter inch drill bit then selected the drill hammer action and high speed. With the drill in his hand, hidden under the backpack, he walked around the corner, behind the Chevy and crossed to the opposite side of the street, walking towards car. Outside the Chevy's s rear door, he could see the shadows of three people in the Chevy, two in the front and one in the rear. He pressed *talk*.

'Hills. All clear? Over.'

There was that long delay again.

'Affirmative. Over.'

'Coming out. Over and out.'

He dropped the radio in his pocket, waiting a second to give the thugs in the car time to lean forward and concentrate on the building's entrance. He flung the back door of the Chevy open. The thug inside on the back seat was sitting forward, concentrating on the front door of the building, gun in hand. He turned at the sound of the door opening but was distracted and slow. Peanut hit him hard in the side of the head with the heavy battery base of the drill. He then swung the drill over and hit the guy in the front seat on the temple with the drill base, seeing him slump. He rammed the drill bit hard against the ear of the stunned thug in the rear seat beside him and pulled the trigger. The drill emitted a thudding mechanical scream as the bit disappeared into his ear and head. The victim's eyes opened in surprise and his body jerked as he collapsed on the rear seat.

Hills saw her opportunity and hit the thug in the front seat in the neck. Peanut extracted the drill and reached over the seat as Hills knocked the stunned thug's gun away. He jammed the drill bit into the rear of the front thug's head and pulled the trigger. The drill again screamed and thudded as it buried itself four inches into his skull, his body jerking, then collapsing and lying still. Hills went into shock when Peanut extracted the drill bit from the guy's head. He slammed the rear door shut as she stared transfixed at the blood pouring out the hole in the thug's head and Peanut pulled the body out of the way so she could drive.

'For fuck's sake, Hills, drive! We're not waiting for a fucking bus!'

Chapter 9

'We have to get rid of these bodies,' Peanut said as a moan came from the guy up front.

Hills accelerated into the street as she checked the rearview mirror. 'If I give you my key, will you clear my room? And clear yours as well. That way we can get going. I don't feel all that comfortable with these guys in the car, either,' she said, her voice shaky.

'I don't think they'll attack you,' said Peanut.

'It's not that. They were dropped off. They'll have backup and they'll know where we're staying.'

'Christ! If that's the case, forget the hotel and the clothes! Head straight back to camp. If I drive, can you call and talk to Chas?' asked Peanut.

'Yeah, okay. I'll pull over.'

She eased the Chevy over and Peanut took the wheel as Hills climbed into the back seat. He eased the big Suburban back out onto the road as Hills put her phone on speaker.

'Chas, I was waiting for Peanut and I got jumped. Peanut sorted it, but those guys had backup. We can't go back to the hotel. We're heading for the camp.'

'We'll handle the hotel rooms. Did you happen to get the license plate of the other vehicle?' asked Chas

'Black Ford Taurus. Plate FY 6956,' replied Hills.

'Okay, leave it with us. Was Peanut successful?' Chas had a hopeful tone in his voice. Peanut nodded.

'He says yes.'

'You are on speaker?' asked Chas.

'Yep,' said Hills.

'How did it go, Peanut?'

'Good. I have the hard copy. I could only find the one and I have a digital copy on a thumb drive that was with it. That drive contains some pretty hot stuff. Well worth a second look.' He chuckled. 'Now I know why the Department of State wanted it back. Someone could blackmail the shit out of them.'

There was silence. 'Thanks, Peanut. We'll see you back at camp.'

Hills put the phone away and wound down the window as the smell of feces filled the car.

'This one is dead,' she said.

'Figured that. This one is stirring, but he doesn't look good.'

'Can we move him to the back? I need to get away from the smell,' she said.

'Will do. Wait till I find a place to pull over.'

A few minutes later, he pulled the car over and opened the front door, reaching in and dragging the guy out, hoisting him up and into the back of the wagon as Hills helped. She was impressed. Peanut was full of surprises. That guy was beefy; yet Peanut, all five foot four of him, had used a fireman's lift to put him in the back with ease. He did the same with the dead back-seat guy, chucking him into the rear beside the barely alive one. Hills checked their pockets and their legs for any more guns. Peanut noticed that she was thorough. Her police training had been extremely professional. For some reason, that standard of training gave him confidence in her, despite her being surprised by those guys. He had a feeling that Hills was the sort that would have his back in an emergency, not that it meant anything.

Peanut took the wheel and they set off again, Hills asking Peanut a question that had been troubling her.

'How did you know that they were in the car with me? I tried to signal.'

'Your crossed fingers pretty much said it all and your slow responses on the radio confirmed it.'

'Thanks.'

'You're welcome.'

'Do you think we're safe?' she asked.

'No.'

'Why?'

'They knew you were sitting there. What's the first thing they would do to make sure they never lost you?'

'Tracker?'

Peanut grinned. Hills wasn't slow.

'Yeah. We need to stop and take a look. It'll be under the back or the rear-wheel arch. A little magnetic box,' he said.

'Yeah, I've seen them. Where's the next stop?'

'Interchange lights up ahead. Could be a truck stop,' he said.

Peanut turned off at the interchange and stopped in among the rows of loaded semi-trailers.

He pointed to the road. 'Let me know if anybody suspicious drives by.'

Hills walked to where she could watch the highway without being noticed or get in the way of the trucks entering or leaving. Then, two minutes later, a white Toyota Camry drove slowly past, before speeding up through the interchange. Peanut gave a whistle and she ran over, climbed in, and they drove off.

'What did you do with it?' she asked.

Peanut pointed to a truck pulling out behind them, going in the opposite direction. She laughed. It was an infectiously happy laugh that made Peanut give a reluctant smile. The night had come close to being a disaster, but it had been saved.

'Map us a course, Hills. Get us home.'

She reached over and gave his arm a gentle squeeze. He glanced at her. He was still wearing a smile, but it faltered when he saw she had that look again, that funny look. The one where he really didn't know what she was thinking. Then it was gone. Replaced by a smile as she turned to the GPS and set their destination.

They pulled up in front of the camp bunkhouse. It was eerie and dark.

'Herman was given time off because we were going away, but never mind, we can still get something to eat,' said Hills.

'I can do scrambled eggs.' Peanut said and laughed.

'Fuck your scrambled eggs! You're supposed to have greens as well, you know.'

'I always put chopped chives or parsley into them,' he said.

She rolled her eyes and grimaced. He was enjoying winding her up.

'Ahh..., fuck you!' she said.

'Yeah. Fuck me. The last two weeks have felt like that.'

'Like what?'

'Everybody wanting to fuck me over. And they succeeded. I'm a confirmed murderer as well as a confirmed killer and professional thief. Let's get some food. My engine is running low.'

Hills stood stock still beside the Chevy as the realisation of what he had said sunk in. They had kidnapped him and then she and Boris both had had a go at him, two days in a row. Then they'd used him to steal what they wanted. He was right. He had been fucked over. Completely. Somewhere inside him there was probably a nice guy. She wasn't yet sure. His actions had already confirmed that he was ruthless. She had seen that. He hadn't shown any remorse in getting that piece of shit Chuckie ready for the high road. Then tonight, killing those two guys in the car, he'd shown no hesitation. He just rammed the drill in their heads and pulled the trigger; he did it without blinking. He was tough and hard, resilient to a level she had never seen before. He might have come off the streets, but she was coming to the distinct realization that maybe he wasn't a thug, though she was still unsure. Her police training told her that once a thug, always a thug but was Peanut ever truly a thug? The one thing he had shown was that he would do whatever the situation required, illegal or not. But did that make him a thug? Still unsure, she followed him into the building.

'Does Chas have an office here?' Peanut asked.

'I'll show you.'

He followed her to the back of the building where there was a small office. He took out the file and taped the thumb drive to the cover and put it into the top drawer. Hills locked the office door after they went out.

'Does he always leave the key in the door?'

'Yep. Chas works on the basis that the more people know, the better they will perform.'

'No argument with that. Hey, failing scrambled eggs, how about some toast and raspberry jam?'

'Jesus fucking Christ!' Hills declared loudly in exasperation, suddenly noticing Peanut's lips twitch. He'd been winding her up, again, and she gave him a you-got-me smile and rolled her eyes.

***

It was the door slamming that woke him. He jumped up and stealthily opened the door of his room. He had jammed a piece of wood in the lock to stop it from working. If anyone had noticed, they hadn't objected. The sound of inebriated voices drifted towards him. He pulled on his jeans and tee shirt and walked towards the conference room, peering around the door. Chas, Boris, Peter, and the corporal were there. He had to think for a minute, then he remembered. Rawlings, Blue Rawlings. He wondered what they were celebrating? Hills came out of her room and stood beside him. She had pulled on her jeans, but she still had her nightie on. She moved close and leant on his shoulder as she peered around the door.

'What da'ya think?' she asked.

He felt uncomfortable with her that close and moved away slightly. He hadn't forgotten the hit.

'They're too far gone to make any sense,' he said. 'I've never been interested in joining in and playing drunk catch up. By the time you are lubed up enough to be happy, the rest are falling asleep. I'm going back to bed. Lock your door.'

She had noticed that he had moved away but reached out and took his arm. 'No, please. There's a spare single mattress on the floor in my room. You can sleep there, just for tonight. I don't trust that corporal.'

He followed her to her room and she dragged a mattress out from under the bed. Peanut lay down, tired, ready to carry on sleeping. She locked the door and tiptoed back into bed, turning out the light as she settled in.

'Night, Peanut,' Hills said in a loud whisper.

'Night, Hills.'

***

The door rattled. She was awake instantly.

'Hills, are you in there? Come out and have some fun. Come on!' a voice said in a loud whisper. She knew it was Blue.

Peanut rolled over. 'One of yours, I believe. Mine all went home.'

'Would you do the honors, please?' she asked.

He shook his head and stood up. 'Last time I'm doing a sleepover at your place. It's like fucking Grand Central Station.' He swung open the door.

'You have the wrong bedroom, buddy. Buy a map.'

'Ahh...! What are you doing here?' asked Blue.

'Telling you to fuck off.' Peanut knew the corporal wasn't happy, but he also knew he wasn't going to do anything. He had obviously heard about Boris and Hills getting dumped. 'Amanda has had a very busy day and a very busy night, and she needs her beauty sleep.'

'Ahh ... I suppose so.' Blue was flummoxed.

'You're saying she's ugly?' Peanut asked.

'No! I was wondering if she might join us for some drinks and fun, that's all.'

'What do you think her answer will be, given that you've already decided she's ugly and doesn't need her sleep?'

Blue's mouth sagged open. His sozzled brain was struggling to keep up.

'Go to bed, corporal,' Peanut said as he shut the door and locked it.

Hills burst into giggles.

'I think I'll keep you on as my doorman.'

'No. The wages you pay are shit. Night.'

'Night, and thanks.'

***

The banging on the door was loud and insistent.

'Hills wake up! It's an emergency,' called Chas.

Hills got up, unlocked the door and peered around the edge.

'Fucking Peanut has gone! He hasn't slept in his bed. Get dressed and we'll meet in the conference room in five minutes. There's no saying how long he's been gone. Fucking Christ! He's got those documents with him. What a fucking disaster!'

Hills peered back at Peanut, who was shaking his head in disgust as she opened the door wide.

'You invited me to stay the night and I can't get any sleep with all this fucking racket going on. First Blue and now you. The documents are locked in your office in the top drawer of your desk. Hills has the key. I'm going to *my* bed, in *my* room.' Peanut picked up his shoes and turned towards the door.

Hills touched his arm as he walked past.

'Thanks, Peanut.'

Peanut gave the briefest of nods and walked out the door.

Chas looked at Hills and then at the back of Peanut and the mattress on the floor before he shook his head and walked off. Hills grinned at his retreating back as she closed the door. She had no doubt there would be gossip. She didn't care. Peanut might be a killer, but he had also shown that he was a gentleman. Although he still scared her, for some weird reason she was beginning to feel safe around him. It was as if she sensed that he wouldn't hurt her unless she tried to hurt him first. The fleeting thought of what he might do if she did try to hurt him sent a small shiver of fear down her spine. She instinctively knew that he would kill her immediately.

***

Chas was sitting in the dining room having coffee with Hills, Peanut, and Peter. Boris and the corporal had not yet surfaced. They were still recovering from last night's celebrations.

'The Department of State is pleased. Well done, Hills and Peanut,' said Chas. 'The car that dropped off the kidnappers was a rental and we've handed the information to the FBI. As for the guys who tracked you on the way to the interchange, who knows? We don't know who they were. And well done, Peanut, on rescuing Hills. The FBI are checking the fingerprints and DNA on the two bodies, but that will take some time. Despite it all, success. You're a good team.'

41

Peanut shook his head. 'With respect Chas, that's shit. You don't have squat. You have someone ratting you out. We only decided on Friday to do the job Saturday and they knew. They were waiting. You have an informer in your ranks. I suggest you sort that out before you plan any more missions. You could get someone killed. It was close enough with Hills.'

Peter snorted. 'Listen to the security expert. Tell you what, dirtbag, when you're lying waiting for the needle you can discuss it all with the priest. You know squat all about security,' said Peter.

'Yeah, and as the attack happened on your watch, you know even less, dipshit.' Peanut's tone was blunt.

Peter's face coloured and he started to rise.

'Settle down, now!' Chas was angry. 'I agree, we do have a leak and until we find out who it is, we watch our backs. Any idea where we should start?'

'Only one. Check all the mobile calls made from here in the last two days,' said Hills.

'Good idea. Even so, it was a successful mission. As I said, well done all. Meeting over. Peanut and Hills, you two stay back. I want a word,' said Chas.

Peanut and Hills exchanged glances. They were both puzzled.

Chapter 10

'Any ideas as to the leak?' Chas asked.

Peanut and Hills shook their heads.

'I'd like it to be Peter, but somehow I suspect it'll be someone else entirely,' Peanut said. 'I remember when we sorted out the time we were to go, Boris wasn't there. Might mean something and then again it might not. It would have been easier for them to stop us if they'd known the exact time of entry. They could have sat in the office and waited. So it's just a guess.'

'Did you look at the documents you recovered?' Chas seemed thoughtful.

'Of course.'

'All of them?'

'Yes.'

'We might have to arrange a security clearance for you so you fall under the coverage of security laws and their requirements. You'll have to sign a statutory declaration.'

Peanut burst out laughing.

'Given that I've been blackmailed and accused of murder, that's a bit ridiculous, isn't it? Like what you see in a comedy. If you don't like what I'm doing or seeing, you can lock me up on fucking death row!'

'There would have to be a trial first and that could get messy, especially now that you've read the documents.'

'That really only leaves you with one real option, doesn't it?' said Peanut.

Chas winced.

'We are not going to shoot you!' he said.

'And if your boss tells you to tidy things up, would you disobey a direct order?'

'He wouldn't tell me to do that, but if he did, yes, I would disobey it, absolutely!'

Peanut gave a quiet chuckle.

'Maybe press-ganging me wasn't such a hot idea?' He paused. 'By the way, who or what is the ICT?' he asked.

'How do you know about that?' Chas was stunned.

'Two loose-leaf folders on the ICT were in the secure room. Stuff about setting up memos and a chain of command. No names were given, just things like responsibilities, allowed actions, surveillance, copies of emails sent and received, that sort of thing. Only four pages were about what they are allowed to do. It's really scary reading.'

'You read it all?' asked Chas.

'Yep.'

'Shit! How did they get that information? You should have taken that as well,' said Chas.

'Yeah, now you tell me. But if you want it, I know where it is. It's easy to get.'

'Can you retrieve those files?'

'Yeah.'

'Tonight?'

'Yeah, but we'll have to do it differently. You have a leak and there are guys out there, unaccounted for, trying to hunt us down.'

'What are you suggesting?' asked Chas.

'I go alone. That keeps Hills, you, and everyone else out of the firing line.'

'So, what do we do?'

'Keep the bar stools warm. If I don't come back, you'll know I've been caught and I'll be dead somewhere. And if I do come back, I'll have a lemon, lime and bitters.'

'Bad idea,' Hills said. 'As you have already pointed out, we have a leak. They will be waiting again.' She shook her head.

Chas cleared his throat. 'I have to agree with Hills.'

'It's not a matter of whether you agree or not. It's the only way it'll work. Let me handle anybody stupid enough to be waiting. I'll need my swords and my phone, please.' He stared at the unhappy faces of Chas and Hills. 'You didn't answer my question, Chas. Who is the ICT?'

'It's us,' replied Chas.

Peanut stared hard at Chas and Hills.

'Shit!'

***

Peanut walked to his room to get ready for a run. It was a mess. The mattress was on the floor and his bedclothes were scattered. The clothes he had bought were in a pile in the corner. He walked back to the conference room where Chas and Hills were still talking.

'Would you like to tell me who wrecked my room?' he asked.

Chas stood up with a scowl on his face. 'Show me.'

Chas took one look at Peanut's room and turned and walked away, his face angry. 'Wait here,' he said.

'Chas authorised a search of your room to see if you were concealing anything. It was meant to be done discreetly,' said Hills.

'By whom?'

'Blue. He was probably still miffed because you told him to fuck off last night.'

Peanut grimaced. He'd had a lot of bad things happen that were worse than that, but it was the principle.

'Chas only had to ask,' said Peanut.

'We know that now, but he didn't this morning. He'll sort it.'

Chas came storming back, followed by a red-faced Blue. While Chas stood over him Blue got busy remaking the bed. As Peanut watched he saw the years of military training showing through. Blue made a very neat bed. Peanut looked closely at him. Blue was over six feet by a couple of inches and rangy, not solid like Chas and Boris but Peanut could see the strength in his bare arms. He had a feeling that Blue would be strong.

'Thanks, Blue. Are you available most mornings? You do an excellent job, if I say so myself,' said Peanut. There was anger in Blue's eyes as Chas waved him away and waited until he'd left, then turned to Hills and Peanut.

'We go tonight. You're on your own, Peanut. Any ideas on the start time?'

'Nine o'clock. But tell everyone else that it'll be at eleven o'clock. Have you got my swords?'

'Yes,' replied Chas. 'I'd prefer if you had a gun, but my boss would kill me if he found out. Swords it is. Come with me and we'll get them. Then you can get moving. You and Hills can get on the road. I'll call with the hotel details when I've booked it.'

Peanut was delighted. He would be able to get the thumb drive and the money tonight, as well as the documents. It couldn't be better.

***

Hills parked the Chevy three blocks away from the building, both of them watching, making sure the way was clear. He opened the door and left so quickly and smoothly that she was surprised; suddenly he was gone. She started the Chevy and moved a further three blocks away. She would get into position when Peanut called. No earpieces, nothing that could give the game away. This seemed too rushed, coming back the night after a near disaster. She sat quietly in a small pool of worry, watching everything, the Chevy's doors locked, the motor running, ready, just in case someone tried to sneak up on her.

44

Peanut did a quick walk around the building, checking all was clear before quickly retracing the previous night's steps and accessing the walkway, removing the ceiling panels, dropping down and taking the folders out of the safe room cabinets and putting them in his back pack. He climbed up the rope and then he heard it. The sound of the outside office door being quietly opened. He quickly pulled the rope up out of the way and replaced the ceiling panel. As he scaled the rope up through the old ceiling to the walkway, the sound of the door to the strong room being opened came up to him. He heard the door close and male voices drifted up clearly. The so-called acoustic ceiling panels didn't really muffle much sound. He took out his mobile phone and pushed record. Checking the time told him they were early, it was just past nine thirty p.m. He held the phone in the open space between the new and old ceiling, just to get the best reception. They talked shit for ten minutes, obviously walking around the safe room as the volume and direction of their voices changed. It was mainly sport, then girls and then girls' personal private parts and then the one guy said what Peanut wanted to hear. It was still partly muffled by the ceiling panels but the words were reasonably distinct.

'That fucker's not here yet.'

'Not till eleven, Boris said.'

'Where will we sit to wait? To get the best shot at the fucker?'

'Does it matter? Bam, Bam, good night, sucker!' They laughed. Peanut desperately hoped that his phone had picked up the voices. He heard more crude talk about girls; they were getting fainter, hard to hear and it got more muffled, as if they were sitting close together on the floor on the far side of the safe room, talking quietly. He heard one say he couldn't wait to get back to base in … The rest was too muffed to hear. He'd heard enough. The muffled voices made it impossible to pick up anything more clearly and from the way they were talking, they were back to the rude photos on their mobile phones.

Peanut gently lowered the old ceiling cut-out panel into place and fitted the screws by screwing them in by hand. The sound of the drill would have immediately given him away. He quietly drew back onto the central walkway. It was time to go. He walked to the door, removed the bundle of cash and the thumb drive from under the walkway and put it all into his backpack. He went downstairs and was about to go outside when he saw it through the window. It was the white Camry that had followed them last night. Leaving via the front door was out. He ran back up the stairs on light feet. From behind the balustrade on the balcony he watched the Camry as it eased out from the curb and drove around the corner. He made his escape over the roof and down the quoins as fast as he could and when he was more than a block away, he hid in a doorway and called Hills.

'Hills.'

'Don't come and get me,' he said. 'That white Camry is hanging around.'

'Whereabouts?' she asked.

'The shopping center where you bought my gear.'

'Okay.'

Then he checked the recording on his phone and realized that he had been right to place it in the open space of the ceiling; the words were slightly muffled but just clear enough.

He set out at a slow jog, the weight of the backpack annoying him. He stopped and tighten the shoulder straps to stop it bouncing. If he had his wallet, he could have caught a taxi. He couldn't use the bundle of cash. It would raise suspicions if he pulled out a wad like that. There was no doubt about it, these ICT pricks who had taken his freedom away were a right bunch of assholes.

When he reached the mall, he gazed out over the parked cars. It was hopeless. There were too many. He rang Hills again.

'Where are you parked?' he asked.

'East entrance, by the sign.' He jogged around the corner and climbed in. She raised her fist and they bumped knuckles.

'Ring Chas. Tell him we need an emergency meeting, just him and us. Not in the bar, somewhere private,' said Peanut.

'Seriously?' she asked.

'Yes. Don't tell Chas, but I know who the informant is.'

'Shit! Who is it?'

'You'll see.' Peanut pulled the papers out of his backpack and placed them on the rear seat. 'That's what Chas wanted. Don't lose them.'

She smiled at him, then reached over and rubbed his arm yet again. He was getting used to her touching him. It was friendly but, given their history, it also seemed a bit weird. He hadn't forgotten the pain she'd inflicted on him.

***

They met Chas in a small conference room at the back of the hotel. Peanut started talking as soon as they sat down.

'Sitting inside that safe room are two guys waiting for me to arrive. Outside, driving around the block is a white Camry, two guys inside that look like rent-a-mob. The Camry is the same one that followed us last night; it has a dent in the boot lid. Maybe the FBI would like to have a talk to them. As we have nearly an hour to go until I should be in the room; you have time to deal with it. And the raid was successful, again. You owe me a lemon, lime and bitters,' said Peanut.

'From where I stand, you can have the whole fucking factory that makes the horrible fucking stuff. Give me a beer or a whisky any day. I'll call the FBI now,' said Chas with a smile.

They waited as Chas called his contact at the FBI and explained the situation, then Peanut pulled out his phone.

'Listen,' he said and he played the recording. 'That was the two guys talking underneath me in the safe room. I was in the ceiling, but the sound is fairly clear.'

Chas was stunned.

'Boris! He's been with us for a year, nearly from the beginning. Shit! Why'd he do it?'

'Maybe because I showed him up. Can you use him to sow some misinformation?' asked Peanut.

Chas looked at Peanut then glanced at Hills. She smiled and punched Peanut lightly in the shoulder.

'You're more than just a pretty face,' said Hills.

'I'm not so sure,' said Chas.

Hills raised a questioning eyebrow.

'Not about Peanut's pretty face but about using Boris. Once a rat, always a rat. But we'll see how he reacts. Let's go see,' Chas said.

***

Peter, Boris and Blue were surprised when they walked in. Peanut sat beside Boris, while Hills walked over and sat beside Blue.

Chas brought them up to date.

'The mission was successful. Well done, team. We have a recording for you to listen to,' said Chas. 'This was taken of a conversation between two guys who had entered the safe room to wait for Peanut to arrive. They had been tipped off. Play the recording, Peanut.'

As Peanut pushed the play button, he noticed Boris was moving uncomfortably in his chair, straightening up, like he was getting ready to run. On full volume the words were clear.

46

'That fucker's not here yet.'

'Not till eleven, Boris said.'

'Where will we sit to wait? To get the best shot at the fucker?'

'Does it matter? Bam, Bam, good night, sucker!'

Peanut stopped the recording. Chas stared hard at Boris.

'Well?' he asked.

Boris abruptly leapt to his feet and pointed a snub-nosed pistol at Chas.

Peanut shrugged his jacket clear of his shoulders and stood up as Boris stepped back to cover the room. Then he changed his mind, stepped forward and put the pistol to Peter's head instead. On his face was an evil smile.

'Stand up, old man. We're going for a walk,' said Boris.

Boris was concentrating hard on Peter and Chas and didn't notice Peanut move back, out of his line of sight. Then when Boris turned to Peter, his back was towards Peanut.

Peanut's hands blurred as he stepped forward. His swords flashed, as one blade flicked up and pricked a startled Boris under the ear.

'Don't move! Put the gun down, now!' Peanut yelled at Boris. When Boris hesitated, the blade pricked him more deeply. For a moment he stood rooted to the spot before he let the barrel of his gun drop.

'Drop the fucking gun!' yelled Peanut, gently pushing the sword in a bit harder.

Boris stood still, confused and trying to work out his chances. Peter spun, placing a hand on the gun and punched Boris in the solar plexus. Boris doubled over, sinking nearly to his knees, the gun still locked in his hand. He suddenly jerked it clear, swinging it up to point at Peter. Boris had now run out of options. The sword that had been in a guard position blurred, pointing, thrusting in a flash of polished steel. It buried itself deep into the side of his chest. Boris gave a surprised gasp. He heaved in tremendous pain, dropping the gun as his heart stopped and his body collapsed. A low guttural moan came, then he lay in silence, unmoving on the floor, dead.

It had happened so fast, but to Chas's eyes, it had to happen.

'*Consequences*, asshole,' Chas heard Peanut mutter. Peanut extracted the sword, cleaned it on Boris's jacket and then removed the harness off his back, slipping both swords into the harness and placing it on the table. He slipped his jacket on as he gave the team a wry grin.

'I'm off to the bar to get that lemon, lime and bitters. I don't think they serve them on death row. Tell the cops where I am, huh?' he said as he turned and walked out.

Chapter 11

Peter's body language as he stood in front of Chas was aggressive; he wasn't going to take no for an answer. He spread his hands in a clear *let's fix it* gesture.

'Boss, no argument. We need to stage this. That little crim, sorry, ex-crim, just saved my life. I owe him. We can't have him going to jail for killing a fucking traitor. Right, team?'

They all nodded as Peter kicked Boris's body.

'This is the story. This sucker was fooling around, holding the sword by the blade, just like a sword swallower does, then he slipped on some water and fell on Peanut's sword.' Peter picked up a glass of water, tipped it on the floor and dragged his foot through it to create a skid mark. 'Any arguments?'

Chas gave a grim nod.

'That sounds good. Take one of those swords and put it in Boris's hand for DNA and fingerprints. Make sure it has his blood on it. Lie it next to the body when you have done that. I'll ring my contacts at the FBI.' He paused, thinking, and then carried on. 'Blue—you, Hills, and Peanut were talking and never saw anything. Me and Peter are the only ones who saw what happened to Boris. Is that clear? Hills, go and tell Peanut. Work out what you were all talking about. The FBI will be sure to ask. Now go get Peanut on our side. Use your womanly wiles if you have to.' He paused and gave her a forbidding look. '*All* of them, if necessary. The *last* thing this team needs is bad publicity.'

Hills's blush said it all and Chas knew he had guessed right. She had changed her mind about Peanut. She liked him. But how much? Time would tell. But the question would be whether Peanut liked her? Chas had seen her punch Peanut in the nuts and had shuddered. She had hit him hard. A punch like that would put most men off a woman, any women, for life!

***

Hills found Peanut leaning on the bar in a quiet corner. Their eyes met in the mirror behind the bar as she walked towards him. When she wrapped an arm around him and hugged him, he grunted in surprise, slopping his lemon, lime and bitters on the bar.

'The team says thanks,' said Hills. 'Now this is the official story. You, me, and Blue were busy talking about what sights we were going to see tomorrow and never saw what happened. The only ones who saw what happened were Chas, Peter, and Boris. He was fooling around with your sword. He slipped on some water and fell.' She pulled back, her eyes almost pleading. 'The team needs this; otherwise, we'll all get sacked and you'll go to jail. Peter is adamant that's not going to happen, and Chas agrees. Peter was Boris's friend and he feels betrayed by the prick. You saved his life and we need your agreement.' Peanut snorted derisively.

'That won't work. Peter hates my guts.'

'Not anymore.' Peter's gruff voice came from behind them.

Peanut spun around. Peter was standing in front of him. 'You have some skill with those blades, buddy. Absolutely fucking magical,' Peter said as he gave a weak smile. 'That was really special. I've never been so happy to see some prick die and know that it wasn't me. Thanks, and I truly mean that.' He held out his hand and a surprised Peanut shook it. 'But go back to your bad old ways and I'll fucking nail you. And I mean that as well.' He turned and went to walk away.

'Hey,' called Peanut and Peter turned back towards him. 'For the record, asshole, there never were any bad old ways and if you have ever been told anything different it's fucking bullshit!'

Peter stood frowning at Peanut for a moment. It seemed that he might take it further but he suddenly gave a slight smile and a nod and turned and stalked off. But Peanut knew that was as close to an apology as he was ever going to get. *Dour old prick,* he thought to himself. He glanced at Hills.

'That sounds a shit load better than getting strapped to a gurney and being given the final vaccination,' said Peanut.

'The final vaccination?' asked Hills.

'Yeah, so you can no longer catch the disease called life.' He took a sip of his drink as a feeling of relief flooded through him. Now that they were going to stage the death to protect him and the rest of the team, it made him think maybe he was part of something important, not just there to be used. He dismissed the thought immediately. It was the ICT team they were protecting, not him.

He stood staring at the ice cubes in his drink, thinking about what had happened when he noticed that Hills had put her arm back around him. It made him uncomfortable, like why was she doing that?

He gave her a quick hug, to let her know he appreciated her and the team's support, then moved away and studied her. She seemed almost put out by his moving away. The thought crossed his mind that maybe underneath her ball-bashing exterior there was a nice woman. Somewhere. It was an annoying thought.

Pity she was the enemy.

***

The FBI interviews went on long into the night. Everyone was interviewed at least twice. It was late and the hotel's kitchen was about to close when Peanut, Hills, and Chas went for a quick meal.

There had been some skepticism on the faces of the FBI about all the pat answers, but they couldn't fault the cause of death. It would be classified as an unfortunate accident. The FBI had bigger fish to fry.

The other thugs found in the safe room were refusing to talk. The person who rented the office couldn't be found, and the two guys driving around in the Camry were adamant they didn't know the guys in the safe room until the street video showed them getting out of the car. Even so, they denied following the Chevy the previous night until the highway cam footage showed them driving four cars behind. The FBI were convinced they would eventually get to the nub of the issue. As they had clearly lied, they would be held in separate cells until they got to the truth. And they would. In their books that was more important than a clumsy accidental death. Even if it all seemed a bit too pat.

Chas glanced at Peanut as he sat back in his chair at the end of the meal.

Peanut had enjoyed a chicken burger and at Hills's insistence, a salad on the side. He had to concede it was much better than his own cooking.

'Do you have the paperwork, Peanut?' asked Chas.

'Yeah. It's on the back seat of the Chevy.'

'I'll get it before I go to bed. I'll probably need it for the meeting tomorrow. Incidentally, the FBI is now investigating that firm. Everyone associated with it has vanished. It would appear to have been Russian-backed but how they made money is anybody's guess. The whole thing doesn't stack up. We won't catch them, and neither will the FBI. Those Russians will be long gone.'

Hills frowned at Chas with tired eyes. 'Do we have to drive back tonight? I'm tired, really tired,' she said.

Peanut could see the black under her eyes. Last night she had almost been killed and tonight there had been Boris's attack and just as sudden death. Maybe it was too much for her. Perhaps she wasn't such a tough bitch after all?

'No, we're booked in for the next three nights. Have a break, guys. I have meetings tomorrow but the next few days are free.' Chas gave a weary smile. 'I want to see how successful the FBI are in questioning those guys. We need answers.'

***

It was four in the morning when Peanut left the hotel. Four and a half hours of sleep would have to do. An empty taxi was sitting in the rank out front and he climbed in.

'Dulles Airport,' he said to the taxi driver. It was five-thirty when the fifty-minute flight took off for New York. He wanted to be clear of the airport and into downtown New York before the alarm was raised. Until then, he wouldn't be free. Then again, would he ever be free? He had to change his identity. He needed a computer, a non-smart phone, and several SIM cards. He turned off his existing phone as that could be traced. He also needed a bolt hole, somewhere he could lie low for a while. They would expect him to go back to his mother, but that would be a mistake. He had no intention of going back there, not for a long time. He would call and let her know he was okay.

Peanut watched as the New York skyline came into view as they landed at JFK. With his backpack and his swords now strapped to his back, he took the subway downtown. He got off at Bryant Park and walked along the street, enjoying the cool early morning breeze. As the skyscrapers towered above him, he breathed in deeply. Now he was free. He would call Hills later.

Peanut glanced around the small room, a bed and the hand basin. There was a shared kitchen down one end of the hallway and a shared bathroom down the other. Size wasn't important. It was cheap and clean. He picked up his burner and dialed Hills's number. She answered immediately.

'Hills, it's Peanut. In case you didn't know, I've left. I did the job that you lot blackmailed me into, so, as far as I am concerned, the contract is over. Don't try to find me because I've taken copies of all the documents I uplifted on your behalf and if anything happens to me, my lawyer is under clear instructions to send them all to the news media. If you can, please let Chas know.'

'Peanut! Don't hang up. Chas is next door. He'll want to talk to you!'

'No. I'm free now. But for what it's worth, I think we made a good team. We might have carried on, but not under those circumstances. I'll remember you with affection and thanks for getting Danny boy free.' He laughed. 'And for the smack in the nuts. Bye, Hills. It actually ended up being nice working with you.'

The phone went dead in Hills's hand. He was gone. She could feel tears welling up in her eyes. She wiped them away and steadied herself as she went and tapped on Chas's door.

He opened it without delay. He knew immediately. 'Peanut?' he asked.

She nodded. Chas studied her face and knew she was holding back tears.

'He's gone. He has copies of all the paperwork he retrieved and if we chase him or he has an accident, it all goes to the news media.'

Chas wasn't surprised. He knew Peanut was intelligent. He would've thought it all out. He shrugged.

'We'll leave him alone.' Chas's answer was definite.

Hills was upset. 'We're not even going to try to find him?'

'Nope. Why would we? He's smart and he's canny. Impossible to catch. He will change his name and that'll make him impossible to track.' He saw her wet eyes. 'I know you were getting close to him, but he's gone and it's over. He's walked away and we walk away.'

50

Hills wiped her eyes.

'It's a pity,' Chas said, 'because I had the approval to offer him a permanent job with us and he would've fitted right in. We would have scrubbed the record clean as well. Never mind, we'll have to look for someone else. It's going to be hard finding another Peanut, that's for sure.' Hills nodded as she turned and walked out. Chas stood and paced. He was annoyed. Having someone like Peanut on the team gave them an edge. An unexpected and lethal edge, an edge that was sometimes needed. An edge that even Boris underestimated. Boris had ignored Peanut and that had cost him his life. But it was over. It was time to move on. Chas doubted they'd ever see Peanut again.

***

Peanut strolled up Madison Avenue admiring all the fancy addresses. He noticed the nameplate on the building as he walked by but didn't pause; he just kept on going to the corner, stopped, turned and scrutinized the area. He now knew where they were. He could disappear quickly into the subway where they would never track him. But first things first, he needed to see the warehouse. He took the subway to Queens, then hailing a taxi to take him there.

'Stop, please.' The taxi pulled to the side and Peanut buzzed the window down, peering through the ten-foot-high chain-link fence surrounding the warehouse. He noticed the cameras and that the warehouse was back-to-back with another identical warehouse, both built the same, both painted in peeling yellow paint. The battered red sign said *Global Warehousing.* Whatever that meant.

'Drive around the corner please,' he instructed.

The taxi driver glanced at him through the rearview mirror, his eyes worried.

'Hey, buddy, you ain't casing the joint, are you?'

Peanut snorted.

'Yeah. I'm thinking of buying it.'

'It's not for sale,' the driver said.

'Everything's for sale; you, me, this taxi and especially that warehouse. It just comes down to price. The owner is testing the market to see if there are any buyers. All on the quiet, just so that he doesn't have to pay estate agent fees. He's a real tight prick. That's why I'm here.'

'True! Hey! I can give you a good price on a taxi?'

Peanut shook his head as the taxi drove around the corner.

'This city is too big. I have trouble finding my dick in the mornings, let alone finding my way around this town.'

The driver chuckled.

'It's nice to meet a man who isn't a bullshit artist.' Peanut grinned in reply as he looked out the window.

Peanut could see that the warehouse had been designed to operate as a joint unit or as two separate facilities, with a shared wall down the middle. The loading docks and entrances were on opposite sides but the built-on offices were all side by side on the one end. There was only one camera on this side, pointing at the entrance gate. A faded yellow sign said *Car Restorations.* Both buildings had a worn, unloved look about them. He grinned at the driver in the mirror.

'Back to the station, please. I've seen enough.'

'Make an offer?'

'Absolutely. One they can't refuse.'

'That's the only one to make. You sure I can't interest you in a taxi?'

'And spend all my days getting lost? Not my scene, sorry.'

***

It was one a.m. when Peanut stood in the shadow of a building across the street from the *Car Restorations* warehouse. This side of the street was the blind concrete wall frontage of more warehouses and nobody was watching. The only camera was the fixed type, pointing at the gate in the fence and he was at the opposite end from the gate. He hurried across the street to the chain-link fence, unrolling two pieces of sacking as he walked. He quickly scaled up the chain links beside the steel post and draped the sacking over the barbed wire on the top of the fence, then draped the other sack over the first of the barbed wires on the top outrigger, slipping his body through the gap between the sacks and swinging his legs over. He removed the sacks and then scaled down the inside.

The lack of maintenance showed; the barbed wire on the outrigger was loose, easy to shove aside as he squirmed through. The lock on the office door was old and his pick opened it immediately. He walked in, shut the door and turned on his flashlight when he was in the warehouse proper. The sign was correct. It was a car restoration warehouse, but when he examined the work closer, the restoration seemed to include changing the car manufacturer's identification plates. It was a warehouse chock-a-block with stolen cars. He then wondered if it was connected to the other warehouse. He shone the torch on the dividing concrete block wall. There was a large roller door and a small side door set in the middle of the wall. The roller door was locked. When he couldn't budge it, he tried the side door. It opened with one twist of the steel handle. Both enterprises were linked. No need to be honest when you have crooks on both sides of the wall.

He walked into the office of the other warehouse. Somewhere in here there would be an inventory. He began searching, checking files, checking desk drawers, and he found it. It was a printout of what was going on, where and when. He photocopied it. It was a large-scale business, a staging post, goods in and out really quickly. He walked out into the warehouse proper and began checking the hundreds of pallets stacked on top of each other. The packets on each were marked in batches. It took him no more than a minute of looking at the inventory to work it out. Different drugs, different numbers for different customers, and different destinations. This was payday. His payday. There was too much gear for this to be just a New York operation. He kept looking until he found the phone numbers: Boston, Philadelphia, Pittsburgh, Washington, Atlanta, and Miami. All east coast cities. These Russians were into supply on an industrial scale. He then tried the computers, all six of them. Then he got lucky and found the logon for one of them, written on a Post-it note under the keyboard. There were regular emails, mostly between New York, Los Angles, and Houston. Each supplied the other with drugs. It was an interconnected business. He took note of the LA address of the organisation, the address of the LA warehouse, and the name of the company that handled all the importation at the Port of Houston. Three hours later, he was feeling pleased with himself as he made his way out through the warehouses, scaled the fence, walked four blocks away, and called a taxi.

***

He examined the drab walls of his cheap lodgings. All going well, tomorrow he'd be gone or dead. He didn't plan on being dead. Then LA. It had to be next. A double payday was just too hard to resist. If that went well, a check of the set up at the Port of Houston. Then the hunt for Janice-Rose would begin in earnest. He would have the money to do that. She was far too important to ignore. Hunting for her would mean going back to his old stomping grounds, but that was the risk he had to take. A false identity won't hide you when everyone knows who you are. Then he relaxed and thought about Libby. She wasn't really his girlfriend, although at one stage he had found her sexy. She was just a girl he sometimes hung out with. Libby had made that plain. She wanted someone at least six feet four. He'd found that puzzling. Libby was only an inch taller than him.

'Why?' he'd asked her.

She was blunt. 'Big guy, big cock!'

He wasn't sure if she was joking or not but he knew he was better off single than tied to a silly bitch like that. Nonetheless, she had been a lot of fun, and he was overdue for some fun.

Even so, Ms. Hiller was still at the back of his mind. Hills. She had popped into his mind on the flight to New York and now. It was weird. He knew she would have forgotten about him but the memory of her was nice, despite the punch in the balls. One tough lady, but underneath that tough exterior he had a feeling she could be really sweet. Maybe. He would never know.

He lay down on his bed, cleared his head and then did what he had always done when he wanted to sleep. He thought about the timber-planked cabin in the foothills off the Lee Highway where his mother had once taken him for a holiday. It had been quiet, just the birdsong. He had loved it and decided that was where he wanted a holiday, in the trees, well away from all the mindless pricks in the world. Work in the city by day and hide in the trees at night. It was a stupid dream and he knew it, but it always put him to sleep. He could feel himself drifting, remembering the bush walks, his mother's laughter as they picked wildflowers, as he quietly slipped into sleep. Then the thought gently drifted in, stopping the sleep process dead. Would Hills like having a holiday in some place like that? He rolled over, suddenly awake. Ahh ... fuck it!

Chapter 12

Peanut walked up the steps into the foyer. The noise of the street disappeared as the heavy glass door swung shut behind him. It was a real swanky part of Madison Avenue. The marble-clad exterior of the building smacked of money. Only the best and highest paying tenants need apply. The doorman looked hard at Peanut's casual attire as he walked to the elevator.

Peanut exited on the 10th floor where he couldn't miss the polished brass nameplate *Priest Associates* screwed to the wall. He had a meeting with John Vasiliev, Jordan Priest's fix-it guy. In the anteroom he was surprised they wanted him to wait. He thought he had given them enough to warrant an immediate response. A tall blonde with straight shoulder-length hair and cold blue eyes walked out to meet him. She had an unfriendly look about her as she signaled to him to follow. He watched her ass gyrate in the tight red dress as she led him into an office, and then turned and walked out, throwing him a disdainful glance. He kept his face bland as he wondered what a smile cost. Fuck the bitch!

There was a large fat man seated behind a mahogany desk and a Rent a Thug with designer stubble and a dark suit standing beside him. He wasn't offered a seat.

'What can I do for you Mr. ...' he paused while he studied his notes, 'Conner?'

'Five-hundred-thousand dollars, Mr. Vasiliev,' said Peanut.

Vasiliev leant back in his leather office chair and smiled.

'And what will you do for that five hundred thousand, Mr. Conner?'

'Keep you and your boss out of jail.'

'Really. How?'

'You have a warehouse in Queens, not far from Otto Road. I have full details of all the goods stored there.' Peanut kept his face blank as he dropped the list on the desk. 'I, or my associate, will call the FBI unless you transfer the money to this account immediately.' Peanut dropped another slip of paper onto his desk.

John Vasiliev glared at him. 'This is a shakedown!' His accent was now heavily Russian.

'That's your word for it,' came Peanut's cool response. 'The FBI will be keen to visit. As these goods have been shipped from foreign countries, organized by Russia, and are ready to be shipped interstate, it is an FBI matter. The trucking firms and their destinations are on that goods list. If I were you, I'd consult your boss, Jordon Primakov. And if I'm not on the street within ten minutes, my associate will call the FBI. If the money transfer isn't done within ten minutes, again the FBI will be called. Your choice. Call your boss. I suggest you hurry; we are not patient.' He pulled out his phone. 'My associate is listening. You have ten minutes.'

Vasiliev stood up and turned to the heavy-set guy beside his desk. 'Watch him. If he moves, shoot him.'

'You didn't hear me. If I am not out that door in what is now less than ten minutes, you will be discussing your actions with the FBI. My associate is listening. Cancel that order immediately or he calls the FBI right now and we will wait together for them to arrive.' said Peanut. 'You do not threaten me. I will leave if you do not cancel that order, *now.*'

He stared at Peanut and then looked at the guard, signaled that he put his gun away then stared at Peanut's slight frame and smirked. 'Make me,' he said.

Peanut immediately spun on his heel and walked towards the door. The heavy-set thug lunged and grabbed at him from behind. Peanut knew he would. He dropped to a semi crouch, slipped in close and with one swift movement, swept the thug's legs from under him and sprang back as the bodyguard hit the floor hard and lay still. Peanut's jacket had slid off his shoulders; his hands were a blur as he drew his swords.

Vasiliev was stunned at the speed it happened; he had expected his bodyguard to handle it all. Too late, his hand plunged into his coat pocket and he froze in fear as the steel blade of the sword touched the side of his throat. Peanut glanced at the thug lying on the floor. He was eyeing the steel blade touching Vasiliev's throat and the other sword that was only a foot away and pointing at him. Peanut reached into Vasilievs coat pocket and threw the pistol into the corner. The thug stayed still.

'I gave you a chance. Now you have less than five minutes before I or my associate talk to the FBI. Good day, Mr. Vasiliev. You have the details of where to transfer that money.'

Peanut stalked out, sheathing his swords and ignoring the blonde secretary.

'Mr. Conner! Wait,' shouted a voice.

Peanut turned and recognized Jordon Primakov. 'Yes?'

'Can we talk?' asked Primakov.

'Your assistant has all the details. Your time is running out. You now have less than three minutes. Good day, Mr. Primakov.'

He wasn't surprised when they paid. His smile was grim when he checked his account. Now they would hunt him down. He'd expected that. He transferred the money to a new account and shut down the account they had just used. His new driver's license was in the name of William Flynn and he had used it to set up the new account.

He wasted no time taking the train to JFK and catching the first available flight to LA. They would have already begun to search for him and while he waited for his flight, he emailed the FBI. He was no longer concerned about the money. He would reinvest it in the Cayman Islands or Bermuda later. He couldn't leave it in the States. His false identity could easily be discovered if a government department did a security check because of the amount of money he had suddenly invested. If they found it, it was more than likely they would confiscate it. He was lucky there was seats and bought a ticket for a business-class flight leaving in forty minutes.

Relaxing with a coffee, he people watched, noticing that nobody gave him a second glance. His slight frame made him almost invisible. No one would remember him. He needed sleep and couldn't wait to get into that comfortable business-class seat and nod off.

***

The taxi dropped him off three doors from the warehouse. It was an ugly single-story redbrick building on East 6th Street. He walked past the steel door and took note of the sturdy padlock and the fact that nobody was there. He was familiar with that type of padlock; they were almost impossible to pick. Not only did those locks have internal top and bottom pins, but they also had side pins located on indents in the key as well. He inspected the thickness of the hasp and he knew he didn't have the strength to use bolt cutters on steel that thick.

He carried on walking, pausing from time to time as if getting his bearings. He noticed that the roof had skylights. Maybe that would be his way in. He checked the roof line. An air vent was sticking up near the far corner of the building and he knew he could toss a bit of rope up around that and use it to scale up onto the roof. The rear entrance to the building was accessed by a narrow driveway and there was a camera on the back wall facing the driveway, but the back door was just as secure as the front. The roller door on the loading bay had bars that were padlocked. Then he saw it, above the doors, built into the gable end of the building, a round wooden air vent. About three feet in diameter, it was mounted into the bricks to allow the heat in the roof space to escape during hot weather. That simple vent told him that the building would have been built well over eighty years ago. Smiling to himself, he strolled out of the alley and called a taxi. Tonight, would be the best. They wouldn't suspect another raid so soon. They would still be thinking about his last raid and discussing the "whys" and "what ifs," hopefully with the FBI. He thought they would assume that as he now had half a million dollars in his bank account, he would be spending it on hookers, booze, and drugs. Most of the criminal element that Peanut knew would. They were in for a surprise.

It was one a.m. when he stood at the corner of the building, well away from the camera mounted on the other corner and threw a light rope with a weight on the end, up and over the corner, behind the roof vent, hearing it land with a gentle thud. He walked around the corner and picked up the other end, then climbed up, hand over hand until he reached the corrugated iron roof. He walked to the top of the gable and put on his harness, tied his rope to the nearest skylights and abseiled down to the air vent. He gave the vent a shake. It was solid, but the slats were old, dried-out timber and loose. He had expected that after eighty odd years. He removed the bottom half of the slats and placed them in a bag attached to his waist, then wiggled through the vent and into the warehouse. He released the tension on the line until he was hanging inside and then dropped to the floor, releasing his harness and turning on his torch. He began his inspection

The shed was only a quarter full, but given its size, he estimated there were at least ten tons of what he presumed were drugs, all sorts, just like the New York warehouse. He checked two packets with a hollow spike. He was right. Drugs. This was definitely payday. He walked the length of the warehouse, then into the office area facing the street.

He heard what sounded like a party. Or he thought it was until he got closer and realized that it was the sound of people having sex, loudly, and the closer he got the more it sounded like a full-blown orgy. He took care as he continued on past the row of empty unused offices. This hadn't been an honest warehouse for a very long time. When he came to a crack of light showing under a door, he put his ear to the door and listened. Loud voices, all talking dirty. He eased the door open. He was right; it was an orgy. He glimpsed naked bodies contorted into all sorts of positions and a lone security guard, sitting in the office chair with his pants down, transfixed by porn images on a large widescreen monitor as he masturbated.

Peanut ignored the screen, walked up behind the watchman and hit him hard in the side of the neck with the edge of his hand. He grabbed him as he collapsed into a chair and eased him onto the floor, pulling his shirt up over his head to blind him. He checked in the desk drawers for tape and found it, strong packing tape by the box full. That was logical; they were in the repackaging business. With the watchman's hands and feet secured, silence was guaranteed by stuffing the watchman's own handkerchief into his mouth and then taping it in. He started searching, finding all the information in the main office, turning the porno off so he could concentrate. He retrieved the details of the amount of drugs shipped in, the amount held and for whom and the shipping information with the exact areas the drugs would be trucked to. It was big business and it was the bonanza. He found a lockable storage room, dragged the watchman in, checking that he could breathe, then locked the door, seeing him struggle as he slowly recovered. Peanut was amused at the sight of the once erect penis now dangling down, limp and dirty from being dragged on the floor. All the information that he needed was now in his backpack and he grinned as he walked back to the dangling harness. Fifteen minutes later, he packed his gear up, walking down the street and called a taxi. Time to get some sleep before he meet with Mr. James Gorev.

It wasn't a posh office, just a bit more upmarket but not by much. South Hill Street was a busy area. But it raised a fundamental question. Why did the Russians bother with such nice offices in New York and Los Angles and to a lesser extent, Washington, when the business was only about drugs? Dealing would be at street level with no names, no ID, just take the money and fuck off. Having offices, fancy offices, didn't make sense. He looked up at the office block as he paused by the door. Maybe after he had found Janice-Rose he could spend some time figuring it out, but right now it was just business.

The firm he wanted was on the fourth floor. He knew their name and didn't bother making an appointment. If they fucked him around, they would learn the hard way when the FBI called. He rode the elevator to the fourth floor and took note of the three other companies that were on the same floor. Were they involved with the drug dealers? He would check that out too, after he had found Janice-Rose. The name of the company was etched into the opaque white glass door *Amalgamated Shipping.*

The receptionist looked up when he opened the door and immediately appeared nervous but talked calmly. He knew instantly that she knew about him. They had been warned and would be waiting, despite him giving a different name.

'Yes, sir. Can I help?'

Peanut smiled at her as he examined her name tag, Sharon Reeves. She was probably in her late twenties and she was hot, very hot. Pretty with long dark hair. She was squeezed into a red dress that showed off her well-formed breasts. He automatically assumed she was the boss's girlfriend.

'I don't have an appointment, but I'd like to see James Gorev, please.'

'Just a moment please, sir. Whom shall I say is calling?'

'Barry Wilson.'

'And the nature of your call?'

'Private business. Very important business for Mr. Gorev.'

'Just a moment, Mr. Wilson.'

She stood up and Peanut admired her perfect backside and long legs as she walked away. Yes, very hot. It was ten minutes until she was back. Getting things ready for his reception, Peanut assumed.

'Mr. Gorev will see you now, Mr. Wilson. This way,' she said as she tossed her hair over her shoulder.

She led him through the door behind her desk and along a short corridor to a door with a shiny Conference Room sign. She stood back and indicated that he enter and Peanut put his hand on the door and held it open as he peered around the edge, seeing the three men sitting, all with guns pointed at him, keeping well away at the other end of the table. It was what he expected. He let the door go and then walked in, hearing the door close and the lock snick behind him. Good. No escape, not for him but for them. He examined the men. They were relaxed as they sat together at the far end of a round ten-foot wide conference table, holding Glock 17s. He smiled. They must have bought a job lot. They had been waiting and they thought they were ready, but they hadn't prepared well. Maybe they'd been a bit rushed?

'Welcome, Mr. Wilson. Take a seat. But don't get too settled. I don't think you'll need that chair for long.' The speaker was middle-aged and his dark hair had white showing at the temples. There was only one chair at this end of the table. Clearly, they didn't want him sitting near them. Their pals in New York must have told them about the swords. That was their first mistake. They knew he had swords but had not asked for them. They had seen his slight stature and had dismissed any threat as inconsequential, especially as they had the guns.

He took a good look at the speaker. Even though he was sitting, Peanut could see that he was short, solid, and running to fat. His gold-framed glasses were expensive as was his Rolex. The crisp white shirt and blue tie finished off his professional businessman look. But it was just a look. Peanut knew he was another drug dealer. The two swarthy men sitting on either side of him reinforced this theory. Both wore dark suits, both had designer stubble, and both were unsmiling. Peanut had the impression that they would shoot him with pleasure. They were sitting close to the table, supporting their pistols with their elbows on the table. That was their second mistake. Peanut was surprised when the speaker put his pistol down. But then, why have three guns when two will do? That was their third mistake. The speaker was confident but their mistakes were piling up. As he sat down, the two thugs copied their leader and placed their pistols on the table. Peanut came close to laughing. Of all their mistakes, that was the fatal one.

'Are you James Gorev?' asked Peanut.

'I am,' he replied, his expression grim. 'So, you want to talk business, do you, Mr. Wilson?'

Peanut dropped the two sheets of paper on the table. 'I won't waste your time or mine. This is the inventory of your warehouse. That warehouse is full of illegal drugs. If you don't want the FBI to be informed, then you'll have to pay my fee. The other sheet is my bank details.

'Let me hazard a guess. Five hundred thousand, Mr. Wilson?'

'It is so good to deal with a man who knows figures, Mr. Gorev.'

'Thank you. But it's the other way around. You owe us five hundred thousand in recompense for the five hundred thousand you stole from our New York franchise.' He picked up his pistol and pointed it at Peanut's head. Peanut knew this was not the time to attack. He was not in the right position. He stared at James Gorev without blinking. He had no intention of letting Gorev see that he was nervous. He also knew Gorev wouldn't fire; he wanted the money back. Peanut pulled his chair forward, placed his hands on the table and smiled.

'You understand the FBI will be notified if I don't leave here within the next ten minutes? And if the money is not transferred within that time they will also be notified.'

'Then we shall wait, Mr. Wilson. But be warned, we have a contact within the local FBI who keeps us informed. Yes, we will wait for the ten minutes, then we'll start by crushing your testicles.' He gave a mirthless smile. 'You'll be glad to sign over the half a million and you'll be begging for us to kill you. Which we will. I can't wait, Mr. Wilson. It'll give me and my two friends a great deal of pleasure.'

Peanut kept his face blank. He was sure Gorev was bluffing. If he wasn't, he really was in the shit!

Chapter 13

Gorev was fidgeting. He had got tired of holding his gun up and had placed it back on the table. There were two minutes to go. Peanut grinned at him sensing that he was getting nervous.

'The charges will not just be drugs related, but murder, Mr. Gorev.'

'Why?' asked Gorev.

'If you fire those pistols, that will bring the FBI here quicker than you can blink. The call will go through the moment they are fired.'

'I don't believe you.'

Peanut smiled. 'Your choice.'

Peanut knew all three were on edge and he suspected the thugs had hair-trigger fingers. But not much point in having hair-trigger fingers when your guns are lying on the table. Even so, he knew they were scared of him and his swords, and so were unpredictable.

Peanut's phone shattered the silence. He grinned at Gorev and raised his eyebrows.

'Answer it,' ordered Gorev.

Peanut put it on the table and turned on the speaker.

'Mr. Wilson?'

'Yes, Michael,' said Peanut.

'Is everything okay?'

'No, Michael. Call Clayton O'Neil He's waiting.'

Gorev sat forward in his chair. 'Cancel that! Do you know Clayton O'Neil?' said Gorev.

'Hold the line a minute, Michael.' Peanut took a breath. 'I know him indirectly. O'Neil was given to me as a contact. I spoke to him today.'

'I've heard of that team he's connected to has locked up several of our men,' said Gorev.

'Yes, they have. You really should keep sensitive material somewhere more secure than a crappy safe room with only two shitty filing cabinets. Not very professional, Mr. Gorev. And as for your men getting locked up, if you don't get your ass into gear, you'll be next.'

'Is that a threat, Mr. Wilson?'

Peanut grinned. 'I don't threaten. It's childish. Well, James?'

Gorev suddenly smiled. 'I don't believe you. You're bluffing.'

Peanut pulled a face. It wasn't a pleasant one as the die had been cast. With both his feet firmly planted on the floor, his rubber-soled boots gripped the smooth, timber, while his hands rested on the edge of the table.

'Are you still there, Michael?' asked Peanut as he leaned forward to talk.

Gorev and his thugs leant forward to listen and it was all the edge Peanut needed. He drove forward, using his body and the power of the thigh muscles in his legs to skid the table into the three sitting men. The table immediately shoved them back in their chairs, putting them off balance. Peanut kept rapidly pushing until they were pinned in their chairs and had no foot purchase to push back. The table rammed their chairs further back onto their rear legs and they tipped over backward. The mistake in the way they had been sitting was now evident as they disappeared out of sight behind the table with all three crashing to the floor.

Peanut leaped onto the table, shrugging his jacket back, unsheathing his swords as he ran forward. In three strides he was there, kicking the three guns back along the table. The first thug lunged upwards. It was too easy. He flicked the sword in his right hand around; it went into the thug's eye and into his brain as the second thug lunged up at his legs, arms outstretched. Peanut jumped, the left-handed sword swiping viciously down, cutting across the reaching arms, the razor-sharp sword slicing through the suit coat, into the flesh as Peanut landed on the floor and stepped aside. The thug stopped, realising that his arms weren't working correctly and glanced down, seeing one hand dangling, the blood spurting out of his coat sleeve. He glanced up, terrified, just as the sword penetrated his chest. He was dead on his feet. His body crumpled on top of a scrabbling James Gorev, hindering him as he tried to get into the office behind him. Peanut turned as Gorev pushed to his feet, almost surgically did a short low swipe, cutting one of Gorev's Achilles tendons. Gorev was suddenly unable to walk, collapsing on the floor, now twisting and looking up at Peanut, his face full of terror. Peanut stood looking down at him.

'I think it's time you transferred that money now, don't you? Banks don't like to be kept waiting, do they?' Peanut said as he flicked a sword in front of Gorev's deathly white face. Peanut bent down and frisked him and found no more weapons. For a minute Gorev looked like he might try something, but Peanut placed the tip of the sword tip against his neck and ended any such ideas before he carried out a quick search of the two dead thugs. He picked up the pistols and put them in his pocket and he noticed that they were clean. The markings had all been filed off and it didn't look as if they had ever been fired before.

'Call your secretary in. What's her name? Sharon, wasn't it?'

Gorev pulled out his phone and called.

'Sharon, could you please come to the conference room?'

Peanut snatched Gorev's cell phone and walked to the door, waiting as the door opened, reaching out and pulling her inside, then shutting and locking the door. She saw the bodies and gasped in shock burying her face in her hands.

'Sharon, could you help James into his office please?' said Peanut.

James had a look of desperation on his face. Peanut didn't think Sharon would be much help, not in the elegant sexy high heels she had on. With her half-dragging him, and Gorev pushing himself with his good leg, they made it to Gorev's desk. Peanut pointed Sharon to a chair in the corner.

'Sit down and don't move,' he instructed, watching as Sharon sat. He hoisted Gorev into his chair.

'Go. Log in to your account!'

Gorev had a look of stubbornness on his face. Peanut wondered if he was pretending to be a hero in front of his girlfriend.

'You're not getting half-a-million dollars,' said Gorev.

'You're right. I'm not. Now that your little enterprise is fucked, you owe Sharon severance pay and my bill has gone up. Open your computer and get going.'

'No!' spat Gorev.

Peanut didn't hesitate; he punched Gorev in the side of the head and stunned him, before he grabbed his hand, and bent his little finger until it snapped at the knuckle. Gorev howled in pain and clutched his hand to his chest. Peanut ignored him.

'How much do you want in severance pay?' Peanut asked Sharon. 'I assume you're his girlfriend?'

'Yes,' she answered quietly.

'He's married,' said Peanut.

'Yes, but we're going to leave together and get married in Spain.'

'You really believe he'd leave his wife and children, just to be with you? Why would he do that when he's already got the both of you? He's talking shit. Think about it.'

Sharon frowned at Peanut and then at Gorev. Peanut could see the indecision in her eyes. He turned to Gorev and pointed at the computer. When Gorev shook his head once again the punch was swift. The crack of the second pinkie being broken and Gorev's cry of pain were loud. Gorev clutched his broken hands to his chest and moaned in pain. Peanut knew he had to step it up. Leaving the door of Gorev's office open, Peanut went into the conference room and checked the thug's pockets. He knew he was a smoker. He could smell it on his clothes and he soon found the cigarettes and the lighter. He walked back in and flicked the lighter on in front of Gorev's eyes.

'We're going to move this matter forward. I'm going to start on your fingers, and if that doesn't work, your testicles. Sharon knows what they look like but after I'm finished, she'll never recognize them. You won't ever use them again either, believe me.' Peanut's voice was devoid of emotion and Gorev glanced up and saw the dead eyes, the bleakness and cracked, a look of resignation on his face as he turned on the computer, taking care not to bump the dangling pinkies. Peanut's face was serious as he turned to Sharon.

'Do you know how to operate his accounts?'

'Yes,' she said.

'Get over here, then. You need your redundancy pay and we don't want your boyfriend cheating us, do we?'

She walked over and stood close, almost too close to him, but Peanut knew she was not a threat; she had just changed sides.

Gorev logged onto the account. There was only just over twenty thousand in it. 'Sorry, it's the wrong time of the month,' he said.

'That's what all the girls say, but as you aren't having your period, it doesn't count.'

He glanced at Sharon and she smiled.

'That's just the everyday account. The big one is with BOA,' she said.

'Can you access it?'

'No, I don't have the password.'

Peanut leant forward and twisted Gorev's ear, hard. 'Don't be naughty, James. Go to that account.'

James threw Sharon a pain-filled glance. 'I'll fucking kill you, you stinking bitch.'

The punch was swift and hard and this time it was on the ear that Peanut had just twisted. Gorev cried out just as the BOA sign-on page came up.

'It's rude to talk to your employee like that, or rather, your ex-employee,' said Peanut.

Peanut examined the account. Just over two-point-six million.

'Transfer two-point-six million to that account. Now!' he said as he shoved his bank details under Gorev's nose.

'But you said half a million?'

'That was before you and your thugs tried to kill me.'

Sharon smiled at Peanut. 'I can transfer it.' she said.

Peanut pulled Gorev's chair out and threw him off it. Gorev screamed in pain as one of his broken pinkies hit the floor.

'Is six hundred thousand a good enough redundancy?' asked Peanut.

She smiled and nodded her head. 'Oh, yes!'

'Transfer all that to this account and make the transfer an immediate clearance of funds. When it clears, I'll transfer the six hundred thousand to your account. Okay?'

Peanut watched carefully. He knew it was simple, but as he was unfamiliar with the setup it was easier for Sharon to do it. Five minutes after she had finished Peanut checked his account via the app on his phone. The money had come through.

'Got your bank account details?' Peanut asked.

She gave them to him and Peanut dialed up on his phone and transferred the six hundred thousand on immediate clearance to her account. Gorev lay on the floor beaten, pain and resignation plastered on his face.

Sharon checked her account and then turned and smiled with a look that said it all. 'It's there. I was worried you might cheat me,' she said.

'You've been working for too long with thieves. There are good people in this world, but Gorev and his pals aren't it.' He handed her a thumb drive.

61

'Load this and run it. It's a scrubber. Makes chasing where the money went that much harder.'

He watched as she ran the program and when she finished, he turned the computer off. She stood up, kicked off her shoes, so she was more his height, then kissed him on the cheek, holding him, pressing her body against his, not pushy, just wanting to see if he was interested. He smiled and drew her close for a second. He was.

'Me and Gorev have some business to sort out. Get your things and I'll meet you in reception. You and I are flying out of here, today.'

She left without looking once at Gorev.

Peanut walked over to Gorev and smiled as he slid out one of his swords. Gorev's eyes opened wide.

'No! No! Please, Mr. Wilson! You don't have to kill me! I'll help any way I can!' Peanut gave a wry look.

'*Consequences*, James. I won, you lost.' Gorev's mouth open to plead but any words were abruptly cut off by the pain that slammed into his chest as his heart stopped. Peanut pulled out the sword, wiped the blade on Gorev's shirt and watched as blood gushed out the wound. He slipped the sword back into its sheath as he walked out, closing and locking the door. Sharon was ready to go. He wondered why she hadn't put her shoes on until her lips met his.

They walked out the door onto the street, hand in hand. They passed two heavy-set thugs on their way into the building.

'I need to see a man, let's walk and talk,' said Peanut as he picked up the pace. He knew those thugs would have been going to see Gorev and he was glad that he had locked the doors to the conference room, Gorev's office, and the main door to all the offices.

'You realize you'll have to disappear?' said Peanut.

'Yes. Can I get a few things things from my apartment?'

'Just what you can fit in a cabin bag and one suitcase,' said Peanut.

'That'll be all I need. What's your name?'

'Peanut.'

She laughed. 'Really?'

'Really. It's not my real name, but it'll do for now.'

She understood. She wouldn't get to know his real name until they knew each other better. She didn't care; he had just made her rich!

***

Two blocks later, he smiled as they approached Michael, sitting on the stool he always occupied on the corner. It was a place where he could keep an eye on the newsstand while his brother was busy.

'Thanks, Michael.'

'Shit! Mr. Wilson. It sounded pretty heavy up there. Half a million, I heard?'

'Yes, it was heavy. But you were a great help.' Peanut pulled out his wallet. 'I think we agreed on a couple of hundred, but I think you've earnt a tip.' He peeled off two one-hundred-dollar bills followed by another eight. 'I think an even thousand for your services would be satisfactory. Okay?'

'You bet!' He rolled up the bills and slipped them in his pocket with a broad smile. 'If you ever need anything else, you come to me, okay?' he said.

'I certainly will,' said Peanut as he held up his fist and they touched knuckles. He would use Michael again, anytime.

Chapter 14

Peanut checked the accounts on his computer. He had already moved Gorev's money to another account, one in a different name. He was now a multi-millionaire. He chuckled as he thought about it. *Thank you, Gorev. Your crime did pay, but for me, not you.*

Gorev was a fool. He could have done it so much cheaper and he would still be alive but in jail. The moment he attacked, there was only ever going to be one outcome and it was simple; it was either him or Gorev. Peanut had already notified the FBI and he knew they would be crawling all over the office and warehouse, looking for clues. They wouldn't find them.

Peanut placed his computer into its bag, packed his carry-on luggage, and strode out the door after Sharon.

'Ready to go?' he asked her as he started the rental car.

Sharon nodded, happy.

They drove south heading for San Diego International Airport.

'How long till we get there?' Sharon asked.

'Nearly two hours. Grab some sleep if you can.'

She rolled over in her seat and stared at him. She was wearing the same sexy smile that had first attracted him.

'Are we staying the night? I feel like a bit of excitement.'

Peanut patted her stretched out leg.

'Not a good idea, sweetheart. The moment those bodies are discovered, the police will check the street videos. I never saw any cameras, but all the stores have them facing their front doors. The moment they have us on video, all the airports, train stations, and bus stations will be alerted. We have to keep moving.'

'How much trouble are we in?'

'Until we disappear, heaps, but solving that is only one flight away.'

Three hours later, they walked onto a business-class flight to Atlanta. Peanut slept for the entire flight. He was tired after the all the action and then the driving. He awoke just as the plane began to descend and glanced at Sharon. He watched her looking out of the window. She was pretty. There was no doubt about it. He was happy. At the moment things were looking pretty good.

He'd booked a suite in an expensive hotel. He wanted it to be special, just to see if the magic attraction in LA was more than fleeting stardust. He shouldn't have worried.

It was more than stardust. Much more. Sharon saw the king-size bed, dropped her case, kicked off her shoes and kissed him, gently at first, then as passion built, with an intensity that was hungry and overpowering. She stopped, pulled her dress over her head, then pulled him onto the bed on top of her.

Thirty minutes later when they came up for air, the bed was a mess. He had to admit, it was like nothing he had ever experienced. Sharon was just as beautiful when she was all naked and mussed after passionate lovemaking as she was when fully clothed. How did she do that?

He lay back with her head resting on his arm. 'Lunch, honey?' he asked, feeling the need for the energy that he knew the food would give him.

'Room service would be great, baby. Now that I've a real man in the sack, we are staying here, aren't we?'

That day and the next drifted by. Peanut found her an insatiable lover. She said it was because Gorev used to run out of steam, leaving her yearning for energetic sex, the sort Peanut could give her. He laughed; he thought that was funny. It was purely because he was still young and fit, not old and fat.

But he had his doubts about their future. Enjoying good sex was not the same as building a loving relationship and already he could feel uncertainty creeping in. Was there love between them? He couldn't feel anything deeply emotional developing. Maybe it might change, but that day had yet to come.

Three days later, he knew the relationship was going nowhere. The sex was fantastic, but when they weren't having sex, they had very little in common. Sharon wasn't stupid; in fact, she was extremely bright, but she had a fixation about getting a very rich old man to marry her, just to give her a life of unbridled luxury. When he said it was just a bullshit fantasy, they had another fight. That was the one thing he did love about her; she was just like him. If she thought she was right, she didn't back down. But it was now obvious that, apart from the sex, they didn't share any meaningful mutual interests. He was fixated on hunting for Janice-Rose and she was fixated on hooking a billionaire.

It ended when one petty nit-picking session blew up into a vicious argument. They apologized to each other, made up, had sex again and then agreed to go their separate ways. Peanut took Sharon through the process of becoming someone else, setting her up with an untraceable bank account in her new name. He gave her his contact details, just in case she needed help. She was a fast learner and she was also grateful, very grateful and showed it. They rode in a taxi to the airport holding hands, and parted with a long hug and a kiss, but without another word being spoken. He watched as she walked down the air bridge to catch her flight to Miami.

An old woman sitting at the air bridge waiting gave a quiet wolf whistle.

'You guys really love each other, huh?' she said.

Peanut smiled. 'No, we're breaking up. I won't see her again. It was ever only about the sex.' Peanut smiled at the old woman's astonished expression as he turned and walked towards the international lounge and his flight to the Bahamas.

'I'll never understand this generation,' the old woman muttered just before Peanut was out of earshot.

Sharon still had her looks and she would be a hit—Peanut was sure about that. He wryly thought that the rich single old men of Miami had better watch out. A female heart attack was on her way!

But Peanut quickly forgot about Sharon. His mind was on his el cheapo passport. He hoped it would get him through to the Bahamas. It did.

It only took a one-night stopover for him to invest the money and, despite the beautiful beaches, he knew he had to go back. He had a two-day stopover planned in Houston on the way back to Washington, just to do a quick check of the Houston end of the drug cartel. The hunt for Janice-Rose had to start. Time was passing and he needed to find her. It was then he realized that it was only three weeks since he had left the ICT team. A lot sure had happened.

***

Peanut walked past the small warehouse in the Port of Houston. It was late, nearly midnight, and the area was quiet. The drug cartel had been clever, using a legitimate warehousing business as a front for their drug-supply network. Stuck behind chain-link fencing in a high-security compound, Peanut was convinced this small warehouse was the drug part of the business. It would take time and a lot of thought to work out how to get past the security of the compound. He took a taxi uptown and checked out the main office and the main warehouse of the legitimate business. None of the staff that worked there would ever know what was going on behind the scenes. The more he thought about it, the more he knew he would need a team to pull this one off. Maybe a team of three could do it and four certainly could. But he didn't have a team. The killed the plan before it started so he shelved the idea and flew back to Washington. It annoyed him but some things weren't meant to be.

Peanut climbed into the taxi at Dulles airport.

'Capital Hilton, please.'

It felt good to be back in his hometown. He browsed the rentals in the paper on the drive to the hotel and noticed that apartments were expensive, some extremely so. He resorted to using his phone to look for cheaper options. Further out in the suburbs, perhaps? Somewhere well away from the elevated prices of the central city. He would search for a place tomorrow, using his hotel room as a base. He gazed out the cab window; the day was drab and cold and scattered showers were drifting across the streets. Right now, all he wanted was a hot meal, a shower, and a bed, in that order.

He found a suitable second floor two-bedroom apartment on Blair Road in Takoma Park and paid six months' rent in advance. He settled in and he sent his address to Sharon, just in case. That sorted, he had a phone call to make.

'Danny,' said his brother when he answered his phone. No last name, he expected that. Time inside changes the way your brain thinks.

'Hi'ya, Danny.'

The uplift in Danny's voice was immediate. 'Hi'ya, bro. Where the fuck are you, man?'

'Sorry. Can't say just in case this line is bugged.'

'Really?'

'Yeah. Just in case. Tell me, did Zeb take over from Chuckie?'

'Yeah. He came around and tried to throw his weight around until I mentioned you. I told him how you'd got the feds to get me out. He went all quiet and then fucked off. He's fucking madder than Chuckie, but he don't harm anyone unless it's needed. Fucking Chuckie just loved snuffing out some poor prick, didn't he? Hey, rumour has it that it was you that did for the fat prick. It that right?'

'Nah, Chuckie was shot. I don't use guns. So sorry, Danny. Can't say any more. How's Mom?'

'Misses you and Janice-Rose like mad. She cries about it sometimes, but since I came back, she hasn't had any more shithead boyfriend trouble. Got a really nice guy now. We get on pretty well.'

'Tell her I love her, huh? Zeb hang out in the usual?'

'Yeah, will do. Zeb? Yeah, nothing's changed. Business as usual, just not in our neighborhood. He may be a mad cunt, but he ain't stupid.'

'Good to hear. Got to go, Danny.' He hung up. It was time to visit Zeb.

***

Bellevue was one of the leading areas in Washington for crime statistics: drugs, low pay, drugs, prostitution, drugs, family violence, drugs, crime … all fueled by the gangs. He knew where Zeb hung out and he asked the taxi driver to park. The driver was nervous, but Peanut promised him an extra fifty if he hung around. It was a disused warehouse and maybe it had once been a garage, but it was now boarded up. It appeared empty.

He opened the graffiti-painted door and walked in. Four guys were sitting in old battered armchairs around a chipped coffee table, cards in their hands. They looked up, seeing the small stature of Peanut.

'Zeb around?'

They stared at him. No one spoke. He waited. He could play that stupid game too. Then a dark skinny guy stood up.

'Who wants to know?'

'Me, obviously. I did ask.'

The skinny guy had a glazed look on his face. Peanut figured he was probably a dope head.

'And who the fuck are you, man?'

'Peanut. Pass it on to Zeb that I want a meeting.'

The other three stood up. A short fat guy with tight curly hair held up his hand as the others fanned out.

'Wait here. I'll find out if he wants to see you.'

Peanut shook his head. 'I don't think so. You don't want the feds in here, do you? I got to keep moving, guys. If the feds catch up, it'll be all or nothing and I don't think any of you pricks want to go down with me, do you?'

'You stay here. You killed Chuckie.'

'Fucking bullshit. Chuckie was shot in the side of the head. I don't use guns.'

'So, who did it, then?'

'The feds shot Chuckie and framed me for it. I had info they wanted.'

'About us?'

'Fuck off. The feds don't give a fuck about you drugged-up nobodies. They want the cream with the kilos, not the garbage with the grams.' He pulled a card out of his pocket and flicked it out and as it fell on the floor he turned and walked out. He knew the message would get back to Zeb. As he climbed into the taxi, they walked out the door of the shed and watched him drive off.

'Takoma Park, please,' he said to the driver. Zeb would call tonight. He wasn't the sort to play mind games and make him wait, just to show he was the boss. He might be a nutcase, but he had always been direct with Peanut when he'd dealings with him. Now it was just a waiting game.

***

Chas tossed the folder across the desk to Hills. She raised an eyebrow but nevertheless picked it up and read it. Chas stared out of the window at nothing. He was deep in thought. There was a thump on the table as Hills tossed the folder back to him.

'Peanut!' was the only word she said.

Chas noticed that she was trying not to smile.

'Yeah. He's doing our work for us. First, the warehouse in New York. The feds got a message and picked up nearly all of the shit, but not the organizers. They did a runner back to Mother Russia. The two dummies they did catch said the rumor was that a little runt had done them for a cool half a million. They described him as deadly with swords. Then there was a call to the feds in LA. Three dead bodies later and they're searching the computer in the LA office to see who did that job and how much they got. They think they are linked because the voice on the phone is the same as the one in the New York call. The computer was wiped so any trace on where the money went will be impossible, especially if it has gone offshore. Can't wait to find out if he's got it.'

'Are you going to tell them who it was?' Hills had a worried look on her face as she asked.

'No, of course not. If they arrest Peanut and he talks, we, as an organisation, are finished,' said Chas.

'We should contact him.'

'Yeah, good idea, but how?'

She gave a knowing smile.

'Easy. He wants to find his sister, Janice-Rose. That was what he was doing when we interrupted him with Chuckie. He'll come back to Washington to find her and he'll start with Chuckie's replacement.'

'And let me guess. *You* just happen to know who that is, right?'

Hills picked up Chas's sarcastic tone. She reddened slightly and glared at Chas.

'Yes, I do. A moron named Zeb.'

66

'Then let's go talk to him. See if he knows anything. I assume you know where to find him?' He glanced at her as he stood up. 'Silly me, of course, you know where.'

Hills clamped her lips tight at Chas's dig and again blushed slightly and nodded.

Chas was enjoying himself. He had concluded that Peanut was, in his own way, a good guy. Tough, brutal and honest. Taking down those drug guys in New York and L.A. and then letting the FBI know about the drugs was brilliant. He was lethal, with a habit of making sure the bad guys turned up dead. Not a bad habit at all, in Chas's mind—in fact, a really fucking good one. He had saved taxpayers a hell of a lot of money on defense lawyer bills.

And Chas now knew that Hills fancied Peanut. How much was anybody's guess. She could have had her pick of anyone, but Peanut had made an impression that had stuck. Was it love? Or was it just lust for something she couldn't have? Peanut had made no overtures to Hills, of that Chas was sure. He hadn't even been all that nice as he'd been blunt and indifferent. Chas couldn't really understand it. It was all way too complicated for him, and he mentally waved it away in favor of admiring Hills's ass as she walked down the stairs. He knew it was a man thing and sexist, but the way her backside moved in that dress as she walked down the stairs was lovely, truly lovely.

***

Peanut's phone rang. He was not familiar with the number. 'Yeah?'

'Peanut. It's Zeb. Did the feds really frame you, man?'

'Yeah.'

'Bummer!'

Peanut smiled at the word. He hadn't heard that word since his mother had used it, years ago. Maybe Zeb's parents still spoke like that. That might explain Zeb's love of drugs.

'I'm looking for Janice-Rose and her boyfriend.'

'That creep Dickie Matthews?' asked Zeb.

'Yeah.'

'He's dead, man. Overdose.'

Peanut's spirits fell. If Dickie had been doing drugs, Janice Rose would have been using too. It was not looking good.

'I see. Any word on Janice-Rose?'

'She left him long before he died, man. He wanted her to use her pussy to get him drugs and she told him to fuck off. He hit her so she threw him, kicked him in the nuts and then kicked him in the head and then left.' Zeb laughed. 'He had a real hate for her after that. He didn't know that she could do that martial arts shit.'

Peanut's spirits lifted and he smiled at Zeb's words. Peanut had taught Janice-Rose some of the basic self-defence moves. All of a sudden, he felt proud of his long-lost sister.

'Any word on where she went?'

'Nah. She's not hanging around these parts. If I see her, man, I'll let her know you are looking. I'll let you know if I come across her. Hey, did the feds really kill Chuckie?'

'Yeah.'

'So, you're on the run?'

'It's a knock-for-knock agreement, Zeb. I know too much and so long as the feds don't bother me, I keep mum. And it also helps that they don't know where the fuck I am, just in case they change their minds.'

Zeb laughed. 'Shit yeah. Hey, did you free Danny?'

'Yeah.'

'Wow! The feds must have really wanted what you had, just to do that for you.'

'That part of the deal is over. Just let me know if you hear anything and thanks, man. I won't forget that you helped me out.' Peanut hung up, delighted that Janice-Rose wasn't on drugs but worried that she hadn't been seen. Where could she have gone?

***

Zeb sat down, shaking his head. The other guys around the coffee table looked at him expectantly.

'That was Peanut. He didn't kill Chuckie so forget about any thoughts of revenge. Peanut has contacts. Government contacts. He could be useful. If you see his sister, Janice-Rose, tell me. She could be worth a deal, okay?' They all nodded like monkeys on a chain.

'He really got Danny out, eh?' asked one of them.

'Yeah. Like I said, Peanut and his sister could be useful.' He sat back and studied the cards.

'Deal me a hand, man.'

Thirty minutes later he was smiling, holding a wining hand when the door burst open. A SWAT team stormed in.

'Hands up! Now! Now!' Their hands raced upwards. Nobody argues with six armed men with pointed Bushmaster assault rifles.

A tough-looking man in a suit walked in followed by a cutie with a black skirt that showed some nice leg.

'Which one of you is Zeb?' asked Hills.

There was silence.

Chas frowned and he shrugged at Hills. He sat down on the old couch near the table.

'It's a pity you guys won't speak,' Chas said. 'But I'm not the one with my hands in the air. Gentlemen, we are going to play a game. The first one who drops his arms gets arrested and handcuffed and a nice big bag of Ice will be found on his body on the way to the lockup. That'll get you ten years at least, gentlemen. More, much more, if you've already transgressed into our much-beloved court and penal system. It's your choice whether you cooperate or not. All we want is information about Peanut.'

'What do you want to know?' asked Zeb.

'For a start, which one of you is Zeb?'

'I am, man.'

Chas stood up, walked over and held out his hand.

'Chas Fischer, Federal Agent. And this is Amanda Hiller, also a Federal Agent.' Chas was surprised when Zeb shook his hand.

'FBI?'

'No. But still Federal Agents.'

'Okay, so what do you want?'

'Has Peanut been in touch with you?' Zeb gave a start. He'd rung Peanut and then the feds had come calling. Feds that aren't feds. Zeb was worried. If they weren't the FBI, then who the fuck were they? Were they the ones who got Peanut's brother out of prison? If they had, then they had real power. More than the FBI.

Hills noticed Zeb start and she checked a smile. She could almost see his dope-and-ice-affected brain cells working.

'You guys chasing Peanut?'

'Nah. Just want to talk to him,' Chas said shaking his head.

'He dropped in and left his number, so I rang him. He wanted to know about his sister, Janice-Rose.'

'So, where is she?' Chas asked.

'No idea. Janice-Rose is gone, man.'

Hills butted in. 'Have you got Peanut's number on your phone?'

Zeb opened his phone and handed it over.

Hills smiled her thanks and put the number on her phone.

'Zeb, guys, thanks. Very much appreciated,' Chas said as he smiled.

Zeb's gang seemed nonplussed by the familiarity of Chas and Hills. But then it's easy to be friendly and relaxed when you have a six-member SWAT team standing behind you with Bushmaster assault rifles that, while not pointed at anything specific, were ready and would fire within a heartbeat. Zeb watched Chas and Hills leave and he couldn't help noticing the lady's ass. She might have been a fed, but she was the hottest fed he'd ever fucking seen.

'If they're Peanut's friends, I don't want any part of it,' said the skinny black guy with the curly hair. 'You see that guy? He shook your fucking hand, man, like you're a business partner or something. That prick would cut your nuts off and smile as he was doing it. You see his eyes, man? He was smiling but his fucking eyes weren't.'

Zeb had to agree. As feds went, they were friendly, but why? That scared him.

'If Janice-Rose ever turns up, we leave her and Peanut alone. Okay?'

Chapter 15

Peanut sat on the couch and stared out of the window. The branches at the top of the tree moved gently in the breeze coming up Blair Road. The spring growth was almost fully formed, and the leaves danced, reflecting sunlight off their glossy unfurled surfaces. The heat would soon be here, sentencing everyone to sweating through the muggy Washington summer.

Peanut looked away, his mind elsewhere. He and Janice-Rose had been close, really close, and he thought he knew about her dreams. Despite her being his younger sister, they had shared secrets, lots of them. Their mom had doted on her and Peanut thought that was part of the problem. Janice-Rose was too used to getting her own way. She was also stubborn, very stubborn. The more he thought about it, the more he was convinced that she wouldn't come home until she had achieved something. Finding out that her boyfriend was a loser would have hurt. It would tell her she had made a big mistake and that would have knocked her self-confidence. He knew that she had loved that guy. But he was a pig and he had just used her. It was fortunate that he was dead, but Janice-Rose would still be suffering. She had thrown away her family in favor of a complete tosser. The last row between her and mom had been bitter, vindictive; like any row between a headstrong girl who was nearly a woman and a loving mother who desperately knew the daughter she loved was making a bad mistake. Peanut knew it was all about pride, Janice-Rose's pride. He hoped that now she might see beyond that, admit her mistake, and reach out to her mom. But she was eighteen and headstrong, so that probably wasn't going to happen. He tried to think what Janice-Rose would do. Where would she go? Her grades at school had been good and Peanut had expected her to go to college, but she had said that she couldn't see herself studying shit she wasn't interested in. But she would need money and that meant work. Where could she work? It wouldn't be at McDonald's or Kentucky Fried, that was for sure. All of a sudden it came to him.

He picked up his jacket, but then saw the time. She wouldn't be there now; it was well past the time they shut. He stared out of the window, noticing the light was fading. He sat down and wondered where Janice-Rose was living. Then for the first time in days, he remembered the good times with Sharon. Despite their fights, they did have a lot of fun.

Then it happened again; he thought about Hills. After Sharon left for Miami, Hills had come back into his subconscious. No, he told himself, that was not strictly correct. Hills had often popped into his mind in the small quiet hours, even when he had been lying listening to Sharon's gentle breathing as she slept in his arms. He wondered if his subconscious thoughts about Hills had played a part in him not bonding with Sharon? He shook his head. Why did Hills keep popping into his thoughts? They had barely got past disliking each other. Yes, they had been moving towards a tentative friendship but nothing had started, let alone finished. So why was she stuck in his memory? He knew he had to blot her out. He was becoming obsessive about her and it was beginning to drive him nuts.

His phone rang. He was glad of the interruption. He didn't know the number. He was cautious.

'Yes?'

'Hi, Peanut. It's Hills. How are you?'

Peanut's mouth fell open and he fumbled with his phone, nearly dropping it. It took him a second or two to recover.

'Peanut, are you there? Are you okay?'

He cleared his throat.

'I'm fine, Hills. How did you get my number?'

'Peanut, if we meet, I'll tell you. Can we meet? It's important. I know you're hunting for Janice-Rose and maybe we can help.'

'Is Chas there?'

'Yes, I'm on speaker. We just want to talk.'

'What, no SWAT team, no handcuffs, no putting a gun in my hand to frame me? You and Chas are losing your employment touch.'

'Peanut, we didn't know you then. Seriously, we just want to talk. Just Chas and me. Chas wants to discuss getting all that shit with Chuckie wiped out and you coming back to us as a free agent. Your choice, of course.'

Peanut's laugh was sardonic. 'That might not be so easy, this time. I take it you've seen the results from New York and L.A.?'

'Yes, but who's to say it was you?'

There was a cough in the background and Chas's voice came on the line.

'I seem to remember you were with us at the time, isn't that right? And thanks for doing our work for us. Rumor has it that it has made you quite wealthy, but that couldn't happen, could it? You were with us and it's all just pure speculation, right?'

Peanut sighed. He needed them, but only if they were on the level. He knew Chas was an honorable man and would stand by his word, but like everyone else, Chas had superiors. Could they be trusted? He had misgivings, deep misgivings. Was this reconnection worth the aggravation? He was not an ex-cop like Peter or Hills or ex-military like Chas and Blue; he was just a part-time electronic technician who knew martial arts. He sighed. He did want to see Hills again; he needed to, if only to confirm that there was nothing there and her popping into his mind all the time was just part of his over-active imagination. She had been sweet to him during the last two or three days they'd been together and he thought that was probably all there was to it. Outside of his own family, his mom, Danny, and Janice-Rose, few people had ever been sweet to him. And as far as women went, Sharon was the only one who had accepted him for what he was, although she had made a quip one night when he mentioned his slight stature.

'You're big where it counts, honey, and I'm not talking about your dick!' She had stared at him with open frank eyes and then had kissed him. It had been enjoyable.

Hills's voice interrupted his thoughts.

'Are you there, Peanut? You're not talking.'

'Yeah, sorry. I'm okay. Just a bit stunned. Okay, guys. I'm in a dog box in Takoma Park.' He gave the address and sat back. There was no going back now. He still didn't trust them completely or trust their superiors, but if they were going to take him down, he had enough money to hire the very best of lawyers. He stood up. He needed coffee, even if it was only an instant.

***

The tap on the door was light. He opened the door and Hills and Chas were looking uneasily at him, as if they didn't know what to expect. If they were as unsure as he was, that told him they were on the level. He held out his hand. Hills brushed it aside and hugged him.

'It's so nice to see you again. We thought we had lost you,' she said. He felt uncomfortable with the hug and she sensed it and stood back as he stepped forward and shook Chas's outstretched hand.

'Good to see you. Really good,' said Chas.

They followed Peanut inside.

'Coffee anyone? Sorry I've only got instant.'

'I'd love one. Thanks,' said Hills.

71

Hills and Chas sat down on the lone couch, Chas putting a folder on the coffee table as Peanut made the coffees. He came back from the kitchen, put the coffees and an open packet of biscuits on the table, pulled up a dining chair and sat facing them. Hills had moved along the couch, making room for him but Peanut wanted to talk to the both of them. For a second, she seemed miffed.

'How far along are you with finding Janice-Rose?' she asked.

'I think I know where to start, but I can't do it until tomorrow. This is my priority at the moment, nothing else matters.'

'Understood,' said Chas. 'Do you think you'll find her?'

'I hope so, but it could take some doing, especially if I'm wrong about my destination tomorrow. So, how did you get my number?'

'Zeb gave it to us. Hills was smart enough to remember that you were hunting for Janice-Rose when we interrupted your date with Chuckie.' Chas laughed as he said it. 'She thought you'd come back, so we paid a visit to Chuckie's replacement with the SWAT team. Zeb was helpful, if I may say so.'

Peanut laughed. Zeb would have been gob smacked at Chas and Hills turning up.

'Now tell us exactly what happened in L.A., just in case we need to interfere,' said Chas.

Peanut recounted what had happened, glossing over the gory bits until Chas pulled him up.

'Details, please. You had three guys with guns at one end of the table and you at the other end, yet *they* wound up dead. How did that happen?'

Peanut sighed.

'I should make you promise that neither of you will tell the cops or the feds, but that would be a waste of time. If you were ordered to tell, you would.'

They both shook their heads.

'No, not in a million years,' said Hills. 'We'd lose all credibility with Blue and Peter and the team would be finished. It wouldn't happen. We would deny all knowledge of what went on.' She was emphatic.

Chas laughed.

'You have to understand, and you might not have thought it through, but this whole team is basically illegal. There's only us to get things done and we have to stick up for each other. We need to when so many of our actions are borderline illegal. You should know us better than that by now, I hope.'

'No, I don't. Not really,' said Peanut. 'I know nothing about either of you, just what I saw during your day-to-day activities, so excuse my caution. I don't think I can trust you after the way I was … ah, hired.'

'More press-ganged, I'm afraid,' Chas said with a contrite look on his face. 'We needed a skilled burglar and you were it. We had a time constraint put on us by the State Department so we rushed it and now we've probably put you off working with us for life. Pity.'

Hills nodded her head.

'Whatever you think of us, we are very effective at what we do and you make us that much more effective,' she said. 'So no pressure, but we would really like to have you back.'

Peanut studied her and he saw a pleading look that he had never seen before. Was that for real or was the tough bitch just playacting? He didn't think he would ever find out.

'You're part of the team,' Chas said. 'Or were part of the team. Peter has been giving us hell since you left. Called me a moron and told Hills that if her looks weren't good enough to keep you in the team, then she should have pulled her panties off!' Chas laughed as he said it and Peanut gave a wry grin as he took in Hills's annoyed expression and Chas's sly grin. He had the feeling Chas had enjoyed repeating that in front of Hills.

'So how did it happen? That L.A. thing?' Chas asked.

Peanut shrugged. 'It was easy. They thought they were safe and they pulled their chairs up to the table and put their guns on the table. Even a Glock gets heavy after holding it up for ten minutes. They didn't even ask me to hand over my swords. When the time was right, I shoved the table back and tipped their chairs over. By the time they started to get up, I was across the table with my swords out. The rest, as they say, is history.'

Hills now knew what had happened. It was just another display of Peanut's lethal skills.

'So, you killed the thugs outside the office?' asked Hills.

'Yes, in the conference room. Gorev tried to get to his office, but I hamstrung him. I then got him to call his secretary in to help him into this office. I put him in his chair behind the computer. When he refused, I persuaded him to log on by cracking his knuckles. After that his secretary completed the transfer.'

'She helped you?' asked Hills.

'Yes, she changed sides and the money was transferred quickly.'

'Why did she do that?' asked Hills.

'I offered her a redundancy payment because Gorev's business was finished.' Peanut gave a noncommittal shrug, but Hills wanted all the details.

'How much?'

'Six hundred thousand.'

'Was she worth it?'

'Initially, yes. Later, I'm not so sure, but I didn't ask for it back. I figured that as she'd put up with that pig Gorev lying on top of her, she was entitled to a good redundancy.'

'That's very generous of you, Peanut.' There was a sarcastic tone to her voice.

'I made more, a lot more. But I thought if she had a significant bundle of Gorev's money in her account, it would be an incentive for her to keep quiet and keep out of the way, especially if any of the Russian criminals were still hanging around. She has a new last name and my contact details, just in case she needs any help.'

'That was good thinking. She'll stay hidden I'm sure,' said Chas.

Hills shook her head.

'I don't think she should have your contact details.'

Chas laughed.

'Hills has seen a photo of Sharon. She's a stunner. We also know that you two shared a hotel room in Atlanta. Hills is jealous.'

Hills blushed.

'I'm not jealous. If Peanut wants to have a relationship with a criminal's secretary, that's his business, but I don't think she should have his contact details.'

Peanut raised his hands in surrender.

'I have some doubt, but I don't think I'll see her ever again. She's gone to Miami with the sole purpose of landing a rich old man. And from what I know of her, she'll succeed.'

Chas grinned slyly at Peanut.

'Really?'

'Truly.'

'That good?' said Chas.

'Yes.'

'Will you two shut the fuck up? You sound like a couple of randy college dickheads!' Hills exclaimed loudly, a wounded tone in her voice.

Chas laughed and Peanut grimaced.

'Despite Peter's recommendation, you can keep your panties on,' Peanut said.

Hills blushed again, looking away and Peanut knew that she was uncomfortable with the conversation. Chas intervened.

'How long do you need to find Janice-Rose? A rough idea would be good.'

'I'll have a better idea tomorrow. But how long is beside the point. I need to find her. She's precious. She's the only sister I have and the only daughter that mom has. Until I find her, I'm sorry, the answer has to be no. I can't work for you,' said Peanut.

'Did you make enough money in New York and L.A. to do that?' asked Hills.

'Yeah, I did.'

'Can they come back at you?' asked Chas.

'The New York lot had a pretty good look at me, so I'm sure the hunt is on. They'll start in New York and then move to L.A. and then they'll eventually link those two back to right here in Washington.'

Chas glanced at Hills and stood up.

'Come on, Hills. I suspect Peanut will need to be up early tomorrow. If you find Janice-Rose, give us a call. We do want you to work for us. We don't often get people with your natural talent.'

'That talent took years of hard work. There's nothing natural about it. I'll keep you in mind once I've found Janice-Rose.' Peanut followed Chas and Hills to his door where Chas shook his hand again. Hills's face was a picture of unhappiness as she eased past Peanut. She wouldn't look at him but walked on ahead to the stairs.

The more he thought about it, the more Peanut was convinced that his decision was the right one. He had to find Janice-Rose.

***

Chas turned off Blair Road as he drove them home.

'He still likes you,' he said to Hills.

'Does he? I didn't pick up on that at all. Plus he likes others.'

'You mean Sharon?'

She snorted.

'What is it with you men? You see something hot and fall into bed with it?'

'And you have never met a man that you've lusted after?' Chas asked, seeing Hills blush.

'It's more than that. She has his contact details,' she said.

Chas shook his head. 'You're wrong. Peanut's a straight shooter. If he said it was just in case she needed help, then he was telling you the truth.'

'I think it's more than that.'

He chuckled.

'No, it's not. Look at the facts. She is off to Miami to find a rich old man. Peanut gave her six hundred thousand dollars. He said he has a lot more than that and she knows it—she transferred it for him. She already had a rich man, Peanut. Fit, young, and healthy and yet she left him to go look for a rich old dude. Any romantic relationship between her and Peanut is well and truly down the gurgler, believe it.'

'So, it was just the sex, then?'

'Of course. They spent a few nights together just to see if there was anything else there and there wasn't.'

He glanced at her. She was still looking annoyed.

'If Peanut can put it all behind him, why can't you?' Chas said. 'And for Christ sake, the next time you see the guy, if there is a next time, tell him you really like him, huh? And show him how much. Kiss the fucking guy and stop driving me nuts!'

'Sorry,' mumbled Hills.

Chapter 16

The yard was open when Peanut pulled up at ten after eight the next morning. Business was slow and the garish pink, red and purple signs said it all. *TOPLESS CAR CLEANING. HOT LADIES GETTING ALL DOWN AND DIRTY ON YOUR LOVE MACHINE. DIRTY LOVE IN THE SUDS.*

Peanut stared, gob smacked. It was crass and cheap. It hadn't been like that when Janice-Rose had worked there. The old fellow who had once owned the place then would have a fit if he saw this. Clearly, he was dead or had been bought out.

There was nobody about, no cars in the bays, even though the office had an open sign and the bays were ready for work. He parked out on the street and walked to the door, taking in the signs of decay. A burly guy stood behind the desk and stared down at him when he walked in. Peanut mentally dubbed him Beefcake.

'All cars that need to be washed in the bays, please,' said Beefcake in a bored but reasonably polite voice.

Peanut smiled and held out his hand. 'Name's Peanut, not here for a wash. I need to speak to the boss, please.'

His outstretched hand was ignored.

'Why?'

'My sister worked here. Janice-Rose Patterson. We haven't heard from her in a while. I need her contact number to check if she's okay.'

Beefcake turned without saying a word and disappeared into the office behind the counter and shut the door. Peanut stood waiting patiently, looking around. The office was worn and the flooring was dirty and ratty; the cheap vinyl tiles were cracked and missing in places. It was a business on the way out. Several minutes went by. Peanut thought about knocking on the door, but that might be rude and he didn't want to push it. He needed Janice-Rose's phone number.

The door suddenly swung open and Beefcake poked his head out.

'The boss will see you now,' he said.

There was a fat guy behind the desk, tucking his shirt into his open pants while a woman straightened her top, shoving her large breasts back into her bra. Beefcake was wearing a lecherous grin, clearly enjoying the spectacle. The woman gave Peanut the once-over and dismissed him as she walked past on her way out of the room. She was a worn forty-something, though still pretty, and her half-unbuttoned blouse showed plenty of cleavage.

The fat guy slumped in his seat as he buckled up his studded black leather belt, and Peanut recognized him instantly. It was the old fellow's pig of a son. 'Fat Boy' Peanut used to call him. That explained the over-the-top shit on the billboards outside.

'If you want something that costs, fuck off and fuck off now,' was Fat Boy's greeting.

Peanut refused to react. He wasn't looking for a fight. 'No, it doesn't cost,' he said mildly. 'I'm trying to contact my sister, Janice-Rose Patterson. She used to work here.'

Fat Boy eyed Peanut up and down, then turned to his computer and studied the screen for a few minutes. There was a gleam in his piggy eyes.

'It'll cost you a hundred bucks, buddy.' It was a shakedown and Peanut knew it. But he didn't have any other options. He pulled out his wallet and held up two fifty-dollar notes.

'Happy to pay, but I want the number, please.'

Fat Boy held out his hand. 'Money first, buddy. We don't want you putting it back in your wallet without paying up now, do we?'

Peanut pointed at himself. 'Look at me. Do you think I'm going to hold out? I just want to make sure you have the number before I call the FBI missing persons desk.'

'Yeah, well since you're a bit of a runt, the price has gone up. This is privileged information and the price is now two hundred bucks.'

'I can't afford that. I'll tell the FBI you have her number.' Peanut turned to leave.

'Hold on there, runt. You owe me a hundred for the trouble that I've been put to.' He held out his hand and gave an evil grin. 'Pay up, runt.'

Peanut shook his head. He was done with being polite. 'It was a hundred for the phone number, which you haven't delivered. With all due respect, you can deal with the FBI. So fuck off.'

Fat Boy's face turned red in a flash of anger.

'Grab him!' he called to Beefcake.

Peanut felt arms close around him from behind. Beefcake might have been burly, but he was slow, much too slow. Peanut dropped almost to his knees, turning side on and drove a short hard punch up into Beefcake's testicles. Still turning, he shoved himself up with his thighs, on the way up driving a knuckle punch into Beefcake's throat, then grabbing his upper arm, turning him, and, using his hip for leverage, sweeping his legs out. There was a sickening thud as Beefcake hit the concrete floor.

Peanut swivelled around as Fat Boy struggled to get out of his chair. He was leaning forward, shoving his body up with his hands on the desk. Peanut saw his opportunity. He grabbed Fat Boy's wrists, jerking them off the desk, then slammed his head hard into the desktop. He aimed a chopping blow to the side of Fat Boy's neck, hitting the Vagus nerve, instantly immobilizing him. Peanut watched him fall, sliding to the floor under his desk as he tried and failed to get something out of his pocket. Peanut walked around behind the desk and kicked him in the temple. Fat Boy collapsed unconscious to the floor.

Peanut dragged him out from behind the desk and took a gun out of his pocket, before he turned to the computer. Her name and details were there along with the comment; *stuck-up bitch*. Peanut grinned and wrote down the number. It was clear that Fat Boy had never got anywhere with Janice-Rose. He wrapped Fat Boy's hands around the gun and then dropped it on the desk. He did the same with the nasty little snub-nosed revolver he took out of Beefcake's pocket. Then he found two paper bags, put the guns into them, and waited for Fat Boy or Beefcake to come to their senses.

Fat boy came to his senses first, getting control of his muscles, Peanut watching, bland faced, just waiting until Fat Boy recovered completely. He eventually levered himself up into his chair and, seeing Peanut standing there, grabbed for his phone.

'I'm going to call the cops, asshole. You tried to rob an innocent businessman.'

'Wouldn't do that, Fat Boy. I have your gun with your fingerprints all over it and guess what? It's had the numbers all filed off so it can't be traced. That, I would like to remind you, is a federal offense and automatic jail time. Want to call the cops while I call the FBI? You're such an asshole that I just might do it anyway.' Fat Boy glared at him with hate-filled eyes. 'Tell Beefcake that I have his gun with his fingerprints all over it as well, huh?' He turned to walk out, then stopped and turned back. 'If I find out that at any time you tried to molest my sister, I will be back to castrate the both of you. Clear, asshole?' Fat Boy tried to be a hero and snorted derisively. Peanut dropped slightly, shrugging his coat back and his two swords flashed into his hands and wove a magical track in the air in front of Fat Boy. The one sword stopped and rested against Fat Boy's neck, the other dancing in the air in front of his now terrified face, his eyes wide and staring, his jowls wobbling in fright, his eyes now scared and pleading.

'You doubt that I have the skill to castrate you?' Peanut snarled.

'No! No! I'm sorry. I didn't mean anything by it. I'm really sorry, sir, please, please; how can I make it up to you?'

'You can't. But if I have to come back, I will take your nuts out of their sack while you watch, put them into a paper bag and take them with me to the trash, just so you can't breed any more shits like you. *Consequences,* asshole, are we clear?' He smacked one sword flat on the desk and Fat Boy jumped in fright. His face was pale with fear as he watched the one sword blade still weave a tight little dance in front of his nose. He nodded vigorously and Peanut turned and walked out the door, sheathing his swords in the office before he walked outside to his car. The forty-something lady was washing a late model Mercedes, the old guy inside openly admiring her. He was at least in his late sixties, probably older. Peanut smiled. If that made the old guy happy, who was he to judge? It had been a good morning's work. He now had Janice-Rose's phone number. He just hoped it still worked.

***

If he'd been religious, Peanut would have prayed as he put his coffee cup in the holder on the dashboard and dialed Janice-Rose's number. He desperately wanted to make contact. But he was also nervous, given just how vicious the breakup argument had been. She might have decided to cut all contact, including the number that he had. Then he realised that she might have decided to have nothing to do with family, including him, and that would hurt. She was the only sister he had and he loved her and wanted their family back together, regardless. But he had to remember that she had never tried to contact him—perhaps she didn't want to have anything to do with him. He couldn't bear the thought of his little sister not wanting to speak with him. But he had to try.

'Hello?'

He recognized her voice immediately.

'J.R., it's Peanut. I've been worried sick about you. Can we meet for a chat? Have a coffee?'

There was a pause and he felt his tension grow, but then she said, 'I'd like that. When?' and he felt a sense of relief wash over him.

'Are you busy at the moment?' He wasn't going to let her get away a second time.

'Nah, just studying. How about Starbucks on the corner of Livingstone and Connecticut? Ten minutes?' she said.

Peanut checked the time on his phone and smiled. 'I'll be there. Love you.'

'Love you too, big brother.'

***

Peanut got out of the car and stretched. He couldn't wait to see her. His sister was feisty and he already knew that she had pissed off Fat Boy. He now wanted to hear how it had happened. He had spent a couple of years teaching her self-defence and she was always a bit on and off, but she knew enough to look after herself and, considering the little time she had put into practice, she was pretty good. He had taught her his mix of skills, which he believed made for a better, well-rounded, self-defence strategy. She'd never win an Olympic medal, but she had a better chance of staying alive. Initially, she had lapped it up, but then she'd got bored, tired of always fighting against him, she had said. But he was still proud of her.

Janice-Rose was waiting on the corner outside Starbucks. She had changed. Her long brunette hair now had blonde streaks and it was cut in a business-like bob, the fringe accentuating her pretty face. He reckoned she might have grown taller too—she was now a good inch taller than him, though with the same slight build. She saw him coming and ran towards him, wrapping him in a hug and kissing his cheek. He held her tight, almost overwhelmed that he had found her and she was okay.

'You're fattening up, big brother,' she said with a teasing grin.

77

'Nah, some of the moves I've been learning require a fair bit of strength so I've been using some weights.'

She pinched him hard in the stomach.

'Ow!'

She laughed. 'Just checking the fat level. It must be muscle—there's no fat there.'

'I could have shown you without you inflicting pain, J.R.'

'What'd you used to say to me? Suck it up?'

He grinned at her. She was just as feisty and stroppy as ever. He wrapped his arms around her and gave her another hug.

'Love you, sis. C'mon, let's get a coffee.'

They sat down, happy to just be together.

'I thought I had lost you when no one knew where you were. You really can be a worry sometimes,' said Peanut.

'Isn't that what little sisters are for?'

'Yeah? I don't think so, J.R. So what are you studying?'

'What I was good at. Biology. I'm going to try to get a job in a lab. Decided that getting a job that paid good money was better than bumming around doing shit.'

Her smiling face and glowing eyes told him she was just as delighted to see him as he was to see her. And that raised another issue, family.

'Mom wants to hear from you.'

She looked at Peanut and screwed up her pretty face.

'She kicked me out. There were faults on both sides, I know, but in the end she said to get out and not come back. At the time I was really angry and I told her she'd never see me again.'

'She cries herself to sleep over you. If she could take back what she said, I know she would. Give it some thought. Anyway, how are you doing?' He didn't want to press the point too hard.

'Money is tight, but I'm surviving—just.'

'So, what happened that made you leave your job?'

She paused for a moment and looked angry.

'That fat prick Jameson sacked me and another girl, Helen, when we wouldn't have a threesome with him. He owes me and Helen a week's wages and tips.'

'I imagine the tips were pretty good?'

'Yeah, they were. We've been trying to hold it together ever since.'

Peanut seethed inside. He decided that he would get their money back.

'How short of cash are you?' he asked.

'I'm two months behind in my rent and, unless things improve, I'll be three months behind by next week.'

'Want to come and live with me? No rent and no drugs. I have a two-bedroom dog box, but it's home.'

Neither of them said anything for a short time, Janice-Rose thinking.

'Would it work? I'm eighteen, a girl and messy. I seem to remember that your room at home was clean, like anally clean.'

He grinned at her comment.

'What have you got to lose? Give it a go. If I'm too hard to live with, you can leave and I'll get you another apartment. What do you say?' he asked.

'That costs! Where are you going to get that kind of money?'

He smiled and didn't answer.

'Do you owe any money elsewhere?' he asked.

'Nah.'

'Would five thousand clear all your debts? Give you a bit of breathing space?'

'Shit, yeah! Clear everything and leave a lot over. So where *are* you getting the money?'

He grinned.

'Ask no questions, J.R.'

'This isn't a one way street, big brother. Where did you get the money? What exactly are you into? Huh?'

Chapter 17

'Probably best that you don't know, J. R.'

'Bullshit. Fess up,' J.R. insisted. 'That sort of money couldn't have come from your shitty little job in the electronics shop.'

'Hey, I liked that job!'

'Yeah, but the pay was shit. You didn't answer my question and I'm not moving in with you unless you're honest with me.'

Peanut moved uncomfortably in his chair. 'I stole it.'

Her jaw dropped and she looked at him aghast. He cut her off before she could say anything.

'Before you jump down my throat, it was the bad guys I stole it from.'

'Like when you cleaned out Fellows, the gang and their suppliers?' she asked.

'Yeah.'

'Only this time you didn't dump the proceeds into the river, did you?'

'Correct.'

She sat looking at him for a minute. This big brother of hers was doing things she never expected.

'If I'm going to live with you, I want to know what might crawl out of the woodwork. I don't want to *not* wake up one morning. So buy me another cup of coffee and tell me everything.' She indicated their empty cups.

Peanut sighed but did as he was told.

She frowned at him as he returned with the coffees. 'No bullshit now—I always know when you're bullshitting.'

Peanut began with his arrest for killing Chuckie and the punch in the balls from Hills.

'Ouch,' from Janice-Rose.

And then being used to steal documents for ICT. He ended with his cleaning out the dealers in L.A. She shook her head in amazement. She knew Peanut was good but *that* good? It staggered her to think that he was able to cheat seriously bad guys and win. He really was that good. He skills had moved on from when he was teaching her, that was for sure. He was good back then, but now?

She sipped her second coffee, thinking through what he'd told her. 'Let me get this straight. You gave your girlfriend of five minutes, six hundred thousand—as a gift?'

'No. It wasn't a gift. I had made plenty and it wasn't my money anyway, so she was welcome to it. She'll need all of that money to stay safe and to keep quiet. It costs a lot to hide, it really does. But if Sharon's careful, she'll be okay.'

'Really? Don't bullshit me. I can get you ten girlfriends for one-sixth of that amount. Helen for one.'

'Helen?'

'You know, the workmate at the car-cleaning outfit—the one who got sacked along with me. I showed her your photo and she thought you were spunky.' She grinned when he blushed. 'Don't get your hopes up; she's a mad bitch. She used to make real money from the tips because she flashed her tits and once she gave a guy a peek at her pussy. That made her fifty bucks. As I say, a mad bitch.' She gave him a level look as she sat examining him, an unblinking stare.

'You know, big brother, if I didn't know you better, I'd think that you had shit for brains.'

Peanut protested, 'It was to help her hide and to keep her quiet. Don't forget, she witnessed what I did to those guys.'

'Yeah, I suppose.' When she continued to stare at him Peanut began to feel uncomfortable.

'Six hundred thousand for only four nights in bed! She must have been good, if you pardon the pun. What does a girl have to do to be that good?' She sighed. 'On second thoughts, I don't want to know. But apparently, she was worth it. And then she thanked you by waltzing off to Miami to find a rich old man.' She paused. 'In short, she dumped you.'

'It was mutual.'

'Yeah, right. So does that other woman, Hills, the ball basher, know about Sharon?'

'Yeah.'

'And?' she asked.

'Not happy.'

'So she has a soft spot for my big brother, huh?'

'I don't think so,' Peanut said.

She sniffed, sarcastically.

'My brother, the expert in women. You really can afford the five thousand, can't you?'

'Yeah. And any other bills you need help with. Things like studying, transport, whatever. Okay?'

'Thanks. Love you, big brother. Even though your brains seem to be somewhere south in your underpants. She has your contact details, so if she ever needs another six hundred thousand, she at least knows where to come.'

Ignoring Janice-Rose's mocking grin, he changed the subject.

'How much does Jameson owe you?'

'Six hundred and fifty. Half of that is tips. He owes Helen the same amount.'

'Do you have a record?'

'Sure do. In my purse. And a copy of Helen's.' She grinned. She knew what Peanut was going to do.

'Can I come?' she asked.

'Of course. Happy to drive us?'

'Wouldn't miss this for the world!'

***

The wash-down bays were nearly empty when they pulled in. At this time of the day, the business should have been jumping, especially with pretty women in brief clothing doing the washing. But there was only the one worker, the forty-something woman Peanut had seen that morning. Janice-Rose summed it up.

'Let's get the money before the fat prick goes broke.'

They walked into the office where the burly guy who first accosted Peanut was behind the counter.

'His nibs in?'

Beefcake was nervous and took a step backwards. 'I thought that was all settled.'

'There's the small matter of money owing to Janice-Rose and Helen,' Peanut said.

Janice-Rose produced the pay slips.

'They were paid, buddy,' Beefcake said, not even looking at the pay slips.

'Number one, I'm not your buddy, and number two, the money hasn't been paid but it will be. Today. Now, in fact. Are you going to get Jameson, or do I walk through you and into the office?' said Peanut.

Beefcake tapped on the door and called out. 'Boss, that guy's back again and he wants the money he says is owing to Janice-Rose and Helen.'

They could hear Jameson's voice clearly. It sounded shaky and scared. 'Pay them and tell them to fuck off.'

Beefcake picked up the pay slips, opened the till, and reluctantly counted out the money, handing it over to Peanut with a glare. 'Just because you surprised me once doesn't mean that you can do it again. I'll be ready next time.'

Peanut smiled. 'There won't be a next time. I have more important things than dealing with maggot shit like you.'

Beefcake's face flushed and he again gawked at Peanut's small size. Peanut knew immediately that he was going to hit out. It was fast but at the first twitch of Beefcake's shoulder muscles, even as he brought his arms up to punch, Peanut's hand flashed and he chopped Beefcake's Vagus nerve. He collapsed with a thud to the floor. Peanut glanced at Janice-Rose. 'I thought I gave him a clear message yesterday. Some dicks never learn.'

He spun around and kicked the helpless form hard in the crotch, seeing his body involuntarily fold into a fetal position, and then followed Janice-Rose out to the car. The sore nuts for the next day or two might make Beefcake rethink his ideas, but somehow Peanut doubted it.

***

Hills was reading the report on the deaths in L.A. There could be no mistake, it had been Peanut, and it had been savage. No guns were found and Gorev's secretary was missing. Hills grimaced. On the lighter side, the FBI were amused when they heard kicking at the warehouse and found a guard tied up with his pants around his ankles. Checking the computer, they realized he had been watching porn when he was surprised. They let him go, laughing. As all the principals of the company were dead or had done a runner, he wouldn't get paid, that was for sure.

Hills hoped Sharon would stay away. For the life of her, she couldn't understand why she would leave Peanut to chase some old guy. Hills put down the report and was deep in thought when Chas walked in.

'Penny for them? Anything jump out at you?' Chas asked.

'Nothing. It was Peanut in action, no doubt about it. The stab marks give him away. Lethal, as always.' She gazed thoughtfully at Chas. It had been troubling her. 'Why didn't Peanut smash me? I hit him in the nuts and I wasn't gentle about it. In the gym that day, he could have killed me. So why didn't he?

'That wouldn't have happened. I was there.'

'With his level of skill, death can be inflicted instantaneously. By the time you went to step forward, it would have all been over. A snapped neck is permanent, Chas.'

Chas looked thoughtfully at her.

'Ring and ask him. And ask if he's found Janice-Rose. Or do it the other way around to make it look like it's Janice-Rose you are concerned about. You don't want to make it seem like you are chasing the poor man, do you?'

Hills blushed and snorted, annoyed.

'Chas?'

'Yes?'

'Shut the fuck up. I asked a question and wanted an answer. I didn't ask for lonely hearts' advice!'

Chas smiled. 'Whatever. Just call him.'

***

Janice-Rose surveyed Peanut's apartment. It was a lot nicer than hers. Much more modern and twice the size, but could she live with Peanut?

'What happens if I have a boyfriend over?' she asked him.

'What happens now?'

'If my housemate and her friends are in, I go to the local café or to my room.'

'Why can't you do that here?'

'Yeah, I suppose. You wouldn't mind if I had a guy in my room?'

'You're eighteen. Mom raised you well and I'm sure you'll make good choices when it comes to friends, but regardless, they're your choices, not mine, and you can do what you want. I'll just get annoyed if the kitchen or bathroom or both are left in a mess, that's all.'

'Okay, I'll move in. But you have to behave as well, big brother. This is a two-way street.'

He raised his right hand. 'I, Peanut, do solemnly swear that I won't walk around our apartment wearing my undies on my head.'

She giggled. 'If you do, I'll get that Hills woman you told me about to hit you in the nuts again.'

He didn't smile. He remembered the pain. It wasn't funny.

'So, when are you moving in?' he asked.

'Now, if I can? I only have two suitcases. They're the total sum of my entire wealth. I'll pay the agent my arrears tomorrow.'

'No, we might have plans tomorrow. Let's settle it today.'

***

Janice-Rose sat at the dining room table in a pool of sunlight that streamed in the side window. She was tidying up her finances. Peanut thought she looked happy and that was all that mattered to him. Moving had taken just over an hour and she had already remodeled her room and had given Peanut a list of things she wanted to make her stay more comfortable.

'If you need a hand to get any of that, call and I'll help. It's good practice on setting up a house, big brother.'

Peanut couldn't see why he would want to know about setting up a house. It was not something he particularly wanted practice in. He just grunted.

'By the way, I'm going to go see Mom,' said Janice-Rose, her tone casual.

'Good,' he said with equal casualness.

She hesitated, then smiled at him and dived straight in.

'You know how you said that that Hills lady keeps popping into your mind? That she's hard to forget?'

'Yeah. Maybe I shouldn't have told you about that. Don't hold it against me,' said Peanut.

'When you last saw her, did that fix the problem? You said you thought it would.'

'Nah. But I don't even know her. I probably wouldn't like her if I did. I mean, I didn't like her much at the start. It was sort of mutual dislike and sometimes first impressions are right.'

'Yeah, maybe. But suppose it's more than that? Have you thought about that?'

'Are you trying to annoy me?' asked Peanut, grimacing. It sounded like a wind up.

'Nah. You aren't worth the hassle. But you know how sometimes a spark jumps between you and someone else and you know that person is special? Not to anyone else, but just to you? That obviously happened with Sharon.'

'That was a one-off and it didn't work. Apart from that, it hasn't happened to me recently. Maybe it did when I was at school, but I doubt it. Runts like me are not usually on women's radar.'

'Sex isn't enough, is it? And besides, I'm not talking about sex.'

He stared at her for a long minute. 'You seem to be talking around what you want to say. You are calling an axe a long-handled chopping instrument. Get to the point, little sister.'

'I think she loves you and deep down, maybe you love her too, but you're not sure because she hurt you. Plus the fact that you, like most men, are superficial. You see a nice ass and tits and it's love when in reality it's just plain old lust. Men are very good at confusing love and lust.'

'My sister, the psychoanalyst,' snorted Peanut.

Janice-Rose flounced off to the kitchen and turned on the coffee machine. Peanut was bemused. Whatever the reason why Hills kept popping into his head, he didn't think it had anything to do with love. Janice-Rose again interrupted his thoughts.

'Coffee, big brother?'

'Yep. Thanks.'

Chapter 18

It was late. Peanut glared with frustration at the paperwork lying on the dining table. He was trying to finalize a plan for Houston. Even if Janice-Rose worked with him it could still fail and, besides, she might not be interested. He needed a minimum of three people and even then it would be risky. He glanced at her and she looked up from her book.

'What?' she asked.

He didn't get a chance to answer as his phone rang. He picked it up, noticed the caller, and did a double take.

'Hi, Sharon.'

'Peanut, I need help! I'm at your building and I'm being followed by two men. They've just driven in front of me and cut me off!'

'Blair Road?'

'Yes, hurry, help me, please!'

'Coming.' He grabbed his sheath and ran to the door, glancing back at Janice-Rose.

'It's Sharon; she needs help.'

He ran down the stairs, hearing Janice-Rose's footsteps as she followed. He put his sheath on as he ran and shoved the ground door open, rushing outside. There was a car pulled in at an angle to the curb, parked across the front of another car, cutting it off. Two thuggish looking men were struggling to get a woman out of the car. Sharon! The guy closest to her reached behind him and pulled out a gun as Peanut unsheathed his swords and ran. He was only thirty steps away when he heard the thug yell at Sharon as he jammed the gun against her head.

'Get out of the car, bitch!' Peanut was still ten steps away when they both suddenly realized that they had company. The thug with the gun jerked back. He attempted to turn the gun towards them as Peanut threw a sword. A flicker of orange light from the street lamp played on the blade as it flew in the air. Peanut knew instinctively that the strike wouldn't be fatal. The thug's position meant that it wouldn't hit his heart, just go into the side of his chest. The blade hit and Peanut was just a step behind, the guy reeling back in pain, his gun forgotten as Peanut slashed at the hand of the other man, sending his half-drawn gun clattering into the gutter. The thug held his arm up to protect against another slash, standing with his front leg bent and his back leg straight, just so he could push off on his front leg and defend himself. Peanut turned slightly and dropped to get more leverage, and then heel-kicked with all his power, his two heels driving hard onto the straight kneecap. He saw the locked leg bend backward and snap, the thug collapsing face down, screaming as his knee joint was completely destroyed. He straightened to see Janice-Rose jump and kick high, hitting the gunman in the side of the head and then sweeping his legs out, his body hitting the ground with a sickening thud, his head making a horrible cracking sound as it hit the edge of the concrete curb. Peanut quickly pulled the sword out of the thug's body and sheathed it. He bent and picked up the thug with the broken leg in a fireman's lift and walked around the car, throwing him into the back seat and ignoring the deep guttural moan as the guy's smashed leg got twisted. He picked up the unconscious gunman and threw him in the other side of the car.

'Get their guns, ladies. We're going for a ride,' Peanut ordered. 'J.R., you're coming with me. Sharon, you can follow us in your car. By the way, say hello to my sister, Janice-Rose.'

'He found you! I'm so glad,' Sharon said. 'He was really worried.' She suddenly gave a surprised Janice-Rose a hug.

'Can we move it along, ladies? That commotion might bring the cops. Cuddles and coffees later, I'm afraid.' He noticed Janice-Rose had the thugs' guns.

'In the front, J.R. Any problems, shoot. And don't look forward; we don't want to be seen on any highway cameras.'

He climbed into the driver's side of the thugs' car; the motor was still running. He engaged reverse and quickly backed away from Sharon's car and drove off down the street, checking in the rearview mirror to make sure Sharon was following. As they approached a gas station, he pulled to a stop, and walked back as Sharon pulled up behind.

'Just getting some gas to light a fire. Back in a minute. When we drive off, stay well back like you are just the traveling public, okay?'

She sat quietly and five minutes later he was back with a plastic five-gallon jerry can and stashed it in the trunk. Sharon followed well behind as they drove back onto the highway. She thought things through as she drove. Peanut had handled those guys with ease. He was in control, right from when she saw him running towards her. She remembered the feeling of tremendous relief when he had appeared. He had saved her and she knew that she would never be able to repay him.

She followed Peanut as he turned off the highway and then disappeared along a gravel road, then down a rutted track and into a disused quarry. She parked where Peanut indicated and walked over to the thugs' car as Janice-Rose climbed out. Peanut climbed into her vacated seat to speak to the thug with the shattered leg. The thug beside him was bleeding and his chest wound was frothing, a sign that his lung had been punctured. He was deeply unconscious; unmoving, barely breathing. Peanut had heard the crack of his head on the concrete and doubted that he would ever come around. Peanut had no intention that he would. Janice-Rose stood beside Sharon, watching as Peanut settled into the seat, directly in front of the thug with the wounded leg. He turned and scowled at him.

'What's your name?'

'Take me to the hospital, please!'

'I asked for your name. Tell me now!'

'No! Take me to hospital.'

Peanut reached under the seat, pulled the seat release and rammed the seat back, jamming it against the thug's smashed leg. He screamed in pain as his broken knee joint buckled.

Peanut turned and smacked him hard across the face. 'Listen to me, shit for brains. I won't ask you again. What's your name?'

The thug's eyes were full of tears when he whispered, 'Alex Dyomin.'

'Pleased to meet you Alex. Who's your boss?'

'I can't say. He'll kill me.'

'Guess what, Alex. He's not here and *I'll* kill you and kill you slowly if you don't tell me his name.'

Alex shook his head.

Peanut waved out of the door and indicated to Janice-Rose that he wanted a pistol. She handed him the Glock. Peanut lined it up and pointed the gun at Dyomin's good kneecap.

'Tell me,' Peanut demanded.

When the thug shook his head again, Peanut fired. Another scream filled the air.

Peanut stared at him as he sobbed in agony.

'I've only just started,' Peanut told him, his voice cold. 'It's going to get worse, much worse. Who do you work for?' He jerked the seat forward and rammed it back again. The sobbing thug emitted another scream.

'Talk!' yelled Peanut.

'Milo Volkov.'

'Where does he live?'

'He stays with different people. He never says who. Sometimes in Texas and sometimes in New York and Los Angles. He travels all the time.'

'Overseeing the drug shipments?' Peanut saw Alex's tear-filled eyes open wide at that question. He knew the answer before the thug replied in a pain-wracked whisper.

'Yes, I think so,' he said.

'Who ordered you to chase Sharon?'

'He did.'

'How did you know where she was?'

'She used her phone. We tracked her number.'

Peanut glanced at Sharon. 'Got your phone?'

'Yes.'

'Turn the fucking thing off. You nearly got yourself killed.' He turned back to the thugs, lined up the pistol and fired twice. From Dyomin's pocket he removed his phone before he got out of the car.

He opened the boot, shut the doors and left the windows open. He poured petrol into the car, over both bodies and tossed the half-empty jerry can into the back through the open window. Photographing the dead thugs, he opened the fuel cap and, standing well back, stuck the head of a match under his thumbnail and flicked it into the car. There was a loud *whump* as the car became an instant inferno. He took another photo and put the phone in his pocket.

'Let's get out of here. Back the way we came. You can drive, Sharon.'

Still visibly upset at her mistake with the phone, she drove quietly, concentrating on the late-night traffic.

'Is this a rental, Sharon?' Peanut asked.

'Yes. A cheap one.'

'We'll take it back to the depot and get a taxi to the apartment.'

Peanut went through the contacts on the thug's phone. He found Volkov's name and sent him the photos, just to send a message. Message sent, he threw the phone in a rubbish bin.

The taxi dropped them back at the apartment. The upstairs door was still open, but the main one downstairs had swung shut. Nothing in the apartment had been touched. Peanut hadn't expected anyone to be snooping around at that hour. They walked in and he gave a surprised Janice-Rose a hug. 'Well done, little sister. You put that guy down beautifully and with skill. Congratulations.'

She smiled and they bumped knuckles.

'My pleasure, big brother. Coffee everyone?'

'I'll get it. You ladies get acquainted,' Peanut said.

'Peanut never said you were pretty,' said Sharon as she sat on the couch. 'Really pretty. I bet you have to fight the men off!'

Janice-Rose gave a sardonic snort. 'I'm not really in the mood for men right now after the last prick.'

'What was he like?'

'A drug addict and when the money ran out, he wanted me to sell my *little money maker*, as he called it. I told him to fuck off and left. He OD'ed three months ago.'

Sharon noticed that, despite her tough-sounding words, Janice-Rose's eyes had filled with tears. It was clear that she had once thought she loved that prick.

'I'm sorry,' Sharon said. 'Life can be a complete bitch sometimes.'

Peanut came back from the kitchen with the coffees.

'So, Sharon, tell us what happened. You're welcome to stay, by the way. We don't have another bedroom, but you can have the couch.'

'Thanks. I'm happy to sleep on the couch. At least I'll feel safe.'

'That bad, huh?' Janice-Rose said.

'Worse. They wanted to kill me.'

'Tell us what went wrong,' said Peanut. Sharon nodded and sighed. A lot had obviously happened.

'I grew up in Miami,' she started, 'so I know it and a lot of the people who run the places rich men frequent. Anyway, I got passes to all the ones that I thought had what I was looking for—you know, wealthy older men.' She gave a sardonic laugh. Peanut noticed that there was a sadness that she couldn't conceal. Things hadn't worked out.

She took a breath and carried on. 'Anyway, on my second day there, I met Eric. He's a lovely man who had just turned eighty. Even so he was still running his own company. He had lost his wife two years ago and he'd come to Miami to move on. He was lonely for feminine company, but as lovely as he was he was way too old for me. But he wouldn't take no for an answer. He wanted me to sleep with him.'

'Did you?' Janice-Rose asked.

'Yes, and then he proposed. I turned him down and pointed to the age difference but that's when the trouble started. His late wife's younger brother Christian thought that I was after Eric's money—which ironically I wasn't, at least not Eric's. They hired a security firm to get rid of me. To cut a long story short, when I wouldn't leave Christian threatened me.'

She reached into her bag, pulled out a note, and handed it to Peanut. Scrawled in red ink were the words. *You are a dead bitch.*

'That was when I knew I had to leave. I panicked, got in my car and drove. I thought I was clear. But I wasn't. Miles later, I called in at a roadside café for a meal and some gas and another car with two ugly-looking guys pulled in. One guy got out, checked my car over, and then came looking for me. I was scared, really terrified. I thought that this was it. They were going to shove me into the car and that would be the last that anyone would ever see of me. I walked out the back door of the restaurant and hitched a lift with a truck driver. He was a good guy. I said I was running away from a violent partner and I just wanted a lift. I offered to pay but he refused. Said giving me a lift was the least he could do. He was nice, really nice. My sort of guy but, unfortunately, he was broke.

'Those guys in the car figured out what I'd done and eventually caught up with the truck. They called out to the driver and asked him to pull over. They sounded foreign to me, like Russian or eastern European. He refused and asked what they wanted. They asked him if he had seen a good-looking young woman with long black hair, and he said 'I wish' and kept on driving. I was hiding in the back, in the sleeping compartment, scared for myself and scared for the truck driver too. I didn't want him getting hurt because of me. And then they came back and again wanted him to pull over so they could check his truck. He said he was on a tight schedule and that if they hassled him again he would radio ahead to the cops and have them charged with attempted hijacking.' She looked at Peanut and Janice-Rose. 'I knew then that this was really serious; these guys weren't going to leave me alone. Even though I'd left Eric, they wanted me gone, permanently.'

'And they followed you here?' Peanut asked.

'I didn't think so. I sneaked away from the truck in Richmond, got that rental, and then drove here.'

Peanut shook his head. One mistake after another.

'Those guys that tracked you here are nothing to do with a Miami security firm,' Peanut told her. 'They are all about the drug money that we took from Gorev. They have tracked you to Miami because you used your phone and have now tracked you to here. We'll get you a new SIM card tomorrow. You like your phone so you keep it. But you can't go back to Miami.'

Was Sharon in the clear? Peanut didn't know. If those guys had called in their position, they could expect more visitors.

'As I said before, you are welcome to stay. But until I work out if you're safe, stay inside, okay? Don't go out on your own for any reason; don't even show your face at the window, okay?'

Sharon nodded and gave a sad smile, knowing that she had put them all in danger.

'Do you still have the money?' Peanut asked.

'Oh, yes. That'll keep me in comfort in my old age. It's growing already. I told you I know how to invest in the stock market.'

'Nice to hear.' Peanut yawned. 'Okay, let's all get to bed,' he said.

Janice-Rose came in with a blanket and handed it to Sharon.

'That settee is comfortable. I have snoozed on it. See you in the morning.'

'Thank you. At least I will feel safe here. I always did with Peanut.'

'Yes, I do as well. 'Night.'

Chapter 19

Peanut ambled out into the kitchen, still in his shorts and tee. He turned the coffee machine on and smiled at the sight of Sharon quietly sleeping. It amazed him how some women could still look beautiful, even after a night's sleep on a settee.

The noise as the coffee machine ground the beans woke her up. She sat up on the settee and then stood, giving him a quick hug and a husky 'Morning' as she held the blanket around her on her way to the bathroom.

Peanut sat at the table and re-looked at his plans. He glanced up as she came back and sat down at the table across from him. She squinted at the paperwork and then eyed him up.

'Trouble, sweetheart?' It was a term of endearment that Sharon used for anyone she liked.

'Maybe. How would you like a trip to Houston?' he asked.

'Home of NASA and all those handsome astronauts? You bet!' She thought for a minute. 'It's not a holiday, though?'

'Nope, but it could be.'

'What could be?' Janice-Rose asked from where she was leaning against her bedroom doorway.

'Later, J.R., after breakfast. Get dressed, I'm paying.'

'My big brother, Mr. Moneybags.' Janice-Rose laughed and ran her fingers through her hair.

'Love you too, little sister. You are more than welcome to go on a diet and do without, if you want.'

'Fuck off!' Janice-Rose replied cheerily. 'One in, all in, right, Sharon?' They bumped knuckles as Peanut stared up at the ceiling. Janice-Rose walked over, stood beside him and looked up. 'Needs painting, big brother?'

'Nah. Just looking at all the estrogen dripping down. It wasn't there yesterday.'

She lightly punched him on the shoulder. 'You've been on your own for far too long. You need some feminine cultural influences,' Janice-Rose said, as she headed back into her bedroom. 'Time this lady got dressed,' she said.

Peanut stood looking out of the window, checking the fire escape. Janice-Rose came out of her bedroom ready for the day. She saw Sharon was dressed and noticed Peanut as he gestured to her to come over.

'J.R., I need you to check the street, just in case anyone is watching for us. Take the fire escape, and if you see anything suspicious, call me and we'll use the fire escape as well. Sorry, but they know what Sharon and I look like.'

Janice-Rose climbed out of the window and scaled down the fire escape, then held up her rust-steaked hands. He gave her a stay signal, then threw down some wet-wipe tissues watching as she wiped and then walked out onto the street. He moved away from the window and sat on the settee with Sharon.

She was sitting with her hands between her legs and her shoulders slumped. 'I'm sorry for bringing trouble with me. I never meant too,' she said, close to tears.

'Yeah, I know. I thought you would be safe in Miami. Never mind. Shit happens sometimes.'

She laughed ruefully. 'So much for me wanting an older man. It hasn't worked out, so far.'

'No, but it might,' Peanut said. 'That last guy was just too old.'

'He was, but he was a lovely man.'

Peanut's phone rang. It was Janice-Rose.

'There's a car with two tired-looking guys sitting in it about three hundred yards down the street. They look like they've been sitting there all night.'

'Thanks. We'll meet you in the next street and we'll call a taxi.'

'I'll call and have it waiting. Okay?'

***

An hour later, Janice-Rose leant back in her chair, full. 'Thanks, big brother. I really needed that. So, what now?'

'First things first—a SIM card for Sharon. Then we're off to Houston. I need you two to help me fleece some drug dealers of their ill-gotten gains by being lookouts. We then tell the FBI so they can arrest them for the drugs. We, however, will keep their ill-gotten gains. It'll be a win–win for us and the FBI.'

'How much?' Janice-Rose was wary.

'I don't know, but it'll be substantial. And it'll be an even split.'

'Is this another L.A. job with blood and dead bodies?' It was Sharon's turn to look wary.

'No. This can only be done by stealth because the company's front is a legitimate business.'

'So, no blood and gore?' Sharon checked.

'If that happens, we'll have failed. The blood and gore will be ours.'

'Sounds risky,' said Janice-Rose.

'Initially, but only for me. But if we're not careful to hide our tracks, it could become very dangerous.'

Janice-Rose stared hard at her brother. 'I think we need to know more,' she said.

'Agreed,' said Peanut. 'So why don't we pack up and fly out to Houston today? Leave those pricks with nothing to watch. After we've had a look in Houston, then we can make up our minds.'

'Okay. When you said 'even split', what exactly did you mean?' asked Janice-Rose.

'Even-steven. Equal risk means equal reward,' replied Peanut.

Janice-Rose looked at him steadily. She doubted that the risk would be equal. But then again, she could see that Peanut couldn't do the job without look-outs.

'I think you need to explain more. Big brother.'

'I will be in the secure yard but you two will be lookouts. If I get caught, the cops will soon realize that it is across state lines and call the FBI. They will link it to the other jobs I've done and then link it back to you, Sharon and the LA job. They will find out where I live and then you, J.R. are in the firing line as well. So like it or not, we all have risk.'

'So, give us a ball-park figure, big brother.'

He sighed. It was hard to be precise when he didn't really know. He gave her what he thought would be a rough estimate. 'At least one million.'

'Each?' she asked.

'Yes.'

'Shit! For that sort of money, it has to be worth some risk.'

'Maybe, but it's no good to us if we're dead.'

'Very true. So who will make the final decision?' asked Sharon.

'It has to be all of us,' said Peanut. 'We now need a taxi and we'll sneak in the apartment the way we got out, okay?'

***

Chas threw the police report and two grainy photographs on the table in front of Hills. 'Have a read,' he said.

She scrutinized the photographs and then read the report.

'Intersection of highways 29 and 97. Pretty rough photos.'

'They certainly are. Keep looking,' said Chas.

Hills studied the photos more closely.

'That looks like Sharon in that second car?'

Chas nodded.

'It does. Driving at least half a mile behind.'

'I can't see who's in the front one though.'

'It looks like a woman looking at a car behind, or looking at something in the rear seat, maybe,' said Chas, 'and the driver has the sun visor down and his arm across his face.'

'How did you get these?'

'The cops supplied the first one and I went looking on the camera feed and got the second one. The cops don't know I've got it.' Chas chuckled. 'They'll never prove who it is, but I'm picking it's Peanut. If it is and that's Sharon following, then they've linked up.'

Hills inspected the photo of the burnt bodies. 'These guys still haven't been identified, have they?'

'Nope. Very badly burnt. Each killed by a single shot to the chest. I'm picking that any identification will link them to the Russian drug operation in L.A. and New York.'

'That's a long bow?'

'Is it? Think it through.'

Hills mulled it over.

'I think Sharon contacted Peanut because she was in danger. That means those Russian drug guys know that Peanut is here. We should warn him, Chas.'

'Why? Don't you think he's already worked that out? So, who is the mystery woman? I'm picking it's Janice-Rose. Come on, let's go for a drive.'

***

Twenty minutes later they turned onto Blair Road and Chas drove slowly up the street.

'Do you think he's found his sister?' Hills asked.

'I do,' Chas replied.

'So why hasn't he contacted us?'

'He's busy sorting out the guys who tracked down Sharon, that's why.'

It was then when Hills spotted it.

'Look! On the other side of the road. The blue Camry with two men in the front.'

'Let's pay them a visit.' Chas did a U-turn and parked behind the Camry. Chas tapped on the driver's window as Hills walked around the other side of the car.

The window slid down. 'Yes?'

Chas held out his card. 'Chas Fischer, Federal Agent. I'd like a word. The locals are concerned. You've been sitting here for some time. Can I see your identification, please?'

The driver handed over his license and Chas noted the details. Hills did the same on the other side of the car.

'Why have you have been sitting here for so long?'

'We don't have to say.'

'Yes, you do. It's a lawful request.'

'We're waiting on a guy.'

'Who?'

'It doesn't matter, officer, we're moving. He's obviously not going to show.'

'Good idea. This is a quiet neighborhood and the locals like to keep it that way. If I see you here again, I'll report you to the FBI and they'll drag you in for questioning. Understand?'

'Yeah.'

Chas smiled at Hills as they watched the Camry disappear down the street.

'We'll leave it for now,' he said.

Hills was surprised. 'Aren't we even going to drop in and warn him?'

'And give the game away? Those boys aren't stupid. If we call in anywhere after moving them on, that'll be the first place they'll visit. I'm picking there'll be others around.'

Chas stood on the pavement and peered up the street, then raised his hand in a salute. He was rewarded when a hand came out of a window and saluted in return and Hills chuckled.

'Let's get out of here,' he said. He studied Hills for as second. 'None of my business, but it wouldn't hurt to give him a call, like, keep in contact?'

Hills didn't look at him and didn't reply. Chas sighed. He wanted Peanut back on the team and Hills was probably the catalyst. Her being stubborn wasn't helping.

Peanut had the binoculars focused on the street below. He grinned as he watched Chas and Hills drive off. He half-expected them to call, but they didn't.

'Who were those two?' asked Janice-Rose, standing beside Peanut.

'My old friends at ICT cleaning the shit off the streets.'

'The shit?' she asked.

'Pals of the guys at the barbeque last night.'

Sharon stopped packing. She and Janice-Rose stared at him in confusion.

'Are you sure?' Sharon asked.

'Positive. Now that they're gone, it's time for us to go.'

* * *

They took a slow drive around the outside of the Port of Houston compound. It was secure. The only way in was through the gate and past the security checkpoint. Every vehicle arriving was stopped at the gate; nothing was left to chance. There were sensors on the chain-link fence and outriggers with coiled razor wire strung along the top. There was only one way in. Peanut figured it out after watching the trucks go in. The body of an enclosed truck or one carrying a large container blocked the halogen lights at the gate from shining on the rear of the truck. That caused a dark shadow and due to the tight turn in to the gate, the truck's rear stuck out halfway across the road. Peanut knew what he had to do. He explained it to Sharon and Janice-Rose.

'All good, ladies?' he said as they bumped knuckles.

'All good, big brother,' said Janice-Rose and Sharon leant over and kissed him on the cheek.

Chapter 20

Peanut stood and contemplated the sky, wishing the clouds would roll in. The clear starlit night was no help, but clouds were supposed to roll in later. He could see them building, far out in the gulf, but right now, they were no help at all. He pressed *talk* on his walkie-talkie.

'All good, Sharon? Over.'

'Affirmative, Peanut. Over.'

'All good, J.R.? Over.'

'Affirmative, big brother. Over.'

'Truck coming, ladies. I'm on my way. Over and out.'

As the truck swung in towards the gates, Peanut ran out of the darkened doorway of the building on the other side of the road and into the dark shadow at the rear of the truck. He dived under the tail, into the space between the rear axle and the back of the deck and clamped two magnetic clamps onto both sides of the chassis rail. He grabbed the clamps on the one side and put his feet into the looped straps on the clamp the other side and lifted his body up, just so he didn't sag as the truck changed gear and drove through the gate. The truck stopped inside and the check was the usual thorough scrutiny of the papers and then it drove off and turned up one of the interior access roads.

The speed restriction inside the compound was ten miles an hour, and while the truck was driving slow, he twisted his feet and slid the foot clamps off the chassis rail, then slid the hand ones off just as his body hit the road. Peanut rolled clear into what he hoped was the dark side of the road. The trouble was, there was no dark side. The light in the compound was not brilliant, but with no cloud cover and a brilliant moon, it was more like twilight. As he got to his feet, he watched the truck disappear around a corner. It was time to get his bearings. He didn't want to be on the road when a security patrol came by. He had watched the security in operation and they were thorough. Using searchlights that played over the locked fronts of the warehouses, they didn't miss a thing. He pressed *talk* again on the walkie-talkie and spoke quietly.

'Situation, J.R.? Over'

'Security over on the middle road. Nearing the gate end of the yard. Over.'

Excellent. They were two roads over.

'Situation, Sharon? Over.'

'Security on far road, opposite the end of the gate. Over.'

Without Sharon and Janice-Rose, Peanut knew he would have been a sitting duck. Two, almost non-stop patrols kept circulating the large compound and the only thing that would save him from being picked up was Sharon and Janice-Rose watching and the size of the compound. He could have done with another two watchers, but if Sharon and Janice-Rose were careful, it should work.

He ducked up a side street, heading down toward the wharf side of the compound. He reached the road that ran around the inside of the fence. He had to be alert as the normal wharf patrol ran irregular patrols along the outside of the fence.

'I'm on the target road. Situation J.R.? Over.'

'Clear to go. Over.'

'Sharon? Over.'

'Clear to go. Waterfront patrol is still parked. Over.'

The warehouse was a small building, but Peanut couldn't see why they would need a large one. He ran into the gap between the warehouse and the next building. It was just a two-foot-wide firebreak. He only had to stay out of sight. The setup was simple. The company had two warehouses. The trucks arrived at the first one and unloaded, then some of those trucks made their way to the secure compound to complete their unloading. Peanut assumed it was drugs that came here. This was where sealed wooden crates were lifted out and placed into the warehouse. It was the perfect hiding place for drugs, guarded by the tightest security possible. He estimated that the traffic to here was only one truck in three, but given the size of the crates, if it was drugs, an enormous quantity was getting shipped in. He would soon know.

Just then Sharon came through loud in his earpiece.

'Compound patrol turning onto the waterfront street. Copy that? Over.'

'Copy. Over and out.'

He quickly pocketed the walkie-talkie and began walking up the two walls, a leg on each side, knowing if he stayed in that alleyway, he would be caught. He noticed they always shone their searchlights up the gaps between buildings. He reached the roof as the searchlight played on the front of the building and then up the alleyway. He swung his legs clear of the gap just as the beam probed the darkness. It had missed him! His heart was thumping. He knew what would happen if he was seen. The yard would go into lockdown and the police would be called. There would be no escape. He lay flat as the searchlight flitted over the building. The lean-to roof meant that it sloped from front to back. As long as he didn't go near the front, he would stay invisible. He pressed *talk* on his walkie-talkie.

'On target roof, working to access. Over and out.'

He didn't get a reply and he didn't expect one. He crawled over to the vent and got onto his knees. Although his head hit the underside of the cowling, there was just enough room for him to look down. It was a straight drop to the top of a container. He lifted out the bird mesh covering the top of the vent, and sat it on the roof, tying his rope to the support stanchions of the cowling and dropping the end onto the container below. So far, so good. He squeezed his body up and over the gap between the cowling and the upright vent, working his body head first down the rope. He cleared the ceiling and his feet let go of the rope, his body swinging upright, and he stood on the container. He turned on his flashlight and spoke into his walkie-talkie.

'In target. Over.'

He climbed down the container, using the end door fastening arms and quickly began to check. Stack upon stack of plastic-wrapped packets. He noticed that one or two had been breached and he checked. Heroin. He had found it and he was right—this was another major drug operation.

He walked to the office, noticed the computer, and then glanced out the window. It faced the perimeter road. If he turned the computer on, the light would be seen. He left the office and found the answer. There was cardboard piled up in high stacks for disposal. He picked up a large sheet and placed it over the window and turned on the computer. It asked for a PIN. On the wall there was a four-digit number: 3330. He entered it. Obviously, the guys who worked here were so confident that everything was so secure in the compound that they didn't bother concealing the PIN. It was a mistake that made his job easy. He plugged in the thumb drive and began loading in the programs that he wanted: VPN and keylogger, and extras, just in case. Finished, he checked his access to the computer with the tablet and was straight in, no password required. He then hid the programs and unless someone with good computer skills went looking, they would do their job and never be found.

Job done, he checked the web browser, just to see what sites they visited. It was nearly all porn. He then accessed the company network and searched for the password, but this time it was secure. No password was written under the keyboard and none was listed on anything in the desk drawers. It was a job for the keylogger. It would eventually tell them the log on. He turned off the computer and carried the cardboard back to the stack, climbing up the container and then the rope, squeezing over the top of the vent, freeing the rope and lying flat on the roof.

He spoke again into his walkie-talkie.

'On the roof of the target. Situation, J.R.? Over,'

'All clear, gate end. Patrol having a break. Over.'

A raindrop hit his neck and he looked up. The dark clouds were racing in; the rain was coming. He was going to get wet, but he didn't care. Rain would make it harder for them to see anything. It would blot everything out.

'Situation, Sharon? Over.'

'Rear road, far end. Over.'

'Truck situation, J.R.? Over.'

'Middle road, not far from the gate. Just started unloading.'

'On my way. Over and out.'

He ran, just as the moon was suddenly blotted out, the rain beginning to fall. He couldn't stop smiling, the night just kept getting better and better.

He leant up against the side of a warehouse, halfway along the middle road. The truck was backed into the loading bay and there were three men up on the loading dock. One was on the forklift and the other two talking, joking, laughing as they watched. The front of the truck was in darkness but the loading bay was bathed in bright light. He spoke into his walkie-talkie.

'I'm on the middle road, one hundred yards from a loading truck. Situation, J.R.? Over.'

'Patrol on perimeter road, all clear. Over.'

'Sharon? Over.'

'Patrol approaching middle road, about a hundred yards from intersection. Over.'

'Copy. Over and out.'

Would they turn into the middle road? He couldn't stay where he was. He ran for the truck. The rain was getting heavier. He dived under the nose of the truck, getting down on his belly as he scrambled under the cab and towards the rear deck. He saw patrol lights swing into the road. They were coming his way. The noise of the forklift drowned out any of the sounds he made as he scrambled to the rear, getting in behind the rear wheels and axle, and waited for the patrol to pass. The searchlight played over the buildings opposite and then played forward as they went past. There was friendly tooting to the guys on the loading dock. He eased to the rear and fastened the clamps into position and waited. The forklift paused and he heard a guy call out.

'Give you a spell?'

'Nah, only three more trips.'

He waited as they finished, then heard the rear doors on the container slam shut and lock, then the guys talking.

'Thanks, guys. Back in a week.'

'Same time?'

'Depends on the ship. Easy overtime!'

'Home to a warm bed and a hot mom, huh?'

'I wish. The hot mom went cold and fucked off with some guy she met through the kids' school. See you, guys.'

Peanut saw a pair of legs come into view as the driver climbed into the cab. Peanut swung his feet into the straps as the motor started. He raised his body as the truck moved off and began to travel rapidly toward the exit. So much for the ten miles per hour speed limit. He had to take this into account. If it sped up like that as he turned out the gate, dropping off was a matter of sooner rather than later. Hitting the road at twenty or thirty miles an hour instead of ten would hurt. But would they see him at the gate if he dropped off early? It was a risk he had to take. The truck paused at the gate and the security guard called out to the driver.

'All good?'

'Perfect.' There was a pause, then came the security guard's voice again.

'Good to go, pal.'

The gate slid open and the truck trundled through, turned, and accelerated hard. Peanut twisted his feet and slid the foot clamps and the hand clamps off simultaneously. He hit the road hard and rolled. Scrabbling to his feet, he caught his breath and began to run, heading for the shadows.

'Hey!' the shout behind him was loud. He had been seen! He disappeared around the corner. Glancing back as he turned the next corner, he saw the security guard in the distance giving chase. Peanut pressed *talk* on his walkie-talkie.

'Outside the gate. Guard on my tail. Get the car started! Over.'

'Copy, big brother. Over and out.'

Peanut sped up. Taking a quick look back he could see that the security guard was struggling. He grinned. Security guards were chosen for their size, not for their running ability. He knew they would be calling for backup as he swung around the corner and sprinted to the car, leaping in the passenger seat. He took another quick glimpse back. No guard in sight. Janice-Rose accelerated, turning sharply at the first corner and heading hard up the next street.

'Steady on. He didn't get a look at the car. Don't draw attention to us,' Peanut told her.

Janice-Rose slowed down and five minutes later she pulled over and Sharon climbed into the back.

'All good?'

'As far as I can tell.'

'Well done, sweetheart!' Sharon reached over and patted him on the shoulder.

Janice-Rose glanced at his wet clothes. 'Hotel, then a coffee?'

'Yes, please. I'm drenched. A change of clothes and then a nice night-time café.'

Chapter 21

Hills knocked on the door; there was no answer. She glanced at Chas. He raised his eyebrows. She knocked again, waited a minute and then, shoulders slumped, turned and walked down the stairs with Chas following.

'I expected this,' said Chas as they went out of the door that led to the pavement.

'Where do you think they went?' she asked.

Chas gave her an unhappy look. 'I'd love to know because we have a job coming up. We could do with Peanut on the team. But I don't blame him if he doesn't want to see us again. He's not the sort of guy who sits around getting fat.'

'It's my fault. I should have contacted him,' Hills said. 'I was miffed that he had found his sister and hadn't contacted us. I think we have to accept that he doesn't want to work with us anymore.'

'That might be the case, but for some reason I don't think so,' Chas said.

She was about to walk out of the door when he grabbed her arm. 'Our friends are back,' he said. She looked up in time to see the tail end of the blue Camry disappear down the street.

'Think they spotted us?' she asked.

'Nope. If they had, they would have driven off much more quickly than that. Let's go and make sure they understand we know they're hanging around.'

They hurried as they walked back to their car. As Chas buckled up, Hills spied a gap in the traffic and accelerated hard. The blue Camry would be up ahead somewhere, probably just doing a repeat circuit of the neighborhood, hoping to spot someone. She spied the blue car in the distance as it turned off. They followed, easing closer as they turned onto a small back residential street and parked. Chas saw immediately why. It enabled them to watch the apartments and Blair Road. Cunning. They were spying, just keeping out of the way by sitting there, hoping to see Sharon. Pricks.

'Doesn't that beak the law?' Hills asked with a grin.

He laughed. 'It does now. Wait till they get the binoculars out.'

They pulled over and waited. Sure enough, a small set of binoculars was soon spotted. Chas indicated that Hills drive up and park. They walked up to the car. The driver had seen them coming and had buzzed his window up. Hills tapped on the glass. The guy inside ignored her and turned away. Hills pulled her pistol out and pointed it at the driver as Chas hit the window with the hard corner on the butt of his gun. The window shattered and glass fragments sprayed all over the driver.

'Out! Put your hands on your heads and get out now!' Hills shouted. They both sulkily obliged and Hills indicated for them to sit on the ground. Chas squatted in front of them.

'We tend to get mighty pissed off when our good advice is ignored,' said Chas. 'Do you mind telling me why you're still loitering around?'

'We heard he was back in the area, so we decided to drop by.'

'Dropping by isn't driving around in circles and using binoculars, is it?'

The guy didn't say anything.

Hills snorted with disdain. 'These lying pieces of shit can explain it to the FBI. Maybe they're looking for those guys who got fried the other night. The police are now looking for leads.'

The driver shook his head. 'Don't know what you're talking about, lady.'

The other guy chipped in. 'We've done nothing wrong. You can't hold us.'

Hills scoffed. 'Haven't you dumb bunnies heard of the terrorism laws? Driving around, looking for targets, unable to name who you're looking for? Using binoculars? What you're doing means you're liable for preventative detention. That's weeks or maybe years in the slammer if you don't tell the truth. The first step in avoiding that is telling us who you are looking for. Want to give honesty a go for once in your shitty little lives?' she said.

He said nothing.

'Let me help you. You're hunting a beautiful woman with long black hair,' said Hills.

She watched their faces and knew she was right.

'We want her as well and you two fucking turkeys are getting in our way,' said Chas. 'We've had a gutful of you maggots. You're hindering a federal investigation and we're not happy. Get in your car and drive or we'll take you to where those last two pieces of shit got cooked and throw a match on you. Only I won't be nice and shoot you first. Believe me, it will be a slow, very slow barbecue with the both of you screaming all the way to hell. Understand?' said Chas.

'Look, man, we don't want to upset you. Who are you anyway?'

'All you need to know is that we're federal agents and we make sure things get sorted, one way or the other, get me, asshole? I repeat, you are in our way and are hindering a federal investigation.' Chas prodded the thug in the chest. 'If I see you again, no one else will *ever* see you again. This is your last warning, asshole, fuck off!'

'Think it will work?' Hills asked once they were back in their car.

'Nah. Their boss will insist that they find her. Call Peanut and let him know. He'll sort it out.'

When her call went straight to voicemail, Hills left Peanut a message.

'Well, I tried,' she said.

'He'll call back,' Chas said. 'Don't worry about it.'

***

They were in a taxi travelling back from Dulles Airport when Peanut heard his phone beep, and he listened to the message.

'Is it from Hills, big brother?' His sister was getting too good at reading him, but then, she was family. It was allowed. She nudged him, hard. Ignoring her was not an option.

'Was that Hills? You didn't answer me.' Janice-Rose had obviously been listening while Peanut played the message. 'What'd she want?'

'She was letting me know that those meatheads are still hanging around. She and Chas scared them off again, but they don't think they'll stay away for long. She wants to meet you and Sharon. And she wants me to work for them.'

'Why?'

'Why not? It's a free country?' he replied.

'Is she nice? After all, she did hit you where it hurts!' she said. 'Mind you, there have been plenty of times I've felt like doing that, so I can't hold that against her.'

'We have the job on in Houston. I don't want to be part of ICT while we're busy nailing that down,' Peanut replied.

'I'm assuming that the pay with ICT would be nothing like what you make on your own,' Sharon interjected.

'I never stayed long enough to find out, but I'd assume not.'

'Why go back then?' asked Sharon. 'Stay as you are, rich and single. It makes sense to me.' Sharon smiled a knowing smile and rubbed his arm. Noticing his serious expression, she added, 'Let me guess, sweetheart. It's what you told me in Atlanta. That it's all about making a difference. Getting paid more money is just a bonus.'

'Yep. If we can make some money and put some shit behind bars, there is no downside.'

He relaxed in the back of the taxi as they made their way into Washington, but his mind was elsewhere, thinking things through. Janice-Rose caught Sharon's eye and flipped her

99

eyes upward. When her brother was like this, all moody and contemplative, he was fucking hopeless and there was no point talking to him.

Peanut knew that getting back into the apartment was going to be awkward if any thugs were hanging around.

'Let's have a coffee and cake, ladies. I'm paying,' he said.

Peanut sat in the café listening to Janice-Rose and Sharon talk. He could tell that a real friendship was blossoming between them, but he wasn't really paying attention to what they were saying. He couldn't stop worrying about getting back into the apartment. He didn't want to give up the apartment. He felt settled living there. It was his home and he was annoyed that these thugs were disturbing him. Then he realized the answer was obvious. Draw them out. That's what he needed to do. He sent a text to Hills.

Make of car and plate for bad guys?

The answer was immediate.

Dark blue Camry, FP 6031. Where r u?

Downtown, lunch.

Call if u need help.

He was pleased with her response and glanced up into the knowing eyes of Janice-Rose.

'Hills,' she said. It wasn't a question.

'I needed the make of the car and the plate for the bad guys. She's a cop, she remembers shit like that.'

'I seem to remember you do as well,' Janice-Rose said.

'It's not a hard skill to acquire,' said Peanut.

'So, what now?' Sharon asked.

'You and Janice-Rose walk to the apartment and I'll follow well behind and keep watch.'

'I don't fancy being bait, big brother.'

'As soon as you're inside the building, run upstairs and lock the door. Grab the pistol out of the drawer, just in case. Just don't shoot me. Have you got a better plan?' he asked.

She shook her head.

The taxi dropped them well away from the apartment. Peanut followed well behind on the opposite side of the street, looking out for any cars. The thugs that Hills and Chas had scared off had probably changed their car, but it didn't pay to assume anything—the basic stupidity of most of the criminal element never ceased to amaze him.

As Janice-Rose and Sharon walked in the main door of the apartment building, Peanut hid behind a tree. Sure enough, he soon saw a dark blue Camry slow down and cruise by. The girls had been spotted. Peanut knew the scenario. The thugs would come back in the middle of the night, smash in the door and kidnap them. Regardless of how much he liked the apartment, it was now time to get out. Then the car stopped, did a U-turn and parked. He wondered what the fuck was going on. Were these boys trying to be heroes or what? He watched as they opened the bottom street door and went inside. Peanut ran across the road and followed them in. 'Open up! Police!' Peanut heard one of them call as he ran up the first flight of stairs. They were standing outside his apartment door and one had put a policeman's hat on. He crept closer.

'Show us your warrant card or your badge,' Janice-Rose called from the other side of the door.

'Lady, we don't want to break your door down. We're just asking about some drugs being sold on the street.'

'You'll have to show me your identification.'

Peanut drew his swords as the heavier built thug stood back, lifted his leg and was about to kick the door in.

'I wouldn't do that,' said Peanut.

The thugs spun around, noticing the small, wiry frame of Peanut. One gave a snort and then noticed the swords in his hands. The other thug began to move his hand behind to go for his gun. With a seemingly gentle flick, Peanut threw the sword. At that short distance he couldn't miss; the sword buried itself deep into the guy's chest, right into his heart. Peanut strode the five steps forward as the other thug with the policeman's hat desperately reached for his gun. He wasn't quick enough, the gun only half out as Peanut stuck the blade of his sword under his chin.

'I wouldn't do that either, Mr. Policeman'. The man let his hand drop to his side. He lost his composure and looked scared as Peanut called out.

'J.R., Sharon, it's me. Open up!' The door swung open and Janice-Rose and Sharon stood there, taking the scene in.

'Get this one's gun, J.R., cock it and watch him while Sharon and I pull this dead prick inside.' She took the pretend policeman's gun, then shoved him hard in the back.

'Sit in the corner over there.'

'Fuck off, girlie. Who the fuck do you think you are?'

She gave him another quick shove and swept his legs out, watching him crash to the floor. He peered up, stunned, his eyes unfocused and his head disorientated as he tried to get his bearings. He noticed the body of his mate hauled roughly through the door and dumped in the other corner.

Sharon had seen the move Janice-Rose had done and contemplated the guy on the floor.

'You will have to show me how you do that. It looks like something every lady should know.'

'With pleasure, but I learned it from big brother. He's a very good teacher.'

Peanut glared at the thug on the floor, big, beefy with designer stubble, his long dark hair hanging way past his collar, accentuating his white skin. To Peanut's eyes he appeared to be Russian and was used to using his size and weight to scare people. Peanut noticed the arrogance getting replaced with worry. He slipped one of the swords back into the sheath and smiled.

'Guess what time it is?' Peanut asked.

The thug looked blank.

'It's time for you to tell us the truth,' said Peanut.

Chapter 22

Peanut's smile quickly faded as he examined the set face of Mr. Policeman. He crouched in front of him and placed his sword on the floor. The man glanced nervously at the sword.

'We know you're not a policeman, so we'll start with the simple things. Like your name,' said Peanut

'Is he dead?' the thug asked.

'As a doornail.'

'A doornail? What's that?'

'An old English saying. Your pal is dead. Believe me.'

The thug shook his head.

'What's your name, asshole?'

Peanut knew he would talk when his eyes kept flicking to the body. Peanut could smell his sweat. This Russian was scared. If he didn't talk, Peanut intended to move it up from scared to pants-shitting terrified.

'Regis Zotov.'

'Is Milo Volkov your boss?'

Zotov nodded.

'Did you contact anyone after you spotted these women?'

Zotov shook his head.

'No, Slava wanted to get them and be a hero. I told him to wait, but he wouldn't. Milo was offering a reward if we brought them in.'

'You were told to stay away. Why did you come back?'

'Milo insisted. And then offered us a reward. I told him about the feds hanging around and he said not to worry. He was sure you were here. One of the men who died in the other car was Milo's friend. Milo is extremely angry.'

'Where is Milo now?' Peanut asked.

'He never says. It's all by mobile phone.'

Peanut sat back. Zotov's bluster was gone, but Peanut had no doubt that if he was released, he would tell Volkov where they were. By coming here, he had signed his death warrant. Silly man. Peanut nodded at Janice-Rose.

'Cable ties?' she said, turning to walk into the kitchen, the gun in her hand no longer pointing at Regis. Regis saw his chance; he suddenly scrabbled his feet under him and threw himself at Peanut. He was too late to stop his lunge when Peanut flicked the point of the sword up off the floor, his hand enclosing the hilt as Regis impaled himself on the end. Peanut continued the motion, now pushing the sword hard into his heart. Regis was dead before his body stopped moving, almost gently collapsing to the floor. Peanut pulled out the sword, wiped it on Regis's coat and put it back in its sheath. He checked Regis's pockets and pulled out a mobile phone. Regis hadn't lied. The last phone call was two hours ago. Milo Volkov's number was listed and he put that number on his phone. He then checked the other thug; his phone showed no contact since early morning and again Milo Volkov's phone was listed.

'You won't need the cable ties now, will you?' said Janice-Rose as she leant on the kitchen bench.

'He's all tied up with the devil, but thanks anyway.'

***

Hills turned the corner and there it was; the dark blue Camry parked outside Peanut's apartment building door.

'They just won't fucking learn. Do we sit and wait for them or go on up?' she said.

'Go up. The car's empty.' Chas was definite. 'Just in case they caught Peanut unaware.' He knew that was stupid as soon as he said it. Those two morons they had stopped the other day were out of Peanut's league. He would crucify them.

They climbed the stairs and Hills remembered the last time she'd been here. The time when she'd thought Peanut didn't want anything to do with her. She fought off a niggle of worry. She hoped Peanut was alright. The door was shut and it was with mixed feelings that Hills knocked on it. An eye blocked the peep hole for a couple of seconds as Hills held up her identification. Then the eye disappeared and the door swung open. Hills saw a very pretty woman standing there.

'You must be Hills?'

'Yes. And you must be Janice-Rose?'

'Yep.' Janice-Rose smiled at her as she eyed her up and down. 'My big brother sure has good taste in women.' She peered behind Hills. 'And you have to be Chas.'

'I am and he has. It's a pleasure to meet you, Janice-Rose.' Chas held out his hand and a surprised Janice-Rose shook it. Hills blushed slightly at the compliments.

'Come on in. We have a slight dead-body problem at the moment, so be careful where you place your feet.'

Chas laughed.

'Let me guess, the guys from the blue Camry?'

Peanut stood up and grinned. The car keys were in his hand.

'Welcome, Hills and Chas. This pretty woman is Sharon. You've already met the other one.'

The kick was sudden and hard.

'Ow!' shouted Peanut.

'Keep it up, big brother, and I'll give you another smack in the nuts, harder than Hills did, believe it!'

Hills gave a nervous laugh. She would rather that episode be forgotten.

'She knows about our meeting then?' asked Hills.

'No secrets here,' Peanut said bluntly and then changed the subject. 'We need to get rid of these two tonight.'

'Same place?' asked Chas.

'Yeah.'

'Okay. We'll follow you, just to make sure there are no problems. We could call the FBI, but the paperwork isn't worth it. I'll have a quiet word with them, just so they don't waste any time on the investigation.'

'Tell the FBI that both lots worked for Milo Volkov,' Peanut said. 'Shady, all contacts by mobile phone. Sharon is the only one to have met him.' Chas and Hills turned and studied Sharon, intrigued

'Volkov turned up at Gorev's office and wanted me to go back to his hotel with him,' Sharon said. 'James intervened and stopped it from happening. He was arrogant and rude. A big overbearing man, somewhere about fifty, I think. The next time he turned up, James hid me in an empty office.'

'James Gorev?'

'Yes.'

Chas had a good look at Sharon. She was a beautiful woman and he could see why Peanut had gone away with her. Hills asked what was on her mind.

'So you got chased up here from Miami?'

'Yes. I needed help and I had seen what Peanut could do, so I arrived, but unfortunately they followed me here.' She pointed at the two blankets folded on the end of the settee. 'At least Peanut and J.R. have given me a bed.'

Hills immediately felt a sensation of relief. It was strange. It wasn't as if she was jealous. Sharon was stunningly beautiful. She knew she couldn't blame Peanut and Sharon for wanting to find out if the initial attraction they felt was real. She now knew that Chas was right—whatever was between Sharon and Peanut had gone. If it was still there, Sharon wouldn't be sleeping on the settee. She was just a friend.

'Coffee anyone?' asked Janice-Rose, 'Or will we all go to a café and leave the dead in peace? Peanut can pay. It's his shout for using me and Sharon as bait.'

Hills saw the look on Peanut's face and knew instinctively that Janice-Rose was enjoying winding him up. Chas gave Sharon a quick glance.

'Did he?' he asked.

'He certainly did. But he had our permission,' she said.

Chas noticed that Sharon was standing close, not uncomfortably close but near enough so she couldn't be ignored. She took his arm.

'Come on, Chas. Coffee.' She led him out the door and down to their car, parked behind the Camry. He opened the rear door and she stood back and smiled at him.

'Chas in the middle,' Sharon said, 'Hills and Peanut up front and Janice-Rose and me in the back.' Hills grinned at the quick organizing of the seating arrangements as she got in behind the wheel and accelerated out onto the road.

'We hoped you'd contact us when you got Janice-Rose back,' Hills said to Peanut. When he didn't answer, she thought for a second he was ignoring her.

'Too much on at the moment,' Peanut said at length. 'Volkov will stop at nothing until he finds us. We have to take him out.'

'Do you think he means to kill you?' Hills asked.

'If he can. But I have a few ideas and I'm working through them. It takes time, as you know.'

Chas leant forward. 'We need a hand in two weeks' time. Can you spare us some time then?'

'What for?' Peanut asked.

Chas looked around at the others, uncomfortable that they would hear what he was about to say. Peanut noticed.

'Sharon and Janice-Rose know everything. We have no secrets. Talk away,' said Peanut.

'Okay. We need to kidnap a potential problem,' said Chas. 'It won't be as easy as you might think. He lands at JFK in two weeks' time. We need to pick him up before he gets away because he'll have people ready to hide him.'

'Can we meet on Monday? You tell me what time. I'm tied up Saturday and Sunday.'

'Can I ask what you are up to?' asked Chas. Peanut just laughed.

'Research, Chas, just research.'

'Okay, I won't ask. Are you happy to look at the feasibility of this job?'

'Yes. But not as an employee. You want deniability and this gives you that. I will work as an unpaid, unsigned contractor, outside of the department's rules and scruples until I am sure that you guys and the department are on the level.'

'Why?' asked Chas.

'All due respect, but you haven't been exactly on the level with me up to now. I want to have the option of walking away as if I never had anything to do with the job or with ICT.'

'I see. I guess we don't have a choice, do we?'

'Not if you want me to do the job,' said Peanut.

'I do, so yeah, okay.'

Peanut could see that Chas wasn't happy. Tough. Hills sat puzzled, wondering what was going on. Was Peanut coming back, or wasn't he? At least she was sitting beside him again and for some reason, it felt like they were the team of old. She noticed Sharon smiling at her;

saw her nod her head towards Peanut and then quickly flicked her eyebrows. The inference was clear and Hills reddened slightly as she glimpsed Janice-Rose's face, grinning as she watched the exchange of looks. For some reason, Hills didn't mind.

Chas knew that something was going on, but what? He had seen Hills blush and wondered what that was about, but the closeness of Sharon had unnerved him. Her perfume was nice, but the hand-holding was something he wasn't used to. She tugged at his hand as she spoke, and when she leaned forward, her leg rubbed unmistakably against his and her cleavage was on display. He was embarrassed at inadvertently peeking. She suddenly took his arm with her other hand to get his full attention as she spoke so everyone could hear.

'I recommend that we have our coffee break, then get back together later and all go out for dinner tonight. Later, much later, we can say goodbye to our inadvertent guests.' Everybody was happy with that. 'Okay, friends,' Sharon said. 'Where do we dine?'

Janice-Rose couldn't resist.

'Let Peanut pick it. He's paying.'

Peanut frowned at Janice-Rose as they all burst into laughter.

***

Peanut drove quietly along the rutted track down to the quarry. The burnt-out wreck was gone as the FBI had arranged for its removal. He pulled to a stop and took the plastic jerry can out of the boot and poured the gas over the bodies in the back seat, again leaving the windows open. He took photos of the bodies and then stood back, flicking a match in the rear window, the loud whump popped the windshield nearly out and he then took another photo. He jogged back over to the car, climbed in, and Hills accelerated away.

Chas turned and asked. 'Is it wise taking those photos?'

'I've got Volkov's phone number. I want to show him what I do to his men. Can you trace his number, just to see if we can pinpoint him?' He handed the phone over and Chas rang, gave the number to someone and hung up.

'Ten minutes,' Chas said.

'Are you trying to piss Volkov off? By sending the photos?' asked Hills.

'I intend to kill him.' Peanut paused for a second. 'Think of him as just another Chuckie.'

'Crims never learn, you know,' said Chas.

They sat back as Hills drove them back to the apartment. Chas's phone rang. He listened for a minute then hung up.

'Volkov's phone is not a smart phone. The last call he received was from the middle of Houston, the call before that was from the Port of Houston, and the call before that was from Atlanta.'

'Thanks, Chas. Just what I needed to know,' said Peanut. He picked up Regis Zotov's phone and attached the photos to a text message, added a short heading *You are next,* then pushed send. He waited for it to send and then turned the phone off and threw it out the window as the car approached Blair Road.

'Witching hour. One o'clock,' said Chas as he noticed the oppressive clouds scudding across the sky. 'You didn't really need us tonight, did you?' he said.

'No, but I appreciated your company. And thanks again for finding out about Volkov's phone.'

'He'll be hard to track,' said Chas.

'No, I don't think so. He'll be where the money is. With the drugs.'

Chapter 23

Peanut walked out of his bedroom and noticed Sharon stirring on the settee. He stretched and then ducked into the bathroom, smiling at Sharon when he came out. She was now sitting at the table and had turned the coffee machine on. They sat at the table in companionable silence, waiting for the machine to do its job.

'Sharon, you worked in James Gorev's front office as his only secretary. What exactly was the firm's business? The reason for the fancy office?'

'I thought you knew,' said Sharon.

'No, I have no idea.'

'Gorev was an arms' dealer. A legitimate one. I did the paperwork. The government compliance forms and all of that sort of shit.'

'Was the New York office a legitimate business as well?'

'Yes. We all worked together. If we had a client who wanted a thousand AK 47s and we didn't have enough in storage, we would put the call out.'

'Did you sell many guns in the U.S.?' he asked.

'No, not really, we dealt in bulk, internationally. But during the last year, we had some reasonable-sized orders from a firm in Texas. Nothing like the international ones but surprising all the same. That nearly cost me my job.'

'How?' Peanut asked.

'Some of the paperwork was false and when I queried it with Gorev, he told me to put it through with no questions asked. Said it wasn't my job to comment on it. When I suggested that it would be easy to work out that it was false, he said no one else would check. He said that no one else was going to look at it and even if they did, they had the political contacts to kill it. He then said to go do the job I was paid to do or fuck off. It hurt. Three weeks later, you arrived.'

'Whereabouts in Texas was that company? Do you remember the name?'

'San Antonio. Southern States Alliance.' Sharon had a good memory. Peanut was pleased. He stood up and went to the kitchen to get coffee. He strolled back to the table.

'We're going to have to get a bigger apartment. We'll have to move from here and we need to change today before the next load of shit heads come looking. Milo Volkov has those photos of the barbeque and he will want revenge. I expect at least three or four teams to come and comb the neighborhood. We have to move today, this morning. Can you get J.R. up? Out of here in an hour, into a couple of motel units or a vacant apartment.'

'Leave it to J.R. and me,' said Sharon.

'Two units or a very large family one,' said Peanut.

'Why don't you buy a house? Four bedrooms would solve all your problems.' Sharon paused a minute. 'If I'm a burden, just say so and I'll go somewhere else.'

'You're no burden. Just the opposite. In any case, don't forget it was me ripping off Gorev that put you in this position. But it's a bit rough for you sleeping on the settee every night. A house sounds good. A new address will make finding us that much harder.'

She rubbed his arm. 'J.R. and I can go look if you like.'

'Go for it. Just get us into a motel in the meantime.'

***

Peanut admired the pretty flower print hanging on the motel wall. It was two a.m. and he was nearly ready to transfer the money. Each account had a different name. The accounts in the Bahamas were spilt into three names, the Shar account, the Rose account, and the Nut account. He knew there would be screams of anguish on Monday when they discovered that the money had gone. There'd be even more screams when the FBI turned up at their warehouse. He wasn't sure what effect this would have on the FBI investigation, but one of the company's principals was Senator Burlington Ford, a good old boy from Texas and a pillar of the Washington political establishment. Was he the man Gorev had referred to as the political contact? The one who would kill any questions about gun shipments? Peanut had checked and Ford was on a lot of committees and had power. But that was a matter for the FBI. He stood, stretched, and went to make a coffee, his tired eyes peering at the clock, wanting the time to race by.

Sharon shook Peanut awake. He wanted more sleep, but Janice-Rose wasn't having a bar of it.

'Wakey, wakey, big brother. Time to rise and shine.'

'What time is it?'

'Eleven. You can take us to lunch,' she said.

'I didn't get to bed until six.'

'Five hours' sleep, that's enough. You'll sleep better tonight if you get up now.' Janice-Rose snatched the bedclothes off him. 'We want to show you a house after lunch. Come on, get up.' He swung his legs out and stood. She was right; if he overslept, he would not sleep tonight.

The house was modern, but it was made to look old-fashioned with stone cladding and solid timber. It was two-storied and had a full-size basement with a big lawn and ornamental cherry trees. It was surrounded by a ten-foot-high imitation wrought-iron fence. The steel arrowheads on the top of the pickets were intimidating. But the large basement sold it to Peanut. As they were looking through it, he kept his face bland as he didn't want the agent to see he wanted to buy it. He intended to drive a hard bargain and get it for a good price.

'We'd have to renovate it,' Peanut said and sighed. 'Too much hassle, I think.' He turned to the agent. 'How much are they asking?'

'Two point five.'

'Nah, too much. As I said we'd have to alter it. Shame though cos we're cash buyers.'

'I'm sure the owners would look at a reasonable offer, sir.'

'It's been on the market for six months. The price must be too high,' said Sharon.

'The last offer they had was two,' said the agent.

'I'll give you two point one,' said Peanut.

'I'm sure if you went two point three, they would take it,' said the agent.

'Two point two. Cash. Paid up today if required. That's my last offer,' said Peanut as he turned to Sharon. 'Where's the next one we're looking at?'

'I'll just check the address,' said Sharon.

The agent was upset as she rang, not sure of anything. Peanut, Janice-Rose, and Sharon walked to the car, leaning on it and talking, waiting for the agent to finish. She came over, still talking, moving away out of earshot again. They could see her stressing points with her hands as she talked.

They were about to get in the car when the agent caught up with them.

'The house is yours. Two point two, cash,' she said.

They sat in the café, the house papers all signed, stamped and in front of Peanut. His phone pinged and then Janice-Rose's and Sharon's phones both pinged as well. Janice-Rose opened her phone, saw the app on the screen and a message. She opened it and saw the details

'Peanut, I have a message from a bank in the Bahamas wanting me to sign in with the details they have provided. Do I have a bank account in the Bahamas?'

'You do, once you sign in, J.R.'

She worked her phone, signed in, and then came around the table and bobbed down to hug him.

'You have delivered, big brother. Two point two five million and a few cents.' She watched as Sharon did the same, and then showed Janice-Rose her screen.

'The same.' Sharon also hugged Peanut and kissed him on the cheek. The other people in the café were looking bemused at the show of affection. He felt Sharon's hug; he had forgotten just how sexy her hugs were. She walked back and sat down. The lady at the table next door smiled at him and asked.

'What's your secret? If I can rudely enquire?'

'It's my perfume,' Peanut said.

'Really? Can I ask the type?' the lady asked.

'The scent of money.'

Janice-Rose kicked him under the table.

'Ow!'

'Don't be rude, big brother. Use words of more than one syllable.'

He glared at her; that had hurt. The point of her shoe had hit his shin bone. He reached down and rubbed it as the lady smiled at him.

'Your sister?'

'Ex sister. She's up for sale. I can make you a pretty good offer. Time payment plan?' The lady laughed again.

'Thanks, but no thanks. My kids are enough.'

'I know the feeling, lady. Feel like another coffee, Sharon? J.R. is paying.'

'You think I'm made of money, big brother?'

Sharon rose to get the coffees but Janice-Rose put her hand on her arm. 'I'll get them. I'm just winding him up. That's what little sisters are for.'

***

They were sprawled out in the motel chairs two hours later when all three phones pinged again.

'Oh my God, Peanut, that's another four million!' shrieked Sharon.

'The total pool we nicked was just over eighteen million. So, one-third each.'

Sharon's eyes were twinkling. 'This calls for a special kind of thank you,' she said.

'No, it doesn't,' Peanut replied. 'It's quite the opposite. All three of us now have targets painted on our backs. We have to be careful, not just once but all the time. If you have any social media accounts, you'll now have to close and delete them, today if possible. Chas might tell us how the FBI raid went as he was my point of contact, but the FBI will want all the glory. I gave them the bank access numbers and codes so they can check both the firm's legitimate and illegal divisions.'

'The crooks will be pissed off,' said Janice-Rose.

'They will want to know who, what and where, and they'll spend large sums of money trying to find out. Chas promised to list the information I gave him as coming from an unknown but credible source. I hope that keeps us safe,' said Peanut.

***

Chas hung up the phone and smiled at Hills, Peter, and Blue.

'The FBI have hit the jackpot. A new shipment came into the warehouse, but they still hadn't disposed of the previous one. They are creaming themselves, if you'll excuse the crude expression. The company is under intense scrutiny and two of the principals have fled. Senator Burlington Ford is helping with inquiries. He was pissed off at being taken to the station on a Sunday afternoon.'

'Where did the data you gave the FBI come from?' asked Peter.

'Source unknown to the FBI but known to us,' replied Chas.

'Who?' Peter asked.

'Our ex-team member, the one who saved your life.'

'Peanut?'

'The same. And that information has to stay with us, for obvious reasons. The good news is that he's going to help us with the kidnapping,' said Chas.

'He's coming back?' asked Blue.

'Yes, but only on a casual basis.'

'Shit, what's he charging for his services? I bet it's more than we get paid.' Blue said.

'No charge. He wants complete deniability about having anything to do with us until he's sure we're on the level. I'm just happy he's going to be on board.'

Peter was puzzled.

'I know we're fucking cheap, but since when did we become a charity organization with unpaid people working for us? I told you before, Hills, you should have worked it harder,' said Peter.

She blushed and glared at him.

'The day I take Agony Aunt advice from a single, fifty-year-old, twice-divorced, ex-policeman is the day I resign from the female side of the human race!' Hills stridently stated.

Peter grinned at her. He was happy he had annoyed her. It might make her do something definite about Peanut. Christ, it wasn't as if she didn't like the guy, silly woman. Chas wanted to keep the peace and butted in.

'I've arranged a meeting with Peanut, Janice-Rose, and Sharon at three o'clock. Be here, please,' he said.

'You'll be able to see Sharon again,' Hills said, pleased that she could give back some of the teasing.

Chas gave Hills a blank stare. He was uncomfortable around Sharon. He had always been single and was used to being in total control of his own life. He was worried that Sharon might be a threat to that life. He dismissed Hills's comment and began to think about what plans they had to make.

Chapter 24

'When do we get possession of the house?' Janice-Rose asked. She was eager to get in and set up her room. She had no intention of living anywhere else but with Peanut.

'Tomorrow. I'm paying the money today. Once it's cleared the keys are ours,' said Peanut.

'Is the meeting still on today?' she asked.

'Yes. At three o'clock. We'll all go. You and Sharon are invited.'

'What are we doing until then?'

'I'm taking a drive past our old apartment just to check the streets, trying to see if Volkov has put any of his men in the area. After Houston, I'm picking that the area will be knee deep with Volkov's gangsters.'

'That's taking a risk,' said Sharon.

'Why is that? I'm driving a different rental car.'

'I think it's a waste of time, though, big brother. I'll bet there's no one watching. They'll be too scared after what happened to the others.'

'We'll see,' said Peanut as he picked up the keys and walked out the door.

***

He counted three cars, each with two men sitting inside them. With this sort of coverage, there would be more waiting as backup. Volkov's men were out in force and it was no real surprise. It then occurred to him that he could use Sharon as bait to get to Volkov. But he knew he wouldn't. Sharon was, for better or worse, one of the team.

A few hours later the three of them arrived at a two-storied, flat-roofed building with featureless concrete walls. Utilitarian government ugly was the design. It had the same bland look inside as the camp building with nearly the same prison-green paint on the walls. There was no reception desk, or a sign saying where they were. Peanut felt unnerved. It was as if he was in a government department that didn't exist. He chuckled; that was exactly what they were. They walked into the conference room. Chas stood by the door ushering them in and Sharon stopped to give him a quick friendly hug.

He waited till they were all seated.

'Introductions, everybody.' He pointed. 'Blue Rawlings, Peter Withers, Peanut's sister, Janice-Rose, and Peanut's friend, Sharon Reeves. You all know Hills and me.'

He turned on a large monitor and then sat at a computer.

'Okay, let get down to business. We've been asked to kidnap the Reverend Jerry Gorman.' Chas put up an image of a fifty-plus man with short grey hair and an almost handsome face, until you saw his eyes. They were chilling, almost dead.

'Gorman travels all over Europe. It's the organization that he founded and heads that causes the trouble. It's active right across Europe and they want to set up here. It's known as the OKTO: Order of the Knights Templar of Orange. They're part of the white-power alt-right movement. The organisation is still a fledgling one and even though they are not banned, they have already gone to ground. But they are worrying, especially in Ireland. Northern Ireland to be specific, but in the UK as well. You will have heard of the Orange and the Green in Ireland, I'm sure.'

Everyone's faces were blank except Peter's. He snorted derisively.

'To clarify,' Chas continued. 'The Orangemen is an organization of Protestant resistance against the green, the Catholics in Ireland. They still put on orange sashes and march in parades each year, just to celebrate the long-ago victory of William of Orange over the Catholic King James the Second.'

'Nutcases, in other words,' said Peanut.

'Maybe so, but hatred still runs deep, especially in Northern Ireland. Whole suburbs are still divided into either Catholic or Protestant. Years of sectarian war have hardened attitudes and it's a nightmare-like process undoing the generational damage that has been done.' Chas paused, debating what to say next. Peanut's cynical face did not escape his attention.

'Gorman founded OKTO in Ireland. He has Germanic heritage and he's a supporter of Nazi fascist ideals.'

'They're nothing but troublemakers. I don't see how they are getting the time of day, let alone any credence,' said Peanut.

The occupants of the room murmured their agreement and Chas carried on.

'Yes, I agree, but it's rumored that they have warehouses full of arms and explosives. They have money and lots of it. They're using the internet to recruit young people and take them to training camps. Last count, and these figures are what Gorman claims in his speeches, so they have to be regarded with some suspicion, is that they have around three thousand active, trained members in Europe and twice that number who are donating members. The first part of their training is the swearing of them to secrecy. And they enforce that. Four recruits were murdered when they dared to speak out.'

'Violent radicals! How come they're not banned?' Blue asked.

'They haven't done anything wrong—nobody can prove who was responsible for the murders. We know they are putting out feelers towards the Protestant Bible belt over here, to get donations and membership support going. But they are doing it quietly, just to avoid getting noticed. They fly in members who travel around Protestant white churches and drop leaflets.'

'So, what's the problem?' Peter asked. 'The respective governments can clean out their warehouses whenever they want, can't they?'

'If they knew where they were, sure, but that's the problem. As I said, they're underground in secret locations. Apparently, the warehouses are stacked, floor to ceiling, ready to go. We know this because one of the British donors was shown one, somewhere in Germany, just to prove he wasn't wasting his money. He was shocked and after some soul searching, he spoke to MI5. Two weeks later, he was found dead, murdered. The Brits are not happy. He was a major donor of funds to the Conservative party.'

'Is the Reverend at large?' asked Hills.

'He's wanted for questioning, but he's very elusive. No arrest warrant has been issued because there's no proof that he has done anything wrong or broken any laws. And that leads us to the crux of this issue; how does he pay for all these weapons? He has connections with Russians who deal in the Afghanistan drug trade. It's rumored that he ships drugs to Europe and then over to here. Those warehouses that you discovered, Peanut, are rumored to have been supplied with drugs from him. Drugs he got from the Russian mafia. But as with everything this guy does, there is no proof.'

'Christ, Chas, why don't Immigration just deny him entry?' said Peanut.

'He has large amounts of support, including political support for his right-wing racist views and he's being sponsored to come here. The senator who is currently under investigation, Senator Burlington Ford, is one of his supporters.'

Hills grimaced.

'To understand the threat, you need to understand who they oppose. They have no tolerance for Catholics, Jews, Muslims, anybody with brown skin; that means Asian, African or anyone from the east, including India.'

Peanut laughed. 'That's about three-quarters of the people in the world!' he said.

'Yes, they have a wide target, but you know that fascist brainwashing shit works well in some fundamentalist religious communities. Especially when they preach about white people and the Protestant religion being deliberately oppressed.'

'What do you intend to do with the prick?' asked Peanut.

'We're not called the ICT for nothing.' Chas gave the room a stony look. 'For the record, the Brits and their European friends would be very happy if Gorman disappeared, so long as they find out where the munitions are stored. We intend to work on that with Gorman.' He glanced at his notes and carried on.

'During the Irish troubles, Gorman was involved in attacks on several homes that were suspected of passing information to the British Army. In every case, the occupants of the houses were slaughtered. In one house that meant a baby was shot in the head in her cot, and a four-year-old boy machined gunned, along with his mother and father. Gorman was at the scene of the crime, but all the witnesses eventually turned up dead, each time with a bullet in the head. Our boy is a cold-blooded killer. But keep in mind that the IRA was just as brutal.' He glanced up and saw the visibly distressed face of Sharon.

'What's the matter?' asked Chas.

'How does someone justify that? The killing of a baby and a child?' she asked.

'They don't. They don't care. Empathy is not part of these criminals' makeup. If it was, they wouldn't commit crime.'

'So, when does the Nazi piece of shit arrive?' asked Peter.

'JFK in nine days' time, so if we are going to plan anything, now is the time. We need to get things moving.'

'Do you know where he's staying?' asked Peter.

'That's the problem, we don't. We've checked. There's no accommodation booking attached to his ticket.'

'That's normal,' said Blue.

They all turned to Blue. 'I did military training on crossing borders and making it hard to be tracked. He'll book when he gets off the plane. He'll have the phone numbers of selected hotels on his phone and will have checked to make sure that accommodation in them is available. That way, he'll see who follows him and he'll be able to spot them on the way to the hotel.'

'Right,' said Chas. 'That makes it hard. We have to track someone from JFK to a hotel in New York in what will be rush-hour traffic. And someone who is used to being tracked.' Chas was concerned.

'Why not go with him?' asked Sharon. They all gawked at her. 'Janice-Rose was telling me how good she is at cadging taxi rides. I'm probably better even if I say so myself! I walk up to whoever it is and offer to pay.' She stood up and gave a sexy little shimmer. 'How could he resist? I've always get the ride.' All the team laughed except Chas.

'Sharon, this man is dangerous. If he suspected you were up to something, he'd kill you,' said Chas with an uncertain look on his face.

'In my experience, I think I would have more to fear from him trying to jam his tongue down my throat than anything else,' said Sharon with supreme confidence.

'You don't know him,' said Chas.

'Oh, but I do. I know him very well. He is one of the homo sapien species named man.' The room erupted into laughter. Chas held his hand up for silence.

'Come on guys, this is serious. Sharon, are you sure you can pull this off?'

Sharon looked at him with wide-open eyes and he knew what he said had come out wrong.

'Can I cadge a lift into New York city with Gorman? Yes. As for pulling it off, I'm not a slut, Chas. I don't even believe in kissing on first dates, silly old conservative me.' The room again burst into raucous laughter and Chas blushed in embarrassment. Peanut chuckled. He was impressed with her cool. Sharon glanced at him, winked and he smiled. She knew what he was thinking.

Hills couldn't help but notice the byplay between them guessed they were recalling the time they had spent in Atlanta together. She was surprised at how much it hurt.

Peanut noticed her looking at him and Sharon. She had laughed with the rest of them but she now looked sad, almost lost. He wondered why. He sort of wished that he and Hills could be close enough to do what he and Sharon had done but that wasn't going to happen. They were both just members of the team. He focused his attention back on Chas.

'Where do we take him?' asked Blue.

'The safe house in Philly and then the camp. The department doesn't know about it.'

'He's not bringing his wife?'

'He's not married, as far as we know. Although he's apparently a ladies' man. So, watch out, Sharon.'

She smiled at him with her eyes again wide and challenging.

'Chas, I can think of better men than that piece of shit that I'd rather have put their tongues in my mouth.'

Chas again blushed slightly and the room laughed at his discomfort. He quickly recovered and carried on.

'Right, now for the boring details. Let's get a coffee before we go through flight times and other stuff.'

Two hours later, the plans were almost finished.

'Tomorrow at nine, everybody? We should be able to wrap it up then,' said Chas, bringing the meeting to a close.

Hills had sat beside Peanut during the planning.

'Interested in a lemon, lime and bitters?' she asked as she packed her papers away.

'Yeah, thanks, Hills.'

'You guys going for a drink?' asked Sharon.

'Yep. Want to come?' asked Hills.

'Only if Chas invites me.'

'Happy to Sharon,' said Chas.

'Don't mean to be a gooseberry, but if you two are going for a drink, I am too,' said Janice-Rose.

'Of course you can come,' said Hills.

Blue and Peter glanced at each other and grinned. 'You're not leaving us out. One in, all in. That makes an official ICT shout, right, Chas?'

Chas sighed. 'In the interests of team harmony, it's an official liquid team meeting. Shall we go?'

Sharon took Chas's arm as they went out the door and, to Peanut's surprise, Hills did the same.

Peanut never got to talk to Hills. She and Janice-Rose ended up deep in conversation and Chas was totally engrossed in what Sharon was telling him. He ended up between Peter and Blue. He was glad to learn more about his team members. Peter leaned over towards Blue.

'Break-up all over?'

'Papers signed, money and lawyers paid, visiting the kids established. You know, the ex and I now get on better than when we were married. Strange.'

Peter shook his head. 'Don't go there. The number of men who get divorced and then after the divorce go and have affairs with their ex is ridiculous. It always ends in heartache. The reasons for the divorce are still there and they don't change. Hear me, Blue, don't go there.'

Peanut glanced at Peter.

'Hard experience, Peter?'

Peter sighed.

'Yep. I learned the hard way. Us men always do. When it comes to affairs of the heart, we're dickheads, and that's because it's just our dicks we think with. Fools, the lot of us.'

He grimaced towards Sharon and Chas. 'I've never seen Chas so tied up. That lady has him around her finger. But she seems nice.'

'She is nice,' Peanut said. 'The fact that she's beautiful is just a bonus. She's a really good person. Smart as well. J.R. has been teaching her some self-defense. When you're that pretty, you get hit on and some men just don't know when to quit.'

'She any good?' Blue asked.

'Not yet, but she will be. Our new home has a basement gym so regular practice is now required.' He nudged Peter.

'Rumor has it that you are a good pistol shot. The basement has a pistol shooting range, courtesy of the previous owners. Want to give us all some lessons? Believe me, we need it.'

'Happy to. I don't live all that far away so it would be handy, especially if I can come and practice myself.'

'More than welcome,' said Peanut. Blue leaned over.

'Let me know when. It's time to upgrade my skills on pea shooters,' he said.

A guffaw of laugher came from Chas as Sharon told him something; from the nature of the laughter, it seemed a bit risqué. Blue grinned.

'It's nice to see Sharon and Chas together. He's never met the right girl. Twenty years in the military, a leader in the Seals and the right lady never showed up. Then he left the military to look after his sick mom. She died three months ago. So, are your sister and Sharon part of this team or what?'

'I'm just a contractor and Janice-Rose is my sister and Sharon is my friend.' He smiled at Blue and Peter. 'As I have read the rules and the setup manual and know what is allowed or not allowed, we all come under the phrase: "Operations and people as required at the ICT leader's discretion." We are at Chas's discretion.'

Chapter 25

'Hills is cool, big brother. You get to talk to her?' asked Janice-Rose.

She sat in the chair across from Peanut, feet up on the settee as the motel television played quietly in the corner.

'Yes, she is, but nope,' Peanut replied. 'You had her tied up. I'm glad you like her.'

'She really smack you in the nuts or is that just a bullshit story?'

'It was for real,' he said.

'And you let her? Losing your touch, big brother.'

'I was handcuffed at the time and Hills wanted to prove a point.'

'And did she?'

'Nah. I still have my nuts and I think that they still work.'

Janice-Rose gave a slight smile and changed the subject.

'You think Sharon and Chas will hit it off? They have gone to his house together.'

Peanut gave a dismissive grunt.

'I hardly think Sharon giving Chas advice on interior decorating is really all that romantic,' he said.

'Yeah? You really do have shit for brains. By the way, Hills is coming to the house tomorrow afternoon after we finish. She's going to help us make a list of what we need to set up home.'

'Why?' he asked.

'Does there have to be a reason? She's a friend and wants to help me set up my room. Don't you want her there?'

'No. I'm happy she's coming. Just wondering if you and she had something else organized, that's all. Later on we could go out for dinner, if you like.'

'We'll see tomorrow,' Janice-Rose said. 'I think I would rather sit on the floor of our new home and eat pizza.' She stood. 'I'm tired. See you in the morning.'

He gave a wave goodnight and got up to make another coffee. His phone rang. He noticed the caller. Hills.

'Hi. What's up?'

'I've rung to apologize. Wanted to talk to you but Janice-Rose and I got into a really good discussion. She's a good kid.'

'I'll never admit that to her face but yes, she is.'

'I'm coming tomorrow afternoon. Do you mind?' she asked.

'No, and I suggested dinner out afterward but J.R. said she would prefer a pizza on the floor of the new house.'

Hills laughed. 'Actually, that sounds pretty good. Hey, do you still run?'

'Yeah, every day if I can. You?'

'I'm a bit slow on it at the moment but still trying. J.R. said that you have a gym in the new home.'

'We have a basement with a wooden floor and yes,' he said, 'it will be a practice gym.'

'I'll have to come over and get a few pointers.'

'More than welcome,' Peanut said.

'Okay, see you tomorrow.' She rung off.

Coffee made, he sat down and mulled over the conversation. That call was almost strange, he thought. Hills could have called him plenty of times in the past but had waited until he was back working with ICT before calling. Why? He decided that tomorrow he would ask. His phone rang again. Sharon.

'Hi, sweetheart. It's getting late and Chas and I have had a few drinks so I am staying over. See you tomorrow?'

'Thanks. I was getting slightly worried. You have a nice night.' He put down his phone. He wondered if Sharon and Chas could make it work, but it was not his business. He put his coffee down; it was still half-full. Time for bed.

***

Peanut opened the front door inwards and stood back, looking from the outside at what was needed for the security upgrade. He found it incredible that the house didn't even have a basic burglar alarm.

He got bumped out of the way by Janice-Rose.

'Ladies first,' she said as she and Hills squeezed past.

He could see that Hills was surprised at the outside look of the house; the elegant stonework, the imitation wrought-iron fence, the engraved heavy oak front door and the beautiful decorative leadlight windows. She walked in and Janice-Rose began to show her around.

Peanut continued his survey of the house, jotting down what they needed to make the house safe. The front and back doors were losers. Beautiful to look at but not designed to withstand any sort of attack. People assumed that by living in genteel neighborhoods they were automatically safe. They weren't. The windows needed steel bars and the porch access at the head of the outside stairs needed some sort of decorative imitation wrought-iron doors that locked. Made in high tensile steel, of course. But it could be made safe.

Hills came down the stairs with Sharon and Janice-Rose, her eyes shining as she walked up to him.

'Peanut, it's beautiful.' She gave him a quick one-armed hug as she admired the kitchen. 'Have you made a list of what you need?' she asked.

'Like lounge furniture, bedroom furniture, dining furniture?'

'Yes,' she said.

'Nope. Not at all. Start shopping tomorrow, I guess. My priority right now is to get a security firm to beef up the doors and windows and other things,' Peanut said. 'The place doesn't even have a security alarm and neither do the fence gates.'

'If you do the security, J.R., Sharon and I will do the furniture including freezer and fridge. Okay?'

'So long as I don't get a pink girly bed with mauve sheets.'

'Promise. The man who dumped me hard on the floor has to have something he-man.'

Janice-Rose saw the opening.

'A single bunk with ropes hanging down for him to climb up?'

Hills laughed as Peanut frowned at Janice-Rose.

Sharon gave him a quick reassuring hug. 'You won't get that,' she said. 'Mandy and I will get you something really classy. Something any lady would want to fall into and cuddle you.'

Janice-Rose snorted.

'I wouldn't bank on that happening soon, if ever,' she said. 'When it comes to women, my brother has shit for brains. I'm never going to be an auntie.'

She picked up her list and flounced off upstairs, Peanut scowled at her retreating back. He ignored the grinning faces of Hills and Sharon, picked up his list and headed to the rear door, needing to work out what was required. He glanced back and saw Hills and Sharon deep in conversation, already making their list. He thought for a moment and smiled. He knew he was lucky to have such people as his friends.

He went outside and again realized the back of the house was closed off from the front. With everything else, he had forgotten. The ten-foot-high fence not only enclosed the backyard, but also cut the section in two, extending out from the rear sides of the house to join the perimeter fence. It was secure, just a few extras needed to make it really safe Access

116

to the back had to be through the locked gate in the short fence from the house to the perimeter fencing. The lock on the fence gate would need replacing, just like all the others.

He was sitting on the floor measuring and checking the rear door when he felt a gentle tap on his shoulder and jumped, startled. He hadn't heard Hills coming back. She sat on the floor beside him.

'Don't take J.R. to heart,' she said. 'She just wants what's best. She sees you not having a girlfriend as something serious. It's not.'

'I know it's not. It's what she loves doing, winding me up. She's a really good person and I love her to bits, but when I get the opportunity, I will hand it straight back, believe it. It's just like self-defense. If you hand it out, you have to be prepared to take it.'

'Speaking of that, when will the gym be up and running?'

Peanut surveyed the house in his mind's eye, seeing all that still had to be done.

'It depends on how fast we can get the house finished and furnished,' he said. 'I've called a carpenter and he can be here pretty promptly, so one week, maybe two. Don't forget we have a kidnapping to do.'

She gave a short nod and stood. 'I'm glad you are back, really glad. I think we make a good team.'

He stood and regarded her, not smiling, serious.

'I think we do too.' He suddenly leaned in and gave her a quick hug. 'Thanks for helping.' He realized he had surprised her with the hug. She was uncomfortable and he eased back and gave a slight smile as Hills looked at him, uncertain, confused. The hug was totally unexpected and she wished she had reacted differently. There was a sudden catcall from Janice-Rose.

'Christ, big brother, is that it? You're supposed to kiss her now. Jesus!'

Peanut and Hills both blushed and gave embarrassed laughs as Janice-Rose shook her head with a sad expression and went back into the lounge. Peanut gave Hills a rueful grin as he sat back down to his notes.

***

They were sitting having a coffee when Peanut remembered.

'Sharon, did you do any research on the Southern States Alliance?'

'That was the problem with the paperwork,' she said, 'it didn't check out. Any half-brained investigator would see that they were just a front; a post box in San Antonio for an address, no physical location, no listing in the companies register. But I did find that it had been set up by one person, a Melissa Albanese. No address supplied other than the post box number.'

'Find anything out about her?'

'Told to drop it, remember?'

Peanut sat thinking. Was Melissa Albanese in any way tied in to the senator? He was from San Antonio. Unlikely, Albanese was not a common name. He would check, just to make sure.

'Peanut, were there any bad guys hanging around the apartment?' Sharon asked.

'Yep. Why?'

'I left a package of personal notes there. I'd like to get them back, if possible.'

'Don't even think it. Those guys know you. You would sign your death warrant and ours as well. They would make you talk, believe it. Let me see what Chas can do. He should be able to arrange for someone to get those notes. I think Hills may still have a key.'

'Would it be safe for them?' she asked, looking worried.

'Should be. They know how to be careful.'

After calling Chas, he picked up his keys and headed for the door. Janice-Rose peered up at him from the couch.

'Going somewhere?' she asked.

'Groceries. We're short. I'll clean out the fridge and freezer at Blair Road after we finish. No point wasting the food over there.'

Janice-Rose stood. 'Can I come?'

He gave a come-on gesture with his hand and she grabbed her coat and followed him to the car.

***

Hills and Chas noticed two cars parked outside Peanut's old apartment but figured even if they belonged to the bad guys the latter wouldn't recognize them. All the ones that knew them were dead.

Seeing nothing suspicious, they walked up the stairs and let themselves into Peanut's old apartment, going straight to the drawer in Janice-Rose's old room to get Sharon's box of notes. The box was tied with a neat red ribbon, clearly important to Sharon. They checked the fridge, freezer and pantry. There wasn't that much food left, but it was silly to waste it. They started loading it into a box to carry back.

'What do you think of Peanut's new house?' Chas asked.

'It's impressive. It'll make a great family home,' said Hills.

'That's what I thought.' He paused a minute then hesitantly asked. 'What do you think of Sharon?' Hills noticed the slightly embarrassed face as he asked. She knew he liked Sharon but was still unsure.

'She's sweet,' said Hills. 'I wonder why she worked for Gorev?'

'She was his girlfriend. But she knows she made a mistake. She told me meeting Peanut and then meeting us has given her a new life and a family. Her parents are dead, by the way. Killed in a car accident by a drunk driver when she was thirteen. Her grandma raised her.'

'That's sad. You and her an item?'

'No. I think that I'm too old. I've never been married and I have to admit, I'm set in my ways,' Chas said.

'Did you tell her that?'

'Yes. She just said that it could be cured, whatever that means.'

'She likes you. Go with it. What have you got to lose?'

'My sanity?' he quipped.

'Is that all? I always thought you were half-mad already!'

He glanced at her and laughed.

The sudden crash of the door bursting open made them both jump. Two heavyset guys stood there. Their guns were pointed ominously at them. Chas and Hills knew the type. Rent a Thug.

'Get your hands up or I shoot,' said one of the thugs.

They raised their hands.

'Well done. Now, sit on the floor, with your backs to the wall.'

'We are federal officers and we're conducting an investigation that you are hindering,' said Chas.

The other thug pressed his gun into Chas's stomach and put his face up close to Chas's.

'Get it clear, bozo. We'll hinder whatever we like. What are you investigating anyway?'

'The people who lived here are of interest to us,' said Chas cautiously.

'Yeah? So, what federal lot are you? The fucking housing inspectors?'

'We're the ICT. We work between the FBI, the NSA and the CIA.'

The thug eyeballed Chas and kept his gun pressed to Chas's stomach. 'That's a fucking mouthful. What exactly do you do?'

'We make sure an investigation goes to the right team so there's no overlap. So matters that are important don't get lost. Put the gun away. You are committing a serious federal offence.'

Without warning the thug smashed Chas in the head with the butt of his gun. Chas slumped to the floor. He bent and removed Chas's gun before putting his gun to Hills's head while he took her gun out of her waist holster.

'On the floor, bitch. Sit with your big-mouth pal. You another Fed?'

'I am and I am cautioning you—you've broken the law and you will be charged.'

'Yeah? No judge and jury here, sweet cheeks.' He held up his pistol. 'This is the only judge here and when it goes bang, your sentence is served.' He noticed the box in her hands, bent down and tore it out of her grasp, opened it, shuffled through and leered when he held up a picture of Sharon.

'Success! This is the bitch we're looking for. Who is she? More importantly, where the fuck is she?'

Peanut and Janice-Rose had finished the grocery shop and were now on their way to Blair Road. He remembered the notes Sharon wanted and he could pick up those notes and check if anything else had been left behind after he and Janice-Rose cleaned out the fridge and freezer. He was surprised to see three cars parked outside. He recognized Chas's car but not the other two. They must belong to the thugs who were watching the apartment. He felt an immediate sense of disquiet. Something was wrong, badly wrong.

Janice-Rose was thinking the same thing.

'They must be up in the apartment,' she quietly stated.

Peanut took the Glock 17 out of the glove compartment and passed it to Janice-Rose.

He ran to the street door, hearing Janice-Rose close behind. It was locked. Grateful that he hadn't yet got around to returning his keys, he gently eased himself inside and motioned to J.R. to follow. The stairway was empty. They ran quietly up the stairs to the door of the apartment. He heard a moan. Hills! They had her! Did he want the cops? No, not yet. He signaled Janice-Rose to come close and whispered, 'We don't want the cops. Only fire if you have to, okay?'

She nodded as he shrugged his jacket back and took out his swords. Gently he opened the door.

There was a guy standing with his back to them with a gun pointed at Chas and he saw blood running down Chas's face. Two other thugs were squatting, their hands holding Hills's legs down and spread apart, and a guy with his pants around his ankles was lying on top of her. Peanut didn't hesitate. The sword in his right hand plunged into the guy who was standing, just to the left of his spine. He gave the blade a quick twist. That quick cutting twist would destroy the heart completely. The sword in his left hand simultaneously plunged into the left side of the chest of one of the guys squatting. The other guy squatting realized something was wrong when the guy that had been standing collapsed onto him. He threw himself back, wondering what was happening. He shoved the body off him, realizing he was dead, and found himself staring up at Peanut. He went for his gun, terror rising in his eyes as the sword swished towards him. Chas lifted his legs up and kicked him in the side of the head, the slight delay giving Peanut time to do the half-turn and plunge his sword in.

The thug lying on top of Hills suddenly became aware that things weren't right. He turned his head and saw a sword buried in his pal's chest. He jerked in panic at the sight of his other men lying dead on the floor.

With her legs now free, Hills saw Funny Man looking desperately for his gun. Feeling him lift his hips up to get traction, she lifted her hips up to his, wrapping her legs around him, crossing her ankles and clamping on tight. His movement now restricted, Funny Man struggled desperately to get free. Hills's martial arts training, her running, and the workouts with weights now showed. It had made her legs strong. Ankles crossed, she squeezed. Funny Man couldn't get out of her clamp. Now in a blind panic, he swung his fist back to punch her and felt a sudden sharp sting in the back of his fist. He looked at his hand as the sword disappeared through his fist and out the other side and another sword pricked the side of his neck. It stung; it was sharp and it had penetrated the skin.

The voice was calm, almost conversational.

'If I plunge this sword into your neck, the damage is irreversible. You'll bleed out and be unconscious in two minutes and dead in four. I suggest you get off Ms. Hiller before I get really annoyed and remove your cock and balls, preferably while you're still alive to watch.'

He flicked the sword out of the thug's fist and gave him a quick prick in the ass. The thug's face froze in fright.

'Can you move?' Peanut asked Hills.

'Yes.'

'Chas, can you untie Hills, please, and pass me that tie.'

121

Chas crawled over and untied Hills. She sat up and then stood, her skirt dropping down. Chas stood, groggy on his feet and handed her his jacket to cover her breasts. Janice-Rose hugged her as Hills tried not to cry.

Peanut apologized to Hills and Chas.

'I'm sorry. This is my fault that these guys are here. I want to find out how they knew.'

Hills stared at Peanut through her tears as he tied the thug's hands behind his back and tied his ankles together.

'Whatever you have to do to find out what you need from that maggot,' she said, 'do it as painfully as possible, please.'

Peanut grimaced.

'That will be up to him.'

He squatted in front of Funny Man and put his sword back at his throat.

'That lady you tried to rape is special,' said Peanut as he poked the thug under the chin with his sword. Funny Man jerked his head back as a trickle of blood ran down the blade. 'All your second chances are gone. Answer my questions or I'll make sure your last days on this earth are extremely painful. I'm very good at it.'

'Can you pull up my pants, please?' asked Funny Man.

'No. What's your name?' asked Peanut.

'You might be a federal agent, but I have my rights and you have to hand me over to the police so I can get a lawyer.'

Peanut sighed again. 'Yes, we are federal agents, but not the sort that you want to meet,' said Peanut as he picked up Hills's torn blouse and panties. 'What's your name?'

Funny Man stared at Peanut with a belligerent look. Peanut punched him in the nose and as the thug reeled backwards, he punched him in the testicles. Funny Man fell forward and huddled into the fetal position. Peanut grabbed his nose and when his mouth opened to breathe, Peanut rammed in the balled-up blouse.

Peanut took his other sword and drove it into Funny Man's thigh and twisted it hard in against the bone. Funny Man tried to scream, choking on the blouse. Peanut twisted the sword into a calculated spot. He knew he wouldn't hit an artery or a major vein as the sword ground against bone. He pulled it almost out, then plunged it in again. The muffled scream echoed around the apartment, then stopped as the thug fainted.

Peanut stood up, walked to the kitchen and filled a pot with water. The thug began spluttering when Peanut sloshed the water over his head. He slowly came to his full senses and looked up at the bleak face of Peanut, his face was now a mask of terror. Peanut leant forward and grabbed one of his testicles and squeezed, as he flicked his penis with the point of the sword. The thug moaned as he tried to speak. Peanut removed the gag.

'Well?' he said.

'Ivan Popov!' His voice was hoarse.

'Who's your boss?'

'Milo Volkov.'

'And who employs him?'

'He's his own boss.'

'He brings in the drugs, does he?'

'Yes, he's the major distributor.'

'How did you find us?'

'Elimination. We went through all the tenants listed on this section of the street and we found only three apartments that could be yours.'

Peanut was stunned at the tenacity of the thugs. They would never give up. Peanut glanced at Chas, Hills, and Janice-Rose.

'Shall I load them into the car and take them to the usual place?' Peanut asked Chas.

'Yes. I'll help you and get the petrol,' replied Chas.

Peanut bent and picked up one of the dead thugs using a fireman's lift and carried the body to one of the thug's cars, as Chas came behind him with another. Peanut let Chas lift out the last body as he turned, crouched, and hit Funny Man hard in the temple, knocking him unconscious. He carried him to the car and put him in the center of the rear seat, latching the seat belt in, slamming the door shut and speaking to Janice-Rose.

'Could you get my car and follow Chas? These guys had three cars here the other day, they might be back.'

Janice-Rose took Hills's hand and led her down the stairs. Tears had started running down Hills's face and she didn't even bother to wipe them away.

Chas drove off, Janice-Rose and Hills following. Peanut pulled out behind them. He arrived at the quarry and, getting out of the car, took photos of the bodies. Funny Man had regained consciousness, his words indistinct through the gag.

'You have to take me to the hospital. I need medical attention. Please!'

Peanut stood outside the car, ignoring him. This thug was the last one alive of the four heroes that were going to commit rape and torture and then murder Hills and Chas. He was now begging for help. No chance. He had noticed that not once had Funny Man said that he was sorry. It was all about him. He was a pathological piece of human flotsam.

Chas and Hills arrived, Chas carrying the jerry can. Peanut offered to take it, but Chas shook his head.

'Hills is one of ours. My pleasure this time, Peanut.'

Chas poured the gas over the bodies and over Funny Man, standing back as Hills quietly stepped forward. She stood looking for a few seconds, holding up the match so Funny Man could see what was going to happen. Funny Man was now one scared piece of turd, shaking in terror as he sat there. Hills could smell the gas and smell the feces from the emptied bowels of the dead and she wondered if Funny Man had emptied his in his terror. If he was a reflection of his boss, Volkov, then she intended to work with Peanut to get rid of him, permanently.

She stepped back, clear of the car as she put the head of the match under her thumbnail, and then flicked the match in through the window. An instant whump and then a small explosion of flames gushed out the windows as the car went up, the muffled screams echoing around the quarry and then fading. Peanut took photos and stood beside her for a second, watching.

'*Consequences*, Hills. They just caught up on those turds. Well done.'

She glanced at him. His face was bleak and hard. She gave a slight smile and nodded as she turned and they walked to their cars.

'I'll go with Peanut and J.R., Chas,' Hills said.

Chas gave Hills a quick nod and glanced at Peanut.

'Look after her, big guy.' He studied Hills a second. 'You need anything, anything at all, just call.' He gave Peanut a nod as he drove off, his mind full of the night's events. It had been so close.

Peanut followed Chas back to the main road. Hills now appeared remarkably calm.

'You okay, Hills?'

'Sore tits, Peanut, but that prick never got his dick in. You and J.R. arrived just in time to save this maiden's virtue. Thanks. But I will still go and get a check; you never know where filth like that have been.' She leaned over and gently kissed him on the cheek; he peered in the rearview mirror and saw Janice-Rose smiling in the back seat. The kiss on the cheek was nice, it was just like old times and he noticed that as she sat back, she gently caressed Sharon's box, still largely intact though minus the pretty red ribbon.

That box had nearly cost them their lives.

Hills said no when they asked her if she wanted company and to talk.

Peanut reached over and touched her arm.

'Anything at all, just call. Please.'

She clasped his arm and squeezed and then climbed out of the car. She wanted a shower to scrub herself clean of that dirty piece of shit that had touched her. She had stood close to the car before she lit the match. She had held it up high so that piece of trash could see it wasn't him and his gun passing sentence; it was her and she was both judge and jury.

She stood in the shower, scrubbing, soaping her body and her vagina, wanting to feel clean, knowing it would probably take some time, if ever, to feel really clean. Peanut and Chas and Janice-Rose had been so supportive. She knew that if she rang any one of them, they would come. But right now she needed to sleep, to block out the horror of the day.

Late that night, she jolted awake, the thug's words echoing in her mind.

Lie still or I'll rip your fucking tits off, bitch!

She then wished she had someone to hold.

Chapter 27

Peanut sent the pictures the next day to every contact on Popov's phone, then turned the phone off and threw it into a trash can. He wanted all Popov's contacts to know Volkov was sending them to die. He knew the psychology of the Volkovs of this world and he would be angry. Thugs ruled through fear and when that fear was broken, their rule was over.

He had been thinking about Hills off and on, hoping she was okay. He started to dial her number, then he changed his mind. It would be better to keep his distance. Let her contact him if she needed anything. He gave a wry grin as he thought about it. He didn't want another smack in the nuts for asking annoying, prying questions.

They spent four hours that morning doing small arms practice, but when Peter arrived to assess their standard, it became clear a lot of work still had to be done. In typical fashion Peter bluntly told them that all, except Chas, were below standard. He wasn't polite.

'Fucking rubbish!' were his exact words. However, he was impressed with the range in the basement. It was a 'professional' set up he informed them.

'There are now no excuses if you miss what you are aiming at, huh?' he said. 'Practice is all it is.'

That afternoon, the new furniture they had ordered would be arriving along with assorted household effects that the women had chosen. It was a major change from a fully furnished apartment. Tomorrow the metal workers would be fitting the security screens on the windows. The day after that they would have the practice runs for the kidnapping of Gorman. Then they would all move to New York for the final week of checks. Peanut hoped it went well for all their sakes.

Sharon walked in. 'Sweetheart, did you check on Melissa Albanese?'

Peanut smiled ruefully. 'Sorry, not yet.'

'Leave it to me, I'll do it.'

'Thanks. Hey, I know you are seeing Chas, but regardless, you have a home here—you know that, don't you?'

'Yes, sweetheart, I do. Why?'

'If you and Chas hit it off, don't feel bad if you decide to move out. We love having you here. Just come and go as you please and if you need a shoulder, I'm here.'

'Peanut, I think Chas and I as permanent could be some time off, if ever. He's set in his ways but maybe with a little bit of re-education? I still don't know. Time will tell. But I do think he likes me.'

'He likes you, Sharon, believe it.'

The furniture began to arrive and Peanut left it to Sharon, Janice-Rose, and Hills. He was busy talking designs and strength with the metal workers and then the security guys arrived to set up alarms, cameras, sensors, monitors, automatic hard-drive recording, and finally, a new burglar alarm. He finished talking with the metal-work guys and noticed the security guys leaving.

His early feelings about the house was correct. It needed alterations. The current layout meant that it would be almost impossible to fend off a planned and organized attack. As the nearest police station was thirty minutes away and then add the time for the SWAT team to get ready, Peanut estimated that any meaningful help in defending against an organized attack was near to an hour away. No security had been ever considered when the house was built. Even with a new lock on the side gate, the gate could still be forced open and an attack on both front and back was then possible. The house layout meant that it could not be defended from that sort of attack. The layout had to change. That meant a remodeling of the center of the bottom story. He began drawing up plans, knowing that the result had to be aesthetically pleasing as well as practical. It was their home, after all.

Two hours later he was happy he had the basics. He knew there was no defense against stun grenades being fired through the windows or high-powered weapons being used but blunting an attack to gain time until help arrived was the aim. And that raised the sixty-four million dollar question. Would it happen? Would the bad guys find out where they lived and attack? Peanut suddenly realized he was nodding. Of course they would. This was all about survival. He began to make a list of all the weapons they would need. He felt quite despondent when he studied it. It was a long list. They had to be stored in a handy place. He relooked at his plans. Storage for all those weapons would have to be built in. He sighed and began altering his plans.

He was finished and sitting daydreaming when he got a gentle tap on his shoulder.

'Come see the new furniture,' Hills invited.

The next hour was spent being shown from one new item to another, including a classic plain dining table, large comfortable lounge chairs, and new beds. He couldn't stop smiling; they had turned the house into a beautiful home. They finished by showing him his bedroom. Janice-Rose couldn't help herself.

'We argued over the size of the single bunk. We knew you wouldn't want anything more than two-foot wide.'

Peanut stared at her and frowned. He knew she was winding him up. As they walked into his bedroom, he was stunned by the sight of a king-sized bed with beautiful carved oak ends. In the large room, it didn't look a bit out of place. The quilts and duvets were the perfect match. He turned to them.

'It is stunning. It's beautiful. Shit, it must have cost, but it's worth it. Who?' Peanut asked.

Hills smiled, delighted that he liked it and happy to share the credit. 'I picked it, with Sharon's and J.R.'s help of course.'

He turned and hugged her.

'Thanks, Hills.' He noticed that this time she responded and it felt nice really nice. She pulled back.

'I'm glad you approve,' she said.

'The only thing left, big brother,' said Janie-Rose, 'is giving it a speed test, like rebound efficiency, sag response when there are two of you in action in the middle, huh? It's a workbench after all.'

'J.R., there is more to a bed than sex.'

'Yeah? What planet are you on, big brother?' She glanced over at a grinning Sharon and Hills, sighing and shaking her head. 'See, I told you; I'm never going to be an auntie!'

***

Peanut watched Janice-Rose and Sharon try the moves that he had taught them.

'Whoa, Sharon, when you make that move,' he walked over and tapped her leg, 'move this leg back by about four inches to give you more power, more leverage. Try that series of moves again.' He watched closely and was pleased with the improvement. 'Now roll those moves into the next lot that I showed you. You know them, J.R. Help Sharon if she forgets. It should be one seamless flow. Then go through the moves you need to disarm someone. Both rifle and pistol.'

He turned and walked over to Hills, going through a series of striking moves he had taught her, using a punching bag. He watched; she was nearly perfect. She stopped and grimaced at him, sweating hard. He grinned and put a padded vest and helmet on. The vest had a front that hung down and covered his groin.

He pointed to himself. 'Go through that sequence against me.'

She turned, took a deep breath, and hit out. His blocking was too good; she couldn't get a hit in. She paused, breathing heavily and bending over to get some air in, then straightened as he grinned at her, taking the padded top off and handing it to her.

'Your turn.'

She was able to keep out some of his hits but she knew from the force of the hits that he was pulling his punches. He held up his hands to stop.

'Well done. Two days ago you wouldn't have stopped any of those, but now, I'm impressed, Ms. Hiller. You are a very good student. Let me show you the slight errors you are making, just before we stop for the day.'

He stood behind her and took her body hard up against his. 'When you see that move, pull this leg back,' he hooked his leg around hers and pulled it back, 'and then move your body this way and forward and block here, in front of your lower rib cage. That will deflect that hit.'

She was suddenly aware of how close they were standing, of how tight their bodies were as he moved her from position to position and was barely aware of what he was saying as he moved away.

'Are you sure you are not practicing those moves at your apartment?'

She turned and gave him a slightly embarrassed how-did-you-know look.

'Just a little,' she admitted. 'I didn't want to look like a complete nincompoop, did I?'

'You're definitely not a nincompoop. When we come back from New York we will step it up a bit. For now, those blocks are the key to everything else. All the other moves build on them.' He smiled. 'We'll go through those moves together again next session, just to get it right, okay?'

Sharon and Janice-Rose saw them talking and came over. They were both sweating heavily.

'That it for the day, boss?' Sharon asked with a cheeky smile.

'Yep. We can all go for a short three-mile run, if you like? Just to cool down?' Three heads shook vigorously. He knew the day's exercise was over.

He turned to Hills. 'Stay the night, Mandy? You might as well. It's getting pretty late.'

Hills was about to shake her head and then saw Janice-Rose nodding furiously and mouthing, 'Please? Please?'. Sharon smiled at the byplay. She had a date with Chas and Janice-Rose would be left alone with just Peanut. Hills shrugged, figuring it would be nice to try out one of the new beds she'd help select.

'Huh, okay. Thanks.'

'Big brother is cooking, okay?' Janice-Rose smiled at her frowning brother.

'Whatever is in the freezer and is pre-made and easy,' Peanut said.

They sat in the lounge in their dressing gowns after dinner. Peanut had put the dinner dishes in the washer and was ready to relax, sprawled in a recliner chair, the television playing quietly up on the wall. He went over the house plans with Janice-Rose and Hills, and Hills pointed out some weaknesses. Her time with the SWAT team showed as she talked about the homes they had attacked and had found hard to enter. The changes were slight but significant.

'You think that they will attack, don't you?' asked Janice-Rose.

Peanut gave his sister a flat stare. 'Yes. Put odds on it? Eight to two.'

'That sure, huh?' asked Hills.

'Yes.'

'Shit!'

Hills and Janice-Rose began talking, and Peanut started writing more notes on his laptop. Hills wondered what that was about. She felt at home sitting there. It was like it was her home. She assumed it was because she had helped furnish it, but it just seemed that it was a home to them all. But not her, she reminded herself. She and Janice-Rose talked until the day's hard exercise took its toll and Janice-Rose stood and yawned.

'I'm off to bed. That exercise has wiped me out. You are too hard on us, big brother. I need my beauty sleep.' She quickly glanced at Peanut, seeing his mouth open to make a quip. 'Not a word, big brother!' She made a zip-it sign across her lips.

'I wasn't going to comment on your beauty sleep,' he said. 'I was going to wish you good night. For the record, you are beautiful, just a pain at times, but then, hey, so am I.'

'You surely are. Love you. Talk to Mandy about how to make me an auntie, will you? She might give you some advice. You need it. Night.'

She flounced up the stairs, as Peanut gave a snort and then a chuckle as Hills blushed and laughed. She glanced at him.

'Do you?' she asked.

'Do I need any advice on making my sister an auntie? No, I don't think I do. Not the practical side, anyway.'

'And the unpractical side, the romantic side?'

He was uncomfortable at her query.

'The romantic side never seems to work out. Probably my fault. I suppose that maybe one day it might work out, but in the meantime it's better to get the New York thing out of the way.'

She felt disappointed. He wasn't going to be anything more than a friend anytime soon.

'Night, Peanut.'

'Night, Hills.'

Chapter 28

They sat in the bar of the hotel on 8th Avenue, yet again looking over the plans for the next day. It was drab New York weather outside. The occasional squall battered the floor-to-ceiling windows. It had been damp and miserable all day.

They had been through the arrivals' section at the airport three times and they knew how it would go down to the exact minute. But as in all things with a human element, there was always uncertainty. Peanut knew that Chas was worried. It showed, all during the last week as they practiced. Something had changed. Sharon was now more than just a team member to him, she and him had become close and Sharon had stayed at his house for most of the week. Peanut figured that if that if Sharon was now an item, Chas would be terrified that Jerry Gorman would harm her. Clearly, Chas was afraid that something might happen to her. If Gorman suspected anything, if there had been a leak, he would kill her, and kill her in in public, if he was forced to. Jerry Gorman's record for violence was well known. He might be sophisticated, but he was still a heartless killer and just a bit too clever to get caught.

'After the pickup, we'll drive to Philly and stay in the safe house for the night,' said Chas. 'The following morning we'll travel to the camp. Our guest will be handcuffed and locked in a room with no windows. All good?'

Everyone murmured their approval.

***

Blue sat on a seat near the luggage carousel and spoke to Peter.

'No sign yet, still unloading.' Him and Peter were the cover guys. If Gorman was being met, they would step in before he got near a taxi and arrest him and his friend or friends, whatever the case may be. Chas was hanging back, ready to move, depending on the circumstances and if needed would be there to assist. Not that Blue or Peter expected any problems.

'Gorman's arrived, walking to the carousel' Blue watched. There was already a line of two deep around the carousel but it didn't bother Gorman. Blue noticed he looked at the line and then pushed two old folks aside so he could stand next to the carousel. Typical. He didn't push in where there were people who might object, he pushed in on the old couple. Blue absolutely loathed people who did that. If Gorman wasn't the target and he wasn't on a mission, he would have sorted it. At six three and solid, Blue tended to sort most things. The old couple protested but Gorman ignored them, standing firm up against the carousel. The alarm went and the carousel started. The old couple got their bags and moved off, Gorman now looking pissed. He had pushed in and still had to wait. Blue chucked to himself, Maybe there was a god after all. He rang Peter.

'Yeah?'

'Gorman on his way. Watch him. He's a rude prick. If we have to arrest him and he objects in any way, we dump him, hard.'

'What's got into your pants?' Blue chuckled and told Peter about the old couple. Peter was quiet a minute.

'Okay Blue. Pass it on to Peanut. He's over at the taxi stand. If Gorman has to be dumped, Peanut is probably the best one to do it.' Blue grinned. Peanut was definitely the best one to do it.

***

'Ready?' Chas asked.

'Yes,' Sharon replied.

129

Chas admired Sharon. She was gorgeous in a dress especially bought for the hijack, a light yellow jacket and perfect makeup, slight heels in elegant shoes. With a gold watch, and minimal gold jewelry, it all smacked of money, wealth and prestige. The sort of look that makes someone take a second glance and it tends to make a polite request hard to refuse.

As the passengers from the London flight filed out through the exit, Peanut and the team stood out of direct sight, waiting. Jerry Gorman walked past with an arrogant self-assurance that spoke of being in charge, his bearing almost ex-military.

'Here we go,' Peanut said quietly. Chas had disappeared, as he was in one of the tracking cars. Janice-Rose was the emergency backup if anything went wrong with Sharon. They simply could not afford to lose sight of Gorman. Peanuts' phone bussed silently in his pocket. Blue.

'Yeah?'

'Careful with this prick Gorman,' Blue said. 'He walked to the luggage carousel to get his bag and shoved an old lady and an old man out of the way, just to be first. The old man complained and he just ignored them. He is one arrogant rude prick. When he got his bag and left, he deliberately bumped the old man into the carousel. A complete shit head.'

'Thanks. Getting him in custody will be revenge enough, I would think.'

'Yeah. Just don't fuck about if you have to do any strong arm stuff. Just take the prick out.' Peanut grinned at Blue's comment. He knew Gorman's history. Fucking about was the last thing he would do. He stood well out of Gorman's line of sight as he scanned the crowd and watched Gorman.

He watched as Sharon walked up to Gorman as he stood in the taxi queue. He noticed as she stood close, just as she had once done to him. Not too close to be pushy, but close enough to not be ignored. She placed a hand on Gorman's arm as she talked and Peanut knew instantly that she had success. Gorman was smiling, talking and he couldn't keep his eyes off her as Sharon listened intently. The smiles were all mutual, her hand had slid up to Gorman's elbow, and she and him mutually nodded. She didn't mind as he took her arm as a taxi pulled up and he escorted her into the taxi, easing in beside her. Sharon had done it. She had cadged a lift with the target. As the taxi pulled away Peanut sent a text to Chas and Hills.

'Sharon and target on their way.'

The reply from Hills came instantly.

'I'll pick you up just outside the drop-off point,' she said. Peanut waited as Hills pulled up and he settled into the seat as she drove off.

'First impressions?' she asked as she turned onto the main exit road.

'Sharon looks like she's in charge. She's cool, calm and collected,' Peanut replied. 'Blue called and said that Gorman was rude and arrogant at the luggage carousel. He shoved two old folks out of the way getting his bags. Just a rude prick.' They rode in silence as they concentrated on keeping the taxi in sight. It wasn't easy with the road being a major airport access way and yellow taxis ducking in and out of the lines of flowing traffic.

***

They were coming up to the Queensboro Bridge and Hills began concentrating even more as the traffic was becoming really heavy. She knew she would have to turn off and park as soon as Sharon called in their destination.

Peanut's phone rang. Sharon.

'He's staying at the Plaza, right on Central Park. Pick me up around the corner on 59th Street.'

'We'll be there in five, Sharon. We're only three blocks away.' His phone went dead and Hills viewed the GPS and then gave Peanut a querying look. How did he know how close they were? He pointed to his mobile sitting in between his legs and it was showing exactly

130

where they were. She smiled and five minutes later, pulled to the curb. Sharon climbed in and Hills eased back out into the stream of traffic. Peanut glanced back at Sharon and congratulated her.

'You did good,' said Peanut. She high-fived him. 'We know where he is now.'

'I watched him check in. He's definitely staying there,' said Sharon.

'You went in with him?' he asked.

'Yes. We were talking. We're having a drink this evening.'

'Really? Shit, that'll help no end. I'll ring Chas.' Peanut rang and quickly explained to Chas what had happened. Chas's response was blunt.

'A meeting, Peanut. The café around the corner.'

Five minutes later they walked in and Chas was already sitting there with a row of coffees set up. He stood and hugged Sharon. Peanut heard him whisper quietly.

'Thank God you are safe' and she kissed him gently on the lips. Peanut grinned. He was surprised at how easy it had all been to get this close to Gorman. Why wasn't he met at the airport? It could only be that he was sneaking in. Did he use his own name on his passport? He had a feeling that he might not have. If that was the case, they would have to be doubly careful, just in case the authorities noticed. But they could check that out later, when he was under their control. He kept grinning at Sharon and Chas; it was nice they were now an item. Janice-Rose noticed the kiss then congratulated Sharon.

'Well done. Shopping, then a drink. Brilliant.'

'Not just that either.' said Sharon. 'I told him a fib about my little brother. I said his name is Neville and he and his girlfriend could pick us up and take us for a drink. He wants to meet both of you. He loves America and Americans! He's never been here before.'

'Well done,' said Chas, now looking even more worried. 'When are you meeting him?'

'At six. Thirty minutes from now,' said Sharon.

'Shit, that soon? We cannot afford any mistakes now. We have made contact, now we have to execute the pickup.'

'Does the department know where we are taking him tonight?' asked Sharon.

'Nope. They know nothing about this operation,' replied Chas.

Peanut suddenly felt decidedly uneasy. What they were doing was illegal, criminal, and if the department decided on a different approach, it could throw them to the wolves. That was the last thing any of them wanted. He grinned to himself, the precautions he had taken on deniability made it impossible for him to be held accountable. In the meantime, he was going to keep it like that. He just didn't trust the department.

Chapter 29

Peanut had expected the traffic to be heavy outside the hotel where Gorman was staying, but at that time of day, it wasn't. He watched Sharon walk elegantly into the foyer, and two minutes later stroll out of the door with a smiling Jerry Gorman on her arm. In the flesh, Peanut thought Gorman looked threatening, his craggy face and hard blue eyes that questioned everything, despite his easy smile.

'Jerry, this is Neville, my brother,' said Sharon.

Peanut held out his hand. Gorman's grip was a little too firm. Was he trying to show he was the boss? But Peanut also detected a reserve in Gorman's body language and he tried to set him at his ease, grinning cheekily as he opening the SUV's doors. Sharon got in and took Gorman's hand, pointing to Janice-Rose and Hills as he climbed in

'That's my kid sister and that's Mandy, Peanut's girlfriend. I asked her along as she really knows fashion.'

She smiled up at Jerry and cuddled in.

'Neville can go get a coffee or something, can't you?'

'Yep, glad to. Women and fashion are not among my strong suits.'

Hills butted in.

'Amen to that!'

Gorman chuckled, leaning forward in the seat and smiling at Hills. Peanut smiled inwardly. They were right. Gorman fancied himself as a ladies man.

Standing on the pavement, Peanut caught movement out of the corner of his eye and looked back towards the hotel. Shit! They were coming. He could see the bulges in their jacket pockets. They weren't running, but it was a very hurried walk.

'Time to go, guys,' Peanut called as he slammed the car door. 'Go, sis, go! Don't wait for me.'

Janice-Rose started to accelerate out into the traffic as one burly thug shoved Peanut aside and reached for the door handle, calling out to stop. His feet were swept out from under him and he went down face first into the gutter. The second guy bashed into Peanut, grabbing at his jacket. Peanut chopped him in the neck, hitting the Vagus nerve and incapacitating him instantly, watching him slump to the ground. Peanut spun on his heels, noticing the first guy on his knees, getting out of the gutter. He kicked him in the head, aiming for the temple and then turned, and sprinted in the same direction as the SUV. It was all about putting distance between him and the scene of the crime. He pulled out his phone and rang Hills.

'Where are you?' she asked.

'Running up the street.'

'Okay I see you. I'm half a block in front. There's nobody following you.'

He kept on running and saw the car moving slowly into the curb. He pulled the door open and jumped in, shoving Gorman into the middle, grinning as he noticed Hills, sitting sideways in the front seat with her pistol pointed back at Gorman. Gorman stared at Peanut as he got his wind back.

'I've just been told you are federal agents sent to keep me safe, is that correct?' asked Gorman. His accent was Irish and he didn't look the least bit upset. In fact, he appeared quite calm.

'We will let Chas, our boss, fill you in. We're on our way to meet him now.' Peanut phoned Chas. 'There's been a leak,' Peanut said to Chas. 'Some guys were waiting for Jerry. We'll have to dump this car. They had radios and they'll call in its license plate and the last position.'

'Drive on a bit further to make sure no one's following, then pull over and park,' Chas instructed 'Lock it and I'll pick you up. I have a seven-seater dark blue SUV. Look out for it.'

When Hills squinted back the blue SUV was only three cars back.

'Turn left,' said Hills.

'How come you knew this alley was here?' asked Peanut.

'I used to be New York cop,' Hills replied.

Peanut grimaced.

'See what I mean when I say I know nothing about you and Chas, and for that matter, Blue and Peter.' She glanced at him as Chas pulled up behind.

'Yeah, but you do now,' she said. 'And as time goes on, you will know even more. Let's get on board Chas's wagon, everybody.'

Chas watched as they climbed on board, letting Hills take over the driving, noticing the now slightly worried look on Gorman's face. Hills eased out into the street, accelerating quietly away.

'Hills, will you ring the rental company when we get to the safe house and tell them where the SVU is?' Hills nodded. 'Good, we are going to the safe house in Philadelphia. Okay? We'll have a bit of a drive, but it will give us plenty of time to talk.'

Gorman studied the team.

'Do you guys have any identification?' he asked. Chas handed over his ID.

'You are not FBI? What is this ICT?'

'The FBI wouldn't handle this because you're a foreign national.

'Any idea about those guys at the hotel?' Chas asked Peanut.

'Not ours. Russian by the sound of the accent. Clumsy and not well trained. A New York cop would eat them alive,' said Peanut.

'Like Hills?'

Peanut laughed. 'Hills would kill them. Metaphorically speaking, of course.' He watched as Hills blushed slightly with the praise.

'Why were they after me?' asked Gorman. I'm just here on vacation.'

'We know you are *not* here on vacation,' said Chas.

'Then you tell me; what am I here for?' Gorman asked.

'To drum up support among white Protestants to support your cause.'

Gorman gave a noticeable start.

'So, tell me, what is your role in this?' he asked.

'We're just the pickup and keep you safe, guys,' Chas said.

'Have you notified the authorities about those men back at the hotel?'

'I have and they have vanished.'

'Will they find them?' Gorman asked.

Chas gave a noncommittal shrug. 'Greater New York has twenty-five million people. The airports will be watched, but if they rent a car and travel, they're gone.'

If Chas wasn't mistaken, Gorman seemed happy they had got away.

'My belongings are in my hotel room. I suppose they are lost, now?' Gorman asked.

Chas pulled out his phone. 'Peter, we need a hotel room cleared. Take Blue with you, just in case someone is watching. What's your room number?'

'Five ten.'

'Hear that Peter?' Chas laughed at something Peter said and ended the call.

'Take us to Philly, Hills. Peter's going to pick up some pizzas. I don't know about the rest of you, but I'm hungry,' said Chas.

It was a quiet trip to the safe house.

***

Peter and Blue arrived with the pizzas and Gorman's bags and everyone, including Gorman, gathered in the lounge to eat. Gorman didn't say much apart from the odd remark to

Sharon who was sitting next to him. As yet he hadn't worked out that he had been kidnapped. Peanut nudged Janice-Rose.

'J.R., did you get to see Mom yet? You said you would.'

'Yeah. I paid a visit. It was awkward for about five seconds and then we hugged and we both apologized. I won't ever get another mom, so I'm going to keep in touch. When this is all over, that is.'

'That'll make Mom happy. Thanks.'

'Hey, I saw in the rearview mirror you take those guys out,' Janice-Rose said. 'When are you going to show me some of those moves? I need more practice, big brother.'

Hills reached over and nudged her.

'We'll practice together,' Hills said. 'I have to get his nibs to upgrade my skills as well. I thought I was good and he dumped me like I was a novice. Hurt my head and hurt my pride.'

Janice-Rose shook her head.

'You're a rough fucking prick, brother.'

'I said I was sorry!'

'He did and I accepted,' Hills said. 'Besides, I had hit him in the nuts.'

Janice-Rose winked.

'Yes, but you can rub them better sometime, eh?'

Peanut glared at his sister. 'J.R., would you like to go sit somewhere else?'

'Nope. And I'm sorry if I offended.'

Hills lightly touched her arm.

'None taken. Just ignore Peanut. The mention of nuts makes him a tad uncomfortable. It does with most men.'

Hills glanced over at Peanut, seeing the bland look.

'You seem very mellow about things?' she said.

He gave an evil little smile.

'Just wait until J.R. brings her next boyfriend home,' Peanut said. 'Boy, am I looking forward to that!'

'What goes round, comes around, right?' Hills said.

'Precisely.'

After the pizza was finished, Gorman went to the small room Chas had allocated him. Chas followed and turned the key in the lock as soon as he was inside.

'Hey! What are you doing? Let me out! What the hell's going on?' Gorman shouted. Chas put the key in his pocket and walked away with a self-satisfied smirk on his face.

Gorman kept up his hammering on the door for quite some time, but no one paid him any attention.

Chas held the meeting in a small conference room at the safe house. There was seating for around fifteen or twenty, a large whiteboard on a stand at the front of the room and a monitor fixed to the wall above it. Chas knew he wouldn't need any of it. He smiled at Janice-Rose. He knew what he was about to say would be welcome. When he had first met her, he was unsure but she had integrated herself well into the team, despite her youth. He had been staggered at her rapid development, mainly due to Peanut and Hills. Peanut had taught her not just defense but attack and on attack she was just as deadly as Hills. But what had convinced him was Peter. He had taken a shine to Janice-Rose and they had become friends, and she had blossomed with the extra firearms training.

Chas had walked down to the pistol range in Peanuts basement and saw J.R. doing rapid firing at a moving target. The Glock in her hand was firing nearly as fast as a semi-automatic rifle. She was countering the recoil of each shot and hitting the moving target every time. He had glanced at Peter and raised an eyebrow. When Janice-Rose walked off to replace the target, he raised an eyebrow at Peter.

'She's that good?' he asked.

'Yeah.'

'Good as you?'

Peter had grunted.

'Tell you what, Chas, it would be that close that I wouldn't put any money on it.'

'Team member?'

'If she isn't already, she should be.'

Chas had nodded and walked out the door, his mind now made up.

'It is my pleasure to announce that Janice-Rose is now officially a member of the team. At the conclusion of the meeting you'll need to sign an oath of secrecy, Janice-Rose.'

'Way to go! Just like the Secret Service, eh?' Janice-Rose was happy. Chas chuckled.

'Not quite, J.R.,' he said. 'Every government department requires that these days, unfortunately.' Janice-Rose's face was one large delighted smile.

'Okay, now let's get down to business,' said Chas. 'Where do you think those guys at the hotel came from?' he asked Peanut.

'I'm sure they were Volkov's men. They spoke like they were foreign, the way Russians speak English. The same as those thugs of Volkov's that we've already run into.'

'So how did they know where Gorman was? Did they follow him from the airport?' Chas asked.

'The only person who knew what hotel Gorman was using was Gorman, right?' said Peanut. 'That means we must have been followed. You suspected that might happen and it did, I believe. Are you sure no one knows about the camp?'

'You could be wrong. Gorman said in the taxi he was meeting friends later on,' said Sharon. 'When I left him in the lobby and I looked back, he was on his mobile. He could have told someone else where he was.'

'If he was followed, that means the department's security was breached. Highly unlikely, but not impossible. I think it's more likely that there's a tie-up between Gorman and Volkov.'

'If security has been breached, they'll be waiting for us at the camp.'

'There goes our night's sleep. We need to get back to the camp and make sure it's secure before you guys arrive,' said Hills.

'Just you and Peanut?' asked Chas.

'Yes, we can handle it,' she said. 'Especially if the thugs at the hotel are any indication.'

'Okay then. Off you go. Keep in touch. And please no heroics. Have you got that?'

Chapter 30

Peanut was driving the second leg. Hills had driven the first one until she found herself becoming sleepy and losing concentration.

The miles rolled by. Peanut was still feeling fresh when they approached Baltimore. The camp was over an hour's drive from Washington and they would get there before midnight.

Peanut glanced over at Hills. There was no doubt about it, she was a very attractive woman and he couldn't escape the fact that he liked her. Really liked her. It was different from what he had felt for Sharon, but he was unsure. Was it love? Truth be told he thought that he had probably fallen in love with her. But the big question was, did she want him? Regardless, now wasn't the time for any of that. They had a job to do.

The gate slid closed behind them and they pulled to a stop and parked around the side of the building, well out of sight of the gate. Hills had her torch out, shining the beam on the steps as they walked up to the door. The whole camp was eerie, the dark trees standing black against the starry sky.

Peanut followed Hills inside and locked the door behind them.

'How easy do you think it'll be for them to find this place?' she asked.

'They sure as hell won't find it in the dark,' he replied. 'We've still got time on our side. I'm guessing they won't be here before lunchtime tomorrow. I wish we had a chain and padlock for that gate. That would stop them from forcing it open.'

'We have. The place gets padlocked up when we know we will be away for some time. Come on, we'll do it together.'

They walked over to the gate, Peanut with the heavy chain and padlock over his shoulder. With their eyes now adjusted to the dark, they left the torch off. Peanut threaded the chain around the gate and post and padlocked it. As they walked back, he felt her take his hand and she entwined her fingers in his, their arms touching, saying nothing, happy. She locked the door behind them.

'Hungry?' she asked.

'No, I'll wait until tomorrow. Right now, we need sleep. 'There's only one gate in and out of here, isn't there?' asked Peanut.

'Thanks for reminding me,' she said. 'There is a back gate, but it hasn't been used since we've had this place. It's probably not working. Can we check it tomorrow?'

'Yeah, I'll do it at first light.'

'Your room or mine?' he asked, half-joking, not really sure, despite the handholding.

'Mine. I've got two beds, remember? You can have the mattress on the floor.' Her face gave nothing away.

'Okay,' he said, slightly dejected. His pick-up line hadn't worked. Perhaps he shouldn't have been so subtle.

'By the way,' she said, 'Your mattress on the floor comes with an accessory.'

'What's that?' he asked, puzzled

'Me,' she said as she took his hand and led him to her room.

***

They lay in each other's arms, happy. She nuzzled his neck.

'That was really nice,' she said.

'Yes, it was. Special'

'Can I ask something really personal?' she asked after a pause.

'Depends on what it is.'

'We shouldn't have secrets,' she said.

'No, I agree, but this is just the first night. Let's not spoil it.'

'You think that if I asked you why you're so untrusting of people that it would spoil it? Spoil what we have shared tonight?'

'Maybe,' he hesitated. 'No, probably. There are some things in my past that you don't want to know. Not yet, anyway. Maybe not ever. I know it's a lot to ask but can we just enjoy the now? Just until we see how it goes? Just as we get to know each other?'

'Okay, but you must promise me you'll tell me when we're settled. When you are sure that this is for real and we are not just having a one-off bonk, okay?'

'Amanda Carolyn Hiller, you could never be a one-off bonk. I love you and I promise. But at this early stage, let's leave my past behind. Believe me, it's for the best.'

***

Peanut left Hill's sleeping form curled up. He got dressed quietly and slipped out the door. In the half-light, it was cold and the stars were still out. He could feel rain coming. The air felt damp and heavy clouds were rushing across the dawn sky. Trees were being battered by wind and a piece of paper cartwheeled across the compound.

He found the gate and was surprised it wasn't overgrown. But it was padlocked. He knew where the tools were and went and got a hammer out of the shed. With one hit he knocked the padlock open. He was surprised at the lack of a good padlock until he discovered that the gate led to nowhere. Just a few steps and then the forest. Maybe when they were building the place they once had a plan but it had never got started, let alone finished. But it was still another way out.

He pulled the gate shut and rigged the padlock on the hasp to make it look like it was closed.

He saw that the light on in the kitchen when he strolled back in. Hills was standing at the stove, poaching eggs and cooking toast. She turned and smiled at him.

'Don't get any ideas. The sex might not be a one off, but this is,' she said.

'It was lovely,' he said as he watched her cook.

'What?' she asked when she noticed he kept staring at her.

'I just want to tell you how much I loved last night.'

'I did too. So do you still respect me this morning?' she teased.

'Yep!' Peanut grinned as he rubbed his hand across the stubble on his chin. He must remember to shave, he told himself.

They ate quietly together, Hills's legs touching and rubbing his under the table, both of them happy. They cleaned up, leaving it neat for Herman.

They were sitting in the sun, resting when they heard it. A motor vehicle coming up the road. The SUV stopped at the gates and Peter and Blue got out.

'What's with the padlock? Keeping the peasants out, eh?' said Blue.

'No. Keeping out the men with the guns. Have you seen anything?' asked Peanut.

'Nope, not a thing,' said Blue. Peter stood looking around, taking a new, hard look at the place. He glanced at Peanut.

'What'cha think?' he asked them.

'This whole camp is surrounded by trees,' Peanut said. 'Anybody could take pot shots at us from outside, but we can hide in the buildings so they won't do that. They want us dead.'

He pointed to the low hill behind the camp, overlooking the compound.

'That's the only high ground,' Peanut said.

'Yeah. Hold that and you don't have a problem,' Blue said. 'If you don't have that hill, this place is nearly indefensible.'

'Any further ideas about defense strategy?' Peter asked them.

'There's a gate out the back that leads to nowhere, but there could be a track from there to the top of the hill. It's just a matter of us taking a hike up through the trees to find out.'

'If I can get a clear line of fire, me and the Barrett here could stop an armoured truck,' said Blue as he patted his rifle case.

'Ex-army sniper, Blue?' asked Peanut.

'You betcha. Five long-range verified kills; twelve unverified.'

Peanut knew then that Blue was a crack shot. That was why Blue was in the ICT. If a long-range cleanup was required, Blue would make sure it happened.

'Shall we go take a look?' Blue asked.

Hills shook her head. 'We'll all go. There's nothing here to defend. We're a team and we stick together.' They locked up and began the slow climb to the top of the low rise, the trees not so dense as they neared the top.

They stood on the top of the hill. The view of the camp was partly obscured by trees and Blue pointed out the weakness.

'From here, you can shoot anyone using the main gate or coming and going out of the front of the building.' He bent down and took his rifle out of its case and checked the view through the scope. He moved position three times before he was satisfied, then marked the ground. 'From here, I could take out their vehicles at the front gate.' Blue stood and took a pair of binoculars out of their case and scanned the countryside. The hill was only three hundred feet higher than the surrounding landscape, but the view through the trees was magnificent. Farms spread out across the far valley, the main highway visible in the distance and minor roads meandered into the hills and disappeared behind green folds in the landscape.

'I think that back gate must have been put there so this hill could be used,' said Peanut.

'That makes a lot of sense,' said Hills as she stood admiring the view. 'Do you want to stay up here and keep a lookout?' she asked Blue.

'Suits me,' said Blue.

'I don't think they will search for this camp,' said Peanut. 'If the department knew about the safe house, these friends of Volkov's will know. Remember, Burlington Ford is a friend of Volkov's. Why search for the camp when Chas could lead them straight here? He will have Gorman on board so it makes sense to leave us alone and follow Chas.' Hills nodded at Peanut. His untrusting nature just might have hit the nail on the head. She picked up her phone and rang Chas. She spoke and hung up.

'They are approaching Harrisonburg. They have a truck following,' said Hills. 'Chas said to be ready.'

Peanut glanced at Peter and Hills and asked, 'Ideas, guys?'

Peter snorted derisively.

'Someone in the department knows about the safe house and the fact that we have it,' he said. 'We have a fucking traitor in the ranks.'

'Yeah, Peanut replied. 'Call Blue and tell him what's going on. Let's follow Chas's advice, eh? Let's get ready for their arrival.'

Chapter 31

Chas was driving. Janice-Rose sat beside him and Sharon sat beside a handcuffed Gorman in the back. Chas was wary. The guys meeting Gorman at the hotel had unnerved him. He was now certain they were Gorman's friends and had come to take him into hiding. He was also sure that they wouldn't give up. The behavior of the thugs hunting Sharon proved that they never gave up.

They were passing through Harrisonburg when he noticed the white twelve-ton truck behind him, just the sort that does large-scale city deliveries. It was sitting there, not catching up, but not dropping back when he speeded up. He wasn't worried, despite them turning off Highway 81 onto a two-lane blacktop. There was far too much traffic to make any attack likely. He decided to put the problem to rest. He pulled into a service station before he cleared Harrisonburg, pulling up to a bowser. There were cars at several of the bowsers and he got out and began to fill the SVU, standing at the pump, opening the fill cap and watching the truck as it went by. He placed the nozzle in the tank. The head of the guy in the passenger seat of the truck turned and studied him filling up. That proved it; they were definitely being followed. There was no doubt left. There was a leak somewhere in the department. What now? He paid and climbed back in.

'Check your guns, ladies. Our passenger has some of his friends up ahead.' He didn't add that there were probably more behind as well. He was now beginning to wonder if they'd make it to the camp. He hoped so. He checked his GPS before he drove off. He was familiar with the back roads into the camp and he would turn off soon and hopefully confuse anyone who was following.

It wasn't long before he caught up with the truck. It was like they had been waiting, as they stayed just in front of him. He checked behind and saw them coming up fast. A white SUV followed by a red SUV. The lead vehicle came close, threateningly close, and he was expecting to be rear ended, but it just sat there, two car lengths away. Chas quickly checked the GPS. There was a mile to go before he could take a back road to the camp and all he had to do was get there. His options swiftly began to narrow as the truck began to slow and the white SUV ease out to overtake. He could see it had four guys in it. There was only one man in the red SUV behind the white one but that still made it five armed thugs against the three of them. That was not good odds. The white SUV was getting close. It was a maneuver to box him in behind the truck and then force him off the road. He swung the SUV violently out to overtake the truck, and the truck swung out to cut him off. He immediately swerved back and floored the accelerator. He was nearly past the truck when its driver realized that he had been outsmarted and swung the truck back. Chas had chosen well. The hard shoulder of the road provided plenty of traction for the SUV's four-wheel drive and he was past and racing for the corner, breaking hard and swinging the SUV around the ninety-degree turn onto the loose grave surface. His chasers had miscalculated; the truck was now following him instead of letting the white SUV follow. He could soon outrun the truck and there was nowhere for the white SUV to pass. All he had to do was get to the camp alive.

'Good driving, Chas,' said Janice-Rose.

'Thanks. Ring Peter, will you, and tell him about our tails? See if he can slow them down at the gate or better still stop them.' Janice-Rose rang Peter and put it on speaker.

'Leave it to us,' said Peter. Chas laughed. Peter would sort it.

***

Peter turned to the team.

'Action time. I'll man the gate and shut it behind Chas when he arrives. Blue, you get up the hill. Can you take out both vehicles?'

'Blue only has to take out the rear vehicle. That blocks the track. Leaves him with more ammo to keep them pinned down,' said Peanut.

Blue and Peter grinned at each other.

'Isolate the fuckers,' said Blue. 'Love it. Hunt and kill at leisure. Beautiful.'

'That's the plan then, guys?' Hills asked. She saw the nods. Peanut pointed to the Barrett.

'Blue, do you need more ammo?' Peanut had seen the box of ammunition Blue had carried into the camp.

'Yeah, if things get sticky, it'll help. I've got enough armor-piercing shells to take out three or more vehicles, incidentally.' Blue grimaced at them with a deadpan face. 'Army 101. You can never have enough bullets.'

'I'll go get it. Got the keys?' asked Peanut. Hills chucked him the keys and he set off at a fast lope down the hill, with Peter following. Blue grinned up at Hills.

'You guys an item, huh?' he asked.

'Yeah, Blue. I think he's a nice guy. But like all new things I still have a few reservations. I hope we can work it all out.' She gave a wry smile. 'He don't take no prisoners.'

Blue grunted. 'I noticed.' He grimaced unsmilingly at Hills. 'In this line of work, that's not a bad thing. Necessary in fact.'

'I always thought it was, Blue.'

Blue examined the road to the camp through the binoculars.

'Nothing happening at the moment, but I don't think it will be long.'

Peanut opened the back door and headed to Blue's room. The ammunition was sitting on the small table and he picked it up and headed to the door, suddenly stopping and thinking. He went to his room and grabbed his knapsack, then picked up his and Hills's jackets and headed to the back door. If they got stuck, they could at least keep warm. His phone beeped. A text. Hills.

Chas at gate.

He ran to the front window and watched Chas race through, pushing the gate-close button and Peter padlocked it shut. He waited until Chas pulled up outside, then walked out carrying the ammo. He pointed up the hill.

'Head up there, guys. They are ready and armed.'

Chas pulled Gorman out of the back seat and marched him over to the back gate, following Peter, Sharon, and Janice-Rose up the hill. Peanut's phone beeped again. He read the text.

Enemy at the gate.

He ran to the front window and saw the truck parked, four men getting out and looking around. Running out the back door, he locked it and jogged through the back gate, closing it and aligning the padlock to make it appear locked and then jogged in amongst the trees. The ground rose steadily from the back of the camp; thirty feet up the track he could see the truck parked at the front gate and changed direction so he wouldn't get noticed. He started to climb. Ten minutes later he was walking out onto the hilltop and handing the ammunition to Blue, who grinned his thanks and pointed at the front gate.

'They can't make up their minds what to do,' he said. 'They were on their phones for a while and then they climbed over the gate. They're looking around, but they haven't moved yet.'

'Can I have a look?' Peanut held out his hand for the binoculars and after a moment said, 'They're not the ones who were outside the hotel.'

'Unless Volkov turns up, doing anything is probably wasted,' said Hills. We need him to end this shit.'

Peanut shook his head. There was a black look in his eyes.

'Not quite. If he doesn't arrive, we need to know where he is and they just might be able tell us.'

Peanut swiveled the binoculars and saw that the white SUV had arrived.

'It's the two from the hotel, plus two others,' he said.

Chas was puzzled.

'There was a red SUV behind that white one. It's gone. It appeared to have just one person in it. Maybe it's Volkov?' he said.

'None of these guys look like the guy Sharon described as Volkov,' Peanut said, 'so it could be him. If it is, he won't come anywhere near until he has us helpless or dead.'

'Can you disable those vehicles?' Chas asked Blue.

'Oh, yeah. Just watch me.' Blue opened the box of ammo and took a spare clip out of the case. It was loaded with black-tipped amour-piercing shells. He held the clip up. 'These little beauties will go right through an engine block.' He slipped the existing clip out of the rifle and loaded in the new one.

'I'll stay with Blue,' said Chas. It'll give him protection if anyone breaks through. Hills, you, Peter, Peanut and J.R. go back down. Gorman here won't do anything.' Peanut grinned; Gorman was handcuffed to a strong sapling.

'Give us four minutes. We'll give them a warning and if they don't respond, fire. We'll watch from the back gate,' said Peanut. He could see that Blue was in his element and itching to start shooting. They walked down to the back gate, stopping twenty feet from the fence, hidden in among the trees.

'I'll guard the gate,' Peanut said and Hills and Peter agreed, then moved twenty feet to either side of the gate. Janice-Rose had followed them down and Peanut pointed to a spot ten yards behind him.

'J.R., if they get past me, kill them. We have to protect the hill top.'

Janice-Rose gave a nod to show she understood and checked her pistol. Peanut knew that she wouldn't miss.

If their vehicles were disabled the attackers would be isolated. Unless they could clear the front gate and use their vehicles, they would be locked in, isolated. From where Peanut was standing, slightly uphill from the camp, he could just see the truck parked at the gate a n d the white SUV just behind it. The last of the thugs climbed over the gate and they heard a door smash as the intruders broke their way into the camp. Peter called out a warning, his voice loud and commanding.

'You are surrounded by federal agents, come out with your hands up and leave your weapons behind or we'll shoot!'

There was no response. Peter repeated the call.

A minute later, Hills called out. 'Go, Blue!'

The sound of the Barrett was deafening. It echoed around the camp and Peanut involuntarily flinched. The SUV behind the truck outside the gate jumped with the impact of the bullet, then the second and third shots reverberated through the trees. Smoke and flames billowed from under the bonnet as the fuel system ignited. At that moment Hills's phone buzzed.

'Rear vehicle immobilized, now taking out the front one,' said Blue.

The loud crack of rifle fire echoed around the camp once more. Peanut watched as bullets tore into the front of the truck and smoke began to pour out of the engine compartment.

Hills's phone rang again.

'Front one fucked, changing to anti-personnel ammo,' said Blue.

'They aren't going anywhere anytime soon. They are well and truly fucked,' Peter said to Peanut. Peanut grinned.

'Careful, guys, movement,' Hills called out when she saw movement at the rear door.

The back door opened and someone peeped out. A head came into view, peering around the edge of the door.

'Get ready, guys, this gate is their only option,' Peanut said. It was sudden and unexpected. Two of them charged out, a single-bed mattress held in front of them for protection, running hard for the gate. It was stupid—as if the stuffing of a mattress would stop a bullet. Peter and Hills fired together but the mattresses kept on coming. They kept on firing, emptying their Glock 17 magazines into the mattress, then trying to reload, seeing the mattress stumble but stay up, reaching the gate as Hills and Peter both frantically tried to reload new magazines in the Glocks. The gate was jerked open. The guys behind the mattresses poked their guns over the top, firing wildly, then shoved the mattresses aside and stormed through the narrow exit. Peanut saw that they had been clever, using a piece of old construction ply held up behind the mattress as protection.

As Peter clicked the fresh magazine home, the first thug through the gate turned, his gun swinging on Peter as Peanut stepping from behind a tree and slashed down on his gun hand. Turning, he saw the other thug running towards the tree Hills was behind as she reloaded. Peanut threw his sword as the guy raised his pistol, the blade burying itself in his back as Janice-Rose fired. He staggered, then went down as Peanut turned back to the first gunman, still trying to make the remains of what was left of his hand function, the gun lying on the ground. Peter fired and the man collapsed instantly. Peanut noticed another two guys had reached the gate, one turning and running back to the cover of the camp buildings as Hills, Janice-Rose, and Peter fired together and the other guy at the gate folded over, dead. Three out of the eight dead. Hills held up her hand, fingers and thumb outstretched. That said it all. Five left. Peanut retrieved his sword and Hills came over and gave him a quick kiss and gave Janice-Rose a quick hug.

'Thanks, J.R., Peanut.'

Peanut grinned.

'Just doing our jobs, right?'

She gave a thumbs up, smiling.

Peter called out.

'Thanks, Peanut. And I'm not kissing you.' Blue's voice coming from behind startled them.

'Live a little, Peter! Give it a go.' They turned and saw Blue cheekily grinning, cradling the Barrett. Peter's face didn't change.

'Live a little? You first, asshole.'

Hills ended the conversation.

'I'll kill the first one of you mother fuckers that tries, right?'

'Way to go, Mandy,' Janice-Rose said. 'So that big brother of mine is worth it? You guys started on making me an auntie yet?'

Hills blushed as Peanut held his hands up in a peace gesture.

'Come on, guys, we're in a fight here. It's not a kissing contest.'

He scanned the building, seeing movement at the back-door window and at the window of the room beside it.

'See that movement, Blue? At the door and at the window?'

'I see it,' said Blue as he hefted the rifle up, using a tree for support. He took aim and blasted through the middle of the doorway and then through the wall underneath the head at the window. In the silence that followed after the loud deafening din of the Barrett, they heard moans coming from inside the building.

'Bloody big pistol, Blue,' said Peanut with a laugh.

'It wasn't doing much good up top so decided to join the action down here. Maybe four left and one wounded, eh?' said Blue.

'Time to flush them out,' said Peanut. 'Could you put another couple of shots through that door and under that window, just to keep their heads down?'

'My pleasure.'

He hefted the rifle up against the tree again, using the tree as a side support, and quickly fired a bullet through the camp rear door and another through the planking under the window as Peanut set off at a dead run through the gate and over to the back of the building. He paused and was bumped, quickly turning around to see Hills and Janice-Rose right behind him.

'What are you doing here?' he asked. Hills shook her head disgustedly at him.

'Team, Peanut,' Janice-Rose said.

The rifle fired again and they saw Peter run over to them, grinning and puffing as he arrived. He gave a wry grin.

'Four against four. Good odds, guys. Let's go get the pricks,' he said. 'Front porch entry as Blue has the back one covered, right?'

They peered around the front and saw two heads pull rapidly back when they saw them coming around the corner. They ducked down under the veranda edge as a gun came around the corner of the door and fired blindly at where the last were. The gun stopped and Peanut jumped up onto the veranda and ran along to the door, his swords in his hands, stopping to peer inside at a thug crouched over, frantically reloading his pistol, watched by his mate. The guy standing jumped in fright and attempted to raise his gun. He died instantly, the sword penetrating his heart before he had the gun halfway up. The thug reloading tried to struggle to his feet until the sword pricked his throat. Peanut raised a finger to his lips and motioned to Peter. Peter promptly took the gun off him and sat him down as Peanut, Hills, and Janice-Rose walked carefully inside. Peanut retrieved his sword.

'Back door's next,' he said to Hills and Janice-Rose.

There was a dead body and a pool of blood in the rear doorway and they heard moans coming from the room next door. A thug had his gun in his hand and he was peering fearfully out of the window as his mate lay bleeding on the floor.

'On the floor! Now!' yelled Hills as she aimed her weapon at him.

He jerked his head around, dropped his gun, and lay on the floor with his arms outstretched.

'That was easy, eh?' said Peanut. Hills rounded on him.

'Why did you run to the camp without telling us? We could have waited them out. We work as a team or have you forgotten that?' glowered Hills.

'The more time they have,' replied Peanut, 'the better their plan will be. We had them on the back foot. We just needed to push harder.'

'You would have carried on without us if we hadn't come, wouldn't you?'

'Of course. Yes. I would have done some things a bit differently, but the result would have been the same. These guys are a bunch of untrained morons. Talk to Blue. He'll tell you,' said Peanut.

Hills shook her head. No matter what he said, she was not happy that Peanut had acted alone. She rang Chas.

'Volkov's not here, but the coast is clear,' she said.

Peanut quickly turned. 'Where are the binoculars?' he asked.

'On the hill,' replied Blue.

Peanut sprinted out of the door, through the back gate and up the hill, surprising Sharon and Chas, who were getting ready to come down with Gorman.

Peanut grabbed the binoculars and scanned the roads into the camp. Another SUV, a dark red one, was driving away. He pointed towards it as a breathless Hills arrived. He handed Chas the binoculars.

'Volkov! He was here, waiting for his guys to bring Gorman out,' said Chas as he handed the binoculars to Hills. 'That was the second SUV that was following us; he's too cunning. He hung back and let his men take the heat. We've missed him.'

'For now, Chas,' said Peanut, 'but he won't go away. He has way too much money tied up in drugs. He's just a sophisticated version of Chuckie.' Peanut gave a sad smile. 'There have always been criminals, and there always will be. As a wise man once said, *Mankind are a race that breeds criminals. The same ten per cent breeds ninety per cent of the criminals, generation after generation in every society.*' Peanut gave a sad smile. 'There ends the lesson. Let's go have a talk to some of the ten percenters.'

Hills frowned at him, knowing from her studies that what he said was true and it was soul destroying if you thought about it too deeply. No matter what anyone did, no matter how many police, how much money, there will always be criminals, continually breeding more criminals. She tried to blot the thought out of her mind.

'Chas is going to get you to question Gorman. He will be tough. Are you ready for that?' Peanut gave a bleak smile.

'The real question is whether Gorman is ready for that?'

Hills and Peanut walked downhill to the camp with Peanut carrying the gun case while she carried the ammunition. She was reflective. Peanut had summed up the brutal side of humankind and it left her feeling flat. Was that all they could hope for? An endless parade of soulless, pathological pieces of shit to catch and put away? Did hate always trump love? It left her feeling depressed. She knew the ICT team was also part of the brutal side of life, but what else was there, other than letting the thugs of the world win? The rule of law just didn't cut it. And they still had to question the two thugs and Gorman. How hard would that be? But it didn't really matter, they would talk and then they would suffer the *consequences*. Peanut's *consequences*.

She watched as Gorman was bundled into the room Peanut had once occupied and the door locked. She walked over to where the two thugs were lying on the floor, their hands and feet tied. They were scared. Their faces said it all.

'Which one, Peanut?' Blue asked.

Peanut pointed to the guy they caught reloading his gun at the door. 'Him. Take his mate away.' He grinned at the second guy. 'Unless he wants to volunteer?'

Blue dragged the one out of the room.

'As your prisoners, you have a duty to look after us,' the other one pleaded.

'Do we?' said Peanut. 'I think you mistake us for people who give a shit. We don't. What's your name?'

The thug stared at Peanut, his mouth closed almost in a sneer. Peanut sighed. Another hero. Peanut bent over and made to punch him in the nose, but instead, hit him in the testicles. The thug grunted in pain and jerked into the fetal position. Peanut flatted him onto his back, undid his belt, pulled down his pants and took hold of one of his testicles and gave a hard squeeze. A scream of pain erupted from the thug's twisted mouth. When it died away, it was replaced with a whimper. Peanut twisted the thug's head and eyeballed him. 'That wasn't a hard question. Imagine how much more painful it's going to be when we come to the really hard questions. So, your name?'

'Elias Weber.' His voice was gravelly and strained.

'Where do you live?' When he didn't answer Peanut squeezed the sore testicle. The thug writhed and flinched.

'Queens, New York.' he said.

'And where is Volkov residing these days?'

'I don't know. He always contacts us, or more often, contacts Buffet by cell phone.'

'Buffet?' Peanut asked.

'Jimmy Buffet in Queens.'

'Your boss?'

'Yes.'

'Where were you going to take Gorman?' Peanut asked.

'Volkov was going to meet us on the road and take him off us. We were to go home after that.'

'How much were you being paid for this?'

'We were all getting five thousand each for the week's work.'

'So, it's Buffett who pays you, is it?'

'Yeah. He and Gorman are friends from way back.'

'Is Buffet still running guns?' interjected Peter.

When Weber hesitated, Peanut squeezed the other testicle. Weber howled in pain. 'Yes, yes he is still running guns!' Weber gasped the words out, all pretense of being a hero gone.

'Selling them to Gorman?' Peter asked.

'No. He sells them to a woman from Texas,' said Weber. 'A bitch called Albanese. Sold her several boxes of sniper rifles with ammo and some Bushmaster assault rifles.'

'Who else does he sell too?' Peter asked

'I heard that Volkov also took a heap down south to Texas.'

'Who does Buffet get the guns from?' Peanut asked.

'Gorman and some Russian arms dealers. Volkov's friends.'

Hills glanced at Peanut; they both had the same question on their minds.

'Where do all the guns go that Buffet sells?' Hills asked.

'What doesn't get picked up immediately gets stored. He, Volkov, and Gorman have a secure shed in Queens. He stores them all in there until they're picked up. Buffet doesn't care much about that, just so long as he has the money from the sale in his pocket.'

'How many are there?' asked Peanut.

'The shed is full, man, right to the top. And Gorman is getting Buffet to buy another shed.'

'I'm not sure whether to believe you or not, Weber. We'll go see what your pal says, eh?' said Peanut.

Weber's face went pale. What was he hiding? They walked along into the other room. It was the backroom thug and he was clearly scared out of his wits.

'Time for some answers, buddy,' Peanut said, 'Like your name for starters. And don't give me any of that macho not talking shit. Your pal just got his testicles squashed for doing that. Judging by the scream, it kind'a hurt. So, what's your name?'

'Sam Phelps,' he answered without hesitation.

'You work for Jimmy Buffett, do you?'

'Yeah.'

'Tell us about the relationship between Gorman, Volkov, and Buffet.'

'They do business together. They're friends.'

'Gorman stays with Buffet quite a bit, eh?' Peanut asked.

It was a stab in the dark, but Peanut thought it was worth a guess. Sam was nervous and shifted uneasily.

'Tell me the truth, or you are going to learn all about just how sore your nuts can be. You don't want that, believe me.'

'He stayed with him when he came over the last time. He was supposed to stay this time as well. Then he got hijacked.'

'Now the hard one. Where are you staying down here?' Peanut asked.

'Nowhere. We drove from Queens last night. We were meant to grab Jerry and hand him over and then drive back to New York. We would have taken turns driving and sleeping on the way back.'

'So, all you guys work for Buffet?'

Sam shook his head. 'No. The two you killed at the gate in the fence worked for Volkov.'

'Is Volkov one of Buffet's friends?' Peanut asked.

'Sort of. Jimmy seems scared of him and when Volkov says sell, you sell, if you want to stay alive.'

'How many of you came south on this little jaunt?'

'Six of us. Buffet said it would be enough for backup, especially as Volkov gave us two of his guys.'

'You guys were only backup?' Peanut asked.

'Yeah. Buffet said to do whatever Volkov wanted. He sent us here.'

'Well, Buffet seems to have overestimated your abilities.'

Peanut went back to the other room to Weber and his white, scared face.

'I think there's more you can tell us,' said Peanut as he crouched down beside the thug. 'Your pal Sam rolled over without a hand being laid on him.'

146

'They'll kill me if I say anything.' Weber's voice trembled.

'Concentrate on the now. If I have to squeeze your testicles again and put a cigarette lighter under what's left, believe me, you will talk. But with that much damage, we can't have awkward questions from the authorities. So you'll have to disappear, permanently, you understand? We have a deep mine shaft not far from here. Has water at the bottom so if the fall don't kill you, you drown. Your choice. Extreme pain and death, or you talk.'

Weber stared into Peanut's bleak eyes and he drew a ragged breath.

'Gorman was going to be met at the hotel and we were just the backup in case anything went wrong. Nobody was supposed to know he was coming. Volkov thought it would be an easy pickup and sent us in to cover it, but Volkov's morons were blindsided and Gorman got taken. Volkov wanted to move a shipment of drugs and arms south. Apparently, one of his drug suppliers in Houston has been put out of business and he needed his men to guard the shipment. He was worried that the guys who wrecked the drugs supply down south would raid the shipment.'

'When will his men be back?' Peanut asked.

'Tomorrow.'

'How many?'

'He has a team of ten guys and half of them are ex-military.'

The tie-up was crystalizing in Peanut's mind and he asked what now seemed logical.

'So Volkov knows Senator Burlington Ford then?'

When Weber hesitated, Peanut moved his hand to his crotch.

'I heard that Volkov and the senator are friends.'

'And Gorman is friends with the senator as well?'

'Yes.'

'Anything else you would like to tell us? Like where the senator and Volkov hang out?' Peanut asked.

'Texas, out in the boonies.'

'Texas is a pretty big state. Where in the boondocks, exactly?'

'I don't know. Somewhere not far from San Antonio. I'm passing on what Buffet told me. That's all I know.'

When Peanut reached over him, Weber cowered, but Peanut just pulled up his pants and buckled them up before he walked away, Hills and Peter following.

Hills replayed both conversations.

'Pretty clear,' Peanut said.

'Yep. The FBI will love this,' said Hills.

'There goes the glory, right?' Peanut said as he laughed.

'No, it's not the glory,' Hills said, 'I couldn't give a fuck about that, but a pay rise would be good,'

'I'm not even getting paid!' said Peanut.

'Piss off, Peanut. You're already rich!'

'That doesn't mean I work for nothing, does it?'

'No, it doesn't. But then you didn't want to work for money,' she reminded him. 'I'll talk to Chas. He'll want to contact the FBI with this stuff.'

Janice-Rose strolled up.

'Can we organize some food? Sharon and I are hungry. Maybe get that Herman guy back? Everyone tells me his food is tasty.'

Peter grimaced. 'Sorry,' he said. 'Herman's mom died. He won't be back for a week. Good food over in Woodstock.'

Peanut raised his hand. 'I can do scrambled eggs, guys.'

Hills, Janice-Rose, and Peter shook their heads and laughed as they spoke in unison, 'Fuck off, Peanut!'

Peanut attached the tow rope to the burnt SUV and gave Blue the signal; Blue revved up the motor and pulled it inside the compound, parking it around the back next to the burnt-out truck where a tow truck could get to it. He shut the gate. There was no point in locking it; all of the bad guys where dead or in cuffs waiting on the FBI.

Chas sat on the porch and leant his back against the wall. Sharon sat beside him, while Janice-Rose, Peter, and Blue sat with their legs dangling over the edge of the porch. It was peaceful and relaxing, considering what they had just gone through.

'Remember Melissa Albanese, Peanut?' Sharon asked.

'Yes?'

'Well, we just found out she's Burlington Ford's daughter. She set up the Southern States Alliance. That was where the guns have been going. The more we look, the more it all points to the senator and his family.'

'Do we have much of a background on the senator?' asked Peanut.

'No,' said Sharon. 'I haven't had time to look any deeper, but I will. I do know that when he wanted to run for the senate years ago he got told to tone down some of his extreme views. He must have done that because he got elected.'

'Thanks, Sharon. Now we have to deal with Volkov,' said Chas. 'If what Weber said is correct, Volkov has a team of ten, half of them ex-soldiers. If that's the case, I think we could be in a spot of trouble. We weren't set up to function as an army. We'll have to decide how and what we need to do to accomplish our ends.'

'That's simple. We get Gorman to talk and then he disappears. No point in leaving him to them and since we can't take him with us, we have to dump him,' said Peanut. Everyone knew what he meant by 'dump'.

'If we're going to come up against trained soldiers our lives are too precious to throw away guarding terrorist shit,' said Blue.

Peter and Sharon murmured their agreement. Peanut's face was unreadable. He stood up.

'I need someone to help me out. Blue?' asked Peanut.

Peanut and Blue walked into Gorman's room. He was sitting on the bed watching them as they came in and he appeared angry.

'You realize you're breaking the law holding me like this?' said Gorman.

'It's just like days of old in Northern Ireland, isn't it?' said Peanut. 'We just want to talk. Are you friends with Senator Burlington Ford and Milo Volkov?'

'I don't know either of them,' Gorman spat the words out.

'Tie him up tightly. There'll be less of a struggle that way,' Peanut said to Blue. Blue tied Gorman up tight and Peanut pulled down Gorman's pants. He looked Gorman in the eye and Gorman knew that look. It was merciless.

'Last chance, Gorman,' said Peanut.

When there was silence, and Peanut reached into Gorman's crotch. There was a penis but no testicles! He grinned at Gorman.

'Northern Ireland, huh, Gorman? The British troops getting a bit of their own back, huh?' said Peanut with a smirk.

Gorman refused to look at him. Peanut knew he was going to take some shaking up. But he also knew from his training where to find the sensitive nerve endings. He had been shown and then experienced just how painful it could be.

'Hold him tight. This is going to hurt.' Peanut felt around Gorman's bare inner thigh, finding the nerve points and squeezing hard. Gorman let out an anguished scream and after two minutes of writhing in pain, unable to even cry out, he lapsed into unconsciousness.

'Get some water to bring him around for the next little session.'

Blue sloshed half a bucket of water over him and grinned as Gorman spluttered awake.

'Hurt did it, Jerry? There's a lot more where that came from,' Peanut said as he squeezed Gorman's thigh again. Another scream and once again after a couple of minutes, Gorman again passed out. Blue tipped more water over him and when he came round Peanut found and squeezed a similar spot inside Gorman's bicep. He gasped and moaned and tried to tear his arm free. Peanut knew it was a battle of wills as he squeezed harder. No matter how hard Gorman struggled, he couldn't get away from Peanut's relentless grip. He jerked and twisted, his mouth sagging and drooling in pain.

'Enough!' he cried.

'The senator and Volkov are your friends, aren't they?'

'Yes.'

He sniveled when Peanut let go of his arm, just keeping a light hold to let him know it wasn't over.

'Have you been to the senator's compound?'

'No, never. This is my first real visit. I have only been here once before to meet Buffet.'

'Where's the compound?'

'We were given directions. North out of San Antonio, off Highway 39, cross over the Guadalupe River and then it's ten miles on a gravel road.'

'Isolated?' Peanut asked.

'Yes.'

'Why are you stockpiling arms?'

Gorman glanced away and shook his head. 'I'm not,' he replied.

'There are warehouses full of them all over Europe. We need to know where they are.'

'There's only one, on the docks in Hamburg,' Gorman mumbled after a lengthy pause.

'So, the rest is all bullshit?' said Peanut.

'Yes. It was to make us look important, so people would join and donate money to our cause.'

'There's a warehouse full in Queens. All purchased by you,' Peanut scoffed.

'They're not mine. I'm just the front man,' said Gorman.

'Really? For whom?'

When Gorman shook his head, Peanut attacked his arm again.

'John ...' he started to say, then screamed and passed out.

Blue poured more water on him, but he didn't respond. Peanut leant down and checked his eyes. Gorman was dead.

'Probably a heart attack,' Peanut said to Blue. 'Untie him and call Chas. Tell him to tell the FBI we found him in here, dead, okay?'

'We certainly did. What a rude prick to die before he coughed up the info we needed. No fucking manners,' said Blue.

Peanut grinned at Blue's black humor as they heaved the body onto the bed.

'I'm glad you're back, Peanut. You fit the team perfectly. And sorry about the bed. I was pissed at you at the time. It's not often I get told to fuck off. I deserved it.' Blue held out his hand as they walked back to the porch. A surprised Peanut shook it.

'Thanks, Blue.'

They moved out onto the porch with the others.

'Died of a heart attack. Call the FBI, Chas,' said Peanut.

'Is his body marked?' asked Chas.

'No,' said Peanut. 'He confirmed there's a warehouse full of arms on the Hamburg docks and that the stock in the warehouse in Queens isn't his. Belongs to John someone but he died before he told us the surname. He also said the senator's base is north of San Antonio off Highway 39. I've recorded what he said.'

'Thanks, guys.' Chas stood up and walked away with his phone in his hand. It seemed to him that another job was over.

Chapter 33

The FBI gave the camp a thorough going over. They checked the dead bodies against the facts and found no evidence of murder or manslaughter. The deaths were all due to self-defense from an attack on the camp by thugs employed by the drug-dealing criminal element. Jimmy Buffet was pulled in for questioning and it came as no surprise that on the advice of his lawyer he refused to talk and was released on bail. The audio tapes were helpful even though they couldn't be used as evidence. Weber and Phelps, sitting in the FBI truck waiting transportation, were not talking either. The chance of using them as witnesses was negligible. With Jerry Gorman dead the FBI knew that there was no point in pursuing what happened at the camp. It appeared that those who deserved it had received justice, albeit roughly. What happened next would depend on what they found when they checked out the warehouse in Queens.

'Well done, guys. The department is pleased. They have passed details about the Hamburg location to their European counterparts,' said Chas. 'There's only one piece of unfinished business and that's Volkov. I have a feeling that we're not going to get him.'

'That clever prick was watching us. He's just too smart. That's the first failure we've had. Fuck it!' said an upset Peter.

'No, it wasn't a failure,' said Chas. 'It was a success. Our job was to kidnap Gorman and, if possible, find out about the weapons he and his organization had stored. And we did that. The department is extremely pleased. We'll now head back to base and work out the next step. But realistically, we haven't even got close to Volkov and that's frustrating. I also want to know how the investigation into the senator's links to the drug operation in Houston is going. The FBI will have a tough time making anything stick, believe me. And with Volkov around to make sure any witnesses disappear, I don't believe they'll be able to build a case.' Chas also knew that if Volkov's men turned up at the camp, the FBI SWAT team, on standby with their truck already at the camp, would handle any issues.

'Okay, everybody,' Chas said. 'Pack up and out of here in ten minutes.'

Peanut heard the news when they got back to Washington.

FBI bust major drug ring. Long-term senator arrested and charged. Further charges against co-conspirators pending.

He laughed with delight and he and Hills toasted the FBI's success with a glass of lemonade. It had turned into a total victory. There was no way back politically for that fat pig. He was dead in the water and would now have to live without sucking out of the public purse. He would do that hard. Now a criminal nobody. Peanut had the quiet satisfied feeling that they had really accomplished something worthwhile, something for the good. He wondered why the FBI had taken so long to release the news of the bust and then thought about it. It had to be because of the senator. He would have moved every chip he had in play to try to kill it. It clearly hadn't worked.

***

Peanut noticed a strange four-wheel drive pickup parked on the drive in front of Janice-Rose's garage door as he let himself in the front door of his home, hearing nothing, standing in the entrance hallway, listening intently, still nothing. If this was someone new turning up, he should have been told. He liked that the house was on the outskirts of Washington in a genteel suburb. With the ground floor five feet above ground level with wide steps and wrought iron banister rails leading up to the porch, it was almost imposing. Once inside, the reason for the height was explained. The house had a large basement. One half was part workshop and a small-arms range and the other half was now the gym.

He was proud of the gym. It allowed him to train, undisturbed, apart from Hills, Sharon, and Janice-Rose. Light-wood paneling ran around the room and a floor of dark timber made the gym look inviting and warm. He ran lightly down the stairs to the gym and paused at the door, hearing the sounds of hard exercise. He opened the door and saw a body go flying, hitting the floor with a dull thud like a bag of cement hitting the ground. It was followed by a loud 'Fuck!' as Janice-Rose straightened up from the throw and she and Hills laughed. The guy stood. He was lanky, about six three or four, neat brown hair cut reasonably short but still fashionable. He had the build of a professional basketballer and was sweating just about as hard. Peanut noticed the sweat stains where he had landed and saw the sweat running down Janice-Rose's face. She wiped her face and threw the lanky guy a towel. He wiped and then noticed Peanut. He was surprised and looked Peanut up and down, taking in the small wiry frame.

'May I ask who you are, sir?' Peanut noted the 'sir'. Polite, professionally so. A cop or the military. Janice-Rose and Hills spun around.

'Peanut,' he said. 'And you are?'

Hills walked over and gave him a quick kiss and Janice-Rose grinned.

'I'm Michael O'Connor, sir. I didn't realize that you were Peanut.'

'You were expecting someone much larger, I expect?'

Michael blushed.

'I was. Janice-Rose and Hills told me so much about what you had done that it naturally followed. Sorry, sir.'

'Don't be. I don't mind being small, not one bit. You are Police or Military, right?' Peanut asked.

'Yes, sir. State Trooper.'

'Ahh … Let me guess. You met Janice-Rose while giving her a ticket for speeding?'

'Uh, yes, sir.'

Janice-Rose rolled her eyes and sighed disgustedly at Hills. She had hoped to keep that ticket a secret.

'My little sister has a very heavy foot and in that car she is dangerous,' Peanut said.

'You mean the Porsche, sir?' Michael asked.

'Yes, Mick. Call me Peanut. You don't mind Mick?'

'No, sir, sorry, Peanut. Mick is what my family and workmates call me.' He grimaced. 'Among other things.'

'I can imagine. Janice-Rose giving you some lessons? Hard ones by the look of it?'

'She's very good. Much better than me but I only learned the police basic stuff. She tells me that she is nowhere near your standard.'

'I've been doing it for years. All that work shows, that's all.'

Hills gave Peanut a querying glance and interrupted.

'Your mom?'

Peanut sighed resignedly.

'She won't move. She loves the area and her neighbors. We are now going to give her existing house a makeover. Pity.'

Hills snorted. 'Told you so. Work?'

'Yes, a meeting with Chas tonight. He and the team are all coming over. We have another job on. It looks good.'

'Government?'

'Yes.' Hills was delighted. She bumped knuckles with Janice-Rose.

'I suppose the early night is out?'

'Of course. Chas will bring Sharon, and rumor has it that Blue is seeing someone as well. If she comes, it will be really late. Sorry.' He turned to Mick.

'You're staying for dinner?' Janice-Rose smiled at Peanut and interrupted.

'Too late, big brother, I already asked him.' She gave a cheeky grin. 'This is our first date, believe it or not.'

'My little sister can be a pain, Mick. Watch her.'

'I have two sisters myself. As their kid brother, I'm well used to getting picked on.' Peanut grinned.

'No doubt, sisters can really sort the men out. J.R. tell you much about herself?'

'Only that she works in a security firm. I'm assuming that is you?'

'Among a few others whom you'll meet later. That's if J.R. hasn't already sent you packing.' Mick gave a slight grin as Peanut turned and walked up the stairs out of the basement.

***

Peanut had initially thought the house extravagant, but now he realized that Hills, Sharon, and Janice-Rose were right; its size and comfort were what they needed. The weekly mowing of the grounds still annoyed him, but the ride-on mower made it easy, if boring. The house had been decorated before it went on the market and while the style wasn't to Peanut's taste, he was happy to live with it. It was simple and plain, almost austere; near white walls alleviated by the occasional well-chosen bold print and a single color, charcoal-grey carpet throughout alleviated by large jet black, deep red-and-white matts. The effect of contrasting colors throughout the house with the plain near white walls was stunning, ultra-modern. But it didn't have what Peanut called a 'homely feel,' despite the beautiful furniture that the ladies had bought. When he was stupid enough to voice that opinion, Hills had studied him for a second or two with wide-open, challenging eyes.

'It takes children to give it a homely feel, not paint and carpets.'

He had no answer.

It was strange how quickly he and Hills had settled into a happy domestic arrangement. It was like it was always meant to be. They had come back from the camp and Janice-Rose helped move Hills in that day. Every time he looked at her, he knew it was love. No doubts remained.

He instinctively liked J.R.'s new guy, speeding ticket or no speeding ticket. He acted and sounded like a good guy. He just hoped he got J.R. to drive a bit slower. He checked the clock. An hour until the rest of the team arrived.

Chas and Sharon seemed to be getting more and more involved and he suspected an engagement announcement would soon be made. He had to admit Chas was a brilliant coordinator and his deep contacts meant that he was indispensable to the operation of the team. Trust was the word. Everybody that worked with Chas soon found out that he could be trusted without fail.

Peanut was still glad that he was not officially involved. That last job had set him, Janice-Rose, and Sharon up for life. Chas now knew about it; he had heard rumors from the FBI investigators about money going missing and had immediately suspected Peanut. He had laughed when Peanut had told him the full story. But that job had a downside.

The senator eventually got off.

Chas reckoned that the President had a hand in that. The senator argued that he was too busy doing work for the government to keep his eyes on everything and that he hadn't known that a large part of the money came from drugs. He put the blame on the other principals. With two of the other principals still missing, presumed in Russia, and the last one disputing the senator's version, the authorities only had a 'he said, she said' case. Because of that, and his medical condition, it was argued that he would die in jail, so the court showed lenience.

He only got time served with a good behavior bond and a million-dollar fine. Peanut knew that the only medical conditions the senator had were excessive fat and excessive greed.

It annoyed him, but the senator had resigned and was now just a Joe Blow private citizen, despite still being incredibly wealthy and no doubt skulking down in the Texas backwater where he lived.

Peanut had asked Chas about ongoing work and was told that the government had more than enough work to keep them all busy. That sounded good to Peanut and it meant that if he joined back up with ICT, they wouldn't have to touch their investments. The question was, join up and get paid? Become a public servant?

Only after Volkov was sorted.

Hills walked in and found him sitting looking out the window, almost as if he was in a trance, but his eyes gave him away; they were alive and watchful. She walked over and kissed him gently on the cheek.

'Love you.'

'Love you too, honey.' He glanced at her and gave a wry grin. 'I think we might have visitors.'

'I don't suppose you mean the visitors we are supposed to have?'

'No. These are the nasty kind. Time to go on alert. I wish the other guys were here.' She checked the clock. 'Twenty minutes. Is that enough time?'

'It will have to be, there are no other options. Let's go on alert, right now!' He saw the heavy vehicle on its second drive by suddenly turn off the road and slam into the closed steel gates as he turned and raced downstairs, Hills following and hitting the alarm. Janice-Rose and Mick ran out into the front entranceway, Mick looking surprised as Janice-Rose opened a side closet and handed him a loaded Bushmaster assault rifle. Peanut looked out the window by the door as the heavy truck backed up and again rammed the gates. Peanut knew that the gates wouldn't hold against many hits like that. He listened as he heard Hills call the police and their contact at the FBI and then call Chas. They needed help and they needed it urgently!

Chapter 34

'Mick, it's you and me up front and Hills and Janice-Rose at the back. Ever use an assault rifle before?'

'Yep. In training, lots of times.' He gave Peanut a worried look. 'Seriously bad people out there, huh?'

'Mick, this is where you decide whether you want to be on the side of the living or the side of the dead. Personally, we all prefer the living.'

Peanut pointed to the front door.

'The front and rear doors have steel cores behind the paneled timber. Their hinges are welded into steel frames that in turn are bolted with fourteen-inch high tensile three-quarter-inch steel bolts into ten inches of solid timber on each side. You might have noticed that the windows have decorative wrought-iron look bars. They're not. They are all high tensile steel. A gas axe would be required to cut a hole.' He then gestured to four ornamental raised small figureheads mounted on the door. He swiveled one up. 'They look like dark wood but are hardened cast steel. They are our gun ports. Just make sure you swivel down after use. Okay? We don't want them firing in.' Mick heard another crash out at the gate. He took a quick look and saw the gate and posts slowly bend as the shattered decorative stonework of the posts lay spread on the ground. The heavy truck began to walk over the gate, bending it flat and then roaring up the drive and parking below the steps.

'Let's give them a welcome, Mick.' They swung two gun ports open and fired almost simultaneously. The thug climbing out of the passenger door of the truck cab collapsed in a heap on the ground and the driver slumped over behind the wheel. The back doors opened and all they could see were the legs of guys climbing out of the rear of the truck, sheltering behind the steel body. They were obviously surprised. They had thought they would just march in, their superior numbers and fire power scaring all into submission. This was unexpected. Peanut and Mick both heard the order yelled and the thugs behind the truck suddenly made a run for the house, immediately coming into range. Peanut took down two, hearing Mick's rifle firing beside him as the attackers dived desperately for the shelter under the edge of the porch. There was silence as the guys hiding under the porch took stock.

'How many, Mick?'

'I counted twelve plus the driver.'

'Yep, that tallies. I got two on their way over; I see you got one. Five down counting the driver, that leaves eight.'

'Who are these guys?' Mick asked

'That is something we intend to find out.' In the distance he heard the metallic ping of metal snapping. They had broken the side-gate lock. Peanut knew it was a weak point. That would have to be toughened up.

'Heads up, ladies,' Peanut called, 'they're around the back.'

A muffled 'Okay,' from Hills as she replied.

'You must have pissed someone off real bad to get this sort of response,' Mick commented.

Peanut just gave a short nod. 'They have come to wipe us out. This is a razed-ground operation.'

Mick patted the solid door. 'Not unexpected, I take it?'

'No.' He heard firing at the rear of the house and a cheer from Janice-Rose.

'I'd say that sister of mine has just scored a kill.'

'What now?' Mick asked

'To get to this door, they have to climb onto the porch. With the steel doors over the stairs shut, they can only do that at the ends of the house away from our firing line.'

He handed Mick a set of earmuffs and safety goggles.

'Stun grenades will be next, followed by them trying to smash in. Let's move.'

Mick gave Peanut a quick glance. He had seen some pretty composed guys under fire in the troopers but no one like Peanut. He was like ice, no emotion, just dealing with it.

He followed Peanut into the center of the house. It was then he noticed the layout of the house had been planned. The alterations were designed to beat back an attack. The inside wall had been slid back. They could see both front and rear doors and had total control over both entries, no matter what happened. The bar from the lounge covered the front door and the island bar in the kitchen covered the back door. The back of the lounge bar was open and Mick saw a rack of five bushmaster rifles and magazines of ammo lined up, in racks, ready to slip into an empty rifle; pistols sitting in custom-made holders, ready to pull and fire. Turning, he saw the back of the island bar was exactly the same. This layout turned the center of the house into a fortress. He knew then that this attack wasn't something that might happen; they had known it would. He turned and Janice-Rose was watching him and he saw the query in her eyes. He knew that she was summing him up, judging him on how he was handling it. He smiled at her and held up two fingers and laughed when she held up one finger, then grimaced.

'Sorry about the introduction to my family life but it isn't normally like this. Normally we're bored shitless.'

'It never rains but it pours?' he said.

'Yeah, something like that.'

'Situation, ladies?' Peanut asked.

'One dead, one wounded and hobbled away,' Hills replied.

'That leaves six and a possible. They have gone back around the front?' he asked.

'We heard a 'fuck this' as the guy hobbled away after his mate. I don't think they were expecting opposition,' Hills said.

'Front door it is. Someone keep an eye on the rear, just in case, please.' Janice-Rose eased back towards the rear door as one of the front windows shattered and two stun grenades flew into the front room, followed by a loud smash on the front door. The stun grenades went off as they couched down behind the bar with ear muffs and eye shades on, then peered over the bar top and saw that the front door had held. Another smash on the door, then another. The door still held. Mick glanced at Peanut and shook his head in disbelief.

'Christ, that's a brilliant lock. Fucking unbelievable!'

'That it is. Five hundred dollars of the finest quality German-engineered steel. But it will let go, it simply has too. Be ready.' Another smash and the door lock suddenly couldn't take anymore and the door crashed open and two more stun grenades flew into the room. The twin explosions and then two guys burst into the room. They crumpled and died in a hail of fully automatic gunfire from the three rifles. The first two were followed by another two who tried to stop at the door and retreat. The sound of automatic rifle fire from outside meant it was too late; they crumpled to the floor, their bodies lying dead in the doorway. Peanut and Hills knew that they hadn't shot them and they moved rapidly towards the door, rifles on the ready. They peered outside and saw two guys standing and one sitting on the porch with their hands up, their white, scared faces looking at Blue, Peter, Chas, and Sharon, lined up with their Bushmasters at shoulder height, aimed and ready. A lady was sitting in late model nice SUV just outside the gate and Peanut couldn't see her clearly, but she had her hands over her mouth, clearly shocked. It had to be Blue's date. Chas gave the order.

'Cable tie them. Hands behind their backs and put them into their truck. We need to go for a drive and Mick can take us. Anybody hurt?'

Janice-Rose grumped. 'I broke my nail on the magazine doing rapid reloading. Fucking sore!'

Chas laughed.

'If that is the extent of our injuries, I'm happy. Sorry, J.R.'

The three were tied and thrown into the truck, one moaning in pain at being manhandled. Two long-bladed knives were taken off the dead guys and Peanut, Chas, and Sharon exchanged glances. They knew exactly what the thugs would have done with those knives and their faces were grim. They were to be butchered. Mick saw the knives, saw the grim looks and put it together. It didn't leave a pretty image. Peanut gestured to Chas.

'I need a partner. Blue has got a date so can Sharon spare you? Peter can talk to the FBI. He's good at that.'

Sharon shook her head.

'No sparing about it; I'm coming too.' She climbed in the front of the truck with Mick getting into the driver's seat.

Chas leaned out the rear door and talked to Hills.

'The story is these guys ran off and we have gone to find them, okay? Make sure our new guest understands and sticks to the script.' She nodded, watching as Mick fired the truck up and backed it out the drive. Peanut saw Hills and Blue head to the lady in the SUV as he swung the rear doors shut.

'Just drive, Mick,' Peanut said. 'Don't worry if you hear any strange sounds. We need to find out who tried to have us all killed. No nice way to do that, unfortunately.'

'I want to know too. Whatever it takes,' Mick replied.

Peanut turned and stared at the injured thug. The truck bounced over the curb as Mick drove it out onto the road and the injured guy winced. Peanut gave him a hard look.

'Name.' Peanut could see the blood soaking through his dirty jeans. It looked like he had taken a bullet in the thigh. The guy squinted at his mates.

'I'm injured,' he said, 'you have to take me to the hospital.'

Peanut promptly kicked him in the injured thigh. The guy yelled in pain and tried to writhe away.

'You are mistaking me for someone who gives a shit. Name?' Peanut asked. The guy peered up with scared eyes and Peanut kicked him again. He moaned and writhed on the steel floor of the truck. Peanut crouched down.

'It's not fair that you are the only one getting picked on, is it? Peanut said. 'Tell me your name and I'll leave you alone and go pick on someone else.' He stood and drew back his foot.

'Al Rashid!'

'Al as in Alan or Alistair?'

'Alistair.'

'Thank you, Al. Now, who hired you?' Al was trapped. He had given his name and was still being picked on.

'Think we are still picking on you?' Peanut asked. Al was scared and he didn't know which way this was going. Peanut stood, eased back his jacket and pulled his swords out and gently waved the blade in front of Al. 'This is sharp. Very sharp.'

He spun and drove the blade into the thigh of the nearest of the three guys, hit the femur and twisted, the shattering scream filling the van as Peanut withdrew the sword.

'Do you still think that I am just picking on you, Al?' Al shook his head. Peanut squatted down by the guy he had stabbed.

'Name, or I do the other leg and then start on your nuts. Castration is the special tonight. Two nuts for the price of one. And you pay.'

The guy was shaking in fright and the reply was prompt.

'Yasser Alizai.'

157

'Tell me, Yasser, who do you work for?' Peanut asked. Peanut twirled the sword blade around and sat the point on the inner thigh of his other leg. Alizai was terrified; shaking in fear, now knowing what would happen if he didn't answer. Peanut smelt the urine and saw that he had pissed himself in fright.

'Brian Schmidt,' Alizai said.

'And where is Brian waiting at this moment?' Peanut asked.

'At his office.'

'Is that where you were going to meet up after you had killed everyone?'

'Yes.'

'So your orders were to kill everyone at that address, right?' Peanut wanted confirmation. Yasser hesitated slightly and then muttered a faint, 'Yes.'

'Speak up, Yasser. I didn't hear that.' Peanut pushed the tip of the sword slightly into his leg.

'Yes! We were to kill you all!' He was panicked and had confirmed what Peanut and the team had guessed.

The guy lying at the front of the truck suddenly yelled.

'Shut the fuck up, you piece of camel shit. You tell them nothing. I'll fucking get to you, fucking loudmouth turd!'

Peanut picked up one of the knives and walked forward to the guy giving orders. He took out a rag and wiped the knife clean and then pressed the point up against the guy's chest.

'You must think we're the police or somebody else that is law abiding,' Peanut said quietly. 'You have it wrong, pal.' He shoved the knife in, the guy's eyes opened in surprise and he gave a shake, a gurgle and died on the floor. Peanut then took the knife and placed it aside. Al Rashid and Yasser stared at the dead guy, both glancing back at Peanut and suddenly understanding that their lives were on the line.

'Why did you kill him?' Ali asked, his voice husky, shaky.

'Because, asshole, you came to kill us and you lost,' Peanut replied. 'This is what happens when you lose. It's called *consequences*.' He sat in front of a frightened Yasser.

'Directions. Now. Call them out to the driver.' Yasser's voice shook as he called out directions, then turned to Peanut.

'Are you going to kill us?' It was said with a slight sense of hope. It made Peanut give a wry grin and a harrumph as if he found that funny. These thugs had come to murder them all. The men and women. The knives said it all. These thugs were lucky they had lived this long. Sharon glanced back. She smiled at Chas and Peanut. They now knew who was the boss and had organized the attack. They felt the truck speed up as Mick hurried to get to Schmidt's office.

They turned the last corner and raced toward the office as the figure of a big guy emerged out of the door and walked towards his car.

'Cut him off, Mick,' Peanut said as he turned to Yasser. 'Is Schmidt a big guy?'

'Yes, big and fat.'

'That's him.' Mick swerved the van in front of the Mercedes. Peanut had a clear view and saw the smile light up the face of Schmidt. He clearly thought that it was a mission accomplished but the look changed when Sharon leaped out and leveled the Bushmaster at him.

'Out, asshole. Now!' Sharon yelled. Peanut grinned. Sharon was in control and her training with Hills, Janice-Rose, and sometimes Chas was now showing. Schmidt raised his hands as Chas pulled his car door open, cable tied his wrists, marched him to the rear of the van, prodded him in and then kicked his legs out from under him and cable tied his ankles. He climbed in and shut the rear doors.

'Ready to go,' Chas said. Mick pulled out from the curb as Chas's phone rang. It was Hills. He listened and grinned.

'We'll be there soon, Hills.' He turned to Peanut. 'FBI are at the house.'

Peanut turned to Schmitt.

'Time to talk, Schmitt. Who hired you?' Peanut asked.

'Fuck off.'

Schmitt just glared at Peanut with his mouth firmly shut. Peanut didn't hesitate. He kicked him in the balls and watched him curl up in agony. He squatted down and placed his hands either side of Schmitt's neck, and gently pushed his thumbs into his carotid arteries.

'Five to ten seconds you are unconscious and four minutes later you're dead.'

He pushed strongly as Schmitt struggled to get away and then his eyes rolled up and he fainted as the blood loss to the brain took effect. Peanut eased his thumbs out of Schmitt's neck and sat back as Schmitt came around and stared up at Peanut with raw terror in his eyes. He had nearly died and he knew it.

'That was fun, wasn't it?' Peanut said. 'But we don't want you to think that you are missing out.'

He picked up his swords and gave Schmitt an evil grin.

'It wouldn't do for you to tell me to fuck off again. I am in charge here, not you.' Peanut drove the sword hard into the fat on the side of Schmitt's fat ass and hit the upper thigh bone. He twisted the sword a couple of times as Schmitt screamed in pain and fainted.

He pulled the sword out and sat back, waiting for him to recover. Schmitt shook his head, moaning in pain and slowly came around, clearly disorientated, not yet sure where he was. Peanut sat waiting, quietly watching nothing, just letting Schmitt come around.

Chas glanced up at Sharon; she smiled at him and nodded approval. He studied Peanut staring at nothing and reflected. He had been the find of a lifetime. Chas now knew that he was both right and he was wrong. Peanut was a brilliant lone operative but he was also a consummate team player. Today had proved that. He noticed Peanut glance at Schmitt. Peanut could see Schmitt's eyes were open and frightened. The big man was used to bullying people to get his way and now he was lying on the steel floor of a truck, helpless and in intense pain. Peanut smiled wryly; it was probably a first for the fat prick.

'Next time you do not answer, I will do the same to your other leg and then castrate you and stick your testicles in your mouth and make you eat them, clear? As I told your men, castration is on special this week. I do two nuts for the price of one, and as the one is free the second one is as well. So who hired you, asshole?' He began to undo Schmitt's belt buckle. Schmitt was trapped, the pain in his thigh was not easing. He needed hospital treatment and strong painkillers. He answered in a shaky voice.

'Burlington Ford.'

'How much?' asked Peanut.

'Three hundred thousand to get rid of you all.'

'You have the receipts for that payment?'

'Yes,' said Schmitt.

'Overseas bank account?' Schmitt gave a nod.

'So you and Burlington Ford planned to commit mass murder,' Peanut asked.

Schmitt glanced away and eventually spoke. 'Yes.'

Peanut wanted more confirmation. 'Burlington Ford is working with Milo Volkov?'

He saw the look on Schmitt's face. He has hit the jackpot. He placed his sword against Schmitt's other leg and pushed slightly and Schmitt recoiled.

'Yes, he is,' Schmitt said.

'Is Volkov staying with Burlington Ford?' Peanut was relentless.

'Yes.'

'How did you know where we lived?'

'Volkov told us.' Schmitt said.

'How did he know?'

'He said that Burlington had contacts.'

Peanut frowned at Chas. 'That has to be more of the rat's work, Chas.'

Peanut stared at the frightened prisoners.

'I think that all these guys escaped,' he said. 'Any ideas, Chas?'

'Yes. There is an old mining shaft not far from the camp. Dump these bodies overnight into a shed I know, take the truck back to the house, and they can all go down the shaft tomorrow. And we'll clean the truck thoroughly. The FBI will want to inspect it.'

Peanut nodded. He could see the faces of the guys in the truck. They knew what was coming; they knew they were all going to die. Yasser noticed the bleakness in Peanut's eyes; it was chilling. He pleaded desperately with Peanut.

'Please, please, … why? We no longer are a threat. Let us go, please.'

Peanut noticed that not once had he or any of the others said sorry. It wasn't in their DNA as killers. He smiled at Yasser and at the scared faces of the others.

'*Consequences,* assholes. You lost, we won. You okay with all of that Mick, Sharon?'

'Okay with what? The pricks got away,' Mick said.

Peanut stood. It was three short quick stabs and they were dead. It was over that quickly. Chas called out directions to Mick who gave a cheerful 'Aye, Aye'. He was enjoying himself. This was much more exciting than stuck in a patrol car, dealing with speeding motorists. He wondered if Chas would give him a job? And he wondered if Peanut could teach him some of those moves with the swords? They were really fucking effective!

Chapter 35

The FBI gave the returned truck an intense going over and were immediately suspicious. It was clean, spotless. Too clean. No DNA anywhere. Mick, Sharon, Peanut, and Chas watched, amused, then went inside. Their noncommittal answers had annoyed the agents. They had been handed a pile of dead bodies and only one explanation, and they were getting nowhere. The problem for them was that whatever they would like to think, the story was rock solid. It tallied with the positions of the bodies and their injuries.

What didn't gel was that some had got way, especially one that was injured. He wouldn't run far but he had disappeared. There was plenty of blood to show he was, at the least, quite seriously wounded, but he had disappeared. They knew it was bullshit. But he was gone and the truck was spotless. The realization that they would never solve every loose end came after their boss had a talk to Chas and then called his team together.

'Wrap it up, guys. We have enough details. Not going to worry about a pile of dead scum, are we? Everything tallies. Let's get a BOLO out for the runners. My thoughts are that they had a backup car nearby.'

The agents shrugged and began taking the bodies away. As the FBI wrapped up outside, Blue was inside, introducing his date to Chas, Sharon, Mick, and Peanut. They had all tried to reassure her that this was not normal.

'Guys, this is Julie.' She gave a very wan smile; she was still pretty shaken up but said a faint hello and a wan smile as she asked.

'They tell me that those guys were sent here to kill you all. Is that right?'

Peanut played the diplomat as he glanced at Hills.

'We know a bit more than that but what have you been told?'

'Just that they were going to try to kill you.'

'Yes, that's what the FBI thinks,' Peanut said, 'but realistically, they were so bad at it that it was never going to happen.'

'But why? Blue and Peter have sort of dodged that part.'

Chas put the issues to bed.

'We work for the Government. Some of what we do is very sensitive and it often results in people getting found out about their crimes. They don't like that.' He scratched his ear as he grinned at her. 'It's no biggie, Michelle. Thugs like that are two a penny. They will never get close enough to hurt any of us.'

'You sound sure.'

Peanut laughed and gave his cheeky grin, looking like a happy teenager as he held up his hand and put her at her ease.

'The facts. Thirteen arrived, three ran off. The rest are dead, including the guy who organized it. Oh, and Janice-Rose broke her fingernail.' He gave a happy smirk, raised his shoulders with a 'we fixed it' shrug and Julie laughed. A 'fuck off, Peanut' came from Janice-Rose listening in.

'Point taken. You slaughtered them. We're safe now?' Julie asked.

'Unless we get hit by an asteroid strike, yes.' Peanut replied.

She laughed again and Peanut knew that Blue had got a good lady. She linked arms with Blue and raised an eyebrow.

'You promised me a drink? I think I could do with a nice strong whisky.' He led her away, clearly happy that Peanut had minimized the dangers. Hills gave him a quick kiss and then took his hand and led him into the lounge. Blue and Julie ambled in, drinks in hand and Peanut apprised the two of them.

'You two look good together. Incidentally, Blue is really good at making beds. I'd put him to work if I were you.' She laughed as Blue blushed.

'He told me, and yes, he's better at it than I am.'

Chas cleared his throat.

'We were going to have a meeting, but I think, given the lateness of the hour and especially after the events of today, that we do it tomorrow afternoon, okay? Or later if you want? It is just about upcoming work, and none of it is pressing.'

Mick held his hand up.

'I'd like to come but I have to work tomorrow on a twelve-hour shift.'

'When do you finish?'

'Six o'clock.'

'Meeting at seven? Here? Mick, you're welcome.' Nods went around the room and Peanut lifted his glass of lemon lime and bitters.

'Here's to another successful day. We all survived.' He paused and they all suddenly saw the bleakness on his face as he talked quietly. 'But they won't.'

Julie stared at him. He could see the worry lines back on her face and winked at her, hoping she would think he was joking. Hills had noticed Julie's worried look and went and sat beside her. They were soon in deep conversation and Peanut felt sure that Hills would soon allay her concerns.

***

They were followed. Chas knew they would be. He glanced at Peanut and laughed. He had been doing this far too long to fall for their attempts to track him. He swung around the street corner and took a shortcut up an alley. As he turned into the alley, Peanut opened the side sliding door of the van and jumped out into an alcove, hiding behind a stack of used drums as Chas carried on down the alley. The car followed a few seconds later and Peanut grinned as he opened a door into a shed and checked through a very dirty window that they had gone. He walked through the shed and opened a door into a small garage. There was the van, old and dented with an electrical tradesman's logo on the side, sitting ready to go. He climbed in and triggered the garage door open and drove out, seeing the door shut behind him. He accelerated down the highway, winding the window down to get rid of the smell of the dead, then taking a turn about a mile away, heading for the camp, pulling into a rest area two miles from the camp.

'You took your time?' Peanut said.

Chas grinned and laughed.

'They are now following Hills and she doesn't look a bit like me! Silly fuckers,' Chas said. 'The FBI clearly doesn't believe us. I might have to fix that. Ready to go?'

'Lead the way.' Peanut followed Chas and ten miles later, up an old and rutted, disused track, pulled up at a rusted and locked steel gate with chain-link fencing stretching around a large mound. Chas unlocked the gate and waved Peanut through, directing him to back up against the mound. Peanut climbed out and opened the rear doors of the van as Chas pointed at the mound.

'The other side of that is the mine shaft, the one we discussed and you threatened that moron with. A two-hundred foot drop, straight down, into deep, very deep water. We shove the bodies up the mound and let them go rolling. Do not go over the edge or you will be dead. Put a rope and harness on before you go anywhere near the top.'

Peanut put the harness on and roped himself to the van, then dragged the first body up and shoved. It rolled down the other side and disappeared down a fifteen-foot-wide hole. There was silence then after a few seconds the sound of a splash. They did the other bodies, locked the gate and left, taking the van to a service station and used a car-cleaning water blaster to clean inside the rear, parking it back in the shed. Chas stood outside and triggered the door shut as Peanut climbed into the front seat of the SUV.

'Job done,' Chas said.

'Yeah. Now for the pricks that caused this,' said Peanut.

'This time it is not about the money, eh? It's revenge.'

Peanut glanced at him and gave an evil grin and chuckled.

'I wouldn't say that, at least not yet.'

Chas glanced quickly at him; what the hell was he planning this time?

***

Four weeks later, on a desolate stretch of Highway 39, Chas pulled to a stop. He checked his map and indicated.

'Turn off about a mile, I think.' He surveyed the scrubby mesquite that seemed to cover everything. 'Easy country to hide in.'

'Yeah. We'll see what it's like when we're closer,' said Peanut.

Chas eased the pickup out onto the highway and took the next turnoff, heading south towards the river. The senator had picked the site well when he had bought the ranch. Far enough away from San Antonio to deter casual visitors but close enough so that a quick helicopter ride was all that he needed to reach the airport. The homestead was built on a dammed section of the river, far enough off the main road to discourage visitors. The senator liked his privacy; that was for sure. He had bought the ranch not long after he had been elected many years ago and it had become his signature item, anchoring him to his ranching and farming base in Texas. The fact that before he had been a dubious city-boy lawyer was conveniently hidden and then forgotten.

Three miles along the loose-surfaced road, Chas pulled to a stop.

'Here, I think,' he said.

Peanut examined the desolate countryside. Mesquite bushes grew out of the stony ground and some stunted Live Oak trees grew in clumps. He could see a dense thicket of small trees in the distance and shook his head. It would be hard to make a living ranching out here. He climbed out and they unloaded the light little Honda motorbike. Painted in camouflage, it had extra tanks of gas strapped to the carrier and Peanut had food and water stored in his backpack. The only modification to the little bike, apart from the camouflage paint, was the custom muffler. The little bike whispered along, its little four-stroke motor just a pleasant mechanical hum. Chas patted Peanut on the back.

'No risks,' he said. 'We have a helicopter on standby, if needed. Don't be a hero. Use the satellite phone if you are in doubt about anything, right?'

Peanut kicked the little Honda into gear. Chas watched him ride off, handling the little bike with ease. He sighed as he climbed back into the truck, turned around and drove back toward the small town of Ingram. It was time for a coffee and a read of the local paper. It could be a long day of waiting.

Peanut was on his own.

***

Peanut rode away from the road, heading towards the intersection of the driveway into Burlington Ford's property and the road. Ten minutes later he arrived at the intersection, parked the little bike up and began searching. It wasn't hard to find; the telecom junction was just along the road from the entrance, nothing more than a grey plastic tube sticking six inches out of the ground with a rounded weather cap shoved over the top and a side screw to keep it fastened. He removed the cap, quickly clipped on his wires and walked back into the scrubby trees out of sight of the intersection and sat on the ground. He plugged in his small portable modem, connected his computer and dialed in. There were three computers and a tablet and four smart phones on the line. This was a tech-savvy house. Grinning as he packed

163

up his gear, he kicked the little bike's engine alight and rode away from the driveway towards a ridge. He wanted to have a look around, just to see what was here. He eased to a stop and climbed off the bike and then lay down and used his binoculars. This was all part of the plan, just to find out what the senator was up to.

When Peanut had first mooted the idea, there was opposition but he persuaded them about the lack of risk and the chance to see up close what Burlington Ford was really up to. One thing was clear, the senator was not sitting back. One attack had failed. The senator had plenty of money and would simply plan another and another until he won. He had the money to keep on paying proxies to kill them. Sooner or later, they would succeed. That left them with only one option, and this was the first step in ending it for good.

He packed up the binoculars and rode to the next ridge and checked again, repeating the process. He had a fair idea of where he was as he and Mandy had studied Google Earth, and he knew he was getting nearer to the homestead. He crawled up what he thought would be the last ridge and there was the homestead, overlooking the river. It was secluded and quiet. He lay still, his binoculars fastened on the buildings. At this distance, he could see the number plates on the four cars parked out in front. He noted the numbers and would call them in later. He concentrated on the buildings, noting that there was a new one, not shown on Google Earth. It was a large closed-in shed, built in still shiny corrugated iron. It had to be new and it was completely out of place against the other stately and aged wood and stone farm buildings. A lone wasp buzzed his head and he flicked it away, wondering why on a ranch this size there was no movement. He swung the binoculars around and then saw why. A herd of cattle was being worked in the distant yards, at least a mile away. Clever. They had built the dusty yards well away from the house. Or maybe, they had built the existing house well away from the yards. It appeared that the original homestead was still over by the yards, derelict and long since abandoned. He saw the heads of people working the stock; he counted four and he doubted that Burlington Ford would ever go anywhere near the yards. A helicopter squatted behind the house, the refueling tank on a stand up against the side of an accommodation block, the long filling hose hanging in coils off the side of the tank. The accommodation block was in use as he could see clothing on a line just outside.

Then he saw him, Burlington Ford. He came through the wide ranch doors onto the porch of the house, escorted by a really pretty, nearly middle-aged lady. She was definitely not his wife, not from the photographs he had seen. They sat on cowhide chairs on the porch, sipping on the drinks they had carried out. It was all very civil and relaxed. He knew he had to spend the day here so he eased back down off the ridge top and, using the satellite phone, called in the vehicle plate numbers and the helicopter's registration to Chas, easing back up to the top and peering over. They were still sitting on the porch and he used the photo feature on the binoculars to take close up images of both of them. They then stood and kissed. It was not a friendly neighborly kiss; it was passionate and he grinned as the woman had to reach over Burlington Ford's fat belly to reach his lips. He photographed that as well. They went inside and he was back to looking at nothing.

It was late in the day when the pickups started to arrive, the setting sun beginning to cast long shadows and it would be dark in an hour. They didn't stop at the house. They drove past and all stopped and parked on the large bare area in front of the main door to the corrugated iron shed. Each pickup carried at least four men; the occasional one had five guys squashed in and one even had six guys squeezed in. Then four large vans arrived. Five to ten guys in each one. This is what he had come to see. Three weeks of sitting in a motel monitoring the main highway in had shown that on every Friday, late in the afternoon, five or six van loads of men and a string of pickups headed out to the property. They wanted to know why. This was the reason why he was here. The last van arrived was followed by a couple of pickups, just as night finally closed in. He shivered. It was winter and it would be a cold desert night.

He waited and in the gloom saw the fat shape of the ex-senator walking to the shed, flanked by three other men. From what Sharon had told him, the one on the left was Volkov. It was time to move.

He started the bike and traveled down the slope towards the homestead, parking the little bike in among a clump of mesquite and making his way slowly towards the shed, the long side that faced away from the homestead, the yard lights and any watching eyes at the house. It was fully dark when he arrived, and that was his first problem. The shed was sided in corrugated iron, no windows at all. He crept closer and put his ear to the iron. He could hear everything said. It was slightly muffled but that was because there were multiple voices shouting and yelling all at once. It sounded like it was some sort of military training. He heard laughter as well and then more yelling and orders. He was puzzled. Out here in the middle of nowhere? What the fuck was going on? What were they training for? It had to be for a marching parade; the shouted commands sounded like that. He heard Left Right Left Right, repeatedly. Training for a fourth of July march, perhaps? More orders were shouted, and more commands barked. Still puzzled, he slid along the side wall of the shed. He needed to see. Then he found it. A small tear in the iron where passing farm machinery had caught on a corrugate. It was tiny, so he took out his multi-tool and using the short blade worked the hole slightly bigger. It was all that he needed. He pulled out a miniature camera lens on a stem, plugged it into his phone's USB, turned on the app and began to take a series of videos and photos of the inside, keeping the screen of his phone hidden under his jacket in case the light gave him away. He was able to see everything. He was stunned. This was far too big for the ICT.

Finished, he put the phone in his pocket and walked away from the shed, feeling safe as he hadn't seen any sentries. That didn't mean that they weren't there; they were probably stationed in the well-lit areas where they could see and be seen. He walked around in the darkness towards the house, approaching it from the far side, again staying in the dark. He scouted the house, checking through the windows and saw the pretty lady reading in the lounge with a half-full wine glass on the table in front of her. There had to be servants. These sorts of people needed servants to wait on them. How else were they going to feed the guys in the shed? That lady inside, with her long fingernails, had never cooked. Almost as if on cue, four men in white chef's uniforms came out the rear door and carried two large gas barbeques over towards the shed. Peanut didn't hesitate. He opened the rear door and slipped in. It was a short hallway to the now empty kitchen and he eased out into the main central hallway. He wanted the office and he soon found it, along towards the bedrooms end of the house. The door was open and the senator's laptop computer was sitting open, its screen black. He gently closed the door and tapped the keyboard. It came to life immediately and wanted a password. He checked underneath the computer, nothing, and then checked the drawers. Nothing again. He sat and tried the obvious. He entered 'Senator' and nothing. He tried 'BFSenator', again nothing. So he tried 'SenatorBF', again failure. Then he remembered the ranch sign out at the road. 'Senatorial'. He was in. Stupid man. He took out his thumb drive and loaded the programs in, getting the computer's IP address as they loaded, taking the thumb drive out and then logging out, pushing the Windows key plus L to lock the computer. He heard footsteps on the wooden floor of the hallway, ladies' footsteps, and he hid in the corner; the office door was pushed open and then the footsteps walked off, leaving the door open the way it was. He heard the sound of a toilet flushing and then the same footfalls. They went past without stopping and he went to the door and watched as she went into the lounge. He walked quickly back to the kitchen, opened the rear door and was rapidly out across the yard and into the darkness, stopping, turning, seeing two of the cooks returning, talking as they walked. He used the darkness to walk around the house and yard, getting further out until he began to look for his bike. When he had parked, he had lined up the house and shed, but now, in the dark, finding the markers was difficult and he was beginning to feel a slight sense of unease when he nearly walked into it. He turned the little bike away from the house, started the motor and began the slow ride away from the compound. Ten minutes later, he turned the headlight on and stopped. He wanted to re-check what his tiny little camera had obtained, just to see if the images were any good. If he had to go back and reshoot any, it was easier to do it now. He was delighted. They were not just good, they were brilliant. The rushed look he had taken back at the shed hadn't allowed him time to really check them out, but he knew Chas would be impressed. He turned the little bike towards the road and rode it as hard as he could in the light of the headlights. It was still slow going but he needed to get away. He did not want to be caught on the road by those good old boys when they left to go home.

One hour later he was there. Stay the night or keep moving? He decided to keep moving and removed the headlight cover but left the taillight one on. He hit high gear on the road and then kept the little bike's engine working hard, seeing no lights of any other traffic. On reaching the turnoff on Highway 39, he again took the little bike up to its maximum speed. It ran much sweeter on the sealed road but ran out of gas ten minutes later. He eased over into some trees at the side and topped it up. Finished, he rang Chas, who answered immediately.

'Hi, Peanut.'

'Got the lot. On Highway 39 heading to Ingram,' said Peanut.

'Meet you there?'

'Yep.'

'What did you find?' Chas asked.

'The works,' said Peanut.

'The works? What?'

'Best I show you. You won't believe it. See you in twenty minutes. On the corner?'

'I'll be there.'

Chapter 36

Their hotel in San Antonio supplied a small conference room for a full meeting of the team: Chas and Sharon, Hills and Peanut, Blue, Peter and Janice-Rose. Maybe sometime in the future Mick might join, but until then this was now the ICT team. Chas sat and glanced at Peanut. 'Okay, Peanut,' he said, 'I've seen it, but clue the team in. Let's hear it.'

'Burlington Ford is building an army,' Peanut said. 'It's in the early stages I think, but they're training the men and they have the weapons. That's why he needed Gorman, not just to build a support base but for the money he was supplying. Take a look.' He hooked up his phone to the monitor and played the video first before he put the pictures on the screen.

The men inside the shed were being drilled in basic parade-ground marching, military style. Munitions boxes were stacked up in the background. One squad was training with what appeared to be mortars, while another group was working with grenade launchers, and yet another was working with long tubes. It was everything but a live-fire exercise. There was no doubt about it. The senator was building a private army.

'Stop!' shouted Blue. 'That last image. Show it again.'

Peanut took it back to the previous picture. The pictures were much clearer than the video. 'Can you blow that up? I want to see the labels on those boxes.'

Peanut expanded the image and zoomed in on one of the boxes.

'What is it, Blue?' Chas asked.

'Hand-held SAMs. I thought as much when I saw those guys holding those long tubes. That labelling puts it beyond doubt.'

'Really? Hand-held surface-to-air missiles?'

Blue grinned. 'Yeah. Very expensive. We need to go through every video and picture and try to catalog some of those weapons.' Blue frowned at Chas. 'Boss, this is way beyond us. This is NSA shit. Show this to them and let them bring in the National Guard.' Blue turned and gave Peanut a big thumbs up.

'This ain't a can of worms,' said Blue, 'I think you've uncovered a pit of snakes. This isn't slightly illegal. This is totally illegal and it violates terrorism laws. Most of those weapons are military use only. Show us some more, buddy.'

Twenty minutes later, it had been confirmed. Video of the men being shown how to set up and use fully automatic .50 caliber machine guns, anti-personnel mines, the list went on. Sharon typed it all down on a computer as they sat back wondering what to do. She looked up at Chas, then at Peanut a query in her expression. Chas and Peanut both noticed.

'What is it Sharon?'

'Remember when I said I'd do some background checks on Burlington Ford?'

Peanut nodded and Chas looked surprised.

'Well, some of his statements prior to his getting elected years ago were quite inflammatory.'

'Okay, fill us in so we know what we are dealing with,' Chas said.

'He maintained that the *rot*, as he put it, had gone so deep in America that there had to be a two-state solution. The southern states would break away and form their own government and move all Negros, Hispanics, Jews, and Catholics; in short, anybody that wasn't of European heritage and identified as belonging to the Protestant religion, north and out of the new Southern States of America. He maintained that a small and well-trained highly mobile army, using helicopters and armored trucks, could sweep through the southern states and take over. The US military would not be able to intervene because under the constitution they're not allowed to take military action within the United States and that meant that the only opposition would be the National Guard. He maintained that many of them, being true southern men, would support the move to a white Protestant Christian Democracy. Led by him, of course.'

She stopped and peered around at the shocked faces of the team.

'He was really just saying what a whole lot of southern whites think but won't voice, and he knows it. But he's got it wrong. Support for an old-style confederate southern government is supported by less than twenty percent of the white southern population. Over the whole population of Texas the support shrinks to less than five percent. If he succeeded, it would be an unsupported dictatorship and probably, given the extent of the racial and religious hatred, a brutal one.'

'Thanks, Sharon. The question is this:-Is he trying to set up an armed insurrection? Or is this just a show of force to get his way with local politicians? Things that he couldn't get as a senator because his own party wouldn't allow it?' asked Chas.

Sharon noticed the room all looked at her and was a bit embarrassed.

'He wouldn't want an armed insurrection because he'd lose,' she said. 'Even his own party would help change the constitution, if need be, just to allow the use of the military. That idea would be a failure. It would be madness. However, he's against the immigration of people who aren't what he sees as the *preferred races or types,* to quote his manifesto. He also maintains that where public facilities are provided, the respective providers should have it in their power to decide who uses them. That means it's up to each city who uses the schools, public toilets, etcetera.'

'Segregation by another name,' said Chas with a look of disgust on his face.

'Correct,' Sharon said. 'If he could force a few of those changes, I think he would see that as a victory that could be built on.' She paused for a moment. 'Would a private army marching through the streets do that?'

'It would certainly be divisive and that's the last thing this country needs. Let's not forget what he's doing is illegal and doing it with arms that are illegal in the public's hands,' said Chas.

'Chas, this is an issue for the NSA,' Peter said. 'It's well above our pay grade.'

'Yes, but not right now, please,' said Peanut.

'Why not?' asked Chas.

'First, those guys of Burlington Ford's are mostly untrained. Look at the video. They're still being taught the basics, like how to march without tripping over their own feet. Watch it. I've never been in the military and I can see they are rubbish at marching. They have yet to do live-fire training and drills. Remember, these are mostly working men, and this is their free time, so there's no rush. Action day is at least four to six months away, I reckon.'

'You're right. Those turkeys are no match for the National Guard. Not from those videos, anyway,' said Chas. 'And second?'

'Money. I intend to relieve them of some of it. Just to help out with our individual budgets,' said Peanut.

'How are you going to do that?' asked Peter.

'Same as I did in Houston. Infect their computers,' said Peanut.

'How?' Chas asked. 'You can't break into Ford's house. Night or day, you'd be spotted. And they'd kill you. Christ! Control him, Hills. Hit him in the nuts again! That suggestion is just pure madness!'

'Chas, it's already done,' said Peanut with a chuckle. 'I did it the night I took those photos and the video. With Burlington Ford in the shed watching the training, the cooks at the shed getting things set up to feed the troops, there was only one woman left in the house and she was on the wine from early in the afternoon. It's done and I'm already getting data. How often he plays with the accounts is out of my hands. But there is no immediate rush until we have the money angle sorted out, is there?' He looked questioningly at Chas.

Chas studied Peanut and thought it through. It was not immediate. Peanut was right. Raiding Burlington Ford's house was more proof of Peanut's lone operative skills. He sees an opportunity and he goes for it. Chas looked around the table and saw the smiles. They all knew that Peanut had already absconded with a lot of the criminal's money. Blue and Peter openly rubbed their hands. He grimaced at them and shook his head. Greedy pricks.

'Okay. If we can relieve him of some of his operating capital, then so much the better,' said Chas. 'We'll give it until the end of either this week or the next and then see if we can move ahead. I'll tell the department about everything bar the money when you give us the green light, okay? I only have one question left. Will they want us to clean this up or leave it for the National Guard or the NSA or even the FBI? I have a funny feeling that we'll be asked to undertake the cleanup. I think they'll want it kept as quiet as possible and that would be impossible with the National Guard or the military.'

Blue glanced around at the team and then Chas.

'They have an army in there,' said Blue. He then gestured at the team. 'There is only us. What you're suggesting is suicide. Fifty, sixty, against us? Untrained or not, those odds are madness. Christ, Chas, I have no intention of dying young.'

'Understood, Blue, I have no intention of dying young either. Nobody here has, right?' said Chas.

Everyone except Peanut nodded.

'You with us, Peanut?' asked Chas.

'Yeah, Chas, just thinking,' said Peanut.

'Surprise us. What's on your mind?'

'It can be done, guys, and done just by us.'

Chas frowned, now worried. 'Let's hope we don't have to do it,' he said and noticed Peanut's confident grin. That worried him even more.

'Yeah, Peanut?'

'Chas, call your contact at the FBI. And let me at least sit in on the meeting. I have some new information that they need to know. I think this will involve the CIA as it involves a foreign power.'

'Russia?'

'Yeah.'

'Will do.' Chas picked up his phone.

***

Chas and Peanut were surprised at the guys waiting for them in the FBI Washington Headquarters conference room. Chas's contact ushered them all to seats and then did the introductions.

'As Chas knows, I'm John Read, his FBI contact. This is our Washington SAC, Sandy Aarons, and this gentleman is from the NSA, Harold Myers, or Hank as he prefers to be called, and we have Peter McConnell from the CIA. Peter is here just to listen and give an opinion if needed. This guy is Charles Ficher, Chas as he likes to be called. Chas, the floor is yours.'

'Guys, introductions. Neville Patterson, aka Peanut. Peanut, tell them what you know.' Peanut glanced around at the other guys at the table.

'You have seen the video and the photos?' He noticed the nods. 'You will have seen the military training going on. It takes money to do that. Lots of money. All of it coming from drugs originally supplied by Jerry Gorman sourced through his contacts in Afghanistan. You know all this anyway.' He paused. 'But the supply never stopped with Gorman's disappearance. We now know that he was supplied by Russians who had the Afghanistan contacts. They had those contacts as they supplied the Taliban with Russian weaponry for

169

drugs. With Gorman gone, they got cheeky and are now doing it all themselves. They own the supply line, all the way from Afghanistan to the gangs and headmen that supply the drug mules that supply the street dealers. Good business, but that is something that you might or might not know.'

He paused as their blank faces stared at him, giving nothing away.

'I wondered about the fancy offices the Russians had in LA and New York. That was because, just like Jerry Gorman, they were legitimate arms dealers. Nice offices in good locations, just to give respectability. Perfect cover if you are setting up an army and dealing in drugs to do it. Gorman was originally doing this in Europe and then initially over here. But Burlington Ford has taken that over. So what's

behind this, or rather who? The emails I have leave no doubt that it is the Russians. I think it is more than just money; it is them trying to destabilize our democracy here on our own soil. The Russian involved is Milo Volkov. He stays at Burlington Ford's home quite a bit, as does a Russian woman. Name of Nadia Burov. I suspect that she would be an agent as well. I have emails that suggest that Volkov and Burov are members of the FSB. Questions?'

Peter, the CIA man, coughed and frowned at Peanut.

'You have those emails?' Peanut opened his computer case and handed over a stack of emails.

'They are in the order they were sent and retrieved.'

Peter smiled politely and began to read. As he finished each one he handed it over to Hank, the NSA man, who quietly read them and handed them to Sandy, the SAC. The paper was shuffled along the line. Chas's contact, John Read, indicated coffee and they all smiled at the suggestion. Peter looked up; he had nearly finished reading and smiled.

'Why don't you guys go and get them and Peanut can stay and talk to us while we wait?' He grinned at their worried faces.

'We are not going to give him the third degree. We just want to know how the fuck he got these?'

As they filed out, Peanut faced Peter, Hank, and Sandy. Peter raised an eyebrow, waiting.

'Illegally,' Peanut said.

The CIA man just smiled. 'I had already figured that out, but how?'

'When I was snooping, trying to find out what was going on at Burlington Ford's ranch, I accessed his computer and loaded in programs that allowed me to access it remotely but to also access his house's Wi-Fi router. That, in turn, allowed me to access all the other computers, tablets, and phones that accessed that router. That is why you have those emails.'

'And you did this as they held their military training, right? Chas told us how you did that. They would have killed you if they had caught you, you knew that?'

Peanut gave a bland look back.

'That just means that failing isn't an option, doesn't it?' he said.

'Yes, I suppose it does.' The CIA man replied. He studied Peanut as he thought. This guy was cool, way too cool. He had seen that aspect in highly trained agents and this guy was of exactly the same mold.

'What did you find out about their finances?' the CIA man asked.

'All seem to be held in overseas investments. Untouchable. They bring in the money when it is needed,' Peanut said.

'Do you prefer to be called Peanut or Neville?' Peter asked.

'Peanut.'

'Apart from the obvious, why? Most short people would see that as an insult.'

'It helps if people discredit my abilities. I do not mind if people see me as a nothing, inconsequential. That automatically gives me an edge. And speaking generally, I am what I am and I'm perfectly happy with that. I am not going to ever become six feet tall. I have said

170

it before and will say again; I would rather be who I am than some big six foot beefed up jock with five girlfriends and chicken shit for brains.'

Peter gave a wry smile as Hank and Sandy chuckled. Peter contemplated Peanut, his expression thoughtful.

'Well said. We might have a job for you. Chas has said that your only fault in operations is the body count. You are quite lethal, I understand. We will discuss all this when Chas comes back with the coffees.' He glanced at Sandy and at Hank.

'These guys are part of the ICT team, right?' asked Peter.

'Yes,' Hank responded.

'I see their charter allows them full operational flexibility, correct?'

'Yes.'

'So they can do what the fuck they like to achieve a result?'

'Yes.'

'What is the separation? Like from the department?' Peter asked.

'There is no link. They are paid out of the department's road budget,' Hank said.

'The department has a road budget?' Peter queried.

'How do you think all those parking lots and walkways get maintained?' Hank replied. Peter grimaced and stared at Peanut.

'I see your name isn't on the ICT books?'

'I work as an independent contractor,' Peanut said. 'Currently unpaid and not on the books. I have just as much deniability as ICT itself does. If it all goes belly up, I wasn't there.'

'You don't trust the department.' It wasn't a query, but a statement of fact.

'No.'

'Good, neither do I. Assholes the lot of them. If anything goes wrong they will blame you all, deniability or not.'

Chas and John Read walked in with two trays of coffees as Peter finished speaking. They heard the last statement and both grinned.

'Hot-iron marks all gone?' Chas asked.

Peanut smiled. 'Branding finished and my nuts still work.'

'Hills would kill anyone that touched your nuts,' Chas said. 'When she is angry, she is murderous.'

Peter peered at Chas.

'The delightful Amanda Carolyn Hiller, I presume?'

'Yes. One of our best.'

'I know,' Peter said. 'Gentlemen, I am going to suggest to my director that the ICT become part of *our* road paving department. Agreed?' They all agreed and Chas looked hard at Peanut. What the fuck had he said to them? The department would be ropable. Peter asked the important question.

'Operationally, where are you at?' Chas indicated to Peanut that he speak.

'Tidying up loose ends, then informing the department of what Burlington Ford is up to.'

Hank and Phil both shook their heads.

'This is a matter that has to be hushed up,' Hank said. 'The department will see it that way as well. I will meet with them this afternoon. Until you hear back, you do nothing.' He turned to Peanut. 'Tell me, how much time do you need to finish what you are doing?'

'Three days.' Peanut was ready now but the extra time would put a couple of minor loose ends to bed.

Peter stood, smiled and walked out, the other guys standing, shaking hands and leaving. The SAC sat looking at them.

'Let me guess. If you guys do this, there could be quite a big body count on this mission?'

Chas summed it up. 'Given the number of military-grade weapons involved, yes.' he said.
The SAC turned and peered sadly out the window.
'Bummer.'

Chapter 37

Chas saw the message on his phone and rang Peanut back. 'You ready to go?' he asked.

'Yeah. Tell the department and see what they say.' He paused for a second. 'And don't mention the money.'

'I won't. How much?'

'If it works, everyone will get more than two million. Just got to make sure it works. Has that CIA guy, Peter McConnell, been in contact?' asked Peanut.

'Nope. Why?'

'He said he might have a job for us. Whether that is all of us or just me, who knows. If it is just me, it can now come through the ICT.'

'You sure?' Chas asked.

'Yeah.'

'Thanks, Peanut.' Chas relaxed. That was an issue resolved. Peanut was now on board. It was now a waiting game and he wondered what the department would decide.

Peanut rang off and examined his scribbled calculations. If this worked, the entire ICT team would be rich, very rich. The two million was just a teaser for Chas.

***

Chas ambled into Peanut's basement, followed by Blue and Peter, grinning at them all.

Peanut jinked sideways and then forward, trying to wrong-foot Sharon and landed flat on his back, quickly rolling away and flipping to his feet, clapping his hands in delight.

'Well done!'

Hills, watching, was impressed. Sharon was like her; she had naturally quick reflexes. Janine-Rose clapped as Mick stood grinning. Chas was delighted, he could see they were working well as a team.

'Meeting, guys,' Chas said. He waited till they had all gathered around.

'The department didn't want us to handle Volkov and Burlington Ford. They wanted to pass it on to the National Guard and the FBI. At the urging of the NSA and the CIA, the President took advice and has now moved us to the CIA. We have exactly the same function, paid as government roading contractors and, as usual, we stay top secret.'

Peanut caught on immediately.

'So, they want us to handle Burlington Ford and Volkov as the ICT, just to keep it all quiet, is that right? And the FBI will clean it up after we have finished. Correct?'

'Yes,' replied Chas. 'We've been given express orders. They don't want trials for any of the principals.' He grimaced at the team. 'I don't have to spell out what that means. It's business as usual. Peanut, you once said that we could handle this. What do you have in mind?' Peanut gave an evil grin and began to explain, going over to the whiteboard in the gym and showing how it would work. Ten minutes later, he was finished. They knew he was right. They could do it, but not on a Friday night. That was the night of Southern States Alliance military practice.

***

The lights in Burlington Ford's house flickered out. The only lights still on were in the kitchen of the accommodation block so that the lone sentry could make coffee and take a break.

The last of the house lights flickered out and Peanut kicked the Honda into gear and rode out to the phone junction at the intersection. He took out his computer and modem and quickly connected, hooking into their computers, loading up the different banks web pages He logged into them one at a time and began to transfer money from their accounts. The key logger had long ago given him the passwords, and as there was no mobile phone coverage out here in the Boonies, the bank just asked for confirmation with a secure bank email and he obliged. All transfers were made immediately and when he had finished, he transferred the money into offshore accounts. It only took thirty minutes to complete. He had to smile as he shut down the computer and packed it away. He was still smiling as he rode back to his position. He pressed *talk* on his radio.

'Transfers completed. You're all rich.' He injected a serious tone into his voice. 'Whatever you do, don't put yourself in the firing line. You now have far too much to live for. Over.'

There was silence for a second, then the radio clicked and Chas's voice came through.

'Thanks, from the lot of us. And don't forget to listen to your own words of advice. Huh? Over.'

'Copy that, Chas,' said Peanut. 'Over and out.'

***

Peter and Mick had positioned themselves so that anyone running out the front door of the accommodation block would walk straight into automatic machine-gun fire. Spare magazines lay on the ground beside them. Mick had taken a week off, just to be with them. It was a try out to see if he wanted to leave the troopers and join. The fact that he was head over teacup in love with Janice-Rose had a fair bit to do with his wanting the job. Blue was in position, further back from the compound, the Barrett loaded with armor-piercing rounds, the helicopter was in his sights as well as anyone trying to leave by vehicle. Chas, Hills, and Sharon were all stationed outside the house, ready to enter when required. Janice-Rose was floating around towards the back of the compound, ready to take out any sentries that poked their heads up and anybody who might try to run that way. Peanut was proud of her, she was a natural. Her quick reflexes and accuracy had made Peter more than proud. He saw her almost as the daughter he never had.

Peanut was stationed at the rear of the corrugated iron shed, the accommodation block thirty meters off to his right, armed with a 40 mm grenade launcher, its rotating drum fully loaded. The ranch hands bunkhouse was sited well away from the compound and was empty, the hands away for the night, partying it up at a new club in San Antonino. They had picked well; it was a weeknight, a Wednesday, and the personnel at the homestead was small. They had made sure that all the principals were in place, especially Volkov and Burlington Ford.

Peanut's radio buzzed.

'Ready, Peanut? Over,' came Chas's voice.

'Ready. Over.'

'Blue, Mick, Peter?'

'Ready. Over.'

'Janice-Rose?'

'Ready. Over.'

'All yours, Peanut. Light it up, over and out,' Chas said.

Peanut eased his grenade launcher up and aimed from his spot, fifty meters back from the rear wall of the corrugated-iron shed. The internal images of the shed that he had taken on his visit had shown that behind that thin corrugated iron wall was a stack of forty-four gallon drums, the labeling suggesting emergency fuel supplies of diesel and av gas. He had the spot clearly in his sights as he raised himself up on his knees from behind an old farm plow and fired.

He heard the explosion inside the shed, aiming to fire a second grenade as the corrugated-iron walls of the shed seemed to momentarily swell and expand. The sudden whump and the massive explosion ripped the rear of the shed apart, the impact knocking Peanut back from

174

the plow. He could see the heavy steel plow lift slightly off the ground and slump back into place. He crawled forward, knowing another grenade wasn't needed. He aimed and fired into the rear sleeping quarters of the accommodation block, seeing it blow a hole in the wall and then explode inside. He heard the yells and screams coming from the inside. He quickly fired another one into the rear of the quarters, then aimed and fired into the front of the building. He assumed that those still standing inside would be rushing to get out. He saw the hole appear in the wall and then the explosion inside and then more screams and yells. He glanced back at the main corrugated-iron shed. The back half of the roof had fallen in, twisted sheets of corrugated iron lay everywhere; the fire was raging and the flames clearly visible above the walls of the shed.

The sound of automatic rifle fire came to him. He saw two guys drop and roll at the front of the accommodation block, firing at where they thought the automatic fire was coming from, clearly well-trained soldiers. He fired a grenade, watching it explode between them, an arm and a leg flying into the air. The other guys that ran outside ducked and dived, trying to roll out of harm's way, clearly disorientated as to where the gunfire was coming from. The helicopter pilot sprinted out the back door of the house toward the helicopter, dressed only in jeans, and leapt into the pilot's seat. The whine of the turbines started almost immediately. Too far for Peanut's effective range with the grenade launcher but they had decided right from the start that was Blue's job. A guy that was rolling away near the accommodation block got to his feet and crouched over, sprinting for the helicopter, leaping in as the rotor picked up speed as two more guys leapt up, running and scrambling on board. Rats deserting a sinking ship, Peanut thought.

The helicopter began to lift, the turbines screaming as the pilot asked for maximum power from the twin turbines. It rose straight up, leaping into the sky, the pilot turning the helicopter when it was about three hundred feet up, still rapidly gaining height. Where the fuck was Blue?

The sudden loud blast of the Barrett allayed his fears. The helicopter seemed to stagger slightly, then another loud blast and the sound of the turbines changed. The helicopter was no longer stable. Another blast and then a loud metallic crunch as something locked up and the rotor and its connecting plate detached, spinning away; the scream of the turbines instantly increasing. With no lift, the helicopter fell like a stone. It hit the refueling tanks next to the accommodation block with a tinny-sounding metallic crash, rupturing them instantly and then a loud whump as the tanks and the helicopter exploded, flaming av-gas exploding all over the accommodation block, setting the hundred-year-old timbers alight. Peanut knew that there would no survivors from that blast. He noticed Chas, Sharon, and Hills get up out of hiding and run for the front door of the house, automatic rifles at the ready. He saw Janice-Rose sneak towards where Mick was lying, pausing as the accommodation block became engulfed in flames, two guys leaping out the windows, trying to get away. Janice-Rose shot at one and Peanut saw him buckle over. Mick or Peter dropped the other one.

Then his heart stopped cold. The av-gas was running in an eight-foot-wide river of blue and orange fire, heading straight towards the house. It was going to run under the house, setting it alight from underneath, making the total destruction of the house inevitable. The house had gas tanks for cooking stored along the rear wall and when the house burned, they would explode. He had to get Chas, Hills, and Sharon out of the house!

***

Chas, Sharon, and Hills charged up the wide front steps of the ranch house, crossing the porch, Chas throwing the door open, stopping, seeing no one and then moving inside the front entrance hallway, Bushmaster rifles held at the ready.

'We stick together, as discussed. Do not go off on your own.'

It was important they stick together; this was Sharon's first action and she would be nervous, a bit unsure until she had more experience. He had no worries about Hills, other than she saw this as revenge for her attempted rape by Volkov's thugs. They moved together out into the main central hallway, Chas leading, checking doors along the hallway, making sure the rooms were all clear, just to protect from an attack from behind. Chas checked another room, the laundry on one side, the door on the other leading into the large dining room. He wondered why there were no people, not even outside watching the shed and accommodation building burn, let alone the helicopter crash.

Where were they? He began to get nervous. Did Burlington Ford have a plan in case they were attacked? It would surely have included the helicopter for a quick getaway and now that was just a burning wreck. He stood still, thinking, trying to figure it out, then decided to move slowly down the hallway, he and Sharon watching the front and Hills both the front and the rear. They never expected it. The door of the laundry room that Chas had just checked flew open and, before Hills could react, the cold hard metal of a pistol barrel was shoved against her head.

'The lady dies if you do anything.' It was Volkov. He reached out and took the Bushmaster rifle off Hills. He eased out into the hallway followed by a pretty middle-aged lady, who promptly took the rifles off Sharon and Chas and moved back to stand with Volkov as fat Burlington Ford came out the door. Chas remembered the room. It had large storage cupboards at the rear and they must have been hiding in the cupboards. He felt a fool, but it was too late now.

'Take the lead, Burlington.' Fat Burlington Ford began to squeeze past. Chas saw his chance. Hills and Sharon and Burlington Ford's bulk were between him, Volkov, and the lady. He smacked the pistol in Burlington Ford's hand away and then grabbed it and ripped it from his grasp, punching him in his fat gut, ducking and running along the hallway, past the lounge, grabbing the door handle of the nearest door as the sound of a shot came to him, seeing wood splinter, twisting the handle, then the hammer blow of a second bullet hitting his shoulder and tumbling him into the room, the mind-numbing pain lancing up across his shoulder. He kicked the door shut, lying for a second as he fought against the pain, finding he could still use his right arm, his gun hand. He stood, opened the door and a bullet smacked into the door frame. They were watching, waiting. As he jerked back, he saw the hallway door slam shut. If they jammed a chair under the door handle on the other side of the door, he was effectively locked at this end of the house.

What a disaster! He knew the ladies were in trouble but they wouldn't kill them; they needed to question them. He kicked the door of the room shut and hid behind it as he took off his jacket and checked the wound. It hurt like hell but there was no pumping of blood; it just seemed a deep graze across the back of his shoulder and he wrapped his shirt around to stem the bleeding. The pain made it hard to think logically.

That was very good shooting. Volkov was deadly, no doubt about it. Chas had no radio; that was with Hills and he had no way of calling for help. He began to look at his options. He examined the window, it was high and barred and he soon saw why; this was the room they had once paid the ranch hands wages out off, always with cash. It was a strong room. The only way out was to try another room and smash a window and climb out. But he couldn't attack from outside; if he tried, either he or Sharon and Hills would be killed immediately. His options were getting limited. The ladies were on their own.

**

Peanut pressed *talk* on his radio.
'Fire running towards the house! Everybody get out! Over and out.'

He doubled over and sprinted towards the back door of the house, running up the rear steps and into the hallway that led to the kitchen and the main central hallway. The door to the main hallway wouldn't open, clearly locked. He eased into the kitchen and running to the far end door, opened it into the main hallway. Seeing the end door shut, he walked forward and tried the handle; it wouldn't budge. It had been jammed. He walked back up the hallway, heading toward the bedrooms, seeing the slightly open door. He moved into the room and felt a gun pressed up against his head. He stopped as a feeling of dread swept over him.

'Peanut! What the fuck are you doing here?' Peanut breathed a sigh of relief, turned and grimaced at Chas.

'The place is going to burn. The gas from the helicopter crash is on fire and running under the house. We have to get everybody out, as fast as possible!'

'Sharon and Hills are captive in the lounge. We have no way of getting to them unless we smash out the windows and attack from outside. If we do that, they will see us coming and will kill them.'

'We have to get behind them.'

'How?'

Peanut examined the room and suddenly pointed at the ceiling. Chas wondered what he was looking at and then saw it. In the corner was an access hatch into the ceiling space. Peanut ran across the room and using the right angle of the walls, ran up and punched the access cover, dislodging it and grabbing the edge of the hatch with his other hand. Then, taking a two-handed grip, he swung himself up into the roof space and disappeared from view. Chas looked on amazed. They had never taught him that in the Army!

Peanut paused to let his eyes adjust to the gloom for a second. He found a central access walkway of planks laid on the rafter joists and ran along to the other end of the house. He tried to imagine the rooms below, seeing the places the room walls came up under the roof framing, stopping and looking for another hatch. He found it and lifted it gently; it was the dining room, right next to the lounge. Lowering himself quietly down into the dining room, he dropped lightly onto his feet and walked over to the door into the lounge, gently turning the knob, hoping no one would notice. Everything needed to go right if he was to get Hills and Sharon free.

Chapter 38

Peanut eased the door open a slight crack and heard the lady talking her Russian-accentuated English.

'You think we are going to fall for that stupid bullshit? Fire under the house? Give me that radio!'

Peanut put his radio on quiet as he peered through the slight crack in the door.

They were all standing on the other side of the room; only Hills and Sharon were facing him and they were tied up and standing together, watching, upset but not showing fear. Their training was standing them in good stead. It was the lady talking and fat Burlington Ford stood watching with a smile. A tall solid man, whom he assumed was Volkov, was watching, his face emotionless. The lady talked loudly on the radio, her voice clear in his earpiece.

'Put down your weapons and come to the house unarmed immediately or we'll start carving parts off these two beautiful ladies, starting with their breasts. If you are not here in two minutes, I will start on them.'

Peanut saw the lady smiling at Sharon and Hills. They waited, Peanut was ready.

'They coming, Nadia?' Burlington Ford asked. Peanut knew the name. Nadia Burov. Suspect Russian FSB.

'No, not yet. It's time to give them a hurry up.'

He watched as he heard her radio click, then saw her reach forward and grab Hills's breast. Hills's scream of pain roared through his earpiece. He snapped.

He shoved the door partially open and, standing half-hidden by the door, fired, his bullet hitting a surprised Burov, her arms flailing as she went over backward. Volkov's cat-like reflexes moved him out of the firing line. Instantly reacting, he fired at the door as Peanut crouched behind it. Peanut threw the door open, seeing Volkov run and crash through the window. Peanut fired twice at the fast-moving body, noticing the bullet holes in the door just above his head. If he had been any taller, he would have been hit. Sometimes it paid to be short. Volkov disappeared out of sight onto the porch and kept running. Peanut dropped as the door swung wide open and a stunned Burlington Ford began to lift his rifle. He stopped when he saw the pistol pointed at him. Peanut ran over and grabbed the rifle, shoving it up in the air and turning Burlington Ford around, sweeping his legs and dumping him hard. He threw the rifle across the room as he heard the thud and felt the vibration of the large fat body hit the floor. Running over to Hills and Sharon, he expected the worst but saw Hills stir. There was the start of really deep bruise on her exposed breast. He quickly cut her and Sharon free, watching in case Burlington Ford tried to do something silly. Grabbing the radio Burov had taken from Hills, Peanut pressed send.

'Blue, Volkov outside, probably heading towards cars.'

'See him, Peanut. On to it.'

Burlington Ford shook his head to clear the effects of hitting the floor and tried to raise himself up as he grabbed at the pistol in his belt.

'Drop it, asshole.'

He noticed Peanut scowling at him, his pistol pointed. He stopped trying to reach the pistol and Sharon took it away.

Peanut kicked the chair away from the door handle and Chas stood there, his face a ghostly white, looking decidedly unsteady. Janice-Rose ran in, saw Chas in trouble and grabbed him, helping him stay upright. Peanut sniffed; he could smell it. Smoke. He glanced at Sharon.

'Can you get Hills outside? J.R. can you get Chas outside? If that fire reaches the propane tanks, this place will blow. Get everybody well away, like a quarter of a mile away, okay?'

'What are you going to do, big brother?' Janice-Rose asked.

'Clean up.'

Peanut heard the sudden blast of the Barrett from outside. Blue was on the job. He turned and glanced at Nadia Burov. She was in trouble. The bullet had taken her in the upper chest, missing her heart and going right through. With good medical help, she would survive but Peanut wasn't going to help. Not a bitch that would have cold-bloodedly cut Hills's breasts off and then murdered the lot of them. She staggered to her feet. All pretense of a tough stand-over bitch was gone.

'You have to help me; you have to get me to a hospital!' The pleading was in her eyes, desperate.

'The only thing I have to do is what my instructions are. Clean up.' Peanut aimed and shot her in the kneecap, watching her fall to the floor in a scream of agony.

'Smell that smoke, folks? That's the fire we were warning you about.'

Burlington Ford suddenly rolled over, trying to get up and as he sat up, Peanut pulled a sword out and pushed it gently into his neck.

'I'd forget about getting up.'

'Do you know who I am?'

'I do. That's why I'm here. Who are your pet rats in the department?'

'Help me out and I will tell you.'

Peanut drove the sword into Burlington Ford's upper arm hitting the bone and twisting the steel in hard, hearing the scream and extracting the sword.

'I'm not interested in helping. The name of the rats?'

'No, no, I have a lot of inside information. You have to help me; I can make it worth your while, believe me!'

'That's the trouble, I don't believe you.' He drove the sword into Burlington's thigh, hit the bone and twisted seeing him faint in pain. He stood, walked over to Burov. She looked up at him. She was scared but was still holding it together. Well trained.

'Who are you?' she asked.

'It doesn't matter. Are you FSB or not?' She shut her mouth in a tight line. He shook his head. The bitch could burn. He walked back over to the recovering Burlington Ford.

'Who're the rats?' He reached down and hit him in the testicles, watched him fold up and smiled. 'I've only just started. You are going to feel pretty silly when you tell me, and you will, after a bit more pain.' He punched him in the nose, seeing his head jerk back, his hands going up to his face. He mumbled something through his now bloody hands. Peanut put his sword at his neck and jabbed slightly, seeing Burlington Ford jerk his head back.

'Speak clearly.'

'Fredrick Mellon. There is only one.'

'Thank you.' Peanut could feel the heat coming up through the floor and wraiths of smoke were coming up through the cracks in the floor boards. He didn't have much time left; he had to get out. Burlington Ford slowly got to his feet, Peanut took a step behind him and with a quick double slash, cut both his Achilles tendons, seeing him fall down, using his hands to break his fall. His elbows now exposed, another quick double slash and he collapsed flat on the floor, the tendons severed in his elbows. He rolled over and looked up at Peanut, terror written over his face; he knew the fire was coming and he was immobilized.

'You have to help me, please, please!'

Peanut shook his head.

'It's called *consequences*, asshole.'

Peanut turned and quickly walked out and shut the door, running to the office, ripping the laptop off the desk, then running through the smoke to the next room and grabbing the two laptops sitting on the desk. Looking back he saw the flames coming up through the floor and beginning to run up the walls. He opened the window and climbed out, fire now coming up from underneath. The outside edge of the porch was engulfed in a sheet of flame. The heat was now so intense his hair was singeing and, as he looked, an inferno was now running along the roof of the house. He had to get away. He ran and jumped off the porch, jumping through the sheet of flames, hitting the ground, rolling on the ground then getting up and running directly away, smelling his singed hair, knowing that the flames and heat would soon set the Propane gas tanks off. Cries back in the house turned to screams, then he felt himself being lifted up and blown through the air, hitting the ground hard, and rolling over and over and into a drain. A wave of heat blasted over him as he lay face down, again smelling his hair and clothes burning, but just as quickly the blast of hot air dissipated. He lay still, knowing there were several propane tanks. Was that blast all of them or just one? He didn't know and so he scrambled to his feet, still clutching the computers and ran for his life.

***

Hills sat watching, her eyes straining to see if Peanut was coming, knowing that if he was still in the house he was dead, burned alive. Her heart was in her mouth as the fire took hold and raced through the house, the pain of her breast forgotten with worry; where was Peanut? Her worry was now slowly turning into a sense of dread. The house was now fully engulfed and Janice-Rose glanced anxiously at Hills and Sharon.

'Peanut?' Chas asked and they shook their heads and the blast from the propane tanks exploding filled the sky with fire. Nobody could survive that sort of blast and inferno. Hills burst into a sob, putting her head in her hands and quietly crying. Sharon turned away and Janice-Rose stood staring at the flames; she just couldn't tear her eyes away. Peanut was in there. Her brother was dead. She suddenly saw movement, off to the side. A blackened figure was running towards them. She knew that purposeful jog; it was the way her brother ran during his workouts.

'Peanut!' she yelled. Hills looked up and jumped to her feet, unbelieving, looking at the blackened figure, also knowing that run. Her face broke into a smile and she stood, rooted to the spot as he ran up. She took two steps forward and hugged him.

'We thought you were still inside!' she cried, then stood back and examined him. She turned him and could see the burns on the back of his head and his clothes still smoldering in patches. She helped pull the clothes off him, giving him a blanket to wrap himself in. Peanut glanced down at Chas, grinning up at him.

'Cut that a bit fine, didn't we?' Chas asked.

'Worth it, Chas. Ever heard of a guy in the department called Fredrick Mellon?' Peanut asked.

'Yeah, know him well. Handles operational assessments. Why?'

'He's the rat.'

Chas nodded at Peanut, now knowing how their secrets were exposed.

'I'll pass that on to the CIA. They will deal with it.' he said.

'Will they? Wouldn't they just use us?' Peanut replied.

Despite his pain, Chas chuckled. 'Probably. Let Peter handle the cleanup. Peter knows how to handle the FBI; he's good at it. I'm not up to it at the moment. I'm going to call the FBI and the helicopter.'

Peanut knew there was only one piece of cleanup left. Volkov. He took Hills's radio.

'Blue, did you get Volkov? Over.'

'Negative. He tried to take a car and I stopped it. He rolled out and into the scrub and ran. I saw lights come on ten minutes later, way out in the bush. He must have had a vehicle hidden out there, just for getaways. Over.'

'Which way was he traveling? Over.'

'Away from us. He must know another way to the highway. Or maybe another back road. I think he has gone. Over.'

'Copy. All the principals except Volkov are dead, so nearly a complete success. I'll pass it all on to Chas. Over and out.'

He walked back and squatted by Chas.

'Volkov got away. He had a car stashed out in the bushes, well away from here. The FBI can put a watch on airports and border crossings, but he has gone.'

Chas shook his head.

'That's a disappointment. But if he has gone, it will be back to Mother Russia. We won't see him again.'

Peanut frowned sourly at Chas and shook his head.

'He'll be back. He has unfinished business.'

'He's a fool if he tries. The FBI advance guard is traveling on that helicopter so get all your stories straight. They are in contact with a guy called John Case. Who his boss is, is anybody's guess, but he has a direct line into the CIA.' Chas lay back down and Hills pressed *talk* on the radio.

'Meeting, guys. Out in the parking lot where Chas is.'

Peanut waited as Blue, Peter and Mick turned up. Peter spoke quietly to Chas and then took charge.

'We need our stories straight. The FBI are on their way. The guys at the accommodation block fired at us. Right? So we fired back. Then they fired at us from the helicopter so we fired back. It was the same at the house; we could see the fire running under the house and when we went into the house to help, they fired at us. The main ringleader, Volkov, has got away, everybody okay with that?'

He saw nodding.

'Hills, you and Peanut have to go to the hospital with Chas. You need your breast examined.' She glanced at Peanut and knew he also had to go; his burns needed urgent treatment.

The sound of a distant helicopter came to them and Peanut hoped they had a medic on board. Chas was looking worse all the time. He could see the shock of the wound setting in.

Peanut surveyed the compound. It was devastated. The house was on fire from end to end and the explosion had blown the back half of the building away. Peanut now realized that with him running away out the front, the house had sheltered him from the full force of the explosion. The back half of the corrugated-iron shed was now just twisted sheets of cladding, its steel frame all bent and warped, and the accommodation block was now just smoking rubble. Standing in the compound, the stench of burnt diesel and av gas was overpowering and the devastation was almost complete The only building standing was the cowboys' quarters, it was too far away to get caught in the flames and it was untouched.

It had been a clever move, sending the cowboys an invitation to free drinks and entertainment.at a new club in San Antonio, backed up with a night's stay in a nice hotel. It was called "a cowboys' night out" and they all got personal flyers in the mail. It was too hard to resist. They had all gone for a good night out and so were not here to witness the attack and its aftermath. The moment they returned, they would know that their jobs were gone. But they would be alive.

***

The FBI stood in the middle of the compound, stunned. The San Antonio SAC had arrived on the helicopter with the first team and he just stood and stared grimly around. Smoke was still drifting up out of the smoldering ruins of the house and accommodation block and the shattered and burnt remains of the helicopter was still visible, tangled in with the wreckage of the fuel tanks and the charred bodies. He turned around and stared at Peter as Peanut, Hills, and Chas were all loaded into the helicopter.

Peter spoke quietly as he informed the SAC of the issues.

'It's called cleanup. Burlington Ford was engaged in the setting up of a private army with the help of some drug-dealing Russians and a European terrorist called Jerry Gorman. Gorman has disappeared, unfortunately.' He looked blandly at the SAC and the SAC gave a slight grin.

'Gorman's not going to appear anytime soon, I take it?' the SAC asked.

'His name was Gorman, not Lazarus,' Peter replied.

'Okay. Where's Burlington Ford?' Peter pointed at the smoldering remains of the house.

'In there, along with the remains of his girlfriend, a Nada Burov. She is a suspected Russian FSB operative. Her sidekick, Milo Volkov, also FSB, has done a runner and will be heading back to Russia. You will need to notify airports and border security. We have, however, saved their computers from the fire and Peanut over there in the helicopter has all the passwords. You might find it interesting reading. Make sure you contact this guy before releasing anything to the news media or the public.'

The SAC peered at the name on the card Peter handed over.

'Who's he?'

'Connected to the CIA, I believe. Some of this could be sensitive internationally you understand. We don't want Uncle Sam getting a bad name now, do we?' Peter replied.

He surveyed the compound and pointed at the corrugated-iron shed and the remains of the accommodation block.

'Inside the remains of that shed are tons of munitions,' said Peter. 'Get the military. They have been subject to heat and could be unstable. Inside what remains of the accommodation block you will probably find more bodies, some of Burlington Ford's soldiers. On Burlington Ford's computer is the list of the local good ole boys that were training here to be part of his army. Might pay to have a word and tell them just how silly that idea was. That Uncle Sam strongly disapproves.'

'We'll do that all right. Stupid fuckers. So this is to be hushed away?' asked the SAC.

'Publicly, this has just been a terrible accident,' Peter said. 'When the helicopter crashed into the fuel tanks it set fire to everything. Pilot error.'

'Right. And the bullet wounds?' the SAC asked with a sarcastic tone in his voice.

Peter kept his face bland.

'Accidental from ammunition set off by the fire and explosion, all bodies too badly burnt to be identified properly.'

The SAC gazed around, shook his head as he listened to Peter.

'This military setup was called the Southern States Alliance,' Peter said. 'It was set up by Burlington Ford's daughter, Melissa Albanese. Money off drugs was funneled into this to pay for the weapons. Might pay to talk to her. We understand that she knew all about the drugs but getting her to admit that with a lawyer present might be a problem. Nonetheless, see how deep she goes or if she was nothing more than a frontwoman.'

The SAC wrote it down, then glanced up.

'This is going to take some time to clean up.' he said.

Peter shook his head. 'I don't see how. Let the military do the weapons, the undertakers do the bodies, and a bulldozer do the rest. Just keep the news media away from here, like ten miles away, back at Highway 39.'

The SAC looked at Peter and gave a wan smile. 'You have done this before, obviously?'

Peter just shrugged. 'People fuck up, there's no doubt about it.'

He turned and made to walk off, then remembered.

'I'll leave you to get on with it,' he said, 'but don't forget that CIA guy. He needs to be kept in the loop. International concerns, you understand.'

The SAC wondered what international concerns had to do with the destruction that had taken place here in the middle of good old ranching Texas.

***

The main FBI team arrived at daybreak and Mick and Blue walked over to the SUV Volkov had tied to escape in. Mick found the blood and tracked it into the trees, heading directly away from the wreck. Blue saw what he was doing and came over.

'Can you track him?'

'At this stage, it's just join the dots.' He pointed at the blood droplets on the ground.

'I'll come with you,' Blue said.

Blue and Mick set off, Mick indicating that he would lead.

'Blue, keep your eyes skinned. I'll track him and you watch my back. Okay?'

Blue followed as they walked the blood trail. If the vehicle headlights were just a ruse and he had doubled back, it would be dangerous. It was easy at the start, the drips of blood left a trail that a blind poodle could follow. Volkov had moved rapidly, expecting to be followed but then had quickly slowed. A quarter of a mile in, the steps stopped and the ground showed his footsteps scuffed as he bandaged his wound, then set off again. The blood drips were now harder to find but were still leading away from the compound. Then the blood trail stopped. The ground was scuffed, he had sat down and tried to stop the bleeding. The amount of blood he had lost would make him dry, craving for water. The retying of his bandage worked and the drips almost stopped. But it didn't matter; ten steps further on, the tire tracks said it all. Volkov was gone. His vehicle had been parked there, waiting for any emergency. The tire tracks led directly away. He had no intention of coming back. Mick gave Blue a 'fuck it' look.

'Let's walk back. He's gone.' Mick said.

Blue studied Mick. 'I know you are a trooper but are you sure you are okay with all this? All the killing?' he asked.

Mick gave a snort.

'My dad is a Baptist minister. He believes in good and evil and as far as he is concerned, evil is fair game. I tend to think the same.'

'Wise man, your dad. It's very hard to commit evil on your fellow man when you are dead.'

Blue spoke to Peter and then left the matter to him. They had their gear loaded when Peter walked over to Mick.

'Mick?'

Mick turned.

'Welcome to the team. The jobs yours if you want it.'

Peter held out his hand and Mick shook it. Peter gave him a pat on the back.

'You did well out there. I take it you accept?'

Mick's face lit into a smile, a bit surprised at dour Peter's friendliness.

'Definitely. Thanks.'

Peter turned to the team.

'Let's get our vehicles and load up. This gig is over.'

Chapter 39

They sat in the San Antonio hotel's small conference room, watching a bandaged Peanut set up the computer and monitor.

'I hope this video has some naughty bits in it,' Blue said.

'Considering all that you are going to see has been stolen, yes, it's naughty. No naked ladies, though. Sorry.'

'Bummer.'

Peanut gave a grunt and glanced over at Chas. He still appeared a bit rocky. It was going to take some time. The hospital's x-ray had found an embedded bullet. The wound was more than just a shoulder gouge and the operation had taken a long time, trying to avoid any nerve damage. He was now back at the hotel, after a final sign off by the hospital before going back to Washington. He was healing quickly, but the scarring across his shoulder was going to be forever.

Peanut finished and turned to the team.

'You know the FBI will ask about the money when they do their online searches.'

They were all surprised; they hadn't thought of that.

'We know nothing. All the records will show that the transfers took place prior to the raid. They must have had a prior warning. Probably from the rat in the department, Fredrick Mellon. So if they ask, that was your understanding. Okay?'

Chas rubbed his chin with his good hand and smiled. It now made perfect sense. Blame it on the rat. He studied Peanut, knowing he had already thought that out long before the raid started. Peanut saw the nods of approval and Chas's wry grin.

'Sharon, J.R., and I pulled a stunt in Houston where we investigated a drug operation and then passed it all on to the FBI, who shut them down. We got that information by loading software into their computers that allowed us to capture logins, passwords and set the computers up as if they were on our own VPN. It worked, and just prior to the FBI raid, we fleeced them of a lot of money. I also uploaded a scrubber to make tracing of where the money had gone impossible.' He smiled at the team.

'We have done the same with Burlington Ford and his Russian friends. As they were dealing drugs and munitions and cash is the only means of exchange, they had a fair bit of money in their offshore accounts. We have removed it to a very large offshore account in the Bahamas.' He gazed around at the team. 'As this is now our money, I will leave it up to you guys to decide how you want to split it up, but I believe that the principle of equal risk, equal reward applies. In other words, we all get the same, right?'

Everybody agreed.

'There were eight of us at risk in this operation so it gets divided by eight.' He smiled at Sharon. 'However, there is a catch. This money has to stay invested offshore, just for your safety. Sharon has the full details of that.'

Sharon stood and handed out copied notes to the team.

'People, whatever you do, please read this or you could lose your money,' she said. 'Any questions, just ring and ask. The government, if it finds out, might see this money as ill-gotten gains from crime and will want to take it. So please, check before you do anything.'

Peanut laughed. 'I taught Sharon the basics but she has turned it into an art form.'

He turned on the computer display and the monitor lit up. All eyes went to the screen.

'That is the total amount we removed off the bad guys. This is what each of us gets on an equal risk, equal reward basis. Any questions?'

The room was silent.

Total: $28,865,000.00

Divided by eight: $3,607,500.

Peanut smiled at the stunned faces.

'There was a bit more than that, like about eight thousand dollars but as we'll have some bank charges we are keepingng that until it has all been split and paid. With what's left we can have a team party, or if you like, a team holiday. Sharon will produce a final account wrap-up sheet when it's all settled. As we have to go to the Bahamas to set up our individual accounts, I am recommending that we fly there in the next three days or so, enjoy the beach for a day or two, and then fly back to Washington.'

'It makes sense,' Sharon said. 'The interest on this sort of amount is large and the faster it's done the better. Plus, I want to have what is mine.' There were chuckles and smiles all around the table. Chas coughed for attention.

'Guys, I think we owe Peanut a big thanks. Peanut, we all owe you one.'

'No you don't, you owe me fucking heaps. I'll have a lemon lime and bitters, in the bar, in half an hour.'

'Fucking hell, Peanut. I told you before; you can have the whole fucking factory of the awful stuff! You can afford it now, anyway,' Chas replied. Peanut chuckled, amused. He liked lemon lime and bitters but not that much.

***

Hills laid her head on his shoulder and squeezed his hand. He glanced at her, then went back to watching the waves roll in on the beautiful white sand. This was beautiful, restful but after four days, it was getting boring. He wanted to get back home to the gym and to practice. To mow the lawns and have a really good hard run. That was his home and he wanted to be there. She sensed his restlessness and glanced at him.

'Yes?'

'Ready to go home, honey?' he asked. She sighed. Truth be told, she was now getting tired of it as well. It was time to leave.

'What's the plan?'

'Book and fly out tomorrow morning?' Peanut asked.

'Let's go. C'mon, we'll tell the others.'

'Not many to tell now, love. There's only Chas and Sharon left.' They stood and walked into the bar where Chad and Sharon were relaxing, laughing at something said.

'Come to say goodbye, folks,' Peanut said as Hills sat down beside Sharon. 'Want to get back home to the daily routine.' Chas nodded and stood, then took Peanut's arm and steered him away. Peanut raised a querying eyebrow.

'Yes?'

'One loose end left. Fredrick Mellon,' Chas stated.

'Two loose ends. Mellon and Volkov. That CIA guy Peter has been in contact with me. Wants to send a message to Russia. I think he wants me to go pay a visit, just to let him know how unacceptable his behavior has been.'

'Kill him?' Chas asked.

'Yes.' Chas nodded. It had to happen.

***

They watched as Fredrick Mellon's car pulled up his drive, park, and then stroll over to his door, his partner unlocking it and greeting him with a kiss as he walked in, putting his arm around her as he kicked the door closed.

Chas gave Peanut a questioning look. 'Doable?'

Peanut studied the house. It was a two-and-a-half story brown-brick with white windows with small colonial panes; it looked classy in a street of expensive semi-terraced homes. Peanut summed up the odds in his mind. It was a well-lit street and anything from the front was impossible. He had already checked the back; it was much more likely, but the window of opportunity was small. He had timed the comings and goings from the house and it was a very tight window indeed.

Mellon was divorced and his wife lived in another state with their kids and her parents. He had been caught with his present partner when his wife had walked in on them screwing on the couch. Once a rat, always a rat, Peanut assumed. His present partner was pretty, photogenic, and worked as an early morning news reporter. She left in the early hours, returning at two in the afternoon and then went to bed. Sometimes she had come home after work looking disheveled, like she had just rushed dressing. Peanut checked. He followed her, watching her leave the studio early and go straight to a hotel. It didn't take long to work out that the guy she was seeing was the manager at the station; Mellon's partner was screwing her way up the ladder. What goes round comes round. But that left a dilemma. He had to get in the house when no one was there. That meant gaining entry during daylight. Or did it? He had noticed an upstairs bathroom window left slightly open on the back third-floor dormer, one of the three rooms under the roof. He examined the building again. He could hear faint music. Springsteen. Loud. Again. Music every night. He grinned, he suddenly knew the answer. Easy. He turned to Chas.

'Doable.'

***

Peanut gave Hills a quick kiss and climbed out of the car. It was nine thirty and the suburb was quiet, a weeknight and most of the street had work the next day. Not a family suburb; most couples that lived there worked. Closely packed, delightful townhouses, in an area close to the central city with malls, shopping, and cafés, it was an expensive area. It was a fact of life that the mortgage would force both of them to work.

He ran up the narrow path, across the garden to the door set into the wall between the front and back yard. He didn't bother trying it, he knew it was locked. He leaped up, grabbed the top of the seven-foot-high brick fence and snaked his way over the top as Hills gently accelerated away down the street. Dropping to the ground on the other side, he walked out into the tiny backyard and peered up in the half light. He could hear the music faintly pumping. As the place was triple glazed, the volume inside would be nearly deafening. Tonight it was Fleetwood Mac. The melodic guitar of Lindsey Buckingham and the soulful vocals of Steve Nicks coming faintly to his ears.

They slept on the second floor and he would be surprised if they heard any of the noises that he made, listening to it loud down in the ground-floor lounge. He positioned his first corner clamp and rammed the clamp shut, clamping it up on both sides of the corner brick, ratcheting it up tight. It was designed to grip the brick surface. The sharp little teeth on the pads that clamped the house bricks made sure the clamp wouldn't move. He swung up on the clamp, standing on the tiny foot-sized platform, positioning the next clamp at waist height and clamping it shut. He took the light rope clamp release up with him as he climbed onto the second clamp, pulled the rope that released the first camp and lifted up and repeated the process. Fifteen minutes later he was at the roof line. He packed the one clamp into his backpack and then, taking out a light line with a rubber-coated tungsten steel hook on the end, threw it over the roof gable above the central bathroom dormer and pulled it tight. He clamped footholds onto the rope and, standing on them, released the last clamp and packed it away. The dormer window was just ten feet away.

He kept one foot on the rope foothold and, using the other foot to propel himself, shoved himself over to the dormer and checked the window latch. It was just a typical cheap window lock, designed more for stopping the window flying open in the wind than stopping burglars. He released the catch, swung the window fully open and gently eased inside, the loud music now coming clearly to him through the shut internal doors. It was no longer Fleetwood Mac. They had upgraded. The harsh chords of the Foo Fighters echoed up through the house and the volume seemed to have gone up. It still sounded like a full-on party. He pulled the gable roof hook trip cord and it released. He wound it in quickly as its rubber sheathing allowed it to slide quietly down the roof. He closed the widow and eased open the bathroom door and peeped out. The stairs down to the next level were just outside the bathroom door and the two doors into the bedrooms at either end of the house were standing open. He quietly walked into one, the bedroom was nearly bare, not even a bed, just junk piled up along one side, shoved roughly up against the sloping rafters. He walked to the other end of the house and it was the same, just another empty bedroom. Perfect for him. He sat on the floor by the open closet and rested. If needed, he could easily slip inside the closet and he would hear any steps on the stairs. He settled down to wait, knowing that he had a lot of time to pass. An hour later, the music died. Their voices drifted up the stairs as they climbed up, going to bed.

'I've got to get my sleep. I have to leave at two, remember? Gimme a fucking break, huh?' She sounded angry. Maybe having sex in the afternoon meant that she was not up for a repeat?

'C'mon sexy, give your lover a bit, eh? You're not going all frigid on me now are you?'

'Honey, I'll make it up to you on the weekend, huh? Promise.'

Their voices faded as they went into the bedroom and Peanut relaxed back onto the floor and dozed off. It was the best way to pass the time.

The sound of a digital alarm reached him; it jolted him into full wakefulness. He glanced at his phone; two am. She was off to work. He heard the sound of the shower, the sound of Fredrick going to the bathroom, the sound of her footsteps eventually going downstairs and then the coffee machine working in the kitchen. Silence for fifteen minutes, then the front door shutting with a firm click. He waited for a further thirty minutes before creeping down the stairs.

He looked at Fredrick lying flat on his back snoring quietly, his arms spread wide and his mouth hanging open. Lovely, just what the fuck did she see in the piece of shit? He quietly unsheathed a sword, walked forward, stood by the bed, lined up his heart and stabbed the sword in. Fredrick's eyes flew open in surprise; he tried to raise his arms and slumped, dead. Peanut removed his sword, wiped it on Fredrick's pajama top and sheathed it on the way to the door. He used a burner to ring Hills. Any police investigation would soon check all communications from the local cell towers at this time of the morning and this call would show up. Hills answered immediately.

'Honey bunch.'

'Finished.'

'Five.' He hung up and waited, keeping the front door unlocked, ready to step out. The little Toyota pulled up outside in just under five minutes. He strolled out, pulling the door shut behind him, climbed in beside Hills and greeted her, all perfectly natural things for a guy to do when he's getting a lift to work. She pulled out from the curb, turned the first corner and began to work her way across town, avoiding the highways and the major intersections with cameras, before pulling into their drive fifty minutes later. The auto garage door opened and she parked the car inside. They walked into the house where she turned and kissed him; the job was finally over.

She pulled back, smiled at him, and asked, 'Bed?'

'Yes.'

She knew he would still be wired after getting the job done. 'Sex?' she asked.

'Yes please. Next question?'

'I bet I can beat you into bed.' She turned and stepped out to run up the stairs but he heel-tapped her and passed her on the first few stair treads as she staggered to regain her footing.

Peanut grinned as he heard her swear at him as he scooted up the stairs. He had wasted his time. She had pulled her dress off on the way up the stairs and as he struggled to get out of his jeans she leaped into the bed in her bra and panties, laughing at him with his jeans still only half off. He gave up struggling and sat on the chair, seeing her smile at him, her love shining in her eyes. He pulled off his jeans and threw them into a pile with his shirt and pulled the bedclothes back, eased in beside her, moving in close, feeling her warmth, pulling her to him, running his hand down her the side of her body, realizing that she was now naked, her bra and panties gone. He gently kissed her and she kissed him back, then eased her head back and gave him a level look. He knew something important had happened. He studied her, waiting, watching as she regarded him with those beautiful, openly questioning eyes.

'Peanut, have you decided whether you would like to be a dad or not?'

'Yeah, I think that I could handle being a dad, you know, sometime. Why?'

'If you could make that sometime like eight months away, that's fine, but if you are planning on anything longer, we have a problem.'

He knew immediately.

'You're sure?'

'I'm sure. But are you?'

He took her in his arms and kissed her.

'I think it's wonderful, but am I sure I can be a good dad? Honey, I'll try my best.'

'Peanut, that is all any good dad does. Besides, I'm going to be a mom and that's a first for me as well.' She leaned forward and kissed him gently and smiled at him.

'Honey, I think you need to tell me why you are untrusting. I know you trust me and I trust you, but now you are going to be a father …'

She paused thinking about what she wanted to say for a second. '… I think you owe it to me and to junior to be honest. We, the both of us, have a right to know and don't you dare try and fudge.'

He looked at her, his face suddenly sad. She was right, before they became parents she had a right to know. He frowned at her.

'You won't like it.'

'I'll take the good with the bad.'

He snorted disbelievingly.

'Really? Even if it is really, really bad?'

'How bad, Peanut?'

He spoke bluntly, his voice harsh, savage.

'I murdered my father.'

Chapter 40

Hills sat stunned, speechless.

'Danny and I murdered him together.'

She was unable to comprehend what he had just said. She tried to put what she wanted to say into words but all that came out was a chocked, hollow sounding, 'Why?'

'He was a drunk. He was Mom's first boyfriend. She fell in love and then got pregnant and then married. He was always a drinker, so it wasn't like she didn't know what she was getting into, but I suppose, like a lot of women who are attracted to a bit of the rough side, she probably thought she could reform him.' He glanced away, remembering.

'She didn't. He would come home drunk, three out of the seven nights of the week. As I grew up, the sounds of him slapping her around and her crying was natural, normal. It seemed that was just what happened between adults. As kids, we knew to keep out of the way or we would get a belting. But he seemed to get sick of slapping Mom and I knew something was going on when he would come and get Danny. Danny would return crying and not tell me anything. I had just turned eleven when one night he came home drunk and he came and took me. He took me to the shed in the back of the yard and pulled my pants down, bent me over the back of an old school desk and raped me. It hurt, really hurt. I went back to the bedroom crying. Danny asked if he had done me too and I knew then what he meant. He came and sat on my bed and we hugged as I cried. We talked and Danny said that we should kill him. That was the start and we began to plan. I forget how many times he raped me and Danny but I was nearly twelve when we had a plan we thought was foolproof.'

Peanut sat, not looking at Mandy, staring into the distance, knowing that he was now losing Mandy, but aware that she had a right to know.

'He would arrive home drunk. Friday nights were the worst. He always staggered up the path, close to passing out. We liked those nights as he was too drunk to do anything, so we strung a light line across the path and sat in the darkness on either side. He came home late again, staggered up the path and we tripped him. He fell, skinning his hands and his nose on the ground, nearly unconscious. When he fell in the past, he would lay there and sometimes pass out, so we had some bricks set up. We placed a brick either side of his head to keep the back of his head sticking up. We had a really large concrete block we had found and wrapped in plastic. Both of us smashed it hard into the back of his skull. Twice. We dragged his body up to the steps and arranged it like he had just fallen. We unwrapped the concrete block, put the block back and took the bricks and wrapper to a waste bin a couple of blocks away. We came back and checked his eyes. He was dead. We went inside and cleaned up, and then went to bed.'

Mandy sat staring at Peanut, sickened at the brutality of Peanut's and Danny's childhood and the extremes they had gone to, to end it.

'I have never felt any remorse for what Danny and I did. My father was a thug, a drunken thug. Our whole lives changed after that. Life actually became fun. For once we had laughter in the house. It was finally a home.'

'Your mom never knew? About you being taken out to the shed and being raped?'

'Of course she knew. If she had done anything, he would have killed her or worse, chained her up and tortured her, just like he threatened. The nights he was molesting us were the nights she got some peace from him. Not that it was any peace for her knowing what he was doing.'

Hills shook her head, finding it hard to understand that someone could treat their own wife and children like that, but she wasn't surprised. She had seen the results of violent child abuse on the force. She knew what Peanut had gone through. She leaned forward and wrapped her arms around him and hugged him, holding him, wanting to take away the hurt he must still feel. He pulled back and stared at her, a strange unknowing look in his eye.

'You understand?'

'Of course I do. We're partners so we share each other's pain, whatever that is. I love you and whatever you need is what we do. But I had to know.'

'Yes, you did.'

'Did your mom ever know what you and Danny did?'

'We never said. She found his body the next morning and called the ambulance and they called the cops. They knew what he was like and the death was written off as an unfortunate accident caused by his being blind drunk. But she knew. She sat with us at the table the next day, took Danny's and my hands in hers and said "Thanks." She smiled at us and squeezed our hands. She knew and we could see the happiness in her eyes, but nothing more was said.' There was silence. Peanut studied her for a second.

'Even now, I'm still not sorry for what Danny and I did.'

'Why should you be? And thank you for telling me; I know how hard that was.'

She leaned forward and wiped a stray tear off his cheek. 'You will make a great dad.'

She suddenly gave a sexy little smile.

'There is a big plus side to this, to my being pregnant.'

'There is?'

'Yep. We can have as much sex as we want and I can't get any more pregnant than I already am.' She paused as he chuckled. 'Plus, I'm glad.'

'Glad that you're pregnant?'

'Yep. And glad that the smack in the nuts didn't put your little tadpoles off their job!'

Peter McConnell and John Case were sitting at the table waiting as Peanut and Chas arrived. There were friendly handshakes and smiles all round. They were clearly happy with the Texas outcome and the cover-up; even Burlington Ford's sister had accepted the result. Peanut had been approached one month after the raid and then contacted again only last week. This time it was John Case who approached him. Chas was dubious and had come to hear what they wanted Peanut for.

John Case started the ball rolling. 'You ever hear of Patriarch Ponds in Moscow?'

'Nope, why?'

'Exclusive area of Moscow. Expensive, the sort of place that you need to have a very large legal, or in the case of Volkov, illegal income to survive. It is where he lives. We want him gone.'

Peanut was skeptical.

'As the CIA has endless amounts of personnel to use, why me?'

Peter McConnell interrupted. 'The CIA's best personnel are embedded. We do not disturb them. The information they get is a hundred times more valuable than scoring a point. But it is a point that needs to be scored. He lives in a luxury apartment block, guarded and secure. But in summer, he likes to go in the weekends to his dacha, set in the hills, thirty miles out of Moscow. They are having a nice summer in Moscow this year and he will go most weekends. That is your opening. Isolated, by himself, stuck in the hills, he is a sitting duck.'

'Really?'

'Only one road in or out. No escape if you seal it off; he is trapped up a dead-end lane.'

'That works both ways. I get in there and anything goes wrong, the same rules apply. The difference is that I am in a foreign country and don't speak the language.'

'True. As you once said, I believe, a reason not to fail. And congratulations on the impending new arrival to your family. Wonderful news.'

Peanut was staggered. How did they know that? They hadn't even told Janice-Rose or his mom yet. The doctor's visits? They were waiting for another month before the big reveal. He kept his face bland. He assumed they did this to awe and intimidate, letting you know that they knew everything. It was putting him on edge. If they know that much, why did they need him? It doesn't matter who kills Volkov, just so long as the prick ends up dead.

'I really can't see why you would need to use me. A cheap Russian thug that knows the area would be better and much more secure.'

Peter and John glanced at each other.

'Peanut,' Peter said, 'that cheap Russian thug's first port of call would be the FSB and he would cut a deal and blackmail us. We know, it has been tried before. It has to be an outsider, someone unknown to anyone but a handful of people. That leaves us with you and, when the Russians complain, gives us total deniability, especially to our own government and the President. That is invaluable.'

'I'm going to be the sacrificial lamb if anything goes wrong?'

'Peanut, you simply can't afford to get caught,' Peter said. 'They would torture you and you would talk, believe it. We want the job done but with as little risk as possible. You will be given a month of intensive training and then sent.' Peanut glanced at Chas and he spread his hands, palms up in a 'it's up to you,' gesture. Peanut wanted Volkov dead. Volkov would never forget the humiliation of being beaten. He would be back and would take revenge and then he, Mandy, and the baby would be in jeopardy. There was only one way to end it for good. Volkov had to go.

'I'll do it.'

***

'Moscow Marriott please.' The taxi driver gently pulled out of the Sheremetyevo International airport pick-up zone and turned towards Moscow. It was strange how quickly he had become used to working in a team. He had always been a loner, and now he was back to being alone again. It had always felt good, but this time it felt like he had left part of himself behind. He tried to figure the feeling out, finally putting it down to his acrimonious leave-taking of Hills.

She objected and had objected strongly. He had been away training at the CIA but he hadn't told her about the assignment until he was only two days away from leaving and she immediately insisted that she come as well. If she couldn't, then he had to stay. They were more than just partners; they were a team. Peanut shook his head to all objections. She had their baby in her womb and that was precious and that was precisely why he was going, to protect them all in the future. She yelled, cried, then told him to fuck off and walked out.

He traveled to Dulles airport by himself. He couldn't reach her by phone and Janice-Rose said she would find her and talk to her. He didn't want goodbyes as he was instructed to not tell anyone his leaving schedule, but he felt like a thief sneaking out in the night. John Case had insisted that his leaving be kept as quiet as possible so if anything went wrong, anybody checking from Russia would learn nothing. It seemed silly because if things went well he would be on a plane out of there within two weeks.

***

The little rental car made heavy work of the deeply rutted road. It was little more than a graveled farm track. The road wound its way through heavily forested low hills, the scenery nice, but he had to ignore it and concentrate on the road. It would have been years since a grader had been over the road. He eased to a stop as an armed man stepped out in front of him and waved him down. He spoke Russian and Peanut shook his head.

'English?' The burly guard shook his head and Peanut handed him a card with Russian writing on it. The Russian read the card and made a signal to wait and disappeared into the trees. Peanut heard the sounds of talking, clearly a radio. He came back and spoke in broken English.

'Wait, you wait.' He stood back and kept his rifle in his arms, ready to raise and fire. Peanut sat and waited, picking up his map and studying it. It was Volkov striding up the track. He had never seen Volkov face to face. All he had seen of him was the side and the back of him as he had leaped through the window at Burlington Ford's ranch. And he knew that Volkov had never seen him. He stopped by the car and stared unsmilingly at him.

'Name?'

'Neville Patterson. Nev to my friends. I think I'm lost as my map seems to have led me astray.' He handed his map out the window and Volkov peered at it and the pencil marks Peanut had drawn on it. He seemed confused and as Peanut clicked the door open, the guard immediately swung his gun up and Volkov stepped back. Peanut gently swung the door open, stood, and then pointed to the map.

'May I?'

Volkov shrugged.

Peanut laid the map on the car bonnet and pointed.

'I was given directions to the dacha of Mr. Kostos Denikin. I was told to take this road, the fourth road past the highway.'

'Why do you want to see Mr. Denikin?'

'He is an expert on the Russian resistance to the Germans during the Second World War. My mother's family came from Vyazma and they wanted me to get some history from Mr. Denikin. Her family has a lot of history, but it has only been handed down by word of mouth and it might not be accurate.'

Volkov suddenly smiled.

'It is good that you do that. It stops people forgetting the sacrifice that was made. You have turned off too early. It is the next road along that way. Your map doesn't show a minor road that you have counted. Go ahead to the next one and try again. Where are you from, Mr. Patterson?'

'Washington, Virginia.' He held out his hand. 'Thank you, sir, you have been very helpful.' Volkov shook his hand.

'Happy to help.' He turned on his heel and patted the guard on the shoulder, in a well-done gesture, spoke in Russian, then walked back along the track.

Peanut climbed back into his car and, under the smiling guard's direction, turned the car around and headed back the way he had come. He noted that where Volkov turned into the trees there seemed to be a path and as he drove off the guard walked into the trees at the side of the road. They had known he was coming. He drove slowly and watched carefully, and then he saw it. A camera mounted on a tree and further along a tiny beam across the road. He smiled. Volkov was making sure he was guarded and that told Peanut he knew he had enemies. It might not be a simple takedown after all. Volkov was aware and ready.

He reached the turnoff, went along a road, turned up it and drove along to Mr. Denikin's house, stopping up the drive. He got out, tapped on the door and looked around, waited, tapped again, seeing a curtain twitch in a house across the road. He was being watched. There was no answer; he knew there wouldn't be as Mr. Denikin was on vacation in Miami, staying with relatives. All part of a believable cover story. But Volkov would check and then dismiss it. Just a lost foreigner.

Peanut turned up twice to the Denikin address in the next four days, knowing he would get no response, but not worrying, using the drive there and around the area to check where to dump the car at night. He found it, a gateway into a paddock on a small derelict farm; he could drive across the dry summer grass and hide his car in the trees. It was only a mile through the forest to Volkov's dacha. Nearly perfect. He had been informed that Volkov and his wife left Moscow early on Friday afternoons, then left for Moscow early on Monday mornings; it was the perfect setup. But it meant that he had to hide the car late on Thursday, go to the house, enter, hide and wait until Friday night. If he could hide in the house, that is. It might be much too small to hide in. He had no way of knowing until he was there. He had to wait.

The moonlit summer night helped as he drove through the gate into the paddock, closing it and driving into the trees on the far side. There was a fence running through the trees, just a double strand of old barbed wire. It was a cattle paddock. He packed his backpack and, checking his bearings, walked through the trees, keeping well away from the road. It was slow going, but so long as he was there before daylight, he would be happy.

He walked steeply downhill and came to a tiny stream and was surprised; he remembered that the road to Volkov's had no bridge. He checked his bearings and pushed on, again staying well away from the road, his small handheld GPS keeping him on track. He walked quietly up to the sentry house and there was no one at home. Why would there be when Volkov was not in residence? Ten minutes later, he reached the driveway to the house. He stayed in the trees and was soon glad that he had; there was a camera looking directly up the drive, mounted upon the high gable of the house and tripped by a red-light beam on the drive. Any doubts about Volkov being permanently on guard disappeared. In his line of work, it was a given. He would have enemies galore.

He checked his watch. Two o'clock. He walked around the house. It was much too big to be called a dacha. In Peanut's mind the traditional dachas that he had seen were just small weekenders, as they were known back home, but like wealth everywhere, some people had to flaunt it. If Volkov wasn't so secretive, this house would be flaunting it. As he worked his way around, he could see a flashing light inside and walked forward and peered through the window. An alarm system. He checked the window; it was alarmed. He checked another window around the back and it was alarmed as well. Ground-floor entry was out. He glanced up at the roof. Two bedrooms downstairs and three more up in the high roof. By Russian worker standards, it was a mansion. He took out his light line and threaded it through the attachment ring on his gable hook, doubling it up and tying it with a release knot. He threw it up and over the roof peak, pulling it back and hooking on the gable. With the house empty, making a noise was not even a concern. He had been worried about the hook and ropes coming through Russian customs, but his case was never even checked.

He tied the climbing rope to one of the light lines and then pulled the other line. The light line released and he pulled the rope up to the hook and secured the light line to the house veranda post with another release knot, tucking the end of the line into his belt. He began to climb, reaching the roof and then the dormer window. He looked in and checked the window edge. No alarm. He smiled, turned the latch on the window and, surprise, it turned and the window opened. The room was unused, the musty smell hinting at neglect in cleaning and use. He doubted that the windows ever got opened much. An old bed with the springs showing was the only furniture in the room. He eased his body through the window and down to the floor, pulling the release line and then hauling the climbing line and then the release on the hook, pulling them all into the room, closing the window and resetting the catch. There was now no going back.

He packed his bag and scouted the house for a hiding place. The upstairs bedrooms all had large closets, but as he walked down the stairs, they creaked and that ruled out the upstairs. No good trying to sneak up on someone when they would be lying in bed hearing the creaks as you came down the stairs. He checked the two large bedrooms downstairs. One smelt faintly of perfume and had woman's things on the dresser but the other room was just a bed with a man's clothes in the wardrobe. He began to think that maybe Volkov and his wife slept apart. He kept looking for his hiding place and he found it. A large built-in closet in the unused washhouse. Why wash when you are there just for the weekend? There were plenty of boxes in the closet to hide behind; it would do for the rest of tonight and tomorrow. He made a bed and settled down. He would need all the rest he could get. Tomorrow night would be a long one.

Chapter 42

The sound of a car coming to a stop in front of the house roused him. He stood up inside the closet and listened. Keys rattled in the front door, then it slammed shut and the beep, beep as the house alarm was switched off. He heard the noises as the person went into the kitchen and then the sound of running water and a jug just starting on its cycle to boil. The sounds were so normal, domestic, just like the sounds at home in Washington that it made him quickly take stock. But this wasn't the home of a normal man; this was the home of a cold-blooded professional murderer, even if he boiled the jug for a coffee like the rest of the civilized world. Peanut breathed out slowly. The sounds he was hearing were definitely made by a man. The footsteps were that of a heavy man and there was none of the lighter footfalls of a women walking or the sounds of him talking to her. He was on his own. Was that good or bad? Was she coming tomorrow or later tonight? He needed time to get away. If he killed Volkov, left, and then his wife turned up, one phone call and the borders would be sealed immediately. He needed time to get to the airport and clear the country. Peanut was prepared to wait. He could do the job tomorrow night and still clear the country and the extra time would allow him to know if she was arriving or not. He quietly sat back down in the corner, behind the large cardboard box full of kids' toys. Saved for when they have guests with children, perhaps?'

The sound of another car then the rattle of the door keys and the door opening and shutting bought him to his feet. He checked the time: nine p.m. A man spoke, harsh, guttural and it sounded like cursing, his voice was slurred, like he had been drinking. Peanut heard a sudden slap and a woman cry out, then quiet, then her cry out again, then him talking loud, and then another slap. It then sounded like she was saying no in Russian. Easing the cupboard door open, the washhouse door was slightly ajar and he crept across the small room and heard the man's rhythmic grunting. The sound of another slap, a cry from the lady and the man quickly finished. Peanut knew that he had just heard a rape take place. The man spoke harshly; it sounded contemptuous and then the sound of two more hard slaps and cries before the man walked away. The sound of a door opening and then the door slamming and the distant sound of a bed squeaking as the man got into bed. He heard the lady's footfalls and the jug go back on and the rattle of a spoon in a cup. A distant faint snore came from the man as he fell asleep. When she went to bed, he would act.

He walked back into the closet and sat down behind the box. He hoped it wouldn't be too long before she went to bed. The sound of her faint sobbing drifted to him and his heart went out to her, but he had a job to do and he wished that he had Hills with him. She would have known how to handle this properly. He was completely at a loss. Thirty minutes later, he heard a rattle of a cup going into the sink and then a door close. He waited another hour, then eased out of the cupboard. Now was the time.

He pulled on the ski mask and walked into the kitchen, surprised that the bench and sink were clean, that the rattle of crockery he had heard was her doing the dishes. After all that had happened to her, she still did the dishes. It told him that this was almost normal behavior. Amazing.

He walked down the short hall. The bedroom doors were shut. He listened at one door and heard nothing but at the other door the sound of snoring was quite distinct. He eased the door open and peered around the edge. It was Volkov, flat on his back, mouth open, asleep. He looked across the hall. She must be sleeping in that room. He walked into the bathroom and picked up a couple of face flannels and took them back with him into the bedroom and quietly closed the door. Walking over to the bed, he gently put his backpack on the floor and then took out a packet of cable ties and the face flannels. He then leaned forward and, using a solid punch to the temple, knocked Volkov out. He grabbed his nose and stuffed the face flannel into his mouth, swiftly cable-tying his wrists and ankles and then cable-tying the face flannel into his mouth by running a tie around his head. Volkov didn't even stir as he cable-tied his wrists to his waist and then tied his ankles to the end of the bed. He then tied a piece of rope to one side of the bed, ran it over his throat and tied it to the other side of the bed. He did that to his legs, just above the knees to stop him from kicking.

He waited, knowing that he would wake up, eventually.

Volkov slowly came to, stirring, slowly finding out he was restrained. He began to focus, seeing the ski-masked figure looking down at him. Peanut was gratified to see fear flicker across his face and then disappear behind the trained bland exterior. Peanut leaned forward and whispered.

'I want some information, Milo. I'm sure you will cooperate.'

He saw the face set, his mouth in a hard straight line. Silly man. He reached down, undid his flies, reached in and took hold of a testicle and squeezed hard. The cry was muffled and Volkov fainted. He removed his hand and sat back and waited. Volkov slowly came round, shaking his head, seeing the ski mask looking at him, feeling the hand go back into his pants and then the agonizing pain. Peanut watched him slump unconscious again.

It was then that the door opened and a pretty middle-aged, dark-haired lady stood there, a rock steady pistol pointed at him. At a distance of only five feet, she couldn't miss. Her voice was clear, but Peanut could see the tracks where the tears had run down her face. He had made a mistake. He had thought she would be sleeping, but instead she had been lying awake, crying quietly. She said something; it was in Russian. Peanut shook his head.

'English.'

She spoke. 'What are you doing?' Her English was only lightly accented, telling him she had been educated somewhere where English was spoken.

'I want to talk to your husband.'

'Why?'

'Your husband is responsible for the importation of tons of drugs into my country and for organizing the murders of my fellow citizens and anyone who opposed him. I need to know who is behind him. He is not a nice man, your husband.'

She gave a wry smile. 'And then you will kill him,' she stated.

'Yes.'

'And then you kill me.'

'No, that was not part of the plan.'

'But it has to be now that I am a witness?' she asked.

'Why? You haven't seen me. Can I ask your name?'

'Helena. What is your name?'

'Neville, but everyone calls me Peanut.'

She laughed, breaking the tension.

'I sense this is personal?'

'You husband tried to organize the killing of my partner and my friends. My partner is pregnant with our first child. Your husband lost, but I also know that he will try again. I am protecting my family.'

She stared long and hard, not saying anything, thinking things through. She suddenly sighed.

'Now I know why he has been so angry since he came back. He is more violent. He rapes me.'

'I know, I heard.'

'He will do the same again tomorrow, every night until he leaves to go away again.' She looked at him as the tears began to run down her face.

'What is your plan?' she asked.

'I will get the information that I need, kill him, and then tie you up and leave. Unfortunately, you will have to stay tied up until someone comes.'

'That will be Sunday night. The guard always comes and gets paid on Sunday night. He and my husband always have a few drinks.'

She smiled at him as her husband came around, slowly taking it all in, then mumbling through the gag in his mouth. She studied him, seeing his wide-open eyes, hearing him mumble, pleading with her to shoot Peanut. She glanced at Peanut.

'Will you be long?'

'I don't know. It never usually takes all that long. Why?'

'Promise me that you will kill him.'

'I promise.'

'You will come and tie me up when it is all over?'

'Yes.'

'Whatever you do, make sure it is as painful as possible,' she said grimly. 'He deserves it.'

She lowered the gun and walked out, shutting the door behind her.

Peanut turned to Volkov with a smile.

'Bad move raping her, wasn't it?' He grinned as he took Volkov's middle finger and bent it back and snapped the knuckle, hearing a faint muffled moan. Peanut was not a sadist, but Volkov was fair game. He had broken all the rules and Peanut intended to break them all back. He reached into his backpack, took out a small electrical device, connected the clips, one to each of Volkov's nipples and another to his limp penis. He flicked the switch and Volkov writhed and moaned as the current flowed through his body. Peanut raised his head and watched Volkov's face, seeing the pain-filled eyes and he gently turned the power up.

'Tell me when you are ready to talk.' Two minutes later, he heard a muffled, 'Yes, Yes,' through the gag. Peanut smiled. The little toy from the CIA had worked. He turned the power down but left it still slightly on, just to let Volkov know what was waiting. He turned on the record function on his phone.

'Who is your superior?'

'Andrei Sokolov.'

'FSB?'

'Yes, assistant director.'

'You were going back to the United States?' It was a shot in the dark, but Peanut had his suspicions. He saw Volkov's pain-filled eyes look at him and he held the controller up, ready to turn the power up.

'Yes.'

'When?'

'Two months.'

'Why?'

'We have unfinished business there.'

'Who was to be your contact?'

'John Case.'

Peanut was glad he had the balaclava on masking his face; he was stunned; this now changed everything.

'You knew I was coming?'

'No, no. It was never mentioned. Things like this are not supposed to happen. Not here in Russia.'

'Talk to me, Milo. What is the end game? Why is the FSB meddling in America's gangs and drug-supply chains?'

Volkov began to talk. Ten minutes later, he stopped, Peanut could see he was exhausted, he had told all. The big tough guy Volkov was just a big bully boy, using his power and brutality on those beneath him, just to enforce his will. He had broken so easily. Peanut stood beside the bed and pushed his thumbs into the carotid arteries on either side of Volkov's neck and held on. The struggle was weak and futile; Milo Volkov was dead five minutes later. Peanut cleaned up, untied him and left him lying with the bedclothes over him and tucked in like he was sleeping. He gently closed the door as he walked out and knocked and entered the bedroom next door.

'Is he dead?' Helena asked.

'Yes. And we have a change of plan. Do you have a passport?'

'Yes, of course.'

'With you?'

'It's in my handbag. Always, just in case.'

'Now, is a just in case. Would you like to come to America?'

'Yes, but why?'

'The police will be waiting for me. I need to hide in the boot of your car as you leave. We need to go straight to the airport and book the first flight out.'

'What will happen if I stay?'

'They will blame you. They will not believe that you were not part of his death. I have learned a lot. But you have no choice if you want to live.'

She frowned at him, worried.

'How will I survive in America? I would need a job and to work.'

'That can all be arranged. I am not poor and until you get settled, you can live with me and my partner. You will be most welcome. I will tell you all about them on the plane.' She suddenly stood, thinking, examining him closely.

'This is a bad idea,' she said.

'How?' Peanut queried.

She gave a grim smile. 'Russian police are thorough, very thorough. If they are looking, every car leaving here will be stopped and searched.'

Peanut frowned as he studied her. If the car was searched, he would be finished. He mulled over his options and he couldn't see any way out, then noticed her smiling.

'Peanut, I will get us out. Come with me.'

***

Helena set the house alarm on the way out, just to make things look normal. Peanut climbed into the passenger seat as she slipped behind the wheel, the car jolting its way down the driveway and up the narrow road.

They saw the police stop in the distance. Only a mile from the house, they had blocked the only way out. A single car parked with its lights flashing. Helena pulled the car over and parked as the two police officers flagged her to stop. She turned the inside light of the car on and buzzed the window down. She gave her name. Peanut smiled at the officers from the other side of the car, bending and looking at them, his heart racing, pretending to be interested as he smiled again at the two officers. He expected to be pulled out and arrested at any second but he stayed calm, appearing relaxed as the officers and Helena talked. She said something and the officers laughed, shining their torches in the rear seat and then in the boot when Helena tripped the latch. Then more rapid-fire Russian and laughter and a final word and a friendly goodbye tap on the roof as she put the car in gear and they moved gently off, heading down the highway. Helena reached over and patted his arm.

'See, I told you it would be okay. You make a very pretty woman, by the way. One officer couldn't keep his eyes off you!

'Thanks to your makeup skills. This wig is hot!' Peanut gave his well-padded bra a push up. 'Maybe a bit too much padding in the breast area? That always tends to get men interested?'

Helena laughed. 'Now you know what some of us women have to go through to look good for you men.' She was sad for a minute. 'Sometimes, it just isn't worth it.'

She noticed a passing sign. 'Twenty minutes to the airport. We'll park and you can change.'

Peanut chuckled. The flights were already booked and all he had to do was change clothes and pick up their tickets. Then they would both walk into the business class lounge.

He knew that if he was going to be picked up, it would be at the ticket desk. The passport would give him away. His passport had been arranged personally by the CIA and they had assured him it was foolproof. Name of Russell McAdam. Did John Case know his passport name? If he did and had passed it on, he was fucked. There was nothing he could do.

He had cleaned all the makeup off and had slipped into his own clothes. As he approached the desk, he felt his heartbeat go up a notch but he stayed calm. He needn't have worried.

'Have a nice flight, Mr. McAdam.'

They sat in the airline's business class lounge, having coffees while they waited. Would they be stopped from boarding? Again, it was unknown. He glanced at Helena's face and he could see the tension still there. She knew what the brutal outcome would be if they got stopped. But they needn't have worried. Boarding passes were checked and they walked up the air bridge to their seats. Twenty minutes later, the plane accelerated down the runway and they were on their way to Berlin. Peanut saw Helena's face begin to relax. He knew that she knew what would have happened if they had been caught. It would not have been pretty.

Chapter 43

He turned on his mobile and rang Chas from Berlin airport. With their flights to London and then New York now booked, they were having a coffee and a muffin in a café and he explained what had happened. He mentioned John Case and told him to talk to Peter McConnell direct. It was typical Chas.

'Leave it to me. We'll sort it.'

Peanut hung up and smiled at Helena.

'My boss is a good guy. He said he will sort it all out.'

She looked worriedly at him.

'I hope so, Peanut. I don't want to go back.' She tapped her computer bag. 'I have a lot of information on my husband's contacts. When he was drunk and asleep, I would check all his calls on his phone and computer and then copy them to my phone and then to my computer. I have copied most of his emails. That might help?'

Peanut laughed. The CIA would be delighted.

'I think that would help a lot. I'll let Chas know what information you have.' He rang Chas again, told him and got the same easygoing response.

'Excellent. Absolutely brilliant! We will sort it. At this stage, you won't be going through customs. You will be met at the air bridge exit. See you there.'

'Chas, I would like Helena to stay with us until this is all sorted, just to give her some security. She saved my life, Chas. I owe her.'

'Peanut, we all owe her. Again, leave it to me.'

Two young men in dark suits met them at the air bridge exit at JFK. They were polite, friendly and escorted them to get their bags and out to a waiting black SUV. They simply showed their cards to airport security and went straight through. It had been a long flight and they were tired. The agent in the passenger seat turned to Peanut and smiled as the car traveled towards Manhattan.

'I am led to believe that you are one of us, but not official?'

Peanut grinned back. 'As I don't know who you are I can't really say. But who told you that?' The agent laughed.

'It's just that the word that has gone around. We have been told that we are not to know, but as they say, curiosity leads to more curiosity. So are you one of us?'

Peanut laughed and shook his head. 'Sorry, I can't tell you that. It's so big a secret that even I don't know!'

The young guy laughed, turned back to the front and punched the driver on the shoulder.

'Let's get these guys to bed. They will be tried after all that travel.' He turned his head slightly. 'Moscow to Berlin to London to JFK, right?'

'Yes. Helena wasn't able to sleep on the plane. We're really tired.'

'We'll have you back home in Washington tomorrow. Your missus will be glad to see you?'

'She wasn't talking to me when I left, so the jury is out on that one. I might have to sleep in a hotel.'

'Bummer. Life's a bitch, right?'

'Yeah, definitely.'

They were escorted to their flight for Washington the next morning. Peanut had poked his head out his hotel room door at five in the morning and a guy was sitting there, wide awake, watching him grin at him and another guy outside Helena's door. Peanut made a drinking gesture.

'Want a coffee, guys? I'll order room service for both of you, if you like?'

'Shit, yes and thanks. Two large black coffees for me and Phil.' He noticed Peanut's small frame. 'It's Peanut isn't it?'

'It is. I'll order those coffees. I want one myself, just to clear the muck out of my brain.' He walked in and ordered the coffees and then quickly dressed. He wanted to get home and have a change of clothes. The rap on the door and the coffees arrived and he stood outside and talked to the guys; they were polite, respectful, and friendly.

'Your lady friend is nice. She said good morning and was surprised that we were here. She said it made her feel safe.'

'She's starting a new life. Her husband was a pig and a killer and had murdered people over here, so I went to Russia and sorted it. Helena saved my life. I, and whoever it is that I am working for, owe her and owe her heaps.'

'Who was her husband?'

'Milo Volkov. FSB.'

'So he's dead?'

'There is no second coming out of hell, guys. I assume we will be met at Dulles?'

'They haven't told us that but I would expect so.'

'Okay, when do we leave?'

The guy checked his watch. 'One hour.'

'Okay. Could you tell Helena? Women like the time to put on their makeup.'

The guy laughed. 'They surely do.'

Peanut went back into the room to wait. He had some emails to do. He was still unsure whether he should contact Hills or just turn up. He decided to just turn up with Helena in tow. He didn't want to be yelled at on the phone.

They were taken from Dulles to Langley, ushered inside and then walked down the long halls, following the colored lines on the floor to a compact conference room. They sat down and waited, Chas turning up a minute or two later.

'Chas, Helena Volkov. Helena, Chas Fischer. Chas is my direct boss.'

Chas gave a self-deprecating grin.

'Hardly, I'm actually the coordinator, not the boss. We all contribute to whatever goal we are set. It seems to work. Can I ask what your job in Moscow was?'

'Analyst of foreign troop movements. It sounds good but it is just time spent looking at video screens of photos and videos from satellites and aircraft. Boring. But it was a job. In Russia today, no job is poverty and hardship. I was lucky to have it.'

'Your education?'

'Ph.D. in earth sciences. I specialized in topography, earthquakes, plate tectonics and atmosphere. That is what got me the job looking at troop movements. I was good picking out things that shouldn't be there.'

'What a waste of a good Ph.D.'

She agreed. 'It was. But I lived.'

The door opened and Peter McConnell walked in. He nodded to them all, then sat and stared unsmilingly at Peanut.

'Is Volkov dead?'

'Yes.'

'Good. They are currently saying that an outsider attacked and killed a defenseless woman and Volkov was injured but will survive. They are saying it was an attack done by the United States of America against a helpless Russian citizen and they would find out who and then hold them to justice. More of the same drivel. They can't admit that one of their most senior FSB officers has been assassinated. It makes the other officers worry and their government look weak in the eyes of the people.'

He turned to Helena.

'I'm sorry to bring this issue up but we needed to make sure.'

'Don't apologize. He was a beast.' She glanced at Peanut. 'Peanut knows. He is better off dead.'

'Okay, Peanut. How did he die?'

'Carotid asphyxiation. Five minutes, the eyes were dead. I checked and held on a couple of minutes longer. No one survives seven minutes. There was no pulse in the neck or in the groin. He was dead.'

'Good. We have your laptop, Helena, thanks, and it is revealing. We are now tracing his contacts. We just might catch a couple of unwanted visitors. Now Peanut, you specified to Chas that this meeting was to be just me, him, and no one else. Why?'

'Chas has no doubt told you about John Case. It seems he is a spy. Let me play you something.'

He took out the phone and set it on the table, checked the right place on the sound track and pushed play. Peanut's voice and the pain-filled voice of Volkov filled the room. He noticed that he jotted the name of Andrei Sokolov down and sat up abruptly when Volkov mentioned John Case as his contact, leaning forward as Volkov answered Peanut's question about what was the end game.

'Burlington Ford was the first but not the last.' Volkov's voice was raspy and hoarse with pain. 'We were instructed to set up ten training cells in Texas, New Mexico, Arkansas, Mississippi, and Louisiana. We wanted at least a thousand trained men in each cell. Burlington Ford was the template. John had arranged three other ranchers to join Melissa's Southern States Alliance. They were keen and one had already started recruiting.'

'Who?'

'Randy McDarment.'

'Who's Randy McDarment?'

'He's a rich oilman and has a large ranch as a plaything. He lives in Texas and used to come and watch the guys train in Burlington Ford's shed.'

'So Melissa Albanese knows all these people and is active in the Southern States Alliance?'

'Yes, she is a very good organizer. Burlington Ford would have never become a senator without her.'

'And you needed the drug sales to fund the operations?'

'Yes.'

'Did Melissa Albanese know about the drugs?'

'Of course.'

'So why the plan to set up armies in the southern USA?'

'We have our Chechnya and it was decided that America deserves the same. America at war with itself would be good for Russia. A distracted America would leave us alone.'

'Who decided?'

'I do not know. Andrei Sokolov just passed the order down.'

'What was John Case's role?'

'Making sure that any government issues were dealt with. He and Andrei were close. What John asked for, Andrei delivered.'

Peanut reached over and turned off the recording.

Peter was surprised. 'Is that all there is?'

'I don't think Helena wants to hear the death gurgle of her late husband.'

Peter was embarrassed and glanced quickly at Helena.

'No, quite right. But we need a copy of that.'

'Give me an email address and I can email the audio file or you can just copy this off my phone.'

Peter pulled out his phone and grinned as he pushed record and Peanut replayed the recording. He studied Peanut.

'You said Helena made you up like a woman to get you through the police check points. Was that the original plan—to use Helena?'

'No.' Peanut gave Helena a wry grin and she laughed.

'The original plan was to tie up Helena and then leave her tied with Volkov dead but that recording killed that plan. Plus by then I knew I could trust Helena.'

'Really? How?'

Peanut looked at Helena and shook his head. 'No,' he said. 'I don't think you need know.'

Helena smiled at him. 'It's alright, Peanut. You can tell him. It's all in the past.'

Peanut shrugged. 'As I was hiding in the house, I heard Helena being raped by Volkov. It was rough, brutal. When I had Volkov tied up and was going to leave and tie Helena up, she came in with a gun. So I told her what I was doing and how I was going to leave her tied up and alive with Volkov dead. She gave me her blessing and then left. When I heard the recording, I knew that the Russians would be waiting so I had Helena take me out and here we are.'

Peter looked puzzled. 'How did you know? That doesn't make sense?'

'Volkov didn't know I was coming. I was sent there to kill him. I think Chase wanted him dead. He knew too much to ever be allowed come back to America again. If caught he would talk and reveal all. So what other use did he have? He had already ruined their plans. They wanted him gone. They knew I would talk to him and Chase couldn't risk me getting away with the information that Volkov knew so they had to kill me too. And as Helena would have seen me, that meant the Russians, to hush it all up, would have to kill her as well, just to tidy up the last loose end. They will now know that I have got away. I assume that John Case will also know. I'd be surprised if he's still in the country.'

'Oh, yes, he is,' Peter said. 'When you told Chas about him it did raise some suspicions so I had him followed to JFK where he was detained under a rare but appropriate securities law. He will face justice.'

'Is that wise, taking him to court?'

'Court is not an option, but he will face justice.'

'One other point. When we questioned Gorman, he said he was front man for the stored weapons in Queens. I asked who he was front man for and he just said John before he died. John Case perhaps?'

'We will ask. Thanks, you have a recording of the Gorman conversation?'

Peanut pulled out his phone and played the audio file as Peter McConnell recorded it. Peanut glanced at him when he had finished.

'May I ask what role John Case had at the CIA?'

'He was not CIA. He was a highly trusted liaison officer with the Department of State with CIA clearance. We are now looking at all our close contacts with outside organizations.'

He sat back in his chair and looked at Peanut and Chas. 'All I can say is well done.'

He turned to Helena. 'And thanks to you we have our man back. Have you given any thoughts on what you might do over here? We are currently arranging permanent residency for you, under a different name, of course. You will stay as Helena but we will let you choose your family name. You will get a passport and a driver's license under that new name as well. We will do all those details this morning. Any issues, Chas?'

'None, but Peanut has. Hills is upset that he left on this job without her. Quite upset. Bitterly upset in fact. I have spoken to her but she is adamant that she and Peanut are a team. That he shouldn't have gone without her.'

Peter studied Chas and Peanut, a thoughtful expression on his face. 'I would imagine a team of Peanut and the indomitable Ms. Hiller could be quite formidable, right? She has something, in what she says. We just might have a role in the future for a two-person team of that quality. Thanks for that, Chas.'

Chas did not look happy. He did not want to lose two of his team. Peter noticed the look and just smiled. If push came to shove, Chas would not have any say.

'So Peanut is going home to a chewing out,' Peter said. 'Hardly fair after what he has been through. I will call front office and on the way out you will be presented with a voucher for Ms. Hiller, and thanks from the CIA for letting us use you. Okay? It's not much but it might help.'

'Leave it to me,' Helena said. 'I will fix it. She needs to know the full story. If she had come, either she or Peanut would now be dead. Let me explain it to her.' She smiled at Peanut. 'It is, after all, the least I can do.'

Peter stood. 'The lady that will take you through the passport, license and residency will be along shortly. I now need to go and see what John Case has to say for himself. I suspect that it won't be much. He knows the *consequences*.'

He turned and walked out. Chas grinned at the two of them.

'Peter summed it up; well done.' He wagged his finger at Peanut. 'But you do have bridges to mend.'

***

Chas pulled his SUV up to the door of Peanut's house. Peters car was parked in front of the garage. Pistol practice, Peanut assumed. Helena took a long look at the house.

'Is this yours?' she asked.

'Mine and Mandy's.'

'It's beautiful, really beautiful.'

Peanut stared hard. 'Somebody's mowed the lawn?'

Chas laughed. 'Mick mowed it. J.R. made him do it. Said that as they don't pay any rent it was the least they could do while you were away.'

They climbed out and went up the steps, Chas leading. Peanut was feeling nervous as Chas knocked and opened the door with his key and called out.

'It's just me, folks, with two friends.'

Mandy and Janice-Rose came around the corner out of the lounge and stopped dead, seeing Peanut and Helena standing side by side, waiting. Peanut gave a nervous smile.

'Hi, honey, hi, J.R. This is Helena. She has just come here from Russia to start a new life. Helena, this is Hills or Mandy, my partner, and this is Janice-Rose, my sister.' They both stared at Helena who walked forward and hugged a surprised Hills.

'It is such a pleasure to meet you. Peanut has told me so much about you both. It is so nice to meet you face to face. To finally meet the family of the man who saved my life.'

Janice-Rose was embraced as she asked a muffled question. 'He saved your life? Really?'

'Yes, he did.'

Peanut gave an embarrassed cough.

'Actually, Helena saved my life. She got me past the guards that were looking for me. If I was caught, it would have been a very long and very painful death.'

Mandy shook her head and gave Peanut a sour look. He knew then she was still angry with him. He wondered what would happen when they were alone, if that happened. At least, she was still in the house and she hadn't moved back to her apartment. That gave him some hope.

He held the envelope out to Mandy. 'The CIA would like you to accept this as measure of their appreciation for letting me go and work for them. Thanks.' She took the envelope from him and carefully opened it, read it, and then studied him with tears suddenly brimming in her eyes. She wiped her eyes and gestured at the couch.

'I'll make us a coffee and then you can talk,' she said. 'This sounds like a story and a half. Start at the beginning and tell us all.'

Janice-Rose held up her hand. 'I'll get Peter up from the pistol range. He can hear this as well.'

She scooted down the stairs, and they heard her calling out to Peter. He came grumpily up the stairs, annoyed at having his pistol practice interrupted, surprised to see Peanut and a strange woman standing there. He looked nonplussed as Peanut did the introductions.

'Peter, this is Helena Campbell. She has come here from Russia.'

Helena walked forward and hugged Peter.

'It is so nice to meet you. Peanut has told me so much about you. It's like I have known you all for years.' She gently pulled back and Peter gave a slight grunt.

'I suppose they've told you that I'm grumpy?'

'And are you?'

'Yeah, I suppose. Sometimes,' he said. He frowned as Janice-Rose and Mandy laughed. Helena didn't laugh. She kept looking at him with a frankness that they could see was unnerving him, making him almost embarrassed. Helena had somehow got under his guard. He glanced away, not sure of how to handle this. Peanut put him out of his misery.

'Peter, Helena is from Russia. She saved my life over there and she has come back here to live and start a new life. She will need all the help we can give to get her up on her feet, okay?' Peter nodded, still nonplussed. Hills walked in with the coffees.

'Let's all sit down and hear what happened,' she said.

Chapter 44

Twice Hills and Janice-Rose glanced at either Peanut or Helena, especially when he described hearing her being raped.

J.R. butted in. 'You should have stopped that, big brother.'

Peanut shook his head.

'I didn't want to involve Helena in the killing. I had a plan to kill him and not kill her but it involved them being in the bedrooms. Killing him out in the lounge might put some blame on her. He paid the price, J.R.'

'Yeah, I suppose,' Janice-Rose conceded.

Helena reached over and patted her arm. 'The rape was nothing new. It was how he liked his sex; forced and rough when he was drunk. He was just an animal. He can't do any more harm. As Peanut said, he has paid the price.'

Peter was sitting beside her, looking in wonderment at this one tough lady. Repeatedly raped by her husband, yet still dealing with getting on with her life.

Peanut carried on talking, telling how the only choice was Helena driving him to the airport and then coming with him. How she had made him up like a woman to fool the police. That had saved their lives. He looked hard at Hills when he said he had offered her his home to stay in until she found her feet. The last thing he wanted was for Hills to refuse. He needn't have worried. Hills didn't hesitate.

'She saved your life. That is the least we can do. With Sharon now staying permanently with Chas, Helena can have her room.'

He was happy that Hills was on board. She turned to him.

'And despite our fight, I'm still sleeping in our bed,' she said.

'I'm glad, honey. That's where you and I should be together.'

She gave a wan smile at his reply, still not altogether happy. Helena looked at them all, gratitude shining in her eyes.

'It makes me feel humble that you and Peanut have given me somewhere to stay. Thank you so much.'

Janice-Rose and Mandy showed her Sharon's old room, helping her pack her few belongings away. They went downstairs, chatting and happy, ignoring Peanut, Peter, and Chas as they talked. Chas left with a 'Call tomorrow' sign to Hills and Peanut. Helena came and sat with Peter.

'They tell me you are twice divorced?' she asked.

He began to speak, telling her how he had mucked up two marriages, all because he allowed work to rule his life. And he wondered what might have been if he had done things differently.

'But you can try again?' Helena said. 'Why not? You are not that old.'

Peter was lost. He was never much good at the social skills and right now whatever little there was had deserted him.

He didn't know how to take Helena. He could feel his heart racing, her direct gaze was unnerving and her hand was still on his arm, giving it another gentle squeeze. He found it impossible to look away. She talked about why she had to leave Russia and the death of Milo Volkov and how the CIA had given her the name Campbell, a name she liked. He answered her questions and she answered his, but it didn't matter; it was happening again.

He wasn't aware of the smiles being exchanged between the others but even if he had been he would not have cared. He was lost in her beautiful brown eyes, the way they looked sad and then gleamed when she was happy and sparkled with an inner joy when he said something nice. Peter knew he had to know more about Helena.

Peanut coughed loudly and Peter and Helena turned towards him.

'Peter, why don't you take Helena out for a coffee and show her our beautiful city?'

Peter was surprised when Helena said gently, 'I'd like that, Peter.'

He promptly stood and escorted her to the door. She picked up her purse as they left, smiling with unabashed delight at Hills and Janice-Rose. They heard the car start and leave.

Hills and Janice-Rose smiled at each other. Janice-Rose asked what was uppermost in their minds.

'Love at first sight, Mandy?'

Hills was unsure.

'I don't know, J.R., but whatever it is, it has made them both happy. I have never seen grumpy old Pete go all mushy like that. It's a bit early to call it love. But who knows?'

Peanut grunted.

'It would be nice if Peter found someone to share his life with. He's been single for a long time and is now probably too old.'

Mandy gave him another sour look. He noticed that he was still getting a few of them.

'Listen to Mr. Lonely Hearts. You telling me that you won't love me when you get old?'

'Shit, no! Not at all, honey. I was just mentioning that in Peter's case...' he paused and then saw the look on her and Janice-Rose's faces. He was on another losing streak and he knew it. Time to fudge.

'Anybody for a coffee?'

They both nodded and Peanut stood and walked to the kitchen.

Janice-Rose leaned over and spoke quietly to Hills, just loud enough for Peanut to hear.

'That brother of mine, Mandy, he really has shit for brains. And that's a worry. You sure you still want to have his baby?'

Hills burst out laughing and Janice-Rose joined in. Peanut didn't turn around, he knew they were laughing at him. He mentally flagged it away and decided to ignore it. He knew he would lose if he tried. And Hills had told Janice-Rose about the baby. He couldn't put into words just how he felt to be home. The joy of seeing Mandy and knowing that the love was still there. Despite the sour looks he had seen the love and concern in her eyes when she was listening to Helena tell the story. He knew that they would talk all night when they went to bed. He was looking forward to it. He grimaced as he poured the three cups of coffee. It was now time to front up to take his puninshment like a man and do what all men to when losing to a woman.

Sulk!

Later that night, while Peanut was snoring gently, Mandy again opened the card from the CIA director. She read it again.

> *Please accept our thanks for your service to our country. It is harder on those that stay home, not knowing the danger their loved ones are in. Your loyalty to your partner and to your country is appreciated and honored. We all thank you.*

It was signed by the Director and there was a voucher inside for a meal and a night at the Jefferson Hotel.

She wiped the tears that had started to trickle down her cheeks and watched Peanut sleeping peacefully. She was proud of him. She loved him to bits, but if he ever thought he was ever doing that again, he would get another smack in the nuts! She chuckled quietly at the thought and Peanut stirred slightly, almost as if he was somehow aware of what she was thinking as she gently snuggled up close beside him.

Made in the USA
Middletown, DE
17 October 2022

12925326R00123